COLLIDER

By Richard Warwick

Dark Lit Publishing

First published in 2020

Copyright Richard Warwick

The First Experiment

Julius Robert Openheimer had realised his works impact, its historical significance. He knew he had become death, the destroyer of worlds. His most famous quote. Now, just outside Montreux, the grandchildren of Openheimer's work would become life, the discoverer of worlds.

The air seemed to be sucked out of the control room every time the door was closed. It was a crisp sterile environment, permanently monitored by a group of sixteen staff pulling twelve-hour shifts. Four staff during the day, four at night, monitoring the Collider functions round the clock. They worked seven consecutive days on duty, followed by seven days off, then seven nights on followed by seven days off. They were supported by two teams of technicians working day shifts maintaining the vast banks of monitors and equipment which controlled and recorded every aspect of the Collider's functions. It was hard work, with relentless mentally exhausting hours often spent testing each section of the Collider equipment to the point of failure, to then replace large sections of protective shielding or monitoring equipment to ensure that the failure point of every element of the Collider was an exact known quantity before the experiment began at full capacity. Days on end underground in the spotlessly clean gleaming steel encased rooms filled with monitors on almost every wall, bays of computer servers, and a silently operating air conditioning unit breathing clean recycled air into every room, keeping an exact twenty-one degrees throughout the facility in order to ensure none of the equipment ever overheated. The scientists in the facility spent entire days without seeing natural light, starting their shifts before dawn and ending their working day after the sun had set. They lived in a clinical cold filtered artificial blue light which was supposed to be gentle on the eyes, and prevent headaches. In most cases it didn't work, and the combination of the constant pure light reflected off almost every surface of every room resulted in the staff making a number of creative adjustments to the lights in stand down areas, from removing every bulb in one room, to adding a layer of blue paint to bulbs in another in an effort to mask the stark light.

Every member of staff working in the facility had the highest level of clearance within the European Science Directorate, only subordinate to two lead scientists who seemed to be treated with an apparent air of royalty by everyone from their own staff to visiting members of the many Governments who had contributed to the building of the Collider facility. Their application of particle theory was the most innovative leap forward in many years, and was expected to change the relationship between the human race and the universe as it was currently understood.

As the Collider started to accelerate to its initial test velocity the control room internal doors locked closed, a locked room inside a sealed bunker deep within the facility. They were six-hundred metres underground, at the centre of the sixteen-mile Collider loops. The Collider loop chambers formed a figure of eight shape, leading to a ten-mile-long focus tunnel with a steadily looped return tunnel.

A few minutes past midnight, with the pre-start up tests completed, the Collider temperature was equal to that of outer space. Every variable was perfect for the first test run, temperature, air pressure, stability of energy feeds. It was beginning. They would change the world forever.

The particle accelerator reached full test cycle completion within the Collider loops at seventeen minutes before midnight, exactly the predicted time. In the control room Jules

Mathers sat back in his chair and smiled. Everything was as it should be, precisely as had been hypothesised under these exact conditions. He was by far the most relaxed of the four duty staff in the control room, and the most qualified theoretical physicist of all sixteen control room staff. Now it was just a simple matter of activating the nuclear reaction in the feed chamber and firing some sub atomic particles into the focus tunnel. A pre-set function which would happen at the press of a button in the control room, once the pass key command sequence had been entered in the command suite monitoring room by one of his superiors, likely to be Alder. This whole night was Alder's baby, finally being born.

One innocuous LED light on the control room function desk lit up. The function desk looked very similar to a music studio mixing desk, with various rotary dials and long-throw faders spread across an eight-foot-wide control panel. Mathers stood over the desk, leaned forward and tapped the LED with the fingernail of his right index finger. He knew it was utterly pointless, since when did an LED light ever get fixed by tapping it? It was a natural reaction, there was no way that something could have gone wrong, it had been perfect. It had been three minutes since Alder had entered the command sequence. Since they had triggered a nuclear reaction firing the feed from the accelerator loops into the focus tunnel.

The intercom exploded into life. "Are you reading the same warning in there?" Alder sounded pissed. It had been perfect to this point, and they only needed a few moments more data before starting the shut-down cycle.

"Just came on," Mathers replied. He was still calm. If this was an accurate reading, the warning was minor. The Particle Collider had continued to accelerate beyond what they had calculated to be normal boundaries. Mathers slid a long-throw fader back by almost an inch. This should stabilise the rate of particles within the focus tunnel by marginally reducing the vacuum, and give them enough time to measure what may have caused the current anomaly. He could see the other three staff in the control room flicking from screen to screen on their monitoring stations, trying to make sense of this glitch. They were all throwing occasional glances his way.

There was no change to the warning light. Within the focus tunnel the readings were still showing gradual acceleration. The crisp sterile air in the control room was starting to feel heavier, as if it were becoming denser with the pressure of diving deep under water.

There was no reduction in the focus tunnel, every theoretically *safe* shut down procedure had been completed with no effect. Mathers had become aware of a pulse which was not his own. A steady *thrum* sensation within the control room. It almost seemed cliché to Mathers that there was the heavy atmosphere and the apparent pulse in the control room, he thought this seemed to be exactly what he expected that he would be the feeling if something went wrong.

The Collider was reaching critical rate. The pulse stopped. Mathers thought his own pulse had stopped too. A groan was audible, increasing in pitch. It had been there for a few moments and had seemingly changed in pitch by a few octaves in a matter of those short seconds.

There was no explosion, no bang or percussive impact noise. Just a shockwave. It lasted just over a second. Every light went out in the control room, all power in the facility had been lost. Somehow even though the power was off, there was still a fading level of light in the windowless control room.

Mathers was thrown backwards a few metres by the shockwave, taken off his feet. It seemed that he took almost a minute to fall from his standing position at the function desk to the floor a few metres away. It was as if gravity had halved in the room. Mathers barely noticed he was falling, it was more a vague floating sensation. He was in the room, but he was also seeing the room for the first time from the doorway on his first day at work there. He was also being interviewed by Alder and Rosst in an office within the facility administrative block. Driving to a restaurant on his first day in Switzerland. In fact, he realised he was simultaneously in dozens of places at the same time. Strangely he felt a small twang of annoyance as he slammed back into the room and crashed to the floor, he had just managed to almost isolate one of the experiences from amongst the others. He had been losing his virginity again in near perfect clarity, and then snapped back to reality just moments before he had made it to the end of the act. Gone before he had the chance to finish what he had enjoyed starting again so painfully much.

The Collider facility was built just over eight miles from Lake Leman, just outside Montreux. Rosst had always enjoyed the fact that he could visit the shores of the Lake where Frank Zappa's concert incident lead to his favourite song being written. *Smoke on the water* changed his life the first time he heard it, it switched him on to his only real outlet outside study and science; music. The facility lay in a scenic and peaceful area of the countryside between Montreux and Gruyère Pays-d'Enhaut national park, cut into the scenery as subtly as was possible for such a large facility. A deep lake had been drained and the surrounding area had been excavated in order to build as much of the facility underground as could be achieved, leaving only a small number of administration and security buildings above ground. The site was designed to be externally minimal. It had some prominent small security installations, but not so visible as to detract from the amazing scenery enjoyed by visitors to the parks and public areas surrounding the facility.

Within the facility things were anything but calm and peaceful. It was almost five minutes to five in the morning, and power had not been restored to the control room or any of the particle accelerator functions, though the accelerator had been gradually slowing to pretest levels and had automatically shut down most functions within the containment area of the Collider.

A few hours after the power had gone off, the electric locks on the doors within the control room had released. Alder had started working his way from the command suite using the electric locking override keys. He had found his way through the facility using a high-powered halogen torch, one of a number stored for emergency situations across the bunker. Mathers took a spare torch from Alder and switched it to full spread beam. As Mathers looked around in the torch light, he tried to quickly assess the damage to the control room equipment. He was shocked to see no smoke, no fires, no computer screens smashed by some form of impact from whatever it was that had knocked him off his feet. As he looked down it occurred to him, he may still be suffering from an unnoticed injury to his head. In the torch light he was sure he saw ice melting in a puddle on the floor, with a fish flapping and dry drowning a few inches from the puddle.

"Northern Pike," Piers Enlan said calmly from just by Mathers' shoulder. Mathers hadn't noticed Enlan walk up behind him. He hadn't noticed any of the other three staff in the room walk over to him.

"What?" Nothing was making sense to Mathers, but this abstract vision seemed no more or less real or possible to him than any of the memories that had just exploded into his consciousness when the shockwave hit.

"It's a Northern Pike," Enlan said absently. "Big fella, caught one from the lake a month after we got here." It seemed too unreal to even consider, as if by accepting the presence of the fish, the scientists had to accept some greater reality which was simply too implausible to be possible.

Mathers looked at Alder, trying to judge his state of mind. He knew that no-one in the control room was seriously hurt from the limited conversation they had managed to achieve in the darkness while they had waited to be released, but he also knew that they were all in shock. They needed to make their way to the Alternative Control Room to check if any of the equipment in there could be restored, a safe distance from the core of the Collider.

Times change

Anna Bannet heard a familiar frantic scratching at her back door. She had just walked through to her dining room with a fresh cup of coffee which was still too hot to drink, but she had a strong thirst so was blowing into the cup to try to cool it to a drinkable temperature. She absently walked back through to the kitchen and opened the door. Looking out of the door through the steam from her coffee, she blurted out a noise that was not quite a scream, not quite a laugh, but somewhere in between the two, combining with a sort of sigh. The cup fell from her hand breaking the handle on the step and spilling coffee, she stepped through the puddle into the light of the day. On the doorstep as if no care existed in the world, her poodle Gennie was sitting obediently looking up at the door waiting. Gennie had disappeared from Anna's garden sometime after quarter to eleven on October thirtieth the previous year. Anna had let Gennie out to relieve herself while Anna had been preparing some early lunch for friends, and when she had gone out to the garden to call her back in the dog was gone. Anna and her friends had searched the garden, then the house. They had then taken to the streets calling Gennie's name to no avail. She was gone, until today. She looked exactly as she had the last time Anna saw her, as if it had been only minutes before. Home and happy to see Anna, as though she had never left.

Levin Moude was too hungry to fully concentrate on the phone call he was having on his mobile phone, his girlfriend was only interested in talking about the cost of a deposit on an apartment she had seen, rather than telling him what food she wanted him to order for her from the Indian restaurant he was walking to. It was the best place in Bern to order Indian food to take out, certainly that he had been able to find so far in the short time he had lived there. Eve was too keen to move into a new flat, and he knew she was nesting. They had been together for almost six months, and she was trying to take the relationship to the next level, she had brought up the topic of children in almost every conversation recently. It was almost a relief to him to hear a woman scream just ahead of him, an excuse to get off the phone. She could text him her order if she decided she was actually hungry.

"Something's happening, text me if you decide what food you want, I have to go," he muttered into the phone. He hung up, and looked towards the sound of the scream. The street was empty, except for him and a woman who was running out into the road. His eyes panned past the woman to the other side of the road where she appeared to be headed. Levin's mouth had already been dry, he had drunk a few beers after work but the walk to the restaurant had seemingly left him parched and needing another. He was going to need more than a beer after this. A man was lying flat on the floor on the path at the north end of Kapellenstrasse. Blood was gouting from the base of his torso at the top of his hip, he had no left leg. Levin ran across the road towards the man, catching up to the woman who had screamed.

"Call an ambulance," he said to her. She looked at him incredulously, slowly looked down at his hand. Her face was white, her expression understandably shocked and confused, she pointed to his hand. He had told *her* to call an ambulance while he had his own phone in his hand. He passed her the phone and went to the man on the floor.

Blood sprayed everywhere. It pulsed out from an open wound. It made no sense; he could see no severed leg anywhere. No trail of blood where a car may have hit the man, no vicious armed assailant running away. The blood seemed to be being pumped from the man in huge bursts, arcing out to the middle of the road. He felt warmth dot across his face. A spot of red clouded his vision. Levin wiped at his face, and looked at the palm of his hand. It was streaked with splotches of blood. He tore off his jacket and tried to push it onto the wound. Anything to stem the flow of blood for long enough to allow time for the ambulance to arrive. He had momentarily started for his belt, but through the cloud of blood vapour and spray from the wound he could see that the leg was gone from the crotch to the top of the hip, leaving not even the most minor of stump to tie a tourniquet off.

He was pushing the jacket into the wound as hard as he could when the woman knelt down next to him. She was shouting for help, it seemed that a few people had heard her scream, and were approaching slowly from the junction at the top of the road. She shouted to them once again and then turned back to him.

"He was stood here, then his leg was gone. It was just gone. An ambulance is coming now."

The man was mouthing something. The noise he made was barely audible and sounded strangled. His head lifted momentarily, and Levin had to lean forward to make eye contact with the man, to try to hear what he was saying. His eyes rolled back into his head and closed. The man was grey. He looked to have been maybe forty years old, and was a little overweight. A strange thought passed through Levin's head. *Maybe he has all this blood because he is so big*. Levin could feel the thump of the man's pulse, the blood slamming into his hand through the jacket. It was getting weaker.

"How could it just be gone?" he said to the woman.

She looked at him blankly. "Nothing *happened*, it was just gone. He was stood there, he had two legs, then he had one leg, and blood just, it just burst out everywhere and he fell over."

Levin only heard the ambulance as it pulled up to the side of the kerb next to him. Passers-by had started to gather. As the paramedics stepped up to him, he realised that the thump of the pulse hitting his hand through the jacket had stopped. He couldn't tell when that had happened. Maybe a few moments, maybe longer. A paramedic put a hand on his shoulder, moving him away from the man. He stood up and moved back. He was looking at his hand as he moved, and was dully aware that blood seemed to be sticking his fingers together.

The man was dead.

Kapellenstrasse was bustling with pedestrians, the end of the day bringing the first employees out of work excited to be on their way home or to a bar for drinks, some going out to restaurants for dinner. Anywhere that wasn't work. Nearing the junction at the north end of Kapellenstrasse a woman tripped, pulling the man next to her down with her. He in turn grabbed at the couple in front of him, taking their balance and causing them to stagger and then drop too. A scream rose up from the pile of limbs and torsos on the path. As they started to find their feet, the woman screamed again. She had blood on her lower leg, her ankle, and her foot. She moved her leg as if to check that she was unhurt, then sank to the floor again. Her knees buckled under her.

A severed leg was on the floor, blood oozing from the open hip joint. It had not been there the second before she had tripped over it.

They had been in the Alternative Control Room for almost twenty hours before power was finally restored. It had taken the six men almost an hour to work their way from the Command Suite through the facility with the minimal amount of equipment they had been able to carry. Rosst had disconnected as much sensor equipment as he could in the limited torch light while Alder had made the journey to the Control Room, released the four other scientists, and made his way back with them. The group had made slow progress through the secure corridors of the facility, laden with laptop computers, tablets, and two large rack cases filled with pressure sensors, thermal imaging sensors, Geiger counters, and laser diffraction units used to measure particle size and speed. Once they were in the Alternative Control Room and had taken a few moments to rest, three small backup generators were wheeled in from a separate store room and set up.

When the first generator had failed to start, Mathers assumed Alder would blow his lid, but Alder simply stepped past the generator and cranked the second one into life. They had enough electricity to set up a group of flood lights, also kept in the store room that the generators had been stored. The third generator gave enough electricity to power laptop computers, but there was no way that the sensor equipment could be run on these small backup generators. While they waited for the main grid to be restored, all six of the group worked slowly and as thoroughly as possible attempting to analyse the limited data which had been recorded on the computers. They all knew that the real analysis could only start once full power was restored and they could fire up the larger sensor equipment.

They had worked in almost silence for hours, none wanting to admit that they were scared beyond any level of ability to communicate effectively what they were thinking. *Had there been a nuclear incident, a breach in the containment area of the Collider?*

For almost a hundred miles in any direction around the facility, as far as France to the north and west, and Italy to the south east, power had been cut off for several hours. It was gradually being restored, but in Montreux it was night again before the grid returned to full function.

"We've found the other half of her." The voice was familiar, but he was so deeply asleep when the phone had exploded into life next to his ear that Dalpoci could not make sense of the blunt statement. "Assistente?" the voice asked.

He had only been promoted to the rank of Assistente a year ago. It still made him uncomfortable to be referred to by his rank. He had just passed fifteen years' service in *Polizia di Stato,* the Italian state police. "Mauro?" he asked.

"Si." He was significantly more awake suddenly, the words processing in his brain. "*Abbiamo trovato l' altra meta del suo."*

"Found the other half of *her*?" he asked.

"Si."

They had been waiting for so long for this, for some trace of the psycho who had butchered a girl so brutally three years ago. Gone without a trace. He had killed a nineteen-year-old girl, and left the top half of her torso in a ditch at the side of the road, cut clean through from just below her breasts. She had been walking home from her evening job in a local cafe when she was murdered. All that had ever been found was the top half of her body, her arms, and her head. They found no marks on her body, no traces of anything in the wound. There was no murder weapon. No sign of a struggle. There had been no witnesses. Just the horrific remains of her body.

"Are you sure it's her?" he asked.

"Si," Mauro replied. "Stesso luogo." *Same place.* "Cut the same way as the rest of her was. Wearing the same clothes. Just like she was on the security film we watched." They had watched the same footage from the restaurant's only camera over and over again. A beautiful young girl, serving a few local customers during an uneventful evening. Her last evening on Earth.

"Who found her? Are you there now?"

"One of the *tirocinanti.*" A trainee for the Carabineiri. "Just back from il Palazzo Ducale."

"Merda. Non lasciante che quegli idioti dei Caribinieri ovunque vicino." *Don't let any of those Caribinieri idiots near it.*

"They're already here," Mauro said in a defeated voice. The Caribinieri would walk all over the crime scene, trample any potential evidence, and get in the way. They didn't have a single detective amongst them worth half the value of the lowest ranking Polizia di Stato investigator.

"Sto arrivando." Dalpoci was already out of bed when he hung up the phone. He pulled on the trousers and shirt he had dropped on the floor six hours ago when he had gone to bed. At five in the morning who would notice he was wearing yesterdays crumpled clothes?

She had been discovered just after dawn on March fifth by a delivery driver just outside Pinerolo, a small town near Turin. *Cast aside by* Il Monstro di Pinerolo. *The Monster of Pinerolo.* He had murdered before, two young women had been raped and murdered in the last ten years, but he had never taken a trophy before. For three years Dalpoci had investigated the murder. He had come close to solving the other two murders but had found no trace of any evidence which could link anyone to the murder of Luisella Biondi. Now he had something to work with, a chance to finish a case which had sickened him to his core. To find and punish someone more brutal than any criminal he had ever dealt with.

Mauro saw him pull over just beyond the police tape where the Caribinieri had cordoned off the scene. He had virtually jumped out of his car and had walked straight past the Caribinieri Officer who was attempting to control the perimeter of the crime scene. Dalpoci had his badge out the second he stepped from his car and flashed it momentarily at both the Officer patrolling the perimeter and the Caribinieri Sub-Lieutenant who had by his own authority taken charge of the situation.

As Mauro stepped closer to the approaching Dalpoci he heard him quietly tell the Caribinieri Sub-Lieutenant to leave the crime scene. The Caribinieri had been dismissed, it was now a state police matter.

"She is exactly the same. I don't understand it," Mauro said. "It's like she was frozen three years ago and defrosted this morning. There is fresh blood."

"There can't be, she's been dead for three years," Dalpoci replied. His face was as alive as Mauro had ever seen it. For three years they had gradually given up hope of catching Luisella's killer. Now they had something more to work with. The chance of a break in this case, and Dalpoci was desperate to make the most of this chance.

They stood over the lower half of the girl's body. Mauro was right in what he had said, there was fresh blood. A lot of blood. Like the body had been cut in half while she was still alive, barely a few hours before. It was turning black on the ground around the legs, but there was still an apparent dampness to the blood which had soaked her dress. Dalpoci crouched by the remains of the body and opened an evidence pack, removing a swab stick. He lifted the torn fabric at the wound with the swab. It came away from the body stickily, leaving a congealing clot of blood on the swab. He placed the swab in an evidence tube and sealed it. The blood wash fresh, from a wound barely over an hour old.

Her legs were stretched out behind her. She was placed face down, in exactly the same position the top half of her body had been found. Dalpoci's body suddenly felt numb. He had examined this scene three years ago, studied every aspect in minute detail. Poured over photographs. Read coroners reports. And now he was stood in the exact same spot he had been stood three years ago, as if time had stood still. Stood in his own shoe prints. He looked at the fence that ran the length of the ditch where the body was sprawled at the edge of the road. A dying bunch of flowers were rested at the post in the fence. Sad remnants of ageing flowers lay against a post, where a few inches away a small plant was growing.

Planted by her mother at the exact place that the other half of Luisella's body had been found. He took out his camera, knowing that this would lead to something he could not bear to imagine. The photograph he took would marry up with the photographs from three years ago. The top half of her body in the photo from all that time ago would fit perfectly onto the photo he was taking now, in exactly the same place.

The group of scientists in Switzerland had simply been shut off from the outside world, and had worked on attempting to find an answer to the question of what had happened within the Collider during the incident. The facility had gone into automatic isolation protocols following the incident, and due to the power cut they had not been able to communicate with anyone externally. Once power was restored, they had been too busy to even consider making calls to anyone; colleagues, family, friends, they would all have to wait for the six men to complete their work. The facility was on automated lockdown when the isolation protocols kicked in. An email message was automatically generated and sent to the head of the European Science Directorate informing him that there had been an incident at the facility, and that it was now in lockdown.

Mathers was sitting quietly next to Enlan, trying to make some sense of the readings they had isolated as potentially being the point where everything within the Collider had gone from the expected readings to what they had begun to refer to as "the incident". It had seemingly happened in less than a millisecond, and yet the reading from the laser diffraction unit clearly indicated a particle within the accelerator having a mass of immeasurable proportions for a number of minutes, which was definitively impossible. The only conclusion anyone in the Alternative Control Room had been able to reach, was that the equipment had malfunctioned during the incident. This in itself was impossible, as there were duplicate readings from every piece of equipment they had checked.

Mathers' brain had stopped processing the figures he was calculating. He had calculated and re-calculated, checked and re-checked every reading and piece of data recorded during the experiment over the last thirty-six hours or so. He could no longer focus and decided to make himself useful by making a fresh round of coffees for the group.

As he was stood in the kitchen just off the Alternative Control Room, Mathers decided to turn on the television. He had realised there had been no contact with the outside world since the incident. It took some considerable effort to concentrate on the news programme which was playing on the English-speaking channel they always watched during breaks in the small stand-down area within the kitchen. He was barely able to process what he was hearing, what the headline running across the banner at the bottom of the screen was saying. There had been some very unusual events over the past forty-eight hours.

The news reader was explaining that a Guard from the Zurich national museum who was last seen walking along Lowenstrasse in downtown Zurich, had disappeared February twenty-seventh four years previously, at approximately seven in the evening, shortly before his shift was due to start. The Guard had been found walking along Bahnhofplatz in a confused state on August fifteenth, at almost exactly eleven in the morning. His watch read February twenty-seventh, at just after seven in the evening.

While he was listening to this story, Mathers was reading the headline on the banner scrolling across the bottom of the screen. On July twenty-second six years ago, a student from Universite de Strasbourg who was last seen in Marche bar on Rue De Zurich at approximately five in the evening was reported missing. The missing student had apparently been found drunk in the same bar at just before closing time on August fifteenth, six years after he had last been seen.

The news reader had moved on to the story of an incident where a decade prior a Range Rover with a woman and two children had disappeared from Eastgate Street, Chester,

England. The same Range Rover had crashed into a Peugeot just a day ago. The woman and both children were taken to a local hospital with minor injuries. When the missing woman's husband, the father of the children had attended the hospital he had identified them as being his family. He had observed that they were wearing the same exact clothes they had been wearing on the day they disappeared. More relevantly, none of the three occupants of the Range Rover had aged, including their ten-month-old baby son.

The incident had expanded way beyond the Collider facility.

War in peacetime

When the President was first elected, he had taken less than a month to clean house and place his own people in key positions within the White House. Steve Halt had been the first choice for White House Chief of staff. He had the most powerful presence of any politician the President had ever known. He was very charismatic, but also had the ability to not be the sole focal point in a room full of people. He could focus people's attention to whoever was speaking in a large meeting, stay on the periphery of a conversation, and then interject a simple statement which would either confirm whatever point was being made, or could stop a motion dead in its tracks. He was respected by his sub-ordinates enough to know his word would never be questioned, but everyone who worked for him knew he would listen to their opinions without bias and consider what others had said when making his decisions.

The call came through late in the afternoon, the outer office had been silent, but Halt had been so caught up in a report he had barely noticed until the phone broke in on his concentration. His personal assistant had left almost an hour ago, which made a direct call to his phone slightly disconcerting. He looked at the caller identity panel, read the name, and snatched the phone up with a smile growing across his face. General Mal Torsler had been appointed NASA Administrator during the same purge of staff in key positions which had made Halt White House Chief of Staff. Halt had always liked Torsler. He was an American hero, but more importantly, Torsler had time for people. He had absolutely no side to him. He accepted no bullshit, hated bureaucracy when it served no purpose but to delay change and justify people's existence, and would not tolerate obstruction to his vision of a new NASA which would make America great again as the world leader in space exploration.

"General, are you calling me personally to tell me we've made first contact?" Halt joked.

"Well, it's a first of sorts, I'm not sure what to make of this one Steve. Do you remember the moon mission from June nineteen sixty-nine?"

"Hmmm, you know I'm forty-two don't you Mal? I remember there were a couple of strange events before we landed on the Moon in November 'sixty-nine. Lost a few men over that period, didn't we? One Shuttle in nineteen-seventy and a landing module disappeared on the first mission to land on the Moon in nineteen sixty-nine."

"That's right. Have you seen any of those strange reports on the news the last few days about people disappearing and suddenly appearing again years later? No memory of where they've been, just turned up like it was the day they disappeared."

"Couldn't really miss it, every news channel seems to be running a story about it." Halt feigned a hick accent "*Aliens dun abducted me,* to *Ah passed through a black hole in nahnteen eighty-seven and come out yesterday mornin'.*"

"Well you may not buy into some of those stories, but this is something a bit more tangible. We just received a radio call from the two astronauts who were on the landing module which went missing in 'sixty-nine from the Columbia. They just told us they have successfully landed on the Moon. Best part is they're requesting permission to exit the module, to make Man's first steps on the Moon."

"You know its August not April, don't you? Can you confirm any part of this, or is this some hoax by kids with a specialist radio transmitter?"

"No hoax, we have them on Space Fence, they're good and strong on every radar pointed up there. Satellite images are coming on line in about four minutes. The ranking astronaut has given all the right identification codes and is using standard communications protocols for the time. He says there are two of them, healthy, unharmed, but a little confused that the radio operator isn't the same guy he was talking to half an hour ago. Seems Neil Armstrong and Buzz Aldrin just landed on the Moon. Strangest thing is in the back of my mind I'm sure they did that once already, I keep thinking something about *taking a small step*. But we all know Pete Conrad was the first man on the Moon."

"How quickly can you get someone up there?" Halt asked.

"Maybe seventeen hours, maybe twenty-four. Depends on how quickly we can arrange the fitness tests. We don't have guys sitting around in Houston wearing space suits ready to jump into a shuttle, we've never had to put on a rescue mission like this before."

Passengers stepping off the quarter-past-two train at Royal Victoria station tracked the sound in the sky, twisting and turning their heads upwards trying to identify where the unusual droning and buzzing sound was coming from. Most walked from the platform down the steps to the road looking to the sky, moving slowly with this odd distraction holding their attention. It was becoming louder with every step.

The area of the London Docklands adjacent to Royal Victoria station has gradually been built up to a bustling metropolitan landscape with conference centres, hotels, pubs, and expensive flats in blocks which are overcrowded with wealthy bankers and lawyers from Monday to Friday, and deserted at the weekend. They are the weekday home of people who spend their weekends in the country at their *real* homes. A cable car crosses the Thames between the dockside, and the O2 Arena by north Greenwich station.

The sound was coming from the south-east, seemingly becoming louder as it moved towards the north-west. Just as the sound seemed to reach overhead the passengers climbing down the steps of the Royal Victoria station from the now slowly departing train, it abruptly stopped, replaced by a strange whine, growing to a high-pitched sort of whistling noise.

The V1 bomb smashed through the north-west corner of the top two floors of the Thames Royal Hotel on its way to the ground. It slammed into Seagull Lane in a hail of shattered glass and bricks and mortar. The explosion pumped shrapnel for hundreds of feet into the air and along the road. The force of the explosion threw a small BMW the full width of the road, slamming it into the front of an oriental restaurant. Customers eating in the restaurant saw the BMW flying towards the window, unable to move, frozen at the sight of such chaotic destruction. A young couple walking along the path where the restaurant window opened onto the street were obliterated by the flying BMW, hurled through the restaurant window with the airborne car. A bloody mess of flesh, bones, metal, and shattered glass. The impact twisted a bus pulling slowly into traffic from its course along the road, lifting both of its front wheels from the tarmac and tearing the front end of the bus clear away. The driver and passengers in the first three rows of seats were killed instantly. Dozens of other passengers were thrown into the carcass of the back section of the bus, a mess of severed limbs and bloodied bodies writhing in pain.

A fracture ran from the centre of the road where the V1 hit, to the base of the hotel which had lost its top floors. People were at once running to see what had happened, running away from the devastation, or just stood in shock. They started to feel the shudder through the ground under them, an earthquake seemed to be shaking the whole area. Parts of the hotel continued to rain down as the fracture grew from a crack to an open wound in the road. There was a cavernous underground car park below the hotel, where a large proportion of the road, with smaller surrounding buildings, cars, and people, all began to slowly and lurchingly sink, subside, and finally collapse into the subterranean void in a cloud of cement dust.

The sky over Berlin was clear of clouds and brightly lit by the full summer Moon. The perfect night, calm weather with visibility stretching out for miles across the German capital skyline. All seven members of the crew were on edge, their senses heightened by the briefing they had received just a few short hours ago. The Germans would be expecting them on a night as clear as this, and yet somehow there was silence. No flack, no barrage balloons, no other planes anywhere to be seen. They had been somehow separated from the squadron a few minutes before. This made no difference, they had a mission to complete. This was the seventeenth mission this crew had been assigned, the most important of all so far. They would be flying deep into the heart of the German capital at the height of the war on a clear summer night to deliver a blow to the commanders of the Nazi war effort at its very epicentre.

JB661 and her crew were on an Arson mission, loaded with over three thousand pounds of incendiary bombs, and a single four thousand pound 'cookie' impact-fused high-capacity bomb. The cookie was designed to destroy large buildings, or entire streets when used in conjunction with other incendiary loads. This would rain devastation down on the built-up metropolis of Berlin, a sustained attack from an experienced crew on a heavily loaded Lancaster working in conjunction with twenty-three other bombers from 103 squadron, combined with others from 576 squadron.

Flight Sergeant Robert Milner was starting to feel an unusual added concern on top of the usual stress of the mission. He was a knowledgeable and capable radio operator who had flown sixteen missions with this crew. On every previous mission his radar had been lit up with dots of other aircraft, his radio a constant buzz and crackle of blips and static. As he scanned frequencies now, he was aware of many strangely clear transmissions, mostly in German, with no stress in the voice of the transmitting radio operator. Nothing from Bomber command, no transmission of mayday from aircraft damaged by anti-aircraft fire. In fact, he had heard no anti-aircraft fire and they were now deep into the heart of Berlin, moments from releasing their payload.

Pilot Officer Thomas Bird looked from the cockpit of the Lancaster, confused by the view before him. Berlin was lit up like a Christmas tree, yet there were no searchlights crossing the sky around him. No beacon of light burning into the sky to identify transgressors. The countdown was already almost at its completion, the bomb bay doors were open. They were at release speed and an altitude of twenty-one thousand feet. The mission had been perfect to this point. They had avoided any Luftwaffe interception aircraft, their route had been successful in negotiating a course past the German defences at Potsdam, the time was now.

Bird spoke to their bomb aimer in the belly of the plane via his head set. Flight Sergeant Paul Firman had been looking down through the viewing window at the front gunner position. His view was clear, yet somehow the target looked different to the still images he had familiarised himself with from reconnaissance photographs he viewed whilst preparing for the mission. The buildings were somehow brighter, the architecture unusual to him. They were at the correct co-ordinates, this must be the right place, but this just did not look like the Germany he had seen on every previous mission he had flown. He desperately wanted this to be over. He was scared, the fear he felt had increased with every consecutive flight over the war-torn European landscape. He had pulled a lever which had released tens of thousands of pounds of bombs onto their targets over the past few months. Soldiers, weapons, factories, and scores of civilians had been obliterated by the simple pull of the lever in his hand. His currently shaking hand. His conscience said that he was doing the right thing, he was with his brothers who he would never let down, but with each mission he increasingly mourned the inevitable innocent lives which were also lost to this hell. Those below, and those flying in the aircraft alongside him, aircraft either shot down by German fighters, or damaged by flak from the ground and crash-landing before even reaching their targets. His headset snatched him back from the struggle his conscience was torturing him with.

"Cleared for release," Bird instructed.

"Release confirmed," Firman replied.

They were directly over the Berlin Friedrichstrasse train station, tracking their way along the Spree River to the north. Firman's grip on the lever tightened. He gently pulled the lever backward until it rested in the release position. Seven thousand pounds of bombs fell from the bomb bay of the Lancaster into the night sky above Berlin. Firman tracked the fall of the bombs as he lay in the nose of the plane. "Bombs away," he told Bird.

The Lancaster banked to its left, towards the north of Berlin. They would be home and landing at RAF Metheringham in Lincolnshire within a few hours if they encountered no resistance on their return flight.

The Prime Minister had called all Members of Parliament back to session, scheduled for the following morning at nine. He had spent the last few hours being briefed in his office at Ten Downing Street. Sitting behind his desk shortly before midnight, the Prime Minister again lifted the pile of photographs of the devastation in Docklands earlier in the day. The large television screen hanging from the wall of the office showed the CCTV camera footage of the bomb slamming into the ground on Seagull Lane, the resulting explosion, cars and a bus destroyed, and people maimed and killed. The footage continued as the Thames Royal Hotel began to collapse inward on itself, and then smashed down burying itself into the street in a cloud of cement dust. An all too familiar image in the modern world of international terrorism.

"How did we not know about this?" The Prime Minister looked up at Colonel Grey, Section Head of MI5. "How did our intelligence community miss a terrorist attack so devastating? This is almost on a par with nine eleven, and you knew nothing? Our terror alert was at heightened, it's not at exceptional, and you are unable to give me any further answers as to if we may be expecting any other attacks."

Grey had just returned to the room from an office being used to co-ordinate the intelligence from all of the intelligence agencies present. "With all due respect Prime Minister, I have just been informed that initial eye witness statements, combined with the best enhancement of the CCTV footage available to us, suggests that this may not have been an incident of international extremist terrorism."

"Well what the hell else would it be?" The Prime minister bellowed at Grey. His face was almost purple with rage, this was the end of his career. He would be the PM who allowed international terrorism to wreak havoc and destruction on the streets of London on a scale not seen for seventy years.

Grey held out an enhanced still image blown up on a tablet screen from the CCTV footage they had been viewing. "Unless one of the terrorist organisations we have been monitoring have decided to start using V1 flying bombs from World War Two, I have to insist that this is something very different, sir."

"A V1?" The Prime Minister sat back in his chair, then sat forward again and snatched the tablet from Grey's hand. "A relic from World War Two was used to bomb us?"

"That's what the experts say that image is. That's what intelligence suggests the witnesses observed." Grey shook his head slowly. "We are under attack from a new enemy, using old weapons."

"Six hundred people dead and we have no idea where the hell to even start looking for the culprits?" The Prime Minister dropped the tablet on his desk. "What have the Americans said to you?"

The Prime Minister had spoken to the American President almost immediately following the bomb, and the President had promised every bit of help he could provide. Grey knew this meant he would possibly get a dissemination of intelligence from the CIA at some point in days to come, which would be redacted to the point that he could make very little sense of what was left and would then have to start the back-and-forth arguments about the politics of protecting sources and American *assets* against the need to protect the public.

"I spoke to Jim Gronan at the CIA, they have nothing linked to any attack of this nature. They are sending over everything they have on possible groups who may have an interest in this area."

The Prime Minister's telephone began to buzz quietly. Then Grey's mobile started to vibrate too. Grey stepped out of the office to answer his call, as the Prime Minister pressed the speaker button on his telephone. He heard the Prime Minister shout into his phone through the closed solidly built door.

"A fucking what bombed Berlin?" boomed from the other side of the door.

Greys own phone came to life. "Colonel, you are not going to believe what's happened now."

The Lancaster was picked up almost two miles north-west of Berlin by a pair of Eurofighter Typhoon jets scrambled from Norvenich Air base near Cologne in West Germany. As the Typhoons approached the Lancaster both pilots armed missiles and locked onto the bomber. Still almost a mile from the relic of the Second World War, the lead Typhoon pilot requested permission to open fire.

In the Lancaster, Milner shouted forward to Bird through his headset that they had what appeared to be a pair of aircraft on an intercept course, closing in rapidly from the south. Bird took immediate action to pull the Bomber up to as high an altitude as he could, pushing the plane to its limits in preparation for what could be their final battle. His crew had survived three previous combat encounters with German Messerschmitts, the beating they took increasing with each consecutive battle. They must be running out of luck by now.

"They're coming in so fast I can barely track them, let alone locate a sight on them to fire," Milner shouted. "Bearing up on us from the south-west now, very slight course alterations as we started to pull up. They can only be seconds away."

Bird banked left to take the Lancaster into a head-on approach to the incoming fighters. He did not want to be flanked if he could avoid it.

A German accented voice cut through Milner's radio, speaking in crisp English. "Unidentified aeroplane you are ordered to surrender. You will be escorted to the nearest air base where you will land. If you fail to comply with this instruction you will be shot down. Confirm this transmission." Milner tried to process the confusing instruction, Nazis did not order RAF Aircraft to surrender, they shot them down if they encountered them in situations like this. No warning, no discussion.

As Bird scanned the night sky in front of him the loudest aeroplane he had ever heard screamed past the Lancaster in an ear-splitting explosion of thunderous noise, followed closely by a second plane in tight formation. He shouted into his headset to Flight Sergeant Charles Smith, the crew's tail gunner. He hated the fact that he was given the instant nickname 'Tail-End' due to the unfortunate co-incidence that his name was Charlie. Smith saw the aircraft fly past, split left and right, banking a full turn to approach the Lancaster from the rear. He lifted the gun sights to take aim, but could not track either plane at the pace they were moving.

Bird looked to his left as he heard an aircraft approach his flank. From his window he could see an aircraft that looked more like a space ship from a science fiction novel Bird had read as a child. The pilot had no face, his head was like a huge reflective fish bowl. His gloved hand pointed to Bird, then pointed downwards. *Land.*

The Typhoon pilots wanted to blow these terrorists from the sky, but they were still over heavily populated areas of the outskirts of northern Berlin. They had been ordered to hold fire unless fired upon, or if it appeared that further bombs may be dropped. The Lancaster's bomb bay doors were closed, and they had clearly been so taken by surprise by the interceptors, that they had made no attempt to open fire.

Radar had picked up this unidentified aeroplane as it approached Berlin, and as the Typhoon pilots took off, they heard over their radios that the unidentified aircraft had been tentatively identified as a World War Two bomber, and moments later the news came through that there had been bombs dropped on Berlin.

Several conversations were going on in Bird's headset, he could hear at least four different voices of his crew shouting, panicked and confused. They could not identify these aircraft, they weren't ME109s, or any other German plane for that matter. They had not been fired upon. Milner's voice cut through his headset.

"We've been ordered to follow our escort and land."

The Cabinet Office Briefing Room on Whitehall known commonly as *COBRA* was lit up at one end by a bank of eight monitors, split between a number of screens showing various images of the scenes from Docklands where the V1 had come to its final resting place, with the remaining monitors showing satellite images of the damage caused in Berlin by the errant Lancaster. "The Lancaster is at Norvenich Air base," Grey said calmly. "The crew have no idea what happened, and at the moment they are only prepared to give their name, rank, and number to the Germans. Not surprising really, they think it's nineteen forty-four and they are prisoners of war."

"Can we identify the aeroplane they were in?" The Prime Minister asked. He looked at the Deputy Prime Minister, who had been stood just behind Grey quietly listening to the account of the events of the last few hours. "Have we heard from the German Chancellor yet?"

"That's my next phone call, not an easy one," The Deputy Prime Minister said. He looked down at his phone, turning it in his hand anxiously. "We just destroyed an entire road, five buildings including a major railway station, no idea how many killed yet. They dropped a bomb on us this afternoon, but in reality, *they* didn't drop the bomb on us any more than *we* sent that Lancaster. This conversation is going to be the difference between war and peace isn't it."

"No, we are not at war. Whatever is said in this conversation, we are not at war. Call the German embassy, arrange for a conference call. They know what happened here today, they need to know without any doubt that we didn't retaliate."

"I hope they know that. How in the hell did World War Two bombs just hit twenty-first century Europe?"

"Have you both seen the news the last few days about the people who disappeared over the years and suddenly reappeared?" Grey interrupted. He had been trying to make sense of what had been going on and something didn't sit right with him. "The people who went missing ten, twenty years ago and turned up in the last day or two with no idea what happened to them or where they had been. Old stolen cars appearing out of nowhere. Heard about the American thing?"

"The men on the Moon from the sixties." The Prime Minister nodded. "It's the same thing isn't it?"

"Can't see how it could be anything else," Grey agreed. "Our past catching up with us?" Grey stepped back and picked up his wireless tablet with the still screen showing the V1 bomb from a shelf it had been casually left on a few minutes before. "Men on the Moon from the sixties, bombs and bombers from World War Two, this is going to need to be more than us talking to the Germans, I think we need to call the Americans too. They need to be a part of this, it's all linked."

The Prime Minister nodded. "Let's see if we can't get a chat going in the next hour, shall we? I spoke to the President a few hours ago, he offered his assistance. Thought it was bloody terrorists again. Maybe we will get more from them than I expected earlier, I wonder if anyone else has put these all together."

"I think we have some serious problems going on," Mathers said to Alder. They had all gathered in the kitchen area and were watching the news reports for what had become their regular hourly meeting. "Every new report on the news seems to have more and more incidents of time displacement."

"What have we done?" Alder shook his head. "We broke through time itself, and now we need to fix this. Or start it again, if that is the right way to phrase it. I never meant this to." He stopped speaking abruptly. He was visibly shaken, more emotionally struck by what had happened than the others had so far been. He looked at Rosst, who nodded. They needed to make sense of the data they had been scouring through over the last few days.

They had lived in the facility, working around the clock until they had ironically lost all sense of time passing as they worked, of day and night merging from one to other. The facility was well stocked of food and supplies. They had eaten while they worked. Slept in small snatches of rest at their desks. They smelled bad, hadn't washed or cleaned their teeth for days. They were vaguely aware that there was an underlying smell of unwashed humanity and coffee breath pervading the atmosphere, but it didn't matter. They could not stop until they had some answer to what they had caused.

"A fracture," Rosst suddenly blurted out to the quiet room. "Look at it." He had a note book and a pencil in his hands. He held the book up as if to prove something to the others. "Something from a week ago comes through three days ago when the accident happened. Something from a year ago comes through two days ago. Something from a decade ago comes through yesterday. It's moving back in time as we move forwards. A fracture cutting its way backwards, opening up through time."

"We need to inform the ESD," Alder said quietly to Rosst. They had moved to a side office to discuss the situation. They needed to assess what immediate actions were needed. They were sure the European Science Directorate had put two and two together already, but they needed to confirm it. To own up. They had reported the incident to the ESD almost three full days ago and had since then worked non-stop trying to find answers to the questions of how and why the experiment had gone wrong. The growing events in the outside world had to be a direct result of their experiment, and if a solution was to be found, it would be found within the facility.

"What do you suggest we tell them?" Rosst was pessimistic that they could explain the experiment and what had gone wrong to anyone at a level where it would not come across as *crazy scientists blow up time*. "So far, we have worked out that shortly after we fired up a nuclear reaction, we found that we had managed to accelerate a particle or particles to somewhere round about a theoretically impossible velocity, causing their gravitational pull to alter space time. That caused what, a ripple? A fracture in time? I'm not sure how we go about explaining that to *anyone* in a way that doesn't make us out to be maniacs who just may well have put an end to the world as we know it."

"It's a call we need to make. I need everything we've got summarised with a conclusion of our findings and our best suggestion of what we can do to repair whatever damage we have caused."

Rosst stood and started towards the door. "I'll have it for you in an hour."

An explanation

In offices thousands of miles apart, three small groups of politicians watched images of each other start to appear on large monitors hung from clean white walls. Each office looked similar in design, a table at the centre of the room, surrounded by leather covered office chairs. A portrait photograph of the Queen hung from the rear wall of the office in London, a photograph of the Lincoln Memorial on the wall in Washington. The German office differed slightly to the others, in that it had a very modern open glass walled visage, set into a corner of the Chancellors office at the Bundeskanzleramt. The Reichstag building could be seen across landscaped grounds, a magnificent and dignified presence in the backdrop of the office.

The German Chancellor was obviously brimming over with rage, her hands gripping the edge of the table in front of her. She had summed up the self-control to sit for long enough to allow this conference call to begin, but now as the other leaders' images were on the screen in front of her she stood, leaning forward against the table. The bombs which had been dropped on Berlin had been felt for miles, the impact sending a rolling thunder through the ground like a terrible tremor from the past. She knew that in reality Britain had not started another War, they had been the victims of a similar incident, but the pain and anger of the loss of life and brutal injuries, cut into her psyche as they did every German in the Capital. They had been the victims of a historical war which they had spent seventy years making the antithesis of modern German World view. They had become the peacemakers, peacekeepers, the sensible voice of World politics.

"Every German citizen wants to know why we have been brutalized today, why our blood is running from wounds as a result of a British aircraft from the War. We need answers, and we need assurances. I have a military that wants to act in vengeance and a population that are near agony from this tragedy. What can I tell them you are doing?"

The British Prime Minister looked at the screen the Chancellor's face was staring back at him from, he was angry too. A German bomb had killed British civilians too. He looked from the Chancellor to the American President, and back to the Chancellor. "A German bomb landed on London today too. Today British men and women are bleeding with German men and women, side by side as victims. We need to work together to know who has caused this. Have you both been given the ESD report?"

Grey was still reading the report from the ESD, it made no sense to him. It had been given to him in a very short meeting with the Prime Minister, the Deputy Prime Minister, and the Secretary of Defense. They had received the report from a department Grey had never heard of, and it contained some entire sentences Grey struggled to recognize or understand a single word of. He looked up hopeful that someone in one of the other offices he could currently see on a pair of monitors on the wall may be able to explain what the document meant to them all in a very simple way.

"Have your people been able to make any sense of this?" The Prime Minister asked the President.

He shook his head slowly. The President had been sitting with his elbow resting on the table in front of him, his chin in the palm of his hand, the top of his index finger covering his mouth. He was aware that his body language presented a negative image to others and was consciously able to control this force of habit in most public situations, but here, now, he was beyond remembering not to touch his face.

"My people are working on it, I think they have done some similar research but are a little behind those places in Europe on this one. Don't you have a couple of those things in Switzerland?" He didn't understand the explanation he had been given by his scientific advisors, he had given up trying to read the report after the first page. It may as well have been in German. "I want to talk to these people. We want you to know that today's tragedies your countries have both suffered are our first priority. The people of America are the children of Europe, and we feel the pain of our closest friends and allies as if it were our own." He could make a speech that brought people together in any circumstance, which shone some light into any darkness.

"We all need to speak to them," The Chancellor said.

All three leaders turned to their aides, their advisors. Each wanted a conversation arranged with these scientists immediately. No delays, no excuses would be acceptable.

"Have we been given all intelligence you are both holding?" The Chancellor asked. "Everything. Not just scraps, anything. However insignificant, whatever the source. I want to know we can either link these atrocities to a terrorist organization, or be able to discount every possibility one by one until we have absolute proof that this was a concerted terrorist attack, or caused by an experiment in Switzerland."

The Prime Minister looked at Grey and nodded. He turned back to the screen. "You will have it as soon as we can put it together."

"Everything," The President said quietly. He was going to have some problems in Congress for this, they didn't give the world un-sanitised access to their intelligence. "It's on its way."

"The simplest way I can explain it is to imagine a train. That train has an almost infinite amount of carriages being pulled along behind it as it moves along the track. The train continues to move at exactly the same speed forever. That train is time. Right now, or the current time, is the engine at the front of the train. The engine moving steadily through eternity. Five minutes ago is at the front of the first carriage behind the engine. Yesterday is at the back of the first carriage. Ten years ago is maybe ten carriages back, twenty years ago; twenty carriages back. A thousand years ago, a million years ago, they are all getting progressively further back on these carriages, as new carriages continue to be added between them and the engine. Then imagine the theory of motion, kinetic energy. A normal train moving along a track at a steady speed, and it suddenly slows or stops. The carriages it is pulling, the passengers on those carriages, they still have momentum, and will be driven forward by that momentum. If the train comes to a sudden stop, the carriages it is pulling may crash into the back of it, concertinaing into each other one by one until that momentum has been absorbed, or the train starts accelerating from the front again."

"That's the simple part. As we accelerated particles within the collider, we managed to separate very specific sub-atomic particles when the collisions occurred. Those sub atomic particles continued to accelerate, reaching near light speed. Imagine a nuclear reaction, the force generated. That force focussed through a particle so small that there is almost no resistance, in a specially designed, controlled environment."

"Are you telling me that we have passed the speed of light?"

"Not exactly. I don't think we can say exactly what happened yet, certainly not until we can repair our equipment. But as those particles definitely reached something close to the speed of light, they create an almost infinite theoretical mass. And as they are reaching that speed, time surrounding and within that mass begins to slow. The greater the speed, the greater the pull on space-time around the object, due to the increased mass. We cannot theoretically pass the speed of light because of the fact that an object reaching the speed of light would gain infinite mass, therefore requiring infinite energy."

"I'm lost," The President said slowly, his hand unconsciously running across his face and shaking his head. He looked from the screen to the Vice President, and then back to the screen.

"Me too," The British Prime Minister said from another screen in the teleconference room.

"As an item accelerates close to the speed of light, relative time around that item slows down. Faster it gets, slower the time passes around it. The Theory of Relativity, to an observer time passes more slowly, the faster the motion of the observer relevant to space-time. What we are guessing has happened, is that around that item time slowed to a stop. To go back to the first analogy, the train hit a wall. When the train came to a sudden stop, the first carriage behind continued its momentum, smashing that carriage into the engine. Then the second carriage smashed into the one in front of it. And so on."

The American President slowly ran his left hand across his face from his brow down to his mouth as he reached out with his right hand to switch off the speaker on the telephone. He looked up at the Vice President, appealing for some sign that his frustrated confusion was shared, that what they had just been told was impossible.

"These damn nerds make any sense to you Paul?"

The Vice President looked back at the President, trying without much success to not express his own difficulty in following the conversation he had just witnessed. "They can't," he started, and trailed off. He looked down at his pad, the notes he had taken scribbled almost illegibly across the page. "They haven't broken the speed of light, but they think they did something that stopped time, and if I got this right, *that caused a train to crash*?"

The President nodded. "These guys might be good at scientific research and experiments, but they are very poor when it comes to explaining what they've done when they screw it all up." He leaned forward over the desk and activated his intercom. "Briefing room two, thirty minutes. NSA executive committee please." He turned back to the Vice President, took a long gulp of his coffee, and rubbed his face again. The same involuntary reflex action he took every time he tried to process a seemingly impossible situation. "Well if they've stopped time, at least I may get an unexpected extension on my current term."

"Good for you," The Vice President smiled. "My promotion on hold then?" He paused a moment thoughtfully, and then spoke more quietly, a more serious tone to his voice, the cadence of his speech more deliberate now. "You realise we have to consider something before we act on this. If we can control this, it may be of incredible use to us in the long run. Imagine the military applications."

"You want to weaponize this? Have you just gone directly to the right-wing politician's playbook on this one?"

"If I don't suggest it someone else may very well do, and we cannot let that happen. We need to at least bear that in mind, we need some control over this long term. Think of the other possibilities though, imagine what would have happened if we could have lifted Booth out of Ford's theatre before he shot Lincoln, or maybe Oswald from the Texas Book Depository. We may be able to prevent any more terror attacks in this country."

"Are you seriously trying to pass this off as a policing and safety benefit? Look at the damage this has already caused, what further damage could we do if we start tinkering with time for our own gain."

"I am just saying you need to have that thought process one way or another within your thinking on this, let our people assess any value this technology may add to our national security."

In Montreux the room stayed silent, two men staring at each other uncomfortably. "I think he understood most of that," Alder finally said dryly. "Might even push that NASA grant through."

"I'm not sure how likely that is, but hey, if we ever get any funding from anyone after this, I'm buying a DeLorean." Rosst lifted himself out of his chair and stretched his back as best he could, he had been sitting at a desk for almost three straight days. Three crazy days since they realised that the experiment they had attempted had gone so far beyond anything they could have predicted, wrong in such an unexpected way.

The fracture goes worldwide

The French Sociologist Emile Durkhiem was once described as 'having an argument with the ghost of Karl Marx'. Alder had heard this when he was a student, and was reminded of it when his first paper was published by a New York scientific journal. A particularly harsh critic had written a rebuttal of his work, describing him as being 'A hundred years too late for a race with Albert Einstein for the ownership of a working theory on time. A race which he would have lost, if he even managed to make it to the finish line'. Alder was thinking that he had just made it to the finish line of this particular race, only to discover that the finish line had moved, and he had no idea where to.

The direct line buzzed, a video link call he had been expecting. It would be the Americans again. The President, presumably now accompanied by his chiefs of staff, scientific advisers, and any number of military assholes. He hated the military with a passion. He explored, discovered, and created. They destroyed.

He nodded to Mathers, who pressed the accept button on a console under the screen. There they were. The President, the Vice President. A group of men and women sat just behind them in suits. In the far background of the screen his focus was drawn to a small group of men. Men in uniforms recognisable the world over. They were Generals in the American military. Even at the periphery of the assembled group, Alder could see their uniforms were adorned with medals, insignias, and stars. Awards for accomplishments which amounted to a reward for killing, either a perceived enemy by war, or their own men by order.

"Gentlemen, you have informed us that you may have created this issue," The President stated from the screen. "We are going to need to know that there is some assurance from you that you are well under way with a solution."

Alder stepped forward. "We need time, this is not simply a case of putting the Collider in reverse." Alder was keen to structure expectations, this would not be something that wound just go back to the way things were before by clicking a few switches and putting their experiment into reverse gear.

"How long are we looking at?" The Vice President asked.

"Maybe hours, maybe days. I simply do not know at this point," Alder replied.

An advisor stepped close to the President and spoke quietly into his ear. The President's expression changed to something between surprise and anger, he nodded and stepped forward into the centre of the screen. His hand rubbed across his mouth, his tension clear to everyone, both in the room and watching him on screen. Other advisors were rushing to the Generals in the room behind the President. Something else had gone wrong.

"By now you must know there have been some extreme incidents as a result of what you suspect to be the effect your experiment has caused. Hundreds of people have died. We need a solution from you." The President looked down, seemingly deep in thought. When he looked up to the screen again Alder realised there was more to the situation than the incidents in London and Berlin. "I need to know within the next two hours that you have this under control, or that you have put together a solution. Whatever you need." The President turned away. "Turn it off."

The Screen went blank.

"Get me the Russian President. We need to know he is aware of this. Then the German Chancellor." The President sat heavily into a chair next to the Vice President. "They've caused a war."

"We don't know that yet," The Vice President replied. "Maybe we can intercept them."

"What do you suggest we say, *War's over guys, welcome to the twenty-first century?* The Russians are about to be invaded again by the Nazis, I can't see them welcoming them in and chatting it out. I need to see the satellite images we have. How clear is it?"

"Hundred percent," The Vice President replied. "Nothing but countryside, then out of nowhere a hundred or so tanks rolling north. Close ups are conclusive, guess the most evil army the world ever faced just rolled back into town."

Generaloberst Abbey Ahren was pleased with the lack of defence the Panzer spearhead had encountered whilst advancing northwards through the Russian countryside. They had not seen any military encampments, and had not been intercepted by even the smallest force of soldiers. He was at the head of a Panzer division of two hundred and forty German Tiger and Panther tanks moving in combat echelon working its way to the Kursk Salient, to rendezvous with other divisions of the II SS Panzer Corps east of Kursk. He had ordered the destruction of two smaller vehicles they had encountered on the road a mile further back, and then one larger truck a few minutes later.

"Where is our Red Army welcome committee?" he asked the four other men in the tank. Hitler had ordered the delay to this offensive to build up the German tank divisions in an effort to capture this strategic area of Russia in one lightning blow. A Blitzkrieg style victory would give a boost to the morale of the Axis powers, and also provide the German war effort with Russian prisoners of war who could be used as slave labour in their munitions factories. As yet, Ahren had not felt it necessary to spread out the tank formation to deliver a blow to smaller Russian Army divisions, the Germans could backtrack to pick up Russian soldiers who were cut off by a victory at Kursk once the main battle was won. This would be the lift Germany needed to help it recover from the struggles of a protracted battle in Stalingrad which had cost so many lives, and depleted German military resources.

"We have a group of vehicles approximately quarter of a mile ahead," SS-Oberscharfuhrer Klemens Bulmann said to Ahren. He was the tank commander who Ahren chose to ride with, the most experienced commander in the division after Ahren. Bulmann had served in the Ardennes offensive where the Germans had surprised and driven back the Allied forces during the Battle of France in nineteen-forty. "Destroy them, or accept surrender?"

"What level of armament are they equipped with?"

"It appears to be small vehicles, perhaps six. No heavy weapons."

"Capture those who can be taken, use four tanks to advance and pincer their vehicles. None of the vehicles escapes." Ahren looked down at his map, confused. The intelligence they had showed a mass of Russian forces built up to repel any advance towards Kursk, they would need to defend Kursk if they were to stop Germany from reaching Moscow. They were encountering small light vehicles which would not give any resistance to an entire division of German tanks. "Have the four tanks advancing take as many prisoners as possible, hold the rest of the division here. We need to assess the line the Russians are holding. We should never have been able to move this freely."

The French border with Belgium contains the picturesque area of Ardennes, just over two-thousand square miles of forest, mountains, valleys, and lakes. Approximately a mile from the town of Hirson, a single British Expeditionary Force *Matilda* Tank sat at the roadside, facing into the Ardennes Forest. Sunrise had seemed to hit in an instant, dawn breaking without any warning. It was dark, barely a pre-dawn light, then the Sun was above the tree line of the forest. The tanks two-man crew were rested and alert, they had expected little opposition from the Nazis in this area of France. They were posted to the region as part of the Allied strategy to contain the Germans who were now advancing from the north, having taken Holland so easily. Both men were confused by the lack of other British Army patrols in the area, they had last made contact with their regiment over an hour ago.

The noise seemed to start in an instant, crashing, sawing, destructive screeching of trees being displaced by an unstoppable force. Both soldiers on the British tank took their positions, they had the high ground, and were sitting with the sun to their backs in an open field. They may be currently alone, but they had options.

Suddenly the sound of heavy machinery broke through the field from the edge of the forest, and through a yawning mouth in the wall of trees, a Panzer II tank broke cover and advanced into the clearing. A second, then a third tank followed, all Panzers. It was not possible, the forest was too dense, the roads effectively unusable to any significant force. The lead tank turned slowly toward the British Matilda, its twenty-millimetre gun squaring up toward the British target. The explosion from the gun echoed through the field, rebounding from the trees bordering two sides. The British Matilda tank started to move backward and turn to face the German force, but was hit low and hard on its front quarter. The tank then lurched awkwardly forward, limping into position to return fire. The tracks of the tank on its right side were damaged but not destroyed. The driver pushed the accelerator pedal down and pulled had on the right-hand directional lever to turn the tank. A fifth German Panzer broke clear of the forest and seemed to be taking its time to assess the condition of the British opponent. A second report sounded from the German Panzer which had fired on the British, a second impact rocked the tank back, not powerful enough to turn the tank over, but punching hard into the armour on the tank. A third shot hit the ground a few meters short of the British tank, throwing earth and small rocks up into the sky, a cloud of brown and green. The second German Panzer broke to the right of the first, turning without any grace toward the British tank. A shot fired from the second tanks gun, hitting the British tank squarely on its turret destroying the Vickers 303 machine gun mounted on it, and cracking the hull of the tank. Another shot hit the turret a second later, tearing through the outer shell of the tank. The impact of this shot obliterated a section of the metal construction of the tank, hurling dozens of pieces of shrapnel through the tank commander's chest and right arm. Blood rained down onto the tank floor, as the driver turned to check on the commander another hit to the tank rocked him from his seat. As the driver hit the floor of the tank a wet plop sounded just ahead of him. He looked up to see an almost unidentifiable lump of flesh in the pool of blood. He looked up to the commander's seat, and realised the lump of flesh was all that was left of the tank commander's arm. The commander was slumped dead in his seat, barely held in place by the torn hull of the gun turret which was splayed inwards, a grotesque shard of metal skewering into the lower torso of the commander.

The hatch adjacent to the gun turret of the Matilda was hanging open on its hinges, loosely rattling against the hull of the tank. Stunned by the rapid devastation of the lone tank, the driver climbed to the hatch, pushed hard on it and open it fully outward. He looked up to the open sky, blood stained across his face, arms, and uniform. He was panicking and forgetting his basic training. He dove clear of the tank, with no idea of the direction of the German tanks. He was flailing down the side of the tank into the open field when a shot from the German tanks hit the ground a few feet from the Matilda. The driver was thrown clear from the side of the tank in another burst of mud and grass. The sound rang in his ear, a tremendous crack as the shell exploded into the turf of the field. The driver struggled to his feet, stumbling on his left side. He looked down and dully realised that his leg may have been hit by shrapnel from the last impact, but it was difficult to differentiate between the blood he was already covered in from the tank commander, and his own wound. Pain seemed further away from him than he could understand, his senses all dulled by shock. Again, he started to run, blindly hoping for some form of cover from the assault. As he stumbled a few feet from the tank he vaguely heard voices, shouts from his peripheral sense, but he could not isolate direction beyond the idea that the shots had possibly come from beside or behind him. He staggered forward again when the first bullet tore into him. The bullet hit him from his left flank, turning him through ninety degrees as it punched through his hip. He fell, his body thumping against the ground and almost bouncing as he sprawled backward. Again, he lifted himself from the ground, this time unable to do more than stand off balance for a few moments. The next shot rang out from the German Luger less than a hundred yards away. A German officer had stepped from a tank, and was stalking his prey, slowly working towards the wounded soldier. The driver sighed as the air was pushed out of his lungs by the bullet as it slammed into his sternum. Blood ran from his mouth, he collapsed forward onto his face and died where he fell.

Ahren and Bulmann had stepped from the tank and were watching as soldiers moved forward to intercept the remaining Russians from the vehicles ahead. Of the six vehicles ahead of them, four had been destroyed in mere seconds as they had tried to flee the moment the tanks approached. Eight soldiers from the II SS Panzer Corps had dismounted the tanks, and were arresting the Russians from the remaining two cars.

"Hold everyone here until we have interrogated these," Ahren said to Bulmann. "This does not feel right, where are their army divisions? Where are the defences?"

"Is it possible they have pulled back to fortify a defence closer to Moscow?"

Ahren shook his head. "No, they would have burned the ground as they withdrew, this is something different." He looked back towards the tank division. They were at the head of a two-hundred and forty tank division, yet his quick estimate as they dismounted suggested more than half of the tanks had fallen back somewhere overnight. He could see the tanks organised into standard formations, with the regulation distance between sections of the division. There were maybe almost a hundred tanks remaining in formation. There had been no radio communication to suggest the rear sections had fallen back. No obstructions or possible Russian ambush. Bulmann's radio lit up "Herr Oberscharfuhrer?" It was the scouting party ahead.

"Ja?"

"We have five prisoners, they have no uniform or weapons."

Bulmann looked at Ahren for direction. "Have them hold the prisoners where they are. We will go to them, you and I. Have the rest of the men wait here, tighten the formation to defensive positions."

"Sprechen sie Deutsch?" The Russian looked at Bulmann and said something incoherent, he looked simple to Bulmann; a peasant.

"English?" Ahren asked. The Russians looked at each other, something unsaid passed between them. A soldier pushed his Luger into the back of the head of one of the Russians, a woman who looked to be at least sixty. "Nein," Ahren said calmly to the soldier. He lifted his hand and gestured the soldier to step back. "Now, English. Yes?" He turned back to the man who had responded to Bulmann's question in Russian; the patriarch of this little family.

"Yes," the man said. "Some." He looked into Ahren's eyes for the first time. "You cannot be. The War, it is over."

"Lie." Bulmann stepped forward and shouted. He pulled his Luger from its holster. "This is a trick." He raised the Luger towards the man.

"Look around," Ahren said, and again raised his arm, this time horizontally across Bulmann's chest stopping him from stepping further forward. "Look at the vehicles." Bulmann was at Ahren's shoulder, his anger and frustration clear, but he would not go against Ahren's judgement.

"You are a farmer, Ja?" Ahren said to the man. The Russian nodded.

Ahren turned to Bulmann. "This is over. Look at the vehicles; they are farmers, but they have vehicles like that. What Russian farmer has motor vehicles? Where is their cart, their horses? Look at their hands, he works on the land. Cracked hands, dirt ingrained. His face, Sunshine has darkened it because he works outside. They are too scared to lie to us."

"It's over?" Bulmann asked. Ahren pushed Bulmann away from the small crowd of Russian farmers and German soldiers.

"I am not sure what is over, and what still remains the same." He looked back towards the soldiers. "Have them take the Russians out to the field. It is a fine day. Tie them and leave them."

"Not kill them?" Bulmann asked. "They will give us away as soon as we leave this place."

"There is no need for them to die. We are soldiers, we kill soldiers. They are not armed, they give us no strategic advantage by dying." Bulmann looked questioningly at Ahren again. "Trust me, we will take their vehicles, they cannot give away our position. Give the order for the remaining sections to continue north."

"And us?"

"We are taking a vehicle from these Russians, and turning around. Get a map. Once our men are moving north, take off every insignia you have on your uniform. Take off all but your under shirt and trousers. We are driving south, to Germany."

History gets personal

Remis Stoffel had been employed by *P2 Security* for over a decade. A private security company operating across Europe since the eighties. Remis had enjoyed his job at first. It gave him a small amount of power over others. He was often self-absorbed, and felt that by working in a security company which served government sites, he may be noticed. He may be asked to become something more important than a security guard. It had never happened, and now he was sitting in a gate lodge at a scientific facility waiting. He had not been relieved for almost two days. His manager had called to ask him to remain at his post, an accident had happened and the facility was now in lockdown. Other staff had been sent to patrol the perimeter. He was one of two guards who remained within the facility.

Stoffel was sitting watching tv, the news was the same on every channel. One story overbearing everything else. Stoffel absently clicked the remote once this particular news broadcast ended. He found another news programme. Another suited clean-shaven man sitting next to a crisply spoken woman in a white pants suit. She looked like a bitch to Stoffel. She spoke clearly in the same condescending way the male newsreader spoke. They informed people of great events, with no passion, no emotion. They were all the same, good schools, university, then sit in a chair and tell the world their particular news company's version of the truth. Bias towards whatever political leaning the news company aligned itself to. Stoffel knew they were not telling the whole story. When the news readers finished speaking, the screen cut to a reporter on location. Stoffel saw the fence he was sitting behind. His gate lodge was on tv. This was not the first time today, in fact he was beginning to become bored of seeing it. The image panned out to show a small but growing crowd outside the gate.

Stoffel got up and went to make coffee again. He was fed up of coffee, fed up of vending machine sandwiches. He had been constipated for a day and a half now. He hated the stodge the facility canteen served, but his only other option was a vending machine the security department had installed for times like now when the canteen was closed. Maybe another coffee may help him to shit. His bowels hurt. It felt like he had cement drying in his lower body.

As a child, Stoffel did not have a close family. When he was eight years old, his sister disappeared. She had been thirteen years old. She went to bed one night, and was gone the next morning. At first the police said she had run away. Then his father was arrested and held for three days suspected of killing his sister. His father was released as no evidence was found, and never charged. This was the end for his father, he could not bear to be accused of doing something to his own daughter. He stayed with Stoffel's mother, if only to try to keep some family together. Days then weeks then months went by, eventually the family accepted that she was not coming back. Lucy Stoffel, missing; presumed run away. That was the police assessment of the situation.

Remis Stoffel spent his life from eight years old isolated, his mother distant, his father destroyed by accusations. Remis once heard his mother screaming at his father. *Why did they arrest you? What did you do?* His father's response was the same as it ever had been. He said nothing. His mother was lashing out. His father just walked out and left her to calm down. He returned later, the same way he had returned the last time she was like this. Walking around the small town they lived in until his wife had gone to bed. He would sleep on the sofa, if he could sleep at all.

Stoffel kept running through his childhood in his mind. He remembered his sister the way she was the last time he saw her. He remembered a happy family with love, ripped from him when she disappeared. Then he thought about the years of pain living with parents who stayed in the same house waiting for a daughter who never came home. Anger choked him again, throttling him from within. Almost thirty years of wondering what happened to her, while his family tore itself apart. He had not spoken to his mother for almost five years. He had no idea how long it had been since he spoke to his father.

The main entrance to the Collider facility used the same biometric locks as the internal doors, combined with a conventional lock key card system. Stoffel had a key card which gave him access to the gate lodge, the facility canteen, and the first outer door of the main facility building. He had no access through the doors leading to the internal bunker areas. As a security guard, he had no reason to go further than the entrance areas of the main buildings for routine checks. Stoffel had given up on food, he had decided he was going to find some answers for himself. The news had given him an idea he did not like at all.

As the outer door to the main facility building opened, lights automatically came on. A reception area opened up in front of Stoffel. He was used to this room, it was crisp and clean, minimal in decorations. The glass fronted exterior gave onto a slate floored reception area with a small desk by a set of doors leading to internal offices. There was a waiting area with large comfortable leather sofas to the left of the main doors. Stoffel made his way to the main desk and slipped into the chair behind it. He reached under the desk, and pushed the internal call switch. This was a silent alarm which sounded only within the facility. He had silenced the alarm system in the gate lodge area before walking to the main building.

Inside the Alternative Control Room, a quiet bell rang out, and a bulb above the main door lit up. Rosst looked at the light, and sighed. The bulb was one of four in a bank of bulbs showing various locations in the facility.

"Main entrance to this building," Rosst said to Alder. "I'll make my way up there now; what guards are on duty?"

"I think it was superguard and a new person," Alder said. Most of the facility staff had begun to refer to Stoffel as *superguard* within the first month of being there. He took his job a little too seriously, searching every visitor with a stern almost abrupt manner. He patrolled the grounds regularly, challenging anyone walking around outside if he didn't recognise them, or if he felt that they should not be in the area.

"Great," Rosst said. "He's probably decided we need to show him some ID as he hasn't checked us in over twenty-four hours."

Rosst walked out of the room and made for a bank of elevators leading to the main reception area.

An elevator opened out onto the reception area, Rosst looked out from the doors curious as to what may have caused the alarm. He saw Stoffel stood at the main reception desk looking across the foyer towards him. Stoffel looked uncomfortable, he was rubbing his stomach. Rosst stepped from the elevator and walked casually to Stoffel.

"Are you alright?" Rosst asked. Stoffel didn't reply. He reached behind him over the counter top of the reception desk with his right hand, his left still rubbing his stomach. As Rosst stepped up to Stoffel he froze mid step, realisation dawning on him. Stoffel brought a small smooth looking pistol from behind the counter. Rosst opened his mouth in surprise, words failing him. Stoffel swung his upturned hand towards Rosst, the butt of the gun slamming into Rosst's forehead opening a gash a few inches into his brow. Rosst staggered backward a step, reaching up to his face. Blood trickled from his hairline down his forehead, reaching his eyebrows and then running down either side of the bridge of his nose. Stoffel raised the gun, now pointed directly at Rosst.

"Elevator, let's go and see your colleagues. We have some things to talk about."

Rosst stepped into the elevator a short distance ahead of Stoffel. The thought that he may be able to hit a button for a floor on the control panel and maybe manage to get the doors closed with Stoffel on the outside of the elevator ran through his head. He decided it was not worth the risk, Stoffel looked like he would shoot if he thought things were not going his way. Stoffel walked into the elevator and stood against the opposite wall to Rosst, the gun remaining level, pointed towards him.

"What is this?" Rosst tried to ask.

"Shut up," Stoffel said over him. "We can talk about things once we are with your colleagues, *your highness*." There was venom in the words. Stoffel had always hated the way Rosst and his buddy had been so revered within the facility. They condescended to occasionally acknowledge men like Stoffel, but only thank them as they opened a gate. Never to ask a normal question. *How is your family? How are you today?* There was no time for a little effort on their part, no personal interaction.

Alder heard the lock release on the door to the control room. He looked up as Rosst stepped through.

"What was the emergen…" The word died in his mouth before he could finish, the sight of Rosst stepping into the room with blood running down his face stopping Alder in his tracks. Behind Rosst superguard stepped into the room, a gun in his hand.

"What is this?" Mathers stepped up to Alder's flank and put his hands out in front of him, a simple sign of surrender to attempt to pacify the gunman.

"You are going to help me, we are going to fix something. You are all over the television, your experiment has made you famous." Stoffel pushed Rosst forward with his left hand, leaving his right hand aiming the gun between the three men in the room. "Where are the rest of your people hiding?"

"They aren't hiding, they are working in another room. Just down the corridor," Alder replied. "We can help you, whatever you need us to do, it can be done in here I'm sure."

"Is this where you did it?" Stoffel asked. "Is this where you took her? Where you killed those people, made people disappear?" He seemed angry, but was talking calmly enough. "You scientists." He began to rub his stomach with his left hand again. The gun lowered momentarily, his eyes briefly glazing over as he remembered her. Suddenly they returned to focus, more so than before. An anger turning to rage as the memory spurred him on. "You took her from me," he screamed. "You took her, and when she went it took everything. You ruined everything, you fucks. Your fucking experiment thing, your science." He sprung forward as his right arm raised, again slamming the butt of the gun into Rosst, this time hitting him hard behind the ear. Rosst was stood a few feet ahead of Stoffel, facing Alder and Mathers. The momentum of Stoffel stepping forward and smashing the gun into the back of his head sent Rosst stumbling forward a few steps before his legs buckled under him. His right leg seemed to turn in on itself, and he dropped to the ground, his left leg stiffly pushing out behind him as he settled.

Stoffel stepped back, breathing heavily. The rage in him taken out for moment on the back of Rosst's head. On the floor, Rosst was breathing in odd sighs. Mathers began to step towards Rosst to check on him, Alder held him back. Rosst was breathing. He was hurt, but he was breathing. Better not to provoke Stoffel if they could help it.

Lucas Kobe had heard stories in the last few hours that there had been several explosions around the town of Ypres. There had been reports of armed terrorists working in small groups moving through the Belgian town, and also across the countryside and scattered surrounding villages. The last news report he saw showed a building on the outskirts of the town destroyed, and the news reader was describing dozens of reports of bodies being found in the street. Lucas had always felt safe in Leuven, it was a beautiful and peaceful city. He had moved to Leuven from Ypres to study at the University, and now that he had almost completed his degree he was considering staying here and settling permanently with his girlfriend.

"The terrorists in Ypres are moving out into the country. They said on the news people are being killed in Brussels now," Lucas said to his girlfriend, Carolina. They were walking towards the main University campus exit. The news reporters had warned that people should not leave their homes for the time being, as there had been so many terrorist incidents in the last few days. Lucas had decided that they were safe enough to get some basic supplies from the local shop though, if they were quick. He had heard that the terrorist problems were linked to something in Switzerland, and figured now that they had worked out what was causing this spate of killings, the authorities must be all over it. There were a few students milling around anyway, and safety comes in numbers.

"Do you really think we should be out here?" Carolina asked.

Lucas turned his head to reply to her question, placing his arm over her shoulder, running his hand up her neck into the long dark hair at the back of her head. As he looked down at her face a crack echoed off the walls of the University buildings. Lucas' arm seemed to be slapped from Carolina's shoulder as her right cheek burst open and was blown away in an instant, taking a large portion of her jaw with it. Blood sprayed outward and she jerked against his shoulder, pushing him sideways with her weight. Her knees gave under her and she crumpled to the ground, dead at Lucas' feet. Lucas turned and looked from her corpse to his own hand. The bullet which had killed her had also torn his thumb clean off his hand. The sight of her dead on the ground in front of him seemed to be freezing him to the spot where he stood. After a few moments his vision seemed to lose focus, a tunnel forming in front of him. Balance began to fail Lucas and he stepped back, a half stumble. He wretched, coughed, then bent forward and vomited. Another crack sounded in the small road bringing his awareness back to reality. He looked up in time to see a woman running from what looked to be a group of soldiers at the university gates. A man lay dead on the ground just a few feet from where the woman was running. Lucas watched in stunned silence as a soldier raised a rifle, aimed, and shot the women in the back as she ran. Her body seemed to continue its momentum, now turned slightly as her shoulder seemed to swing limply forward with the force of the impact. A second shot hit her from behind, pushing her further forward. Her legs no longer stepped with her movement, she seemed to collapse to the ground in increments as she skidded forward, going gracelessly down to her knees, her hips bending back and giving way to her lower torso as it hit onto the ground, then finally her head pitched forward slamming face down into the road.

A soldier stepped through the gates. His uniform was familiar to Lucas. He was from a photograph in the pages of a history book. The soldier raised his rifle again. Lucas raised his hand in front of him. Blood ran from the wound where his thumb used to be, staining his forearm as it streaked to his elbow, coursing around the crook of his arm, and dripping freely to the ground. A smile crossed the face of the soldier. He slowly shifted the weight of the rifle against his shoulder, and tilted his head slightly to the right. The smile was still on his face as his head rested against the stock of the rifle, his left eye closing into a sick wink to Lucas. The soldier's right eye lined up along the gun sights. Lucas' hand seemed to be floating between him and the soldier. The soldier breathed in, held it for a long moment, leant his weight slightly forward and squeezed the trigger.

"We can't just turn it off," Alder said. "The Collider is already off, that won't stop what is happening. We can't put it in reverse and put everyone back where they were."

Stoffel took his left hand from his stomach and ran his index finger along the slide of the gun in his right hand. It was a Sig Sauer p226, grey, sleek, a weapon fit for any professional security agent. It said to anyone who saw Stoffel handle it that he was in charge.

"You can create this machine, you can fix it." Stoffel looked up from the gun, looking directly into Alder's eyes. "You took from me, destroyed my life. Now give it back. Put her back." He pointed the gun at Alder, then at Mathers, then at Rosst, who was still unconscious on the floor. "You took from me, I can take from you too."

"We are trying," Mathers said desperately. "We need time to make repairs. To get it right."

"You've had all your time, your machine is making time now, isn't it? Making time run backwards." Stoffel tapped the gun again with his finger. He was not making sense to Mathers and Alder. They guessed he had seen a few news reports, and had put together in his own mind a crazy idea of something that had happened to him in the past, linked that to the Collider experiment.

"Who is missing?" Mathers asked. "We don't know who you are talking about. Tell us."

"My sister. You took her. The police said my father must have done something to her, but you did it. She was there, she went to bed that night. She was in bed and then in the morning she was gone. You did whatever you did to her and she was gone. We loved her." He was rambling. Confused and angry and blaming the Collider experiment for something that happened to his sister. "I saw the news," he said quietly. "The girl in Italy. They found her cut in half. They found her body years ago, and then this week they found her legs in the same place her body was found. Is that what you did to my sister?"

"We can't know that what happened here caused something to happen to your sister. If we can try to stop what is happening now, even if we stop things coming through, it may not put everything back to where, *when* it was," Alder said. "It might not send everyone back."

"Send her back," Stoffel screamed. "Send her back or I will kill you. You don't think I will shoot you because I need you, but I will. I have no life, you took her, you took my life." He kicked Rosst in the leg, hard enough to lift Rosst's lower left leg across the back of his right leg. "Send her back now." He kicked Rosst again.

Mathers stepped forward slowly. He stepped over Rosst as Stoffel moved backwards. Stoffel pointed the gun at Mathers, now holding it with both hands in a defiant stance, warning Mathers not to come closer.

"We will try to help you. We will do as you ask, but we need this man to help us. We need him to fix the machine, and we cannot treat him if you hurt him so badly that he needs a hospital. There are no medical doctors here." Mathers spoke evenly, trying to bring Stoffel back down to a place where he would understand what they needed to do if they were going to get the Collider to work.

"What did he say?" The British Prime Minister asked.

"The Russians are sending their Air Force. I can't stop them," The American President replied. "He barely spoke to me, said *The West* had caused another world crisis and now he would have to deal with it. The Russian people would not accept another invasion by the Germans."

Collider | Richard Warwick

The President stood up from his desk, and started to pace around the room. It didn't help the Prime Minister, as the President kept walking off the screen while he was talking. The Vice President remained in his chair, and exchanged a look with the President. There was something more going on.

"Ok, so what's the next thing then?" The Prime Minister asked. "Have you spoken to the Chancellor? How are the Germans reacting?" As he asked the question, the Prime Minister realised what the problem was. "They are soldiers," he said slowly. "They figure the war is over so the Russians should not be sending any army or air force to intercept them, they should try to speak to them, to tell them the truth."

"That's about it," The President replied. "Technically it's an army invading Russian soil and as far as they are concerned that makes them an enemy to be stopped by whatever means."

"Then there is Belgium and northern France," The Vice President added. "Seems we have soldiers fighting a couple of long dead wars all across Europe right now."

"I was briefed about the tanks in France, will the French try to get through to them? The Belgians, do they have people on the ground to detain the soldiers or do we need to send people?" The Prime Minister was aware that a lot of his resources were spread thin as it was, he would struggle to put a lot of feet on the ground if soldiers continued to appear randomly across Europe.

"As bad as it sounds, I think the Russians may be doing the right thing given the circumstances, and I think the French may need to do something similar," The President replied. "As much as these soldiers need to be given the opportunity to surrender, as it stands, they are fighting a war they still think is very much underway, and they are an invading force briefed to obliterate any resistance. The Germans may see them as soldiers, German civilians now that the war is over, but they are killing people indiscriminately right now and we have to stop them." He stepped back to the centre of the screen, and the Prime Minister understood how hopeless he felt. The Prime Minister felt just the same. "We need to stop the Nazis before they get reinforcements from World War One."

The Vice President stood and handed the President a tablet. On the Screen there was an image from a satellite showing the destruction of a large section of the Nazi tank division in Russia.

"I think part of the problem just got taken out of our hands, The Russians have hit the tanks." The President passed the tablet back to the Vice President. "We need to resolve the French and Belgian problem one way or another. We can't leave divisions of Nazi soldiers roaming Europe."

"Agreed," The Prime Minister said.

"This is turning pretty surreal," The Vice President said as the screen turned off. "Could just leave it and let history sort it out, like some terrible B-movie. *Nazis versus dinosaurs.*"

Enlan chugged back the last of his coffee and put the mug down complacently on a pile of paperwork. He picked up a laptop computer and slipped it under his arm. Enlan was beginning to get bored and frustrated with the way he was being treated. Mathers was working with Alder and Rosst on planning another test run of the Collider whilst Enlan had been tasked with pulling together working equipment to monitor the environment in the Collider facility during the experiment. He had been left with the two other Control Room scientists from his shift, both still in shock from the incident during the first Collider experiment.

Peter Dornel and Steve Ortile had barely spoken for days. Enlan understood that Ortile had been struggling for a number of weeks before the incident, and this was probably contributing to his mood. His wife had left him a few months prior, and she had moved back to America shortly afterwards taking their son with her. Dornel was another story. He was almost catatonic after the incident, and had to virtually be dragged from the room by Mathers.

"Let's get back," Enlan said. "Nothing more we can do in here, almost everything in here is either burned out or not up to the job." Ortile nodded and picked up a pile of printouts and stood up from his desk.

"You ready Pete?" Ortile asked as he walked to the door. Enlan had left the room. Dornel just looked up. His eyes were blood shot, red and puffy. Dornel guessed he wasn't sleeping at all from the look of him. None of the rest of them had managed more than a few hours' sleep in the last few days, but at least they had managed some. "Come on, we're gonna fix this."

As Ortile stepped out of the room he saw Enlan stomping up the corridor towards the Alternative Control Room. He was starting to think Enlan may be bi-polar. One minute he was fishing and not interested in anything, the next he was surly and reacting badly to some random perceived slight.

Mathers was helping Rosst to his feet in the Alternative Control room when the door flew open. Rosst had started to come to a few moments before and they had managed to convince Stoffel that they needed to move him to a chair and treat him as best as they could if they were going to try to start the Collider again. Rosst turned in Mathers' arms at the sound of the door lock clicking as it released, momentarily causing them to lose balance and stagger forwards a step. Stoffel was stood between Mathers and Rosst, and the door which had just unlocked. The door slammed against the wall as Enlan shouldered his way through, his arms laden with random pieces of equipment.

"What the fuck?" Enlan muttered as he turned to face the room, coming face to face with Stoffel who was spinning in shock towards the sound of the new intruder who was bursting into the room. Stoffel's right arm was swinging upward, raising the gun towards whoever was coming through the door.

"No," shouted Alder. "Get back he has a gun."

Enlan's eyes widened as he saw Rosst stood in Mathers' arms covered in blood, and then immediately in front of him a guard from the facility turning to him with his gun raised. Enlan threw the folder he held in his hand towards Stoffel, a flinch reaction to the threat presented immediately in front of him. The corner of the folder hit Stoffel sharply on his left shoulder, making him step back in surprise, at the same time that Enlan also stepped awkwardly backwards trying to find his way back out of the room. The spring-loaded door had begun to close behind Enlan, and his back hit the thin edge of the door as he stepped back, rebounding and pushing him forwards again. Stoffel unconsciously pulled the trigger of the gun as he was stumbling backwards, his reaction a combination of shock and fear, surprised at the way Enlan had burst through the door, and then at being hit by the folder which had been thrown at him. The bullet hit Enlan high up in the chest, slamming him back again into the door. Enlan was turned by the impact with edge of the door, and fell sideways into the doorway. The door closed against Enlan's body, wedging him between the door and its frame.

Mathers let go of Rosst and stepped towards Stoffel, grabbing at his arm as the out-of-control guard turned back toward them. Mathers was outside Stoffel's arm, and as Stoffel turned toward Mathers his upper arm hit against Mathers' body. Mathers grabbed at the arm to try to control it. Stoffel pulled the trigger twice again, firing randomly past Mathers into the room. Mathers heard glass break with the first shot, and a dull thud as the second shot rang in his ears.

Alder had looked around the room as the door opened, his eyes settling on a flat head screwdriver about six inches in length sat on a desk a few feet ahead of him. As Mathers grabbed Stoffel and wrestled with him for control of the gun, Alder rushed forward picking up the screwdriver. He ran towards them with the screwdriver held out in front of him. As Mathers pulled at Stoffel's arm, turning his body towards the room, Alder saw his target. The front of Stoffel's body was opened up in front of him, his right arm held away from his body by Mathers. Alder dived forwards and drove the screwdriver upwards into Stoffel's torso just below his sternum. Alder's shoulder slammed into Stoffel with the all the force he could manage as he stabbed the screwdriver into him. Alder's momentum took all three men off their feet, landing in a pile on the tiled floor of the room. The gun fell from Stoffel's hand and slid across the tiles to the wall.

Alder rolled off Stoffel and helped Mathers to get out up. Mathers had been at the bottom of the pile when they hit the floor, and was bleeding from his nose. Stoffel was breathing in jerky gulps, blood spreading out from the wound in the centre of his body. The screwdriver was buried in his torso all the way to the handle. His right leg lifted and fell a few times, as if peddling a bike. He was trying to sit up, but as he lifted his right shoulder from the ground he coughed, a rasping noise choking in his throat, and he fell back dead on the floor.

Mathers turned and groaned as he leant against Alder. Rosst was half sitting, half laying on the floor in front of them. His head was partially propping him up against the front of a desk. He had a bullet wound in his throat, blood staining his shirt below his chin. His eyes were open but blank, his pupils dilated. He was dead.

Going home

Ahren and Bulmann set off driving south in the farmers small car as soon as the Panzer division had begun to move northwards again towards Kursk. They planned to cross the border into Ukraine near the city of Sumy and then drive directly west past Kiev and into Germany through Poland. After ten minutes of driving they reached a busy road, and were shocked by the number of vehicles moving up and down the road ahead of them. Bulmann selected first gear and accelerated out into the road from the country track they had just driven along. He was getting slowly used to the wide gear ratios in the terrible Russian car.

Thunder seemed to roll over the horizon from behind them, a rumble shuddering along the landscape out of nowhere. The day was clear, no clouds in the sky. Ahren turned to look through the rear-view window of the car just in time to see three Russian jets cut low into a parallel course with the road. The jets flew directly overhead, a few hundred feet above the small car. More thunder from behind them, followed a few moments later by a further three Russian jets. Bulmann broke hard, and pulled the car over the side of the road, skidding as he broke into the dirt of the verge.

"What the hell is going on?" Bulmann asked. "Those aren't Russian aircraft."

Ahren turned back to Bulmann as more explosions of thunder burst behind them. "The Luftwaffe are developing some sort of rocket. I think Von Braun is getting close with some new bombs, and Messerschmitt have spent the last couple of years working on the two-six-two. Maybe they have put them into production." He turned away from Bulmann towards the direction the jets had come from. More rumbling, the ground beneath their car seemed to vibrate deeply against the sound. "That's not thunder. Those aircraft are in formation for a bombing run. The ambush we were waiting for just happened, I think."

"Should we turn around?" Bulmann asked. "We can't leave them alone, the Russians must have been waiting for us." More bursts of explosions crackled and thudded distantly. It was clear to both men now that the noise they were hearing was a battle raging a few miles behind them.

"Did you see those aircraft? Remember what the farmer said to us. The War, it *is* over. Many years ago. I don't know what has happened, but those are aircraft we have never seen before, not like any weapon we have seen before." He looked up again as more Russian jets flew past them, banking away into the distance moving faster than anything he had ever seen before. "We would be slaughtered. We are not deserting now, look at the car we are driving. Look at the cars driving past us. The war has been over for a long time, I don't know where we are but we need to get back to Germany and find out."

The hydraulic spring load on the door kept pushing it against Enlan against the door frame. He had struggled to move out of the doorway into the corridor, but the weight of the door had been too much for him to escape from. He felt like he had been punched in the chest, but he couldn't understand why he was so winded by the punch. He thought maybe he had broken his shoulder when he had hit the door and fallen over. Enlan tried to speak, but as he opened his mouth a burst of pain ripped through his chest up into his throat. He distantly heard himself moan.

Mathers turned away from Rosst's body, realising that Enlan was still alive. Alder had been crouched over Rosst, just holding his hand. He had checked for a pulse at first, and realising there was none, had simply remained still, gently holding onto his friend. Mathers stepped away from Alder and rushed to the doorway, pulling the door open freeing Enlan. Dornel stepped up to him and looked down at Enlan.

"Can we move him?" Dornel asked.

"We have to," Mathers replied. Enlan lifted his right arm and placed it on the door frame, managing to push himself over onto his back. He looked up at Mathers desperately. "We're here, let's get you comfortable." Mathers leant forward and lifted Enlan's head, resting it in his palm. With his other hand he started to lift Enlan's shoulder. "Take his other arm," he said to Dornel.

Enlan screamed out in pain as Dornel and Mathers slid him from the doorway. Ortile had walked closer to them. As Mathers looked up at him Ortile looked away, his face pale, a blank expression gave away how shocked he was. Mathers thought Ortile may be mentally shutting down.

"Let's see if we can stop the bleeding," Dornel said. "Pete, can you put some pressure on the wound?" he asked. Ortile turned back to them, and slowly sat down on the floor by Enlan. He reached over and placed his hand on the wound in Enlan's chest. Enlan gasped as the pressure was applied to his wound. Mathers looked back into the doorway, taking in the brutal scene. He realised that Enlan had lost a lot of blood, it was spread from the doorway out into the corridor where they were now sitting.

"Call for an ambulance," Mathers said to Dornel.

Dornel started to stand, looking down at Ortile who was sitting silently, pushing his hand against Enlan's chest. Blood was still running out through Ortile's fingers, spreading out from his palm. Enlan shuddered briefly his head turning slightly Mathers' hand.

From the floor Enlan could barely see the faces of his colleagues sat above him. The pain in his chest was unbearable now, it felt as though a white-hot wedge was being driven into his chest, splitting his body open. His vision was almost milky, and getting increasingly less focused. He could only make out vague figures through a haze. There were voices, maybe people talking to him, but he couldn't isolate words. He tried to lift himself up on his elbows again, but as he started to move and put his weight through his arms, the pain exploded in his chest again.

Mathers felt Enlan's head lighten in his palm. He was trying to move. Mathers took his other hand from Enlan's shoulder and gently pulled his head back down into his palm. He stroked his hair gently backwards, trying to calm him. He looked over at Ortile, who was still sitting next to Enlan, but now using both hands to try to stop the bleeding. He had both hand on Enlan's chest, leaning his weight forward. He was quietly crying. Ortile met Mathers gaze, his eyes tragically betraying of the truth of the situation. Mathers nodded slowly. He stroked Enlan's head gently again.

Enlan's chest heaved up, then fell. His breath a small sigh. Mathers watched Ortile's hands raise with Enlan's chest. Enlan's chest rose, Ortile's hands rose. It fell again, and with it the hands too. Mathers realised after a few moments that he was breathing with Enlan, each time he saw Enlan take a breath, he would breath. He saw the chest raise and fall. He breathed. The chest raised slightly. Fell again. Mathers stared down, not breathing. The chest didn't rise again.

Colonel Grey had been summoned back to Downing Street by the Deputy Prime Minister. Grey was not a fan of politicians, but accepted the bureaucracies associated with being Section Head at MI5 as an occupational downside. Being summoned on the whim of a politician so that Grey could tell them what they needed to know about an issue was a regular occurrence. He often then had to tell them what it actually was they needed to do about whatever that particular incident of the day was. He had negotiated various British political regimes as an invaluable source of information and advice, with no bias shown to the various political parties, Right or Left. He was simply there to provide impartial information a suggested plan to bring about conclusion or an acceptable outcome. The thing was that Grey was now in his early fifties, and his patience was wearing a little thin with successive politicians who could not process information for themselves, and needed Grey to hand hold them through the most basic of analysis. He was hoping for a quiet last few years before retirement, to be able to take his pension at fifty-five, and spend the next twenty years living in a quiet village in the countryside. Spend his days reading, maybe going for long bike rides or fishing when the weather was nice. No more phone calls at three in the morning. Never having to spend fourteen hours a day in London going from meeting to meeting. No more international trips, he could happily live out the rest of his life without ever leaving the country again.

In the last hour Grey had spoken to both Steve Halt at the White house, and Jim Gronan at the CIA. Neither had any difference of opinion to Grey, the consensus between the intelligence agencies was that this was not a terrorist led incident, but that it must be the result of the experiment in Switzerland. These scientists from the European Science Directorate had created something which had pulled time inside-out.

Grey buzzed his intercom to his personal secretary. "I need my driver in five minutes, I'm going to Downing Street." He thought through the reality of the way the day had turned out. It was almost the middle of the night. He had been in meeting after meeting for almost the entire day, and had been at his office or at Downing Street for almost two straight days without going home. In fact, he had only spoken to his wife once since the V1 bomb hit London, over a full day ago. He pressed the intercom buzzer again. "Call my wife please, tell her I will be home some time tomorrow. Then go home yourself, I will need you tomorrow but there is nothing more for tonight."

"Thank you," his personal secretary replied. "Eight-thirty as usual?"

"I would normally say later as you have been here beyond your usual hours the last two days, but I think I will need you again as normal tomorrow, looks like it's only going to get busier."

Ahren and Bulmann had been driving in four-hour shifts, trying to rest between each stint at the wheel. They had managed just over twelve hours driving without significant incident, but shortly after midnight, the Russian farmers car they had commandeered had broken down. It was clearly not a well-maintained car, which had been perfect for their purpose. The innocuous car had safely got them across the border into Ukraine without drawing any attention to them, only needing to be refuelled twice. They were now facing a new combination of dilemmas though. The money they had taken from the Russian farmers had been enough to buy fuel for the car in Russia, but was now of no use in a new country. They needed to find somewhere to change the small amount of remaining currency they had, and then also find a new form of transport. Ahren had an idea on how they could resolve both issues and also get them back to Germany without incident. About a mile back, he had seen a commercial train yard adjacent to a main train line. If they could find the station depot supervisor, and if he could be bribed, they could work their way back to Germany on a goods train.

Ahren walked back to the car from grass embankment he had used to relieve himself. "Help me to roll the car off the road onto the verge over there," he said to Bulmann, pointing to a dip in the grass verge a hundred yards ahead. "We need to leave it as far off the road as we can manage, I don't want it found before we are a hundred miles from here."

Bulmann grunted and walked to the back of the car. He had barely spoken for the last twelve hours. Ahren assumed he was still angry that they had left the rest of their division to be destroyed by the Russians. There was nothing they could have done, he had tried to justify his decision to himself since it happened. They would be dead themselves now if they had stayed with their men, no way they would have made any difference to the situation. It was just that simple, get away in the car, or stay and die. They had chosen not to die, but there would always be regret that Ahren could not save the men under his command.

They rolled the car into the verge, and then down a short incline the edge of a field. Ahren turned and started walking towards the train yard. Bulmann reached into the car, then turned silently and followed Ahren onto the road and walked a pace behind him.

Grey's driver pulled up to the curb next to Ten Downing Street and stepped to the side of the car as the engine idled, before he could round the car to open Grey's door, Grey had opened the door and was stepping out. He was keen to get through this meeting and return to his office to try to get some rest. There was no end in sight as far as he could tell, this situation was going to get a lot worse before it got better.

Grey walked through the door, into the dimly lit corridor leading to the Prime Minister's office. The Deputy Prime Minister stepped out of the open office door and nodded to Grey, an acknowledgement that the situation was bad, and also a small level of appreciation for Grey being present. This administration had relied on his experience heavily, he was the best advisor they had within the intelligence community.

"Come in Cam," The Prime Minister said from inside the office. A rare informal greeting from the Prime Minister. He used Grey's first name only when he needed an unusual favour, information gathered with some level of tact from a contact, or more rarely, some information sat on by Grey until it was a more favourable opportunity for the information to be released. "What have we got?"

Grey walked into the office, followed by the Deputy Prime Minister. "Steve Halt and Jim Gronan are of the same opinion as myself I'm afraid. This is way out of our control. We are dealing with a situation that was not created maliciously, there is no international terrorist organisation that we can target to stop the current time things we are seeing. From what Jim said, they think it is down to the scientists at the European Science Directorate to try to fix the machine they built, and try to use that machine to restore whatever was damaged by their experiment."

"How far has this gone?" The Deputy Prime Minister asked.

Grey turned slightly, and shrugged as he held out a heavy envelope to the Deputy Prime Minister. "We have gathered as much information as we can, but have no idea what the full extent may be is the honest answer. Small incidents are being reported gradually, but a lot may have gone unnoticed so far. The larger incidents are obviously easier to document. There are some real political meltdowns happening right now. The Vietnamese are parading a small American army unit all over the television over there, apparently, they have six soldiers who were arrested near Khe Sanh following a fire fight with armed police and then a whole division of the Vietnamese army. They dug in and the battle lasted eight or nine hours. Sounds like there was damn near a massacre and the Vietnamese are claiming that the Americans have invaded again. Steve Halt is using all his charm just to keep the Vietnamese from arresting every American over there right now. There are protests outside the American embassy in Hanoi.

We know this thing is worldwide. In that folder is a list of every incident we know about. Seems that we just reached the turn of the Nineteenth Century. The missing fingers from the Statue of Liberty were discovered on Liberty Island a few hours ago. They went missing while it was being constructed, so we are guessing the time jumps are dating around Eighteen-Eighty now."

"What about all the missing people who have turned up? Have they given us any information on what happened to them?" The Prime Minister asked.

"We have selected a range to interview, but we have only managed to speak to a few so far. We have discounted anyone who went missing later than Nineteen-Eighty. It is feasible that a person may have gone missing for legitimate reasons and still remain of similar appearance since that date, making it impossible to confirm that they are genuine *travellers*. We have had a whole load of crazies turning up at police stations who are claiming that they have time travelled in the last week."

"Travellers," said the Prime Minister. He nodded to himself. "I like that. So, what are the stories of the ones you have spoken to sounding like?"

"Varying stories of finding themselves where they were a few moments before, but everything simply changed around them. An Actress just appeared during a matinee of *The Mousetrap* in a theatre in the West End. Strangely she had disappeared from the same play almost forty years ago. She was lying in position for a part where her character had just been murdered. The curtain went up for the opening scene of the play and there she was, laid upon the stage. Most of the audience just thought it was part of the play until some of the other actors came on and one almost tripped over her. When we spoke to her, she had no recollection of any change, she lay down on stage in the seventies and stood up a couple of days ago as if it was moments later. Everything changed around her without her realising.

The original guitar player from *The Drifters* went missing in the sixties, and he was found drunk a couple of days ago near a bar in New York. People actually saw him *arrive*. Just staggering along the road out of nowhere, bumped into a couple who said there was a moment where the air went dry, sort of warm, then there he was. Shame really, I was going to see The Drifters next month, I heard they have a great guitarist playing for them now. Hope the original guy doesn't demand his job back."

"So that's it, they just appear?" The Deputy Prime Minister asked.

"What was the bit about the air going dry?" The Prime Minister asked.

"That has been a bit of a theme, minimal but it has been mentioned a couple of times." Grey made a wavering motion with his hands. "We aren't dismissing it, but it's not a solid confirmation. Couple of cases of people reporting that their mouths have gone dry, a feeling of thirst out of nowhere. Sudden feeling like it's a warm dry summer day, but since it's hot mostly anyway." Grey shrugged again.

"There is one more concern." Grey took the envelope back from the Deputy Prime Minister and opened it, sliding a sheet of paper from it. "A leak at the European Science Directorate. Turns out there have been a few news reports suggesting that the Collider facility in Switzerland is the cause if this incident." He handed the sheet of paper to the Prime Minister. It had a still of a headline in front of a female news reader. The banner across the screen read *Experiment linked to recent deaths.* "Nothing confirmed, but a few news programmes have run with it. The facility was already on lock-down, but they have had some protesters at the gates from the look of it. The news is linking them to the deaths in Europe so far, but it will only be a matter of time before they link the various bigger incidents of the last few days. If they make that connection, we could be looking at mass panic."

The crowd which had started off small and relatively peaceful at the gates of the Collider facility, had swollen in numbers, and become increasingly volatile. There was a very limited police presence outside the gate of the facility, mostly just a single Officer making an occasional walk from their car to the entrance gate and back again.

From inside the reception area of the main facility building, Mathers watched the crowd at the gate on a bank of CCTV monitors. He had walked to the reception area shortly after Enlan had died, intending to call the police. They needed a coroner to collect the bodies if they were to continue to be able to work in the Alternative Control Room. As Mathers had picked up the telephone to call the police, his gaze fell over the monitor screens set into the desk area. Mathers sighed to himself and fell into the chair by the desk. The facility was in lockdown, with one dead security guard and two dead scientists sitting in the main building. They had one security guard patrolling the grounds, new to the job, and from what Mathers had seen so far, probably not of a mind set to protect the four remaining scientists against a raging mob. Mathers replaced the handset in its base and sat watching the monitors for a few moments. Could the facility gates hold back that many people? Probably not was the answer. If they came through the gates, the facility was large, and they would not be able to get into the main Collider bunker, but they may be able to do significant damage to other areas, maybe prevent supplies from getting to them if needed.

Mathers reached down below the desk and switched off the alarm which Stoffel had triggered to get their attention a short while before. He picked up the phone and dialled an internal extension.

"We have people at the gates," Mathers said when Alder answered the phone. "Looks like they are not exactly happy. I think we are going to need the police out there before we try to get someone in with supplies. I'm not sure we will be able to get the bodies moved right now either."

"Come back down then," Alder said neutrally. "We were going to be calling the Americans and the British again shortly, we may as well do it now. Nothing's going to change if we wait, and they may be able to send some help. God knows we need it."

The familiar scene lit up on the screen in front of Alder and Mathers. The American President surrounded by various advisors and a few Generals tossed into the mix again for good measure. The second screen then blinked into life showing the British Prime Minister casually leaning against a desk drinking a cup of coffee. The activity on both screens suddenly ceased, blank faces turned towards the screen staring out at them slowly changing to shocked expressions. Alder looked at Mathers, and then down at himself. He realised that both of them had blood on their clothes and smeared up their arms. Mathers had a splatter of blood on his face too.

The American President stepped forwards toward the screen. "What happened to you? What the hell is going on there?"

"A guard went psychotic in here," Alder replied. "He came into the building with a gun and shot Doctor Rosst and Doctor Enlan. They both died." Alder heard his voice saying the words almost abstractly, the shock hitting him again. His voice wavered as he spoke again, the words barely audible. "The guard blamed us for losing his sister."

"Where is the guard now?" asked the British Prime Minister.

"He's dead," Mathers spoke up. "When he started shooting at us, we tried to defend ourselves. We had no choice."

"Is anyone else hurt?" asked the Prime Minister.

"No, we are in shock and quite sore but no other injuries, nothing that won't heal. We are finished though, we have lost too much experience, too much knowledge." Alder looked at Mathers, then back at the screens. "I have no idea when we could even try to start another experiment now."

"That's not an option," The Prime Minister replied. "You lost two people there and I am sorry for that, but hundreds, maybe thousands of other people are dying around the world. Your experiment has caused that. You need to make whatever repairs you can to fix this as soon as possible."

The American President shook his head and stepped back from the screen. He turned and looked at a General stood a few feet from the back of the room. The General seemed to know what the President was thinking. He just nodded. The President turned back to the screen.

"There is one other option." His hand ran across his mouth as he paused momentarily. "We have no choice now do we? If we cannot fix your equipment and reverse this, we are left with the only option available to us. We need to destroy what is causing the time jumps. I don't take this decision lightly, but we are left with the choice to attempt to save as many lives around the planet as we can. A nuclear strike is ready now. I'm sorry."

Alder and Mathers both gasped simultaneously. The Prime Minister shook his head and looked down, clearly unaware that this was the next step.

Mathers started to speak, but Alder put his hand on Mathers' shoulder and squeezed. *Let me say what needs to be said.*

"Death and destruction is your only way isn't it? How many people would you kill with a nuclear bomb to save how many other lives? Do you really think that a bomb will fix what is happening? All you can do is destroy, your soldiers are going kill indiscriminately on your orders for no reason." Alder was filled with rage as he spoke. It boiled up in him instantly. "What exactly do you think a nuclear bomb will do? Whatever has happened to time is continuing to happen The collider equipment is fully shut down, there is no power supply to it at the moment. If you destroy it there will be no difference to the effect it has already had, and continues to have on time. Think it through for a minute. You won't repair a hole in a wall by throwing a grenade into it. If you cut your finger you wouldn't heal the wound by smashing the knife you cut yourself with."

"How many people would die?" The Prime Minister asked, interrupting Alder before he said too much.

"Thousands. Maybe hundreds of thousands. But how many have already died, and at this rate how many will continue to die each day until we stop this happening?" The President said. He shook his head and looked away from the screen. "What other choice do we have?"

"How big a bomb will you drop?" Mathers asked. "How many bombs do you think you will need? We are in a bunker hundreds of feet underground, designed to contain a nuclear reaction as part of an experiment. How big a bomb do you think you will need to drop to make any difference?"

"Give me an alternative then," The President replied. "Give me something to go on." He rubbed his hand across his mouth again, wondering what hell these people thought they were doing preaching to him about saving lives against taking necessary action at a cost. "You say *we* destroy. People like *you* kill and destroy indiscriminately. That's what you said. Well how many people have you killed already with your experiment, and you judge us for trying to fix this situation. People like *you* invented the guns and the bombs. There is as much blood on a scientist's hands as there is on the hands of a soldier or a politician. The blood you are metaphorically wearing right now runs far deeper than the actual blood you are stained with."

"So, live in the stone age then?" Mathers asked.

"We are almost back there," The Prime Minister shot back, frustrated at the back and forth going on in front of him. "I am sorry for your loss, and I know you now have an even bigger task on your hands, but you have no choice. Start the equipment again, retry your experiment and find how the jumps in time are happening. At the moment however much you are hurting, and however hard it is, the world is desperately relying on you. The future, and the past is relying on you right now."

A jolt in the track lifted the train carriage momentarily, slamming it back down to the rails rattling the crates noisily against each other. The regular shudder of the train returned as it sped across the Polish border towards Cracow. Ahren rolled his head as he sat up, his neck stiff from the position he had slept in. They had found a fork lift operator prepared to get them onto the train for a couple of hours work helping to load the train, the last of the cash they had, and Ahren's gold cigarette case. They would simply climb off the train in Cracow and find a military transport or a train from there across the German border heading towards Dresden, and then on to Berlin.

"When were you last in Cracow?" Bulmann asked as he lit a cigarette.

"Never," replied Ahren. "And you?"

"Almost a year ago. A good posting." Bulmann blew out a lung full of smoke and flicked ash from his cigarette. He pondered the cigarette for a moment, turning it in his hand slowly. "Do you think the man in Russia was speaking the truth? The war is over. We finally won."

"I have no way of telling. They said it was over for a long time. The weapons they used are not right. We need to get back to Germany and report what we have seen."

"We are deserters. That is how they will see us Herr General." Bulmann threw the butt of his cigarette into the floor of the carriage. Smoke rose from the butt of the cigarette and drifted towards the roof of the train, Bulmann seemingly transfixed with the small faint cloud as it wafted upwards. "How can we return as heroes of the Reich on a cargo train as deserters?"

"I have been thinking about that too. The Russian family we spoke to, they knew no German. They spoke some English but knew no German. *We* won the war? I do not think that can be. If we won the war you and I would not be on the back of a train. Those people would have spoken German, and we would have passed at least one outpost by now. A checkpoint on the track we are on when we crossed the border."

Bulmann shook his head adamantly. He leaned forward and ground the cigarette butt into the floor of the carriage, then kicked it away. "A truce? Possibly we have come to some agreement with Stalin? Maybe the Fuhrer moved our attention to the British?"

"Look at the buildings we are passing." Ahren stood up and opened the window slightly, the slats in the window revealing buildings becoming gradually denser lining the track on either side. "There are no signs in German. I was looking out of this window a short time ago. Every sign we have passed has been in Polish. Whatever happened, things have not turned out well for the Reich."

Mathers stepped out of the shower and lifted his towel from the rail, running it gently over his face. He was the last of the four remaining scientists to go to the staff area of the facility and clean the blood off himself. He had been meticulous making sure he thoroughly cleaned Enlan's blood off him. It had been on his clothes, his arms, some on his face, it had even been in his hair somehow. He felt sick to his stomach. Alder and Mathers had moved the three bodies to a makeshift morgue in an office along the corridor while Dornel and Ortile had gone out to the staff area and taken showers. Mathers had spoken to Ortile and asked him to keep an eye on Dornel, who was clearly becoming less and less stable. Mathers had returned to the Alternative Control Room following the video conference the British and American politicians, to find Dornel stood next to Enlan's body, staring down at Enlan blankly. Dornel did not respond when Mathers had spoken to him. He had cowered back from Mathers when he touched him to get his attention.

Mathers dressed quickly once he was dry, and started back towards the main building. As Mathers hurried across the open area of the facility between buildings, he heard footsteps clatter along the path behind him. He turned to see the new guard rushing along the path to catch up to him.

"I'm sorry sir, I saw people moving around but when I saw the last person walking out here, he was covered in blood. There are people at the main gates. I can't find the other guard, I haven't seen him for hours."

Mathers stared at the guard, frozen on the spot flashing back to Stoffel walking into the Alternative Control Room in the same uniform this man was wearing, gun held out in front of him. The guard stepped back from Mathers, confused by his reaction. Mathers snapped back to reality and realised that the guard was very young, and clearly scared.

"I know about the other men with blood on them, the guard you have been looking for had a bit of an issue. Unfortunately, he hurt some people."

"Oh shit," the Guard replied. "Are they alright? Are the police coming to arrest him?"

"No, it's a little bit too late for that. He killed two people. He is dead too. There will be some people coming here soon I hope, one of my colleagues has made a phone call to the police and also to the company you work for. Are you alright out here at the moment?" Mathers thought the guard looked even more scared now that he realised he was alone guarding the external facility area.

"I think so, if you think the police and other guards will be here soon?"

Mathers had lied to the guard in the hope of giving him a little more confidence in the dire situation they were currently experiencing. Alder had spoken to the police and also the security company this guard worked for. Neither were prepared to send anyone to the facility. The police car which had attended the outer area of the facility earlier while the crowd was gathering had also been called away. Incidents of looting and demonstrations were beginning to be reported in most cities in Europe over the last few hours. Relatively minor disturbances so far, but the police departments were clearly preparing for full scale riots. They would be on their own for some time yet, until the Americans and British managed to convince the Swiss Government to send either the police or the army to defend the facility.

"I'm sure people will be here soon, and until then you can call the facility control room from the main gatehouse using line four of the internal telephone system. Just pick up the phone, hit the line four button on the phone, then select extension one. If anything happens out here, don't get involved, just call me on that number. You'll be fine. You are our new head of security." Mathers was convinced the guard would just leave, but to his surprise, the guard actually looked a little more reassured.

"If that's what you think is best, just call you if there are problems and stay out of the way. I can do that."

Mathers gently hit the guard on the shoulder with his open palm, a reassuring gesture. The guard grinned momentarily. His face quickly re-set to a serious expression, he was now in charge of security at a major Government facility.

Grey turned a pen in his hand as the phone buzzed in his ear, he was surprised the phone at the other end of the line was even ringing. It had been engaged every time he had attempted to call it for the last four hours. He was at behind his desk again, his chair creaking as he pushed back into it as deeply as he could, he needed to actually get some sleep, but at the moment his comfortable office chair was the best rest he could hope for. The phone stopped ringing in his ear, replaced by a clutter of background noise. The hum of a very busy office through a phone on hands free.

"Cam, hold on for a moment, will you?" Jim Gronan almost shouted into the phone. Grey heard him barking orders to several subordinates. "Ok I'm with you, thanks for returning my call, several times. I saw the missed calls but every time I hung up from a call, my phone rang again."

"No problem," Grey replied. "Wasn't like I was going to be finishing early for the day and heading home any time soon anyway. What's new, besides Nazi's in tanks, men on the moon, and soldiers in Vietnam again?"

Gronan laughed. He was used to Greys dry reaction to situations others in the intelligence community would be flapping over so much they would damn near take off.

"You want the abridged list? Some fairly small things and some more interesting things which will need a bit of political sensitivity. I think we need to get some people to that facility in Switzerland as soon as we can do. There are growing reactions across the world to what's happening, and if they are our only hope, we are going to need to protect them. You know they are already tentatively linked to the cause of this thing in the press?"

"Agreed," Grey replied. "I was talking to someone at our Embassy about an hour ago, though they are going to be at least eight hours before they can put together a team to get to the facility."

"You are doing better than us then, we are hopeful of a small team from our Embassy, but the reply I received was *some time in the next twenty-four hours*."

"They seemed confident that they would be safe enough underground when they were talking to your boss earlier," Grey replied sarcastically.

"I think that may have been a small amount of bluster on their part, we looked at the facility as soon as the plans were sent over to us. I'm guessing they could hold out quite well for another day or two, but they are going to need food and water, probably technical supplies too. We need to make sure they get everything they need, unhindered by any external interference." Gronan walked to the door of his office, leaned on the door frame for a moment, and closed his eyes. He was as tired as he had been in years. He thought Grey likely was in the exact same position. "Think this may be my last year here. You still thinking retirement and the quiet life too?"

"It's all I think about every time I walk into work, and it's at the back of my mind until I leave work," Grey replied. "These jobs had a way of wearing on you however good you are at them."

"Too right buddy." Gronan walked into his office and closed the door behind him. He sat on the sofa he usually used for informal planning meetings by a small coffee table in his office. "The next problem, a sensitive one." He stretched his right leg out in front of him, hearing hi knee click, then rested his foot on the edge of the table. "The German tanks we saw on satellite in Russia."

"The Russians destroyed them, didn't they?" Grey asked. "World War Two is casting another shadow over Europe. Old feelings coming back to haunt us."

"Well things are looking a little more awkward now. The Russians did destroy the tanks. Unfortunately, when we watched satellite images of the time leading up to the tank division being destroyed, we saw something else though. The Tanks stopped, and outriders along with a few of the tanks apprehended a few local vehicles. Shortly before the tanks moved on, there was an interesting development. Our analysts identified two German soldiers taking a Russian car and turning back, towards Ukraine. The Tanks continued north, and were destroyed a few minutes later."

"So, you are saying we have a couple of German soldiers driving through Europe, OK they are Nazi's, but essentially just a couple of soldiers, aren't they?" Grey asked, slightly confused at what the issue was, compared to all of the other incidents of the last week.

"The problem is two-fold," Gronan replied "The Germans are making some serious accusations about the way the Russians acted by destroying the tanks. The Russians are pissed at being invaded again. Like you said, old feelings coming up, we don't want to have another war start right in the middle of the current problem we are facing. If the Russians capture these German soldiers now, they could use them against Germany, it could be the last straw. We tracked the car, picked it up again on a satellite near the Russian border. It's being followed, we are guessing by a Russian intelligence vehicle."

"Two soldiers? How could that be such a major incident, even if the Russians do get to them?"

"That is the second part of the problem. As with everything right now, I don't know how reliable the intelligence is, it is seventy-year-old information after all. An analyst here has identified one of the soldiers from CCTV footage at a petrol station in Ukraine."

The Bullet train pulled into Tokyo Station in the district of Chiyoda, coming to a steady stop at the platform. The doors opened with the smooth quiet hiss of Japanese modern technological achievement. Dozens of passengers departed the train, an orderly daily activity for most of the passengers. They moved along the platform steadily towards the main station exit.

A large group of people, more a smooth wave than a flood, poured out of the north Exit of Tokyo station. They moved in a conditioned regular formation, all part their daily routine. The group turned out through the individual turnstiles, reforming to a steady collective as they came upon the pathway to the Tokyo business district. From the direction of the Tokyo Station Gallery, a woman dressed in a faded kimono staggered towards the crowd holding her stomach. As she reached the crowd, she leant forward and vomited. A gush of clear vomit splattered onto the pavement, covering the shoes of a few business men at the front of the crowd. One man took the brunt of the outpouring on his trousers. The woman collapsed to her knees as the crowd pulled back in horror. She was babbling as she knelt in her unfortunately self-produced puddle.

One woman from the crowd stepped towards the woman on her knees. She pushed through the retreating crowd, clutching a paper mask over her mouth. She asked the woman if she was alright. The woman on her knees did not reply, couldn't even raise her head to face the woman stood over her.

"I am a nurse," the Woman said as she stood looking down, trying to avoid stepping in the puddle of vomit. As she looked down at the woman in the kimono, she realised the woman had not only vomited, she had soiled herself too. She was as pale as the nurse had ever seen, sweat breaking out on her forehead. The nurse stepped back from the woman, pulled out her mobile phone, and called an ambulance.

It was a matter of minutes between the nurse' call and the ambulance arriving. In that time the crowd had moved away, most almost running from the scene in their urgency to get away. The ambulance crew were unconvinced by the thought that they should take the woman. She looked to have a stomach infection, and they argued with the nurse that she should make her way home or to her local doctor. The nurse insisted the crew take her to a hospital. She was worried she recognised something in the vomit the woman had produced.

Some hours later, a panic set out through The University of Tokyo Hospital. A woman had been brought in by ambulance during the morning, suffering an apparent stomach infection. Her symptoms were consistent with severe dehydration and a bacterial infection. The hospital did the usual tests, and promptly quarantined its entire building. The tests had come back positive for Cholera.

When Mathers walked back into the alternative control room, Alder caught his eye and motioned towards the door Mathers had just entered through. They walked back out into the corridor, and along towards the elevators.

"Feel better now you're cleaned up and in fresh clothes?" Alder asked.

"Very much. There's another guard out there, young lad. He looked like a rabbit in the headlights when he spoke to me. He was looking for the other one." Alder motioned to the office they had transformed into a temporary morgue. "He had no idea what had happened in here, but he saw everyone else going out to shower, he was scared because we were all covered in blood."

"That makes sense, I would worry if I was on my own watching the people I worked for walking round covered in blood, with no idea what was going on." Alder stopped walking and turned to Mathers. "We have to talk about Pete Dornel. He's no better. Steve just told me that he can barely get a response out of him. He's been getting worse for days. Well, since it happened. I think the guard coming in here has pushed him over the edge."

"I know, I saw him stood over Enlan's body, just staring at him. He needs some help, counselling maybe. Problem is we need him, there is no way we can rebuild the monitoring station without him. No monitoring station, no experiment."

"I asked Steve to try to get him working on it just now. They are sort of piecing it together as best they can. What do you think about the Americans, I may have gone a little too far considering we could actually do with some help from them?"

Mathers smiled. "You may have said a few things that were on the angry side considering we are struggling down here and need some help. Then again, they were threatening to drop a nuclear bomb on our heads at the time. Bit rude on their part if you ask me. The British seemed to help calming things down, I think they understood that obliterating this place will make no difference."

"I spoke to Mike at the ESD head office. The British have spoken to them and asked for more people to be sent here to support us. Unfortunately, there isn't much of a chance of us getting more than one shift of staff in here, and they would need to get through a crowd at the gate. Mike said that since the experiment was blamed for everything, we had three staff from the second shift call them to resign."

"The crowd out front is getting worse. The guard out there said he has seen more people arriving constantly. Sounds like it may be getting a little volatile too. I saw the news earlier while I was waiting for you to come back from the shower, they are starting to say we are to blame for the time jumps, and we've caused deaths all over the world. There's a news crew out there right now, when it showed live footage there must have been a couple of hundred people out there."

"Ok, well hopefully they won't get past the front gate, if they do, I guess we will need to ask for some police help," Alder replied.

"Hmmm, the police were great last time we called them," Mathers replied.

Civil war

The call to the police had come from a farmer early in the morning, to report that there were dozens of people trespassing in one of his fields. His farm occupied land on the bank of the Black River, east of the city of Pocahontas in Arkansas. When the patrol car drove up the farm lane towards the farm house, smoke was rising from what appeared to be a few small fires in a field about a mile away. This was the last call Dan Small his partner Chris Tober would be responding to for the shift, they had been on duty since ten o'clock the night before. A farmer was claiming that there was a camp set up overnight in one of his grazing fields, and some of the people he had seen moving around the camp appeared to be armed.

"Think we can have these guys moving on by six?" Tober asked. He was tired and ready to get back home for some food and get to sleep. Tober had hated nights for his entire police career. Eight years of trying to turn his body clock around every week for a couple of nights was wearing hard on him. He would spend two or three nights trying to stay awake, his body insisting he should be asleep while he was at work. Then once he had finished his night shifts his body would refuse to sleep at night, he would wake with his bowels deciding he needed a shit randomly at three in the morning. It was worse than jet lag.

"I hope so," replied Small. "The last thing I want right now is a long conversation with a bunch of travelling assholes who decided to camp out here on their way to finding themselves. I hate those guys. The *we like to live the natural life* guys. Think they have a right to set up camp wherever they feel like, and then complain that the farmer who owns the land and the police that move them on are breaching their human rights. Assholes."

"Worlds full of them." Tober said.

Small pulled the patrol car onto the track leading to the field where the fires were, and saw the farmer walking towards them along the track. He pulled the car over and wound down his window.

"You got some problem with trespassers?" Small asked the farmer.

"Yup." The farmer crouched by the car door to speak through the open window. "Must be nearly thirty of them up there, looks like they are camping. I'm sure I saw one of them carrying a rifle when I walked over to set the cows out this morning. Weren't there last night when I cleared the field. Must have moved in overnight, but how in the hell they got set up without me hearing them overnight I don't know. I want them gone, I can't have some damn people ruining that field now."

"You speak to any of them?" Small asked. "Ask them to move on?"

"No sir. If it was one or two, I'd have been out there with my gun to say something, but with all of them out there I just called you. I don't want trouble or my place messed up. Just want them gone."

Small nodded. "We're on it. Once they're moving, we will drop by the house back there if that's where you'll be?"

"That's where I'll be," the farmer said.

Small pulled away and wound the window up most of the way. It was already getting hot, and the Sun was baking through the side window of the car making his neck sweat. The sweat ran down his back, hot and uncomfortable against the leather seat of the car. The car started to bounce about on the rutted track, dust flying up around the wheels as it shuddered along. This was obviously the track the farmer used to move his cattle out into the fields. After a few minutes, Small pulled the car over and killed the engine.

"That's it," Small said to Tober. "Let's walk from here, this heat and the dust is giving me a headache."

Tober just opened his door and stepped out, he was used to Small's moods. If Small decided they were walking, whatever Tober said, they were walking. Small's mood could change in an instant, and at this time of the morning he was likely to be on edge.

The track they were walking along adjacent to the field had a dip just ahead, followed by a left turn into the field. A small fence and a line of trees stood at the edge of the field, but through the gaps in the trees Small saw a couple of dozen tents set against the far border of the field. The smoke they had seen rising from the field was obviously from a few small fires near to the camp. The cops dropped down the dip in the track, and came up on the turn into the field, an abrupt left turn into a small gate. Small threw the gate open and strode ahead of Tober into the field.

Tober closed the gate behind them and turned, quickening his pace to catch up to Small, who had not waited. Two men were stood just into the field near the fence a short way ahead of the where the cops entered the field. One of them was obviously urinating into a bush on the verge of the field. Small looked at Tober and shook his head. *Assholes.*

As Small and Tober approached the two men, they realised that the men were dressed in some sort of uniform. The uniforms the men wore looked to be a grey, fading to a light brown in patches. The man who was not urinating turned suddenly as he became aware of footsteps behind him. He had a thick moustache, heavy stubble, and a very dirty face. His uniform jacket was open, revealing a dirty white vest.

"Jesus," the man in the open jacket said, stumbling backward. He drew a long-barrelled revolver from a holster attached to his belt, throwing it up level with the cops.

"Fuck," Small managed to say as he grabbed for his Beretta, fumbling the safety clasp on his holster open. The man who had been urinating turned in shock at the sound of the commotion behind him, grabbing for his trousers as he did so. He pissed on himself as he tripped back, falling into the hedge he had been previously urinating on.

The man with the open jacket regained his footing, a look of disbelief on his face. He held the revolver ahead of him, swinging his aim between the two officers. Tober had stepped right and was raising his pistol when the man in the open jacket fired. The bullet hit him low in his torso, winding him and dropping him to one knee. Small had his Beretta out of his holster, and was lining it up with the target in front of him when a thought ran through his head, a moment of recognition. The men in front of him were wearing Confederate Army uniforms, and the man in the open jacket was holding a LeMat revolver. Small fired twice into the trunk of the man in the open jacket, blood bursting from him and staining the dirty white vest a dark red. The man who had been urinating and then fell into the hedge climbed out of the bush awkwardly, struggling with his trousers which were still at his knees. He was grabbing at his belt, which small realised also had a holster on it containing a LeMat. *Asshole* Small thought. As the man stepped forward bent over struggling for his gun, Small shot him in the top of the head, driving him ass first back into the hedge. Small looked down to see the man spread eagle in the branches of the hedge, his head smashed open by a bullet, trousers open around his knees. Voices drifted across the field from the tents, shouts of soldiers alerted to the gunfire.

"We are running the experiment again in twelve hours," Alder said to the screen. He had Mathers, Dornel, and Ortile stood behind him, gathered closely together in their deliberate resolve to rectify what they had caused. "We need equipment and we need help though. We have rebuilt a temporary monitoring station, but there are some supplies we simply must have, and we need more staff here, trained staff from the ESD."

The Prime Minister was slow to reply. "I spoke to our Embassy, we are arranging some security for your facility but it will take time. Your friends over at the ESD may be a little more difficult, they said they have two people they can send. That's not exactly what I would call helpful."

"They had a few resignations in the last few days," Alder replied. "They have asked the few remaining trained staff we had to get here as soon as they can, but that may be a problem in itself. We have some people at the gate, and it's not exactly a support group. Getting through them may be difficult." Dornel stepped back as Alder mentioned the crowd at the gate.

"We will send some security first, and then once they have the area secured, we will get your staff in. Can you be prepared without the staff if they aren't there for seven or eight hours?"

"We can set everything up, but there is no way we can run the experiment without more staff to monitor the process."

"Get it going then, I'll be in touch." The Prime Minister turned the screen off.

Alder turned and looked at Mathers, they had some work to do.

"Think we need to go after Dornel guys," Ortile said. They turned to see the door closed, Dornel gone. "He mumbled something about going through the experiment again and walked out. What did you see? You know, when we ran the experiment the first time, when it went wrong. What did you see?"

Mathers looked down at the floor as he replied. "I had a flash back, my childhood. Sort of focussed on losing my virginity actually. Maybe some of the stuff more recently too, coming here and working. What about you?"

"My divorce actually," Ortile said sadly. "You said you focussed on losing your virginity, I relived the day she walked out, taking my family with her."

"What do you think he saw?" Alder asked. "Whatever it was though, it's bad enough to have damn near broken him. The guard killing Enlan in front of him seems to have been the last straw."

Small grabbed Tober by the arm and dragged him to his feet, looking down at checking for injuries. Tober had been on one knee holding his stomach as Small turned to him hearing the shouts from the camp across the field. There was a hole on Tober's uniform shirt, but there didn't appear to be any blood from the bullet wound.

"I'm just winded I think," Tober said, rubbing his stomach. He lifted his shirt at the waist to reveal his bullet proof vest, a small ragged silver circle cut into the black vest.

"We need to move," Small said, pulling Tober along towards the gate they entered the field by. "You see the uniforms? I don't know if this is some Civil War re-creationist crap or something else, but that was a real gun he shot you with, it's a LeMat Revolver. If the couple of dozen other assholes in that field are armed the same way, we ain't holding out too long with a pair of Berettas.

Tober was getting his wind back, and was able to turn back to look into the field as they passed through the gate. He saw at least twenty soldiers breaking from the line of tents, most carrying rifles, some pulling out pistols. Tober pulled out his Beretta and followed Small though the gate, turning back onto the track towards their car. He thought about what he had just seen for a moment, the image processing in his mind. He realised that at the edge of the camp there had been at least two soldiers mounting horses. There was no way they would make it back to the car ahead of mounted soldiers.

"Wait a moment," Tober said. "They have horses, we need call for back-up, but there is no way we can out run horses, even with the head start we have. You go ahead to the car and make the call, I'm going to hold take down the horse riders from here." Tober pointed to a mound of earth at the edge of the track on the opposite side to the field. Small nodded and turned, running up the track toward the car.

Tober had barely a few moments to get set at the crest of the bank by the track when the first horse and rider broke clear of the gate in the field, pulling back on the reigns to turn the horse mid gallop onto the track towards where Tober and Small had just exited. Tober had a minimal level of cover, but the advantage of surprise, at least over the lead rider. He waited a moment for the rider to start up the track towards him before shooting. The rider was armed with a rifle, held across the saddle of the horse as he rode. Tober aimed central to the rider's chest, allowing for both the lift and dip of the horse's stride, and also the uneven track surface. Tober breathed out gently, settling into the rhythm of the horse's stride. The soldier rose and fell in the saddle atop the horse, approaching him at a fast pace. Tober saw the rider dropping into the sight of his gun at the bottom of the horse's stride, and fired. The rider cried out as a bullet impacted against his chest driving him backward on the horse. The horse bucked and rode upward mid stride as the rider tumbled backward still holding the reigns. The rider fell back off the horse as it reared up, slamming heavily onto the ground behind him. The horse reacted to the sound of the gunshot, stumbling as it stopped mid stride, turned sharply, and galloped back towards the field it had come from. As the horse turned, it stomped the rider into the ground on its way back towards the field. If the bullet and the fall from the horse had not killed him, two tonnes of horse stamping on him will have finished the job.

A second horse turned out of the field just as the first horse galloped up the track past the gate. The rider had to re-adjust mid stride as his horse pulled up suddenly, throwing dust and mud up in front of it as it stopped at the entry to the field. He Looked around, clearly confused by the rider-less horse. Just as the second rider realised that there had been an ambush along the trap, Tober fired, hitting him in the arm and throwing him sideways off his horse. The second horse spooked and turned, running after the first horse along the track away from the field. The rider struggled to his feet, still holding his rifle. Tober watched the man lift his rifle with his left arm, his right arm hanging at his side, blood running from a wound just below his shoulder. He started to turn in the direction he had been shot from, scanning the edge of the track for his prey. His eyes settled on Tober, still lay on the top of the mound at the edge of the track. The soldier was wearing the same uniform as the other soldiers Tober and Small had met in the field, but this soldier's uniform was cleaner, better fitted to him. He nodded towards Tober, an acknowledgement of his nemesis within this fatal duel. He raised the rifle in his left arm with a suddenness it took Tober by surprise. There was a grace and purpose to the way this soldier handled the rifle. Given his injury, combined with the fact that he had just fallen from a horse, Tober was amazed the soldier was even standing. Tober rolled to his right as the rifle fired, the bullet impacting into the mound of earth ahead of him and throwing mud and dirt up into the air. Tober rolled down the edge of the mound as he heard the soldier start towards his cover, footsteps heavy on the dry ground. Tober turned, gun raised. He was at the base of the mound, making for its edge where it opened onto the track. Tober set himself down on one knee, judging the direction of the footsteps. Estimating where the soldier would crest the mound, Tober held his breath again. The soldier broke ground to Tober's right hand side, his battle-hardened experience correctly anticipating Tobers position and his aim. Tober dropped to the ground as the soldier fired his rifle over Tober's head, only a few feet from him. Tober turned on the ground, raising his gun towards the soldier. He fired three times in quick succession, trying to track the soldier's motion. The first bullet missed the soldier as he dived to his left past the bank of the mound. The second bullet hit its target though, punching into the soldier's stomach hard and turning him mid dive. The third bullet hit the soldier in the hip, his leg flailing upwards with the impact. Tober didn't wait to see if the soldier moved after he hit the ground. He ran along the far edge of the track, making his way back to the car. He knew had bought enough time for Small to radio for back-up.

"Right now, we think they are somewhere in Poland on a train, making their way back to Germany," The Prime Minister said. "It would appear that they stole a car in Russia just before the tanks were destroyed by the Russians. They travelled back across the border into Ukraine in the stolen car, and from there they must have bought their way onto a freight train. That or stowed away on it. We think they were picked up by the Russians and followed over the border. Probably FSB agents."

The German chancellor sighed, frustrated at the constant political losses the German people had been forced to accept in the last few days. "So, there are German citizens who have survived the Russian attack, now trying to make their way back to Germany? Trying to come home? What are you doing about this, have you spoken to the Russians?"

"No," The Prime Minister replied. He was becoming as frustrated as the Chancellor. Constantly playing an intermediary between other countries was a near impossible task given the current situation, and he had been the sole voice of reason all too often lately. "We haven't said anything to the Russians because we are assuming that they are following these men with a view to arresting them, or worse. It looks like the FSB, and they are not exactly forgiving in their policy when it comes to what they view as foreign terrorists. To the Russians, this has been an invasion of their land, and an act of terrorism. They were very clear on that, we barely avoided another war, yet again."

The Chancellor's patience ran out. "They were lost soldiers from a war which ended years ago, this was no more an act of terrorism than your bomber dropping its bombs on Berlin earlier this week."

The speaker on the Prime Minister's telephone distorted at the volume of the Chancellors shouting. "I agree," The Prime Minister said slowly. "Nor the V1 which landed on London. We are all hurting, all suffering losses from a war we stopped fighting a long time ago. I have asked that we try to have these men picked up in Poland by some of our men. There is something more you should know though, and it may not be easy to hear. We believe that we have identified one of the men from the tanks. He is a man known as Klemens Bulmann."

"That Panzer division was identified tentatively as one which went missing, presumed destroyed during the Kursk offensive, commanded by General Abbey Ahren," The Chancellor replied. "Klemens Bulmann was serving in the Panzer division. If he has escaped from their destruction, I would want him to be returned to Germany. He represents an unfortunate group of people within the Nazi structure of the Second World War. If he has survived, and is on his way back to Germany now, he must face justice for his crimes. We need some co-operation in this."

"I had assumed you would feel that way. Who do you think would be with him?"

"If Bulmann has escaped the Russians, he must be with General Ahren. General Ahren is not like Klemens Bulmann, the General was a soldier. A great tactician, and a great leader, not a butcher, and certainly not a monster. He was a German serving his country with honour, highly regarded by the German people during the war. His intelligence will be the reason that these men escaped the Russian destruction of the tanks."

The Prime Minister realised this would be his best opportunity to ask for some help from the Germans. "We will do everything we can to ensure these men are returned to you unharmed. If it indeed is who we suspect, Klemens Bulmann will face the justice he deserves. What happens to General Ahren is for your country to decide. In the same way, I was hoping you would look into the return of the crew from the Lancaster. You still have them under arrest."

"They will be returned to you as soon as it can be arranged. We have all suffered enough losses in the last week," The German Chancellor agreed. "We will return your men to you, and you will help to return our men home."

-

Small saw Tober moving up the track towards the car as quickly as he could manage. Even through his bullet proof vest, the gun shot had clearly winded him badly, probably bruised deeply through his abdomen. Small had requested back-up using the high frequency radio in the car, and was about to drive back towards the field to attempt to find Tober when he came into view. Small started the car and rolled forward towards Tober, who slowed to a gentle walk, and moved out to the side of the track as the car pulled up to him. He opened the door and got in gently, wincing as his bruised body contorted to get into the seat.

"Two more dead," Tober said as Small put the car in reverse and worked his way back along the track, looking over his shoulder for an inlet to turn around. "I heard voices from the field as I was coming back, we're going to have a few more soldiers on their way very soon."

Small glanced across at Tober. "Backup's on its way, but we may well need to get to some cover and wait it out. Damn Civil War re-enactment assholes have lost their minds." They had killed four soldiers so far, but it would be difficult to hold off a concerted attack. "Who the hell are these people anyway? Who goes out and gets dressed up like it's the Civil War and starts shooting at police? Did you see the guns they had? That was an authentic LeMat revolver, real thing. Got to be worth a few thousand easily in that condition."

"I'm not so sure about the re-enactment thing you know," Tober replied. "They were wearing authentic uniforms and had authentic weapons. Nothing about those soldiers looked like they were fake to me, especially the way they handled their weapons. Have you heard much on the news the last few days about strange things happening with people turning up from the past?"

"I heard some crazy shit about time travel. Some bunch of head cases claiming they jumped forward in time, that what you mean?"

"All I'm saying is those guys back there looked like Confederate soldiers. Look at how they reacted when they saw us, we're wearing dark blue uniforms." Tober shook his head. "I know how crazy this sounds, but there are things happening all over, it's been on every news program. Stuff in Europe too, not just here."

"We're wearing police uniforms," Small replied quickly. "Dark blue police uniforms."

"Look at how those first two guys reacted the second they saw us stood there, they didn't see police uniforms. All they saw was two armed men stood right in front of them in blue uniforms, they weren't going to check for ID's. They thought we were Union soldiers."

Small spotted an open gate into a field, twisted the wheel hard, and spun the car round. He sped away up the track towards the farm house they had passed on their way in. Tober was gripping the edge of his seat, breathing heavily. He had grunted against the thud of every bump the car went over along the uneven road surface.

"How you feeling?" Small asked as they thudded over a particularly deep rut in the road. He wanted to change the subject, it was impossible to him that people were travelling through time. Even with what he saw, it just wasn't possible.

"I could do with a day off about now if you can arrange it," Tober replied. He would be fine in a day or two, but right now his body hurt with every breath, and every slight movement. He saw the top of the farm house through a break in the trees lining the track. "Think we had best stop at the house and get that farmer."

"I guess it's going to take those guys a few minutes to get up here once they start moving," Small said. "That gives us time to get into the house, but we don't want to stick around too long in there, too much cover leading up to it. Those guys would be in the house before we saw them if they come up here." Small turned into the drive of the farm house and stopped. They stepped out of the car as the farmer opened his front door. He had a rifle in his hand.

The two FSB agents had received a call four hours earlier, and were just driving into Cracow when the phone call happened. They had instructions to intercept the two German soldiers who were on a train due to arrive in Cracow within the hour. The Agent in the passenger seat twisted in his seat as he pulled his mobile phone from his pocket, answering it quietly.

"Da," he said into the phone. "Da," he said again. "Ya ponimayu." *I understand.* He hung up the phone and replaced it in his pocked. "These men are wanted immediately. We are to return them to Moscow under arrest, unharmed if possible."

The driver nodded. They had been tasked to make arrests of this nature before. The instruction that someone was to be returned to Moscow immediately, unharmed if possible, meant that they were to use whatever means were necessary to guarantee the persons arrival in Moscow. If they could be persuaded to return without force, the men would be questioned thoroughly on return to Moscow. Returned unharmed did not guarantee they would remain unharmed after questioning.

A few hours before the FSB agents in Warsaw had received a call which led them to this mission to Cracow, a train depot guard had been found beaten unconscious in Ukraine. He had spent a few minutes arguing that he had not assisted anyone to stow away onto a freight train from his depot. Some small persuasion had convinced him to remember the description of the two men who had paid him for the privilege of a ride on one of his company's trains. He had then suddenly remembered the details of the train they had climbed aboard, down to the exact carriage. He had also remembered exactly what time the train would be arriving in Cracow, the only stop it would be making before returning along the same track to the depot. He had been convinced that he should not remember who had spoken to him before he lost consciousness from a single blow to the back of the head.

As the train pulled into Cracow Glowny train station along a freight track, Bulmann motioned to the window beside Ahren. "We need to be off this train before the cargo starts being unloaded." Ahren looked through the window towards the sidings Bulmann had pointed out. They were moving slowly, passing railway workers preparing to receive the trains cargo as quickly as possible, they were operating a tight schedule in the station for freight. The workers would meet every train as it arrived.

"Open the door now, we'll step off without drawing attention to ourselves," Ahren said. "Don't pick up anything, they may try to speak to you if you have anything. Just step out and walk."

Bulmann nodded. "We need to get to a transport, do you think there are any German bases left here at all?" The train lurched suddenly as the brakes cut in sharply. Bulmann pulled the door open.

"I doubt there are any bases here now," Ahren said as he stepped from the train onto the platform. "We need to get up onto the passenger platforms." Ahren and Bulmann walked away from the train along the platform passing a small group of railway workers starting to step onto the train to unload its cargo. Ahren looked at Bulmann as they walked along the platform, assessing their potential to blend into a crowd. They were going to struggle simply on the stature of the pair. Bulmann was six feet three inches tall, and Ahren guessed he probably weighed over fifteen stone. Ahren himself was six feet tall, though he was less bulky in appearance than Bulmann, having an athletic frame. On top of the hulking appearance of Bulmann, he was wearing a white vest which was stained with sweat, and a pair of German Army SS Panzer division Officers trousers, a unique cut of trousers which would stand out amongst any civilian crowd. The next issue was the fact that both men stunk of engine oil, an unfortunate and unavoidable side effect of life within a Panzer unit.

From a stairway above the main passenger terminal, the two FSB agents watched the unmistakable pair making their way along the platform from the freight train towards the passenger terminal.

Tober and Small walked through the farm house as quickly as they could, assessing the most likely approach the soldiers could take. The farm house opened onto a clear field bisected by the main farm road to the north, was flanked by woodland to the west, and was bordered by the track they had driven along to the south and east. Along the track covering hundreds of acres to the south and east of the farm house were fields used by the farm for both cattle and crops. The fields immediately due east were used to graze animals, the fields to the south crops, mostly corn.

Tober looked through the curtains from a south facing window, his eyes tracing the track they had just driven along. It had trees and overgrown foliage in places along its verge, hedges also lining areas of the track. This would be the obvious choice for any tactical approach to the farm house, natural cover up to the last few metres from the house. The soldiers could cut into the track anywhere along the track from the fields where gates were sporadically placed. Small walked up behind Tober and looked out of the window, following his gaze along the track.

"They'll just stroll right up to the back door, won't they," Small stated, adjusting his belt and thumbing the strap on his holster.

"I doubt they would go to the trouble of working their way west, even in full daylight. Coming from the fields they have the sun at their back. They outnumber us ten to one, I would guess a scout party are behind some cover out there now."

"You think the farmer has any rifles with a scope on it?" Tober asked.

"Nope." A voice came from behind them. Tober and Small turned from the window and stepped along the landing towards the farmer who was stood leant against a wall, still holding the rifle. "Just this and two more shotguns in a cabinet downstairs."

"Let's get those shotguns," Small said. "We only need to hold them off for thirty minutes or so."

"Hold them off?" the farmer asked.

Small nodded. "I radioed in for backup. Thirty minutes. We need to contain those men out there until that backup gets here. Where are your family?" Small had looked around the house briefly, he had seen photographs of the farmer with a woman and two small children, recent photographs.

"At my wife's mother's house. They've been there for two days."

"What about farm hands, any staff you have here today?" Tober asked.

"None this morning. Farm went bad a few years back, I only have someone in weekdays now. Mostly do it all myself or hire casual when the going's good," The farmer replied. Tober nodded and started for the stairs, Small and the farmer following.

"If they follow standard Confederate operating practice, they are going to try to burn down this house and all of the farm buildings, and try to kill us," Small said. "After *Shermans March to the Sea*, The Confederates started to burn any farm or town that they saw as Union suppliers or sympathisers. There was a lot of scorched earth towards the end of the Civil War. That's how they are going to see a farm with Union soldiers in."

"Finally accepted the idea?" Tober asked over his shoulder as he walked down the stairs. A smile crossed his lips for a moment as he looked back at Small.

"Idea of what?" the farmer asked. "What the hell you talking about Confederate and Union soldiers?"

"Not watched much news?" Tober asked.

Ahren and Bulmann worked their way through the station and out onto the street, avoiding close contact with any of the throng of commuters moving about the various platforms and stairways. Once onto the street Ahren took up a brief paced stride towards a small back street, closely followed by Bulmann. He had spotted a Hospital facility just moments from the train station, and made straight for the car park.

Ahren walked through the rows of cars looking at each car slowly, checking doors as subtly as he could manage. He was shocked at how the cars looked, they were nothing like the cars he knew from Germany. The most shocking change Ahren observed was that no cars were open topped. He had hoped to be able to steal a car when he saw the volume of parked cars outside the hospital, but now realised he would need to wait for a viable target to steal keys from. Ahren and Bulmann walked casually to the far edge of the car park, trying not to attract attention whilst looking for anyone making their way towards the quiet area along the fence bordering the car park and the road. Bulmann walked silently behind Ahren, frustrated at the fact that *the great* General Abbey Ahren could not complete the simple task of acquiring transport for the pair of them. He was confused by the lack of German outposts in Poland too. Poland had not only been annexed, it had *become* a part of Germany in every way as much as Austria. There must still be some German Army bases or military infrastructure remaining in the region. He couldn't accept what he was seeing.

Ahren stopped at an empty bay, turning to walk through the space to the next lane. A car had just pulled into a space close to them, and Ahren wanted to intercept the driver whilst there were no other people in the car park.

Ahren watched casually as the man killed the engine of the car and stepped out. The man looked small, and would be easily subdued. As Ahren stepped quietly into the lane where the man was walking from his car, he heard a dull thud from behind him. Ahren turned sharply, seeing Bulmann slumping forward, being held from behind by a thick set man in a suit. A second man stepped from the space beside Ahren, holding a small automatic pistol at waist height, aimed at Ahren's stomach.

"You would be General Ahren." The man with the gun spoke in German, thickly accented with Russian inflection. Ahren stepped calmly towards the men, glancing around the car park. There were no other men he could see.

"I would," Ahren replied. "You followed us from Russia somehow?"

"We were told where you would be," the FSB agent replied. He straightened his ill fitted suit jacket, looking uncomfortable at the situation. "We are not in a position to have a discussion. Please, we will need to move now." The FSB agent glanced to his partner, still holding up Bulmann, who was coming around from the blow he had received, but was clearly stunned. "Help him."

Ahren stepped towards Bulmann, who was thrust toward Ahren by the second FSB agent, who Ahren observed was holding a short wooden baton, crude but well suited this particular task. Bulmann slumped against Ahren, who reached his arm under Bulmann's armpit and stabilised him on his feet. The second FSB agent slipped the baton into his suit and motioned for them to follow him. Ahren glanced at the agent with the gun, who motioned with his open free hand for them to move.

History darkens

The Prime Minister sat quietly behind his desk, pondering the dossier he had been presented a few minutes earlier. Grey stood silently, rubbing the thick stubble growing on his cheek. It had only occurred to Grey that he had not seen a razor for days now. Looking at the Prime Minister, Grey realised he was not the only one who had missed certain personal grooming opportunities recently. The Prime Minister was sporting a heavy five o'clock shadow, which was rare for such a habitually well-presented politician.

The dossier the Prime Minister was reading had been compiled by Grey's section over the last few hours, and was filled with photographs and testimonies, along with a complete biography of Klemens Bulmann. The Prime Minister was holding the thick file open with his right hand, running his index finger on his left hand absently along the edge of the page he was reading. Grey realised that this may take some time, he himself had spent over an hour digesting the dossier when it was handed to him, preparing to present it to the Prime Minister. He understood why the Prime Minister looked so solemn whilst reading the dossier.

Klemens Bulmann had been born in Berlin shortly before the start of the First World War. He had been brought up by his mother alone, as his father had been killed early during the First World War. The Bulmann family had barely survived the Great Depression of the 'Twenties, with Bulmann's mother working as a prostitute after the death of his father.

In Nineteen-Thirty, at seventeen years old, a bitter Klemens Bulmann had joined the Hitler Youth organisation. This was the first record of Bulmann substantiated within the dossier. He had been photographed at a rally receiving an award for excellent service to the

Nazi Party as a young man. The Hitler Youth had led to recruitment into the SS for Bulmann

at eighteen years old. He had trained hard, and shown promise as an enthusiastic young

soldier.

When Germany invaded Poland, Bulmann had seen active service as a member of the

Fourth Panzer division. It was here that Bulmann had been tested by SS leaders. Wermacht

troops had been viewed as not being prepared to undertake mass murders of civilians and the

destruction of small towns and villages, as the Wermacht were seen as professional soldiers.

Bulmann had been selected to be a member of the newly formed *Einsatzgruppen*, tasked with

the killing of civilians once the Wermacht had subdued all military resistance in Poland.

Bulmann had been quickly promoted within the SS, and was becoming proficient in

both tactical warfare and unarmed combat. He had also shown a particular skill for the

unsavoury task of mass murder where necessary. Bulmann had been sent to Russia in the

summer of 'Forty-One, and had again taken up a roll within the Einsatzgruppen, now a leader

of his own unit. Prior to their time in Russia, Bulmann's Einsatzgruppen unit had

experimented in new ways of killing, including using the back of vans to imprison their

victims, who were slowly gassed using the cars exhaust fumes. He had used the experiments

to develop his skills in not only killing, but also torturing and wounding prisoners whilst

leaving them still in a stable enough condition to be very effectively interrogated. Once in

Russia, Bulmann had led his group with an almost passionate obsession to kill. Millions of

Russian Jews in the occupied Russian territories were murdered, with Bulmann's

Einsatzgruppen unit at the forefront of the killing.

In May of Forty-Two, Bulmann had been transferred back to Poland, promoted to SS-

Oberscharfuhrer. He had been selected now by the highest levels of the SS hierarchy to assist

in the implementation of the *Final Solution* at the death camp of Sobibor, near the town of

Wolzek. Bulmann had become gradually more and more brutal after being posted at Sobibor, seeing his work as the guarantee that the mistakes and failures of the German First World War campaign would not be repeated. He had been indoctrinated in the Hitler Youth years before to the belief that Germany had been defeated not by the French and British armies during the First World War, but by German Jews and the German weakness to take the necessary action to stop forces from within from preventing them imposing their superiority on the World.

Bulmann had murdered hundreds of prisoners at Sobibor, which was structured so proficiently that prisoners usually died within an hour of arriving at the camp. For prisoners at Sobibor who lived beyond the first few hours, Bulmann was a living breathing nightmare. He had beaten prisoners to death with his bare hands, tortured prisoners with every manner of tool, and used this experience to learn very specific details of the human anatomy. This had been seen as a very traditional way of becoming a more effective killer within the SS, and Bulmann had perfected the practice.

In the Spring of Forty-Three, prisoners at Sobibor had managed to stage an uprising, leading to a group of nearly fifty prisoners escaping. Sobibor had been immediately shut down and bulldozed, erased from the landscape for the remainder of the war. The Nazis had attempted to erase the camp of Sobibor from history for ever.

Bulmann was the only member of the SS staff of Sobibor to be unhindered by the closure of the camp. He was seen as too valuable to the Nazi war effort, and his experience was put to use as part of the German offensive in Russia once again. Bulmann was transferred back to a Panzer division, and in the Summer of Forty-Three, he had disappeared from history whilst sat in a tank on his way to Kursk.

Tober loaded as much ammunition as he could into his pockets. He had taken one of shotguns the farmer owned, and Small had taken the other. Between them they had less than a hundred rounds, and Tober was starting to wonder just how many soldiers may be out there. He had seen a small camp at the edge of the field they had walked into, but there had been no time to take much more than a cursory glance at the camp before he had found himself in a shootout with a pair of soldiers.

The Farmer stood staring at Small and Tober, seemingly assessing them. "Sam," he said quietly. "Sam Horlit. If I am going to die here today with you, I guess we should at least know each other's names." He was a big man, the classic picture of an American farmer. Strong, thick set, but maybe not the fastest moving man. Tober thought he may be in his late thirties, healthy from the look of his complexion. Tober guessed the farmer may not have ever fired a gun at another person before, but from the way he held himself, today that would probably change.

"Good to meet you Sam," Tober replied. "I'm Tober, that's Small." Small nodded a greeting to the farmer. "We need to get ourselves to a position where we have some cover. They must be on their way up here by now."

Small walked through the farm house dining room, standing momentarily in the kitchen door. "Looks like getting to cover may be a little too late an option now." He pointed to the kitchen window, which overlooked the track to the south of the house. Four figures were running along the track, making their way directly towards the back of the house. Small drew his Beretta and stepped low into the kitchen, followed closely by Tober.

Tober looked back towards Horlit and shook his head. "Is there any view we can get of the fields over there from the side of the house? They may try to flank us."

Horlit looked back through the dining room slowly. "The utility room has a window, you can see the track and the fields from there." He pointed to a door just off the dining room. "You want me to get in there and try to spot them?"

"Keep your head down in there," Tober said. "If you see anything shout." Tober turned and followed Small though the kitchen. "Think we're safer inside or out?"

"Inside," Small replied, crouching beside the back door. He reached up and turned the handle, opening the door a few inches. A crack sounded just above the door frame, followed momentarily by the report of a rifle echoing around the field by the house. Small held his position beside the door, chancing a quick glance out through the opening. "They are using weapons which are only going to be accurate within a hundred yards or so. We should be able to pick off a few of them as they break cover to get into range."

Tober looked through the window, and saw more figures moving along the track towards the house. He stepped over to the door with small, and crouched behind him. Small pointed to an area where two soldiers were moving into the open between the field and the house, running slowly raising their rifles to aim at the door. Small drew his pistol and knelt, steadying himself against the frame of the door. He raised his gun and shot three times in a tight group. The lead soldier lurched with the first impact, his body driven back as his momentum was abruptly halted. He fell backwards, his rifle swinging out as his arm jerked with the impact, falling into the path of the second soldier as he ran. The second soldier sidestepped ungracefully, losing his footing slightly as he avoided his falling comrade. Small waited for the soldier to steady himself, clearly torn between running back to cover, and moving on towards the house. As the soldier paused, Small took the opportunity and fired again, a further two shots in quick succession. The Soldier buckled at the waist, forced to the ground in a sitting position momentarily, reaching for his stomach as he collapsed. He slumped over to his side, still buckled at the waist.

"Two more coming through the trees," Tober said, drawing his own gun and taking aim. He lent against the end of the kitchen counter, angling himself to view an area which had been blind to Small because of the angle of the door. Tober fired once, feeling noticeably more uncomfortable because of the bruising to his torso. A soldier moving between trees jerked sideways and staggered back towards a tree, falling against it as he lost his footing. Tober had to steady himself against the counter before firing again. He once again. The head of the second soldier Tober had spotted snapped backwards as he ran forwards, his legs flailing out in front of him. A burst of red mist was visible from the soldier's head as he fell to the ground.

"Four each," Small said, glancing towards Tober momentarily, a grin crossing his face. "How many more do you think are out there?" Another crack sounded above the door, sending dust and wood fragments scattering across the porch.

"Guess that means there's at least one more."

"So how is it you know who my countryman here is?" Ahren asked the FSB agent stood behind them. They had stopped half way along a small side road, and Ahren had taken the opportunity to lean Bulmann against a wall to rest.

"He is very well known," the FSB agent replied. "Sadly, you are not so well known to us, but as an accomplice to a war criminal I am sure we will be keen to hear your story."

"War criminal?" Ahren asked, looking back towards Bulmann. Bulmann was leant heavily against the wall, still looking unstable. His eyes were glazed and his pupils were still dilated. Ahren thought he must have suffered a concussion from the blow to the head he had received minutes before. He looked back to the FSB agent questioningly.

"War criminal. He committed many crimes against the Russian people during your war. Tortured and killed hundreds of innocent men, women, and children. No wonder you and he fled the country so quickly when you realised what had happened. We have waited sixty years for justice."

Ahren shook his head, looking from the FSB agent to Bulmann and back again. "Sixty years?" he almost said to himself. "When we realised what happened? What has happened?"

The FSB agent smiled briefly. "You do not know? Your war ended with the destruction of the Reich, your expansion across Europe collapsed and your country was cut up and occupied by us and the Americans. Now you appear to us sixty years later, a gift to the Russian people from a failed science experiment by The West." He pointed at Bulmann, a look of hatred crossing his face. "He will be punished for his crimes. Move."

Ahren reached over and took Bulmann's arm, pulling him away from the wall and starting to walk between the FSB agents. He looked at Bulmann, trying to read him. Ahren had heard rumours, stories about members of the SS killing prisoners, punishing villages where there was resistance to the Nazi control in the area. He had worried more and more as the war went on that these stories may be true. He was a soldier, he had killed, but never unnecessarily. He had killed men, soldiers of other countries armies. Only during battle, and only within the rules of a soldier in war. He felt hatred rise up inside him, a rage and hatred of the monsters who had committed crimes against innocent civilians. They were not soldiers, if what he had been told in whispered conversations was truly real, they were criminals, sick criminals who had dishonoured the very core of the German population during the war. If what this Russian had told him was true, the man he had escaped Russia with, was holding now, was not human, he was a monster. He deserved every punishment coming his way, but this punishment should follow a fair trial.

The FSB agent behind them sensed Ahren was starting to realise who Bulmann truly was. "You know of men like this, don't you? Men who killed, not because they were fighting a war, but because they were purifying, cleansing. You know how many Jews, Russians, innocent people died? Millions. Millions on millions, at the hands of shit like this."

The streets they were walking along were becoming less and less crowded as the end of the morning rush hour passed. Cracow had settled into the working day, with its commuters now settled behind their desks, at their place of work in factories or shops. They rounded a final corner into a small street behind the train station Ahren and Bulmann had arrived at a short while before.

"Hold him here." The FSB agent who had been giving the orders instructed Ahren, while the other agent turned, and removed a set of handcuffs from his jacket pocket. "Step away from him, I am sure he can stand long enough for us to cuff him."

Ahren stepped away from Bulmann, leaving him stood between the FSB agents. He felt a surprising increase in Bulmann's stability as Ahren released his arm. Bulmann was more stable on his feet than he had felt whilst they walked. The FSB agent who had given the instructions levelled his gun at Ahren, warning him not to move whilst Bulmann was being cuffed.

Bulmann relaxed as the FSB agent lifted his right hand to apply the first cuff. He could feel the agent's grip on his wrist tighten as he applied the cuff tightly. The agent reached for Bulmann's left hand, momentarily relaxing his grip on Bulmann's right. He took the opportunity presented to him, his speed and strength devastatingly instant. He snatched his right hand through the grip of the FSB agent's hand, breaking against the weakest point of his grip, pulling his hand upwards twisting against the agent's thumb. His hand came free, the loose cuff flying up towards Bulmann's hand. He caught the loose cuff in mid-air, and with one swift powerful motion smashed his closed fist with the ridged cuff arm into the FSB agent's face. Blood exploded from the nose of the FSB agent, running from his nostrils and also from a deep open wound running up from the bridge of the nose to his right eyebrow. The FSB agent slammed backwards into the car they were stood beside, slumping down onto the bonnet as he tried to stay on his feet. Ahren turned from Bulmann to the lead FSB agent, who was stepping forward raising his gun towards Bulmann. Ahren instinctively hit the agent's arm, throwing his aim wide as he fired at Bulmann. Ahren tried to hold onto the wrist, but the FSB agent snatched his arm away, swinging his free hand towards Ahren pushing him back far enough to be able to try to bring the gun back up towards Bulmann. He turned, rage in his face, intent solely on ending Bulmann's life before he had the opportunity to escape. Bulmann had closed the gap in the short moments between punching the first FSB agent, and the second agent firing at him. The agent was stepping toward Bulmann, his arm outstretched trying to aim at the moving target. Bulmann managed to step just inside the arm pushing it outward as the agent fired for a second time. Bulmann had reached down with his right arm as he stepped into the close space next to the agent. He pulled a short dagger from his trouser leg pocket, and as he wrapped his left arm around the elbow of the FSB agent's arm holding the gun, he thrust the dagger upwards, driving the blade deeply into the torso of the agent. Bulmann held onto the agent's arm, looking into his eyes as he supported him, holding the dagger still in the body of the agent. The agent stared back into Bulmann's eyes, he still had the strength to stand and struggle, trying to free his arm holding the gun. Bulmann slowly pulled the dagger up the torso of the agent from where it was embedded just above his stomach. The agent was almost lifted off his feet by the force Bulmann drove the dagger upward. A scream momentarily escaped his mouth, before blood choked the sound in his throat. Bulmann pulled the dagger back, allowing the dead agent to fall to the ground at his feet.

Bulmann turned to the agent slumped against the car, who was pulling himself back to his feet, one hand holding his face, the other reaching for a gun holstered inside his jacket. Bulmann punched him again, knocking him backward against the car. As the agent rebounded from the car, Bulmann used his left hand to grab the agent's shoulder, pulling him forward onto the dagger. He intentionally delivered a wound into the flank of the agent just below the floating ribs.

"This is your car?" Bulmann asked the agent, pushing the agent against the door of the car. The agent nodded, desperately trying to pull himself away from the grip that held him upright. "You have the keys?" The agent nodded again, letting out a heavy sigh as he breathed. Bulmann nodded with him. With a sudden motion, Bulmann cut across the body of the agent, driving the dagger diagonally upwards. He pulled the dagger back as he stepped from the agent, who slid down the car, still barely alive, but unable to move.

"Step over to the wall," Ahren said from a short distance behind Bulmann. He turned to see Ahren aiming the gun of the agent he had killed at him. Bulmann followed the instruction, calmly walking to the wall and leaning against it.

"We need to leave here now," he said. "Someone will have heard the gunshots. The police will be on their way soon."

"Drop the dagger," Ahren replied. "Kick it away from you." Bulmann followed the instruction, dropping the dagger and kicking it a short distance down the road. Ahren stepped over to the dying agent by the car, crouched, and reached into his pocket. He pulled out a bunch of keys, backed to the car, and used the keys to open the door. He stepped away from the car door slightly, still holding the keys. "Get into the driver's seat. Use that loose cuff to cuff yourself to the steering wheel. We are taking a drive home, to finish what these men started."

Tober heard sirens in the distance. They had heard the occasional shots being fired wildly at the house for almost half an hour, but none of the remaining soldiers had broken cover since they had killed the four who approached along the track. Small had moved from the kitchen door to check on Horlit. The farmer had not shouted for any help, but it had seemed that the gunfire had moved to the side of the house he had been keeping watch over.

"Sirens on their way," Tober shouted. "Maybe five to ten minutes away."

"I hear them," Small replied. "Think our friends out there hear 'em too?"

"I doubt they know what they are if they do hear them," Tober said. "I think it may have spooked them though, looks like there's some movement coming towards you again." He watched from the door as figures moved in the distance along the field, just slight flashes of motion between the fence and tree line. Suddenly a crash sounded against the front door of the farm house, followed by the sound of breaking glass. Tober crouched silently for a moment, torn between going to investigate the noise and guarding the door he was posted at.

"You smell that?" Small shouted. Tober closed the back door and moved backwards into the kitchen. The smell of wood burning hit him moments later.

"I think waiting this out till backup gets here just stopped being an option," Tober shouted to Small. "Guess we are going to be waiting for them outside, which way do you want to go?"

Small and Horlit ran through to the kitchen from the utility room. Small was looking around the kitchen for something to use as a shield or barrier. "If we go out of the utility room door it's a short run to the car. We need to send a distraction of some sort out of the back door." Small turned to the farmer, an idea forming in his mind. "Ever see any of those movies where they start the gas running on the oven and set a fire? We've already got the fire, haven't we?"

"The whole place will blow," Tober said, a look of concern crossing his face.

"We will be on our way along the track by that time," Small replied. "Problem is how many soldiers are north of us along the track already. The explosion will stop any of them still coming up from the south. We need to go, now."

"Ok," Tober said. He walked to the oven, running his hand slowly over the top. It was a big risk going out in the open, but there was no way they could stay in the house now. "Get that door open, I will be right behind you. If you can get to the car get it running."

Small nodded, and walked to the utility room with Horlit following. Smoke was starting to drift through the gap around the dining room door into the kitchen. "On three," Tober shouted. He heard Small unlocking and opening the utility door. Tober turned every switch on the oven, starting all of the gas running. He sprinted through the kitchen and out into the utility. "Two, one," he said as he saw Small looking back for him.

Small led the way out to the side of the house, the shotgun in his hands. He saw movement instantly from the field north of the house. Two figures ran forwards towards them across the field, raising rifles as they ran. Small lifted the shotgun and slowed his run, aiming towards the moving figures. Tober took up position beside Small, covering the area behind them as they moved. Small fired twice, not worried by accuracy. One of the soldiers dived to the ground, dropping his rifle as he landed. The remaining soldier raised his rifle to return fire. As Small took aim to return fire, he heard Horlit's rifle fire next to him. The soldier fell instantly, a clean hit to the chest. There was the sound of guns firing from south of the house. Tober returned fire, hitting a tree being used as cover by a soldier.

"We need to keep moving forward," Tober said. They started to run again, past the front corner of the house and out into the open field at the north of the farm. The front of the house was ablaze, burning from the porch all the way across its front aspect. As they spotted the car, two soldiers suddenly broke cover and began to fire at them. They had been waiting to ambush anyone coming from the house and moving north. Small dropped his shotgun and drew his pistol. He knelt and too aim. The soldiers aim was poor, bullets hitting the front of the house, punching into the walls and breaking a window. Small fired twice, both bullets hitting one of the soldiers in the chest. The soldier seemed to run backwards as the bullets hit him. As Small had knelt and fired, Tober and Horlit had flanked him, aiming their guns at the second soldier. As Tober fired at the soldier, a gunshot from their flank exploded, a bullet slamming into the shoulder of Horlit. He swung with the impact, falling on his side just behind where Small knelt. Tober fired again, his second shot hitting the soldier in front of them. Small turned sharply, firing three times at the soldier who had worked up to their flank. The bullets found their target, taking him off his feet as he was running towards the track.

Tober helped the farmer back to his feet, assessing the wound as he pulled him up. He had a bullet in his shoulder, but it had impacted at the back of the shoulder joint, probably bedded shallowly into the bone of his shoulder blade. Blood ran down his sleeve, and his arm hung limply at his side. "We need to move," Tober told him, wrapping his arm around the farmer's waist and pulling him forwards.

Small ran ahead, pulling the car keys from his pocket. He opened the driver's door, climbed in, and opened the rear door just as Tober and Horlit reached the car. Tober pushed the farmer into the back seat, and dived in beside him. Small looked into the back of the car momentarily as he started the engine. Tober nodded to him not to worry, the farmer would be fine. Small slammed the car into gear and accelerated, hearing gun fire from close behind them as they started to move. Suddenly the house exploded, turning Small's view in the rear-view mirror into a wall of flame. Looking out of the rear windscreen of the car, Tober saw the fragments of wood, bricks, and roof tiles bursting outwards and raining down into the fields and onto the track they drove along. Any of the remaining soldiers near to the house must have been killed or injured.

-

In July Twenty-Twelve, following a prolonged period of pain and altered sensation to the left side of his face, Peter Dornel had been diagnosed as having a brain tumour. The tumour had been causing a condition called Trigeminal Neuralgia, regular or constant severe neurological pain to the face. The trigeminal nerve is the 5th cranial nerve, which gives all

facial sensation and controls the function of many areas of the face including the mandibular

muscle and corneal functions. Dornel suffered pain through the whole left side of his face

almost constantly, the only respite being if and when he finally managed to fall asleep,

always by overdosing on the medication he was taking till he passed out.

For a period of approximately 4 months, Dornel had suffered increasing pain and

unusual sensations to the left side of his face. The sensations began as a tingling and

numbness to the left side of his face, progressing steadily to severe pain in his face and left

eyeball. The pain he suffered was similar to an electric shock in his face, with regular

instances of a very sharp pain as if a knife was being dragged across his cheek and forehead.

He suffered odd sensations and extreme pain in his left eyeball, ranging between pins and

needles in the eye, a feeling that he had been poked in the eye, to the intense sensation that he

was being stabbed in the eye.

Dornel was initially mis-diagnosed with what was suspected to be a Meningioma,

which is a benign tumour on the meninges, which is the membrane which covers the brain.

He was signed off work by his doctor for a period of time, with the view to conventional

surgery which would cut out the tumour. Only after consultation with a Neural Surgeon after

months in agony, in limbo waiting for a decision on appropriate surgery, was it was assessed

that he was actually suffering with a Trigeminal Schwannoma, a sheath tumour which grows

on the nerve itself.

Following this diagnosis, it was suggested that he undertake treatment known as

steriotactic radiosurgery, also known as Gamma Knife treatment. This is an intense type of

radiotherapy highly targeted to a specific area of the body which may be inaccessible or may

be difficult to treat using conventional surgery. This treatment was scheduled for late

November Twenty-Twelve, almost an entire year after Dornel had initially begun to fall ill.

In late November Twenty-Twelve, Dornel attended a private hospital in northern England for treatment.

Following treatment, Dornel had a period of about three weeks where he was ill, but felt that he was slowly recovering. Just as He felt he may be almost fit to try to return to the normality that had been his life a year before, in the December of that year his condition significantly deteriorated, and he spent a period of two weeks regularly losing consciousness, and vomiting every day. The pain he felt in his face and head increased massively, and alongside this, his face became completely numb in most areas on the left side.

Due to this concerning increase in pain and other complications, Dornel's family contacted the hospital which had treated him. A neural surgeon duly suggested that the tumour may have enlarged due to the treatment, as cystic expansion is a regular and expected effect of radiotherapy.

In late January Twenty-Thirteen, Dornel decided that he should return to work even though he was very ill, as he was becoming bored and depressed at home. He found it difficult physically to drag himself into work, but managed to work for a few hours a day for a couple of days a week for a period of time.

Later that year, still suffering with extreme pain in his face, Dornel was given an MRI scan, which showed that the tumour had actually massively expanded, significantly beyond what would ever normally be expected from this sort of treatment. The MRI showed that the tumour had expanded so much that it was now pressing on his brain stem, causing several complications.

Over Twenty-Thirteen, he was monitored using MRIs on a regular basis to track the size of the tumour. The tumour didn't reduce in size quickly, and in October was still large, but had reduced enough to now not be pressing on the brain stem. It took almost a full year before he was told that it had mostly melted away, and that although there was even now still residual pain and altered sensation due to either scar tissue and residual tumour matter, combined with damage to the nerve itself from the treatment, the prognosis was good. It was believed that the treatment was successful, and that the tumour would continue to reduce further from the significantly reduced size it had reached.

Dornel's nearly two-year battle had virtually come to an end, he was cleared to return to full time work, apparently fully recovered. The reality was very much different. He had massive mental issues following his illness. He was suffering with severe depression and anxiety, partly caused by the condition itself, and partly caused by the drugs he had been prescribed to manage the pain he had suffered. He had developed an addiction to pain killers, and struggled to go more than a few hours without his next dose. The cocktail of drugs he had taken were easy to acquire, he had a repeat prescription which was rarely reviewed by his doctors, and when he did attend any appointment, he stated that he was still suffering with residual pain. The doctors were worried that he may suffer a seizure due to the pressure he had sustained to his brain-stem, so no-one was prepared to take the decision to take away the medication which controlled the risk of that. He had a constant supply, care of the state. His mental health continued to deteriorate as he isolated himself, spending all of his time alone when he was not at work. He was paranoid, and suffered with undiagnosed post-traumatic stress disorder. His own body had tortured him to the point of suicide. He had mental scar on top of mental scar. The slow diagnosis of his condition had driven him close to madness, the uncontrolled agony in his head pushing him closer and closer to the edge. By the time he was finally correctly diagnosed and treated, Dornel had been at the brink of something drastic for months, constantly considering taking an overdose, just to take away the pain he was suffering.

When the incident had happened with the Collider during the first experiment, Pete Dornel had felt every excruciating moment of the agony he had suffered during the long hard months when he had been ill, every twinge and ache in his face, the pain in his jaw as his muscles wasted to the point where he could barely open his mouth, let alone chew food. In those few moments, he had felt all the pain in his head as the tumour had grown after his treatment, felt it push on his brain stem, the tumour expanding and strangling the nerve it had grown on. He felt the searing agony in his left eye that he could only describe as feeling like a white-hot fork being driven through the back of his eye. The pain in his face like a live electrical wire being passed across his skin. A feeling like someone was slowly, deliberately passing the blade of a kitchen knife through the flesh that covered the left side of his face, running from his forehead down past his eye, through his cheek, and into his lips.

He felt more pain in a few moments than most could ever imagine suffering in a lifetime. Dornel had not screamed out, barely let out a whimper in fact. He recognised the pain instantly, and it overwhelmed him. Before he could pull in enough air to scream, he broke mentally. His conscious mind shattered with the agony so intense his mind just shut down. He had passed out the moment the world had started again.

Protestors, pain, and politics

The crowd gathered outside the Collider facility had continued to swell significantly in size, and was increasingly becoming unrestrained, with fights even breaking out between protesters within the throng of people. The police presence promised had not materialised, and there were attempts being made by some sections of the crowd to breach the gate and fence sections directly in front of the gatehouse. Some protesters had attempted to climb the tight linked fence, most failing due to a lack of available grip and footing opportunity, some reaching the higher areas of the barrier only to realise that there was a significant further obstacle of a roll of barbed wire tightly fixed to the rim at the top of the fence. Some smaller groups of the protesters had attempted to break down panels from the fence, however this had proven to be an impossible task. The fence sections were a dual layer construction, firstly re-enforced steel rods with only a few millimetres gap between each, running both vertically and horizontally. The second layer welded behind the steel rods, a solid screen of sheet steel also a few millimetres thick. Each fence section was five metres high, and two metres wide. At every two-metre interval, each fence section was riveted and welded to a steel pillar set into a concrete base. It was a seemingly impregnable screen holding the crowd at bay for the time being.

Inside the gatehouse lodge, the young guard Mathers had promoted to head of security a few hours earlier sat behind a bank of monitors staring out at the crowd trying to break the gates open. He was scared, plain and simple. He was sitting on his own in a building which was only a few metres from the main gates which the crowd were trying to force open. He placed his gun on the desk in front of him and put a spare magazine next to it, as if to reassure himself that he had some way of protecting himself. He decided to call Mathers and tell him that the crowd looked like they were about to break through the gates.

As the guard lifted the phone to make the call, he saw the crowd part just in front of the gates on the main monitor. He watched frozen in horror as a small van drove through the gap in the crowd, lined up with the gate, reversed a short distance, and then accelerated towards the gates. The van slammed into the centre of the join between the pair of gates, where they were secured together by a large lock and also a heavy iron reinforced bolt. The gates were both also bolted into the ground on the inside. The guard saw both gates shudder with the impact, but held solid on their hinges. The van reversed again, pulling slightly further back this time, the crowd parting slightly further in anticipation of the collision. The impact was significantly heavier the second time the van rammed into the gates. Its driver had clearly given it everything he could get from the van, and as it made contact with the gates the guard heard a scream of metal against metal as the gates moved slightly, twisting and grinding against each other. The crowd cheered with the impact, rushing forwards in anticipation. The van's radiator burst, throwing cooling fluid and steam out from the bonnet. The front bumper of the van had become wrapped in the twisted metal of the frame of the gate, with the van itself turned slightly at an angle to the gates as its momentum was absorbed by their weight. The driver tried to pull the van backwards for another attempt, but it stalled as he put it into reverse, dying enmeshed in the front gates of the facility. The gates sat in place, the dead van rested against them. They had parted by a few inches, and were twisted in places along their edge, but still formed a barrier to entry to the facility. The guard realised that they were unlikely to hold out to another onslaught though.

Gronan sat at his desk in the office listening to the briefing being delivered by a senior analyst on his immediate staff. Things were not looking good from the sound of the briefing. He had tasked three senior analysts to try to assess where in history the time jumps had reached, and attempt to predict what the next likely event could be. If they could find a pattern to the way that people were slipping through time, they may be able to judge the rate that the *fracture* the scientists had described was moving back through time. History had never been Gronan's strongest subject in school, and he was relying heavily on the reports and research his analysts were completing to understand when the events which had occurred had originated.

"The latest and most prominent reliably datable event we have reported was an incident where two police officers and a farmer were involved in a civil war battle this morning," Bryan Barnes said. He was the most accomplished analyst on Gronan's staff, and probably the best candidate to step into Gronan's role when he eventually retired. He had a small hand-held computer tablet which he was using to remotely control a display on a screen mounted to the office wall. The display on the screen showed a satellite image of the farm in Arkansas and the surrounding area. "The officers received a call between five and six this morning, and on attending were confronted by a section of what is believed to be the Confederate army. This dates the time jumps to approximately Eighteen Sixty-One as of zero five-hundred hours today. Our people are attempting to calculate the rate of time passing by using this as a fixed point against the V1 rocket which landed on London earlier this week, which we dated as Nineteen Forty-Four. We should be able to estimate potential threats and events from this calculation, however there is no apparent geographical pattern to the events recorded so far."

"Can we calculate this rate of passage of time only using two events?" asked Gronan.

"We are using these events as a starting point, with an expectation that we can identify another event within these event times to give some comparative analysis to the theory. Unfortunately, these have been the only clearly defined events we can confirm at this time. We have a report of a man who died following his leg being ripped off by a time jump in Bern, Switzerland. This was shortly after the initial experiment, and we are looking to confirm the exact time of this incident and the time and date the leg appeared. This will give us our third fixed point. Unfortunately, there is nothing at the moment to suggest that the *fracture in time* our scientist friends have described is moving back through time at a fixed rate."

Gronan looked from the satellite image on the screen to Barnes, and back again. "So, what is our best bet for the next event? Are the Red Coats coming?"

Barnes laughed quietly. "If they are, I couldn't tell you if it was by land or by sea. I would suggest there's a strong possibility given the volume of soldiers during that time period, some may appear. It is clear that there is a correlation between the scale of a historical event, and the likelihood that there will be a jump from that time. The Second World War involved millions of soldiers spread across almost all of Continental Europe, so we saw a larger quantity of *travellers* from that war, in comparison to Vietnam, where we have seen only a few *travellers*. I'd say our main concern at the moment is the spread of disease. We recently saw an outbreak of Cholera in Tokyo, Japan. They believe a woman traveller who appeared at the Tokyo Central Station brought it through and infected hundreds of people who then spread out throughout the city, carrying the disease way further and faster than historically this sort of infection would travel. Unfortunately, this is likely to be the downside of the modern world, for all the medication we now have, infection can spread almost globally in a day. The world is a much smaller place today.

Gronan tapped a pen absently against the edge of his desk. He was tired, and had taken on more information in the last few days than he had ever processed in his professional life. His best staff were giving suggestions on when they were predicting time travellers would potentially appear from, yet with no apparent pattern the whole situation seemed abstract and random from what he could see. There was seemingly no information to link one jump to another, nothing to suggest that just because the last traveller may have appeared in northern America, that the next would be even on the same continent. He looked from Barnes to Louise Cornell. She was a brilliant prospect, working closely with Barnes even though she was newly promoted to the senior intelligence analyst team. She clearly had something to add, but was deferring to her senior colleague while he delivered his initial analysis. Gronan nodded at her, knowing that she would most likely have several other concerns within her assessment which could cause him a headache.

"I'm a little confused by some reactions in Europe," Cornell said quietly. It was an understated introduction, her forte when taking a large analytical jump. "The British, The Germans, and the Russians are chasing two German soldiers from World War Two halfway across Europe. Why is so much resource being thrown at two men, when for instance, the town of Ypres in Belgium is under siege from soldiers who have *travelled* from the First World War? Other Soldiers in Belgium have attacked students and staff at a Belgian university. We had German tanks in France which seem to have pulled back into a holding position in the Ardennes. What is the relevance of these two men that makes them so special to three countries?"

Gronan tapped his pen against the desk again, impressed with the link she had made. "There is a certain level of sensitivity to the issue of these two Germans. The German Government were distressed by the loss of what they saw as German citizens who were killed in Russia, the war is over, the German soldiers should have been repatriated as far as they are concerned. Obviously one of these soldiers is a war criminal which both the Russians and the Germans want to put on trial. The British are helping the Germans in an effort to keep them on side in a concerted effort internationally to manage this crisis."

Cornell smiled briefly, she had identified some solutions in her analysis which could be of use. "These German soldiers are almost into Germany in a car they stole from two Russian agents. General Ahren may be of use in resolving some of the other situations. If the Germans are prepared to move him towards the other *travellers* from the wars, starting with the tanks in the Ardennes, given his standing within the German Army, he could convince the soldiers to surrender. Tell them that the wars are over."

"Good," said Gronan. He looked at her approvingly. "What else have you got?"

"The protesters outside the Collider facility. At the moment they are attempting to break into the facility grounds. Those scientists have already lost some of their staff to a guard at the facility who went crazy, they need some support in there." She shifted slightly in her chair, adjusting the loose-fitting suit she was wearing. She rarely wore anything neater than combats and a sweater to work, a longstanding bugbear of the other senior analysts. It was obvious she felt suits were not a necessity for her current work environment. Today she was wearing a suit though. Outside the work environment she was a well presented and fashionable woman who thought the generic, deliberately tailored suits that women in the political intelligence profession wore were an unnecessary assertion of equality, and simply did not buy into the peer pressure exerted on her to fit in. She felt like she was trying to make herself look androgynous simply to pay lip service to irrelevant past problems the politically correct world she lived in could not move on from. The men she worked with took every opportunity to wear designer clothes to make a visual statement, to firmly announce their presence visually before ever saying a word. It was something she saw as irrelevant, quality work was all that mattered in her world, and Gronan recognised her ability and drive.

Gronan sensed she was on to what could be the biggest concern they would face. If these protesters made their way into the facility and caused any damage, or got as far as the inner areas where the scientists were working, irreversible damage could be done. "Do we have the blueprint for the facility?" he asked.

"I have it on my desk," Cornell replied.

"Compare it to the satellite image we have showing the protesters, and identify key threats. Possible entry points, power supply, water, anything which could potentially delay the next attempt at this experiment. We meet back in my office in an hour please." As the analysts stood up and left, Gronan motioned to Barnes to stay behind and close the door.

Barnes returned to his seat. "She has some good ideas," he said thoughtfully, if a little patronisingly.

"She does good work," Gronan replied. "We need a full report in two hours for the Vice President. All conclusions we have, best predictions, and key threats. The Vice President will risk assess the best use of our resources and direct our focus to key areas based on the report we provide."

"We need to use small words for him?" Barnes asked. The Vice President had a bad reputation amongst the intelligence community which served the current Washington establishment. He was seen as a political puppet, a buffoon who had the presentation skills to work well with a strong president, but too much style and not enough substance to ever be a great politician. The definition of a fair-weather politician, absolutely no use in a real crisis.

"I think I will be directing his risk assessment very specifically. Giving him some recommendations, which firmly structure his action."

"You think he will listen?"

"He will bluster and re-word some of what I say, but whatever we recommend will be the risk assessment that is made. On his own he couldn't risk assess a fart without shitting himself."

Barnes tried to control a laugh as he stood to leave the office.

As the protestors began to move the mangled van back from the gates, a fight broke out between two small groups stood close to the facility entrance. Some of the protestors had been trying to climb onto the van, with others trying to pull them back in order to move the van in order to try to break through the gates again.

Alder and Mathers stood in front of the bank of screens in the reception area of the facility watching the protesters, quietly losing more hope in their situation. A sea of humanity had built up outside their gates, an unnatural ebb and flow of movement washed through them as more people joined, pushing forwards through the crowd in an attempt to make their protest heard by the architects of this catastrophe. Mathers could see every level of emotion in the range of protestors. There were curious hangers-on just out to try to be part of the global news event, groups of political militants who opposed the global capitalist expansion which had caused scientists such as those in the Collider facility to push the boundaries of what is safe in an effort to break new ground for their own fame and professional advancement, to religious fanatics who believed that the rapture was now in full motion, taking the world back for their particular messiah.

Dornel was stood behind Alder and Mathers, silently observing the scene for himself. He had disappeared from the control room they had been working in, and after searching the various rooms within the corridor they had been working in, Alder and Mathers had decided to work their way through the building looking for him. They found him almost immediately, having decided to start from the reception area and work their way downwards. Dornel had simply been as he was now, watching the protestors with a worrying fascination. His eyes tracked every pulse of the crowd as it moved forwards and back in front of the facility, steadily swelling in numbers.

"They have no idea what we have done, what we achieved." Alder and Mathers heads snapped round at the sound of the first words from Dornel's mouth since the incident had happened. "They protest at something they could never possibly hope to understand. We may have gone a little wrong, but we were trying to improve the world for everyone, weren't we? We can't take it back, but that's not our fault. We tried, hell we did more than any of those people ever managed to achieve in their whole pointless lives."

Alder nodded slowly, looking Dornel straight in the eye. "Yes Pete, we were trying to improve the world for everyone. Isn't that what every scientist looks to do, make everyone's lives a little better in some way?" He stepped towards Dornel slowly, calmly touching him on the arm. "Shall we go back downstairs, see if there is maybe something we could do to help fix this?"

"Won't change what's happening now." Dornel's eyes were wide, the deep pain and fear spilling out from them, he made no effort to hide his emotion. He turned slowly and walked towards the elevators, Mathers and Alder following behind.

For the first few hours Ahren had been sitting silently whilst Bulmann drove out of Cracow and along the busy main road towards Germany. His head was full of ideas he could never have dreamed of. Nightmares of long dead monsters which had become a possible reality in his existence. He had heard rumours of German soldiers who had killed the populations of countries they had invaded during the war, of deep cruelty being used to control the local people in areas Germany had occupied. But in all of his active service he had seen no atrocities of the like he had been told about by the Russian agents he had just encountered. He had never tolerated the slightest indiscretion perpetrated by a man under his command, they were soldiers who acted with honour, not criminals or murderers. He had heard whispers of Jews being relocated, never heard of again. But they were moved to a new life, to live with their own, weren't they? The same thoughts kept running over and over in his mind until he could no longer hold his silence.

"The people you killed. How many? For what reason?" Bulmann stared ahead, silently watching the road. Ahren sat waiting for an answer, his patience burning away quicker than he had expected after he decided he needed to know the truth. He needed to hear all of the painful truth before he handed this disgrace to a uniform over to whatever Government now stood in Germany. But would the Government in Germany be any different now to the men who created this abomination? "How many?" he said again, his voice firmer, demanding now.

"All of them. All of the enemies of the Fatherland I was told to. Nothing the world would miss. *Untermentionables*. I did what you were too weak to do, I made a home for the German people, free of the burden of those who took but did not contribute. We took back what was stolen from Germany in Versailles."

"Who did you murder in the name of German *greatness*? Women, children? What was the price of our greatness? You killed no one in my name, no one for Germany, you were killing for yourself and the monsters like you. Evil twisted perverts."

"You were a soldier, you have killed. I simply killed where you could not, who you could not. Enemies the blind like yourself could never see."

Ahren felt sick. Everything he had heard but never believed was laid out in front of him by a man he had viewed as a fellow soldier. His own honour as a soldier was gone, not just tainted but forever destroyed by his association with men like this in a war which hid crimes no man should ever be a part of.

The drive to Germany took slightly more than four hours. Ahren had returned to silent contemplation after Bulmann's confession. If he had not been bound to return Bulmann to Germany to face justice for what he had done during the war, he could never have returned to his home land. The miles passed quickly, and with every mile bringing him closer to home the weight of reality sat greater on him. Would he be seen in the same light, a war criminal?

Ahren snapped quickly back to the task at hand as they passed over the German Border, his eyes suddenly drawn to a sign written in his own language. He was home. For the first time since he left Russia Ahren allowed himself to think of his family, what may have become of them? Where was his wife now?

Within a day he would have handed over Bulmann to whatever justice this world saw fit, and then his life as a soldier would end. He would simply be a man again, hoping his debt to the world would be repaid by the justice he would bring Bulmann to face.

A light drew both men's attention to their right flank. Ahren turned to try to identify where the sudden blue light was coming from, seeing a car pulling onto the road behind them from a small slip road. A white car with a light on top was following them, a man in uniform behind the wheel. Bulmann began to slow the car.

"So, are you ready to hand me over for my punishment? I doubt anyone in Germany could judge me for what I did for our country, do you think I will be a hero or a villain?"

Ahren looked at Bulmann, suddenly worried he may be a hero to some. "Stop the car. I think the time has come to find out." As Bulmann slowed the car to a stop, Ahren ran his hand against the gun he had taken from the FSB agent. He reached into his pocket and pulled out the key for the cuffs attaching Bulmann to the steering wheel. "Turn off the engine and give me the keys. Then you have this key and remove your cuffs."

"Last chance, we both want freedom. You fought in the same war as me, do you think you can go back to being a soldier, be treated any different from me?"

"I will face any judgement coming to me," Ahren replied quickly, surprised that Bulmann had pointed out such an obvious possibility. He took the keys from Bulmann, opened his door, and stepped out of the car. The car which had pulled them over had *Bundespolizei* written across the bonnet. He looked back into the car at Bulmann, still cuffed by one hand to the steering wheel. Ahren dropped the cuff key onto the passenger seat next to Bulmann and took the gun from his belt. "Take those cuffs of and get out of the car. Let's not do anything too quickly, you wouldn't want to do anything now and lose out on you chance to tell your story."

In the police car a lone officer watched as a man stepped from the passenger door of the car he had just pulled over. The man dropped something back into the car, spoke to the driver, and started to pull something from his belt. Recognition suddenly dawned on him, this was the pair of soldiers he had seen on a dispatch sheet when he began his shift. He was just calling for backup as he realised the man stood outside the car was pulling a gun from his belt.

Ahren turned at the sound of the voice, trying to remain in view of Bulmann but positioning himself in such a way that he would be able to speak to whatever police type of force had intercepted them.

The officer had drawn his own gun as soon as he stepped from his car, and aimed it towards Ahren as he gave his command. "Stand still, and drop your weapon," he shouted in as clear a voice as he could manage. He was nervous, this was the first time he had ever drawn his gun in any situation other than training. He had been proficient with firearms in training, but that was a false environment. Unarmed targets did not shoot back.

"I have a prisoner to hand over to you." Ahren shouted back calmly. He recognised the stress in the police officers voice, and it concerned him. "I will surrender myself to you too, but you need to take this man into custody first. Once he is secure, I will follow any command you give me."

The police officer took a step forwards, still aiming the gun at Ahren. "Drop your weapon now, get on your knees, and place your hands behind your head." Was this the right arrest procedure for an armed suspect? Every arrest procedure he had ever learned was running through his head. Should he make the suspect stand next to the car with his hands on the bonnet, should he be lay on the ground face down? He had never actually made an arrest for anything more serious than drunks fighting or minor assaults. "Follow my instructions now," he shouted, the stress now making his voice break.

Ahren nodded, slowly bending his right leg behind him, moving to one knee. He placed the gun on the ground just to his left, still within reach, but far enough away to relax the nervy cop with the gun pointed at him. "I am following your instructions, now please be careful of the man in the car." He knelt on both knees, placing his hands on his head. "He is a well-trained soldier who has killed many people."

The police officer began to approach the car, moving slowly. He was cautious as he moved, trying to not make it obvious he was scared and unsure of how to arrest both men. Ahren looked the gun sat on the tarmac, and wondered if he had done the right thing. He looked back to the officer walking so nervously toward him. He was taking a position to see into the car through the passenger door.

"In the car. Move slowly over to the passenger seat, show me your hands as you move." He aimed the gun between Ahren and the open car door, watching Bulmann move slowly across to the passenger seat. "Step out of the car, keep hands out in front of you." Bulmann followed the instructions, the handcuff still attached to his left wrist. The other cuff hung open below, swinging gently in front of Bulmann as he stepped from the car. "Get on your knees, hands on your head." Bulmann followed the instructions, looking at the police officer all the time, watching his movements, assessing him. As Bulmann knelt and placed his hands on his head, the cop approached him, still weary, holding his gun ahead of him. He circled around Ahren and looked at Bulmann's hands, puzzled by the single attached handcuff. "Put that other cuff on yourself, now."

Ahren looked towards Bulmann, suddenly aware of his fatal mistake. "He has keys, do not let him cuff himself." He was pleading with the police officer, knowing Bulmann needed only the slightest opportunity, and this guy was going to give it to him.

"Do it now," the police officer said, levelling his gun on Bulmann. Bulmann stared into the police officers' eyes, nodded, and lifted his hands high above his head. He took the loose cuff and placed it over his free wrist, securing it tightly so the cop could see he was fully cuffed. He knelt silently, his hands rested back on his head.

Ahren watched Bulmann stare at the police officer, knowing he was waiting, picking his perfect shot. He saw the cop moving towards him, still holding his gun ahead of him. He worked around behind Ahren and took his cuffs from his utility belt. Ahren felt a cuff snap onto his right wrist clumsily. There was a small amount of relief, the inexperienced police officer had enough sense to use one hand to cuff him, still holding his gun with the other. The second cuff clicked into place on his left wrist, he was now as vulnerable as he could be, having to rely on the reactions of this police officer when Bulmann made his inevitable move. The police officer placed his gun in his holster and moved between his prisoners, this was the moment.

Ahren felt the police officer lace a hand under his arm and lift him to his feet. He looked over and saw Bulmann pushing his way to his feet by himself, pushing himself upright by putting his cuffed hands on his thigh and giving himself the leverage to spring forward. Ahren dropped back, trying to get clear of the now lunging Bulmann. The police officer froze in shock as he saw Bulmann explode upward from a kneeling position, his hands now free from each other. He had taken the cuff key given to him by Ahren from his belt, where he had tucked it when he had released himself, and unlocked one of his cuffs as soon as he began to stand. There was no time to react, Bulmann's left hand shot forward, grabbing the side of the police officers head. He drove his thumb deep into the officer's eye, using his huge hand to grip the man's skull for leverage. The cop let out a scream, which was muted as Bulmann punched him with a hard right hand to the stomach, driving all of the wind out of him. His hands swung out, trying to push Bulmann back. In one smooth motion Bulmann's hand moved from the officer's stomach to his holster, drew his gun, and fired twice into his stomach. He looked at the gun as the police officer stood in front of him, swaying loosely. Bulmann still held the man's head, keeping him on his feet. "Danke schon," he said as he released the man's head, letting him fall.

Ahren rolled awkwardly, his hands remaining cuffed behind his back, scooped up the gun he had dropped on the tarmac a few minutes before, and dived forwards into cover in front of the car they had been driving. He crouched momentarily, his mind racing. How had he been so stupid, he had left Bulmann with keys to the cuffs he was wearing and had surrendered himself to a police officer, he was to blame for the man's death. He heard Bulmann walking along the road towards the car. He was still cuffed, and although he was under cover, he had very little opportunity to get a strategic advantage. Ahren rolled back from his heals onto his lower back, and in one smooth motion, passed his cuffed hands under his bent legs, pulled tight to his chest. In the distance he heard sirens, the dead police officer must have called for backup before he tried to arrest them.

Bulmann's footsteps stopped, then started again, moving quickly away. He was making for the police car. "Auf wiedersehen bruder," Bulmann shouted at him as he ran.

Ahren made his move, pushing himself up above the bonnet of the car, aiming the gun towards the footsteps. Bulmann was ready, firing towards him. The bullet whistled past, barely missing his face. Ahren dived back behind the cover of the car. Before he managed to regain his footing, he heard the police car door slam, the engine fired, and tyres screamed loudly against the road. Ahren stood again, firing at the police car as it swung out onto the road, veering past the oncoming traffic and into the opposite carriageway, sending an oncoming car off the road into the verge where Ahren was stood. The driver managed to miss Ahren narrowly before he smashed into the barrier at the edge of the road. Bulmann was gone.

"We need some supplies as soon as we can get them, most importantly we need food." Alder said into the phone, staring at the emergency rations he had been eating for days on end. Mathers nodded at him and mouthed *get pizza*. "We emailed a list of equipment we need too, without it we have no chance of even trying to start the Collider." He was talking to an administrator at the European Science Directorate who sounded like she was going through the motions on an order for a supermarket delivery. "There are even more protestors outside the facility, you will need to ensure there are security and a full police escort for there to be any chance of managing to deliver anything to us."

Alder mumbled something into the phone that Mathers couldn't quite make out, and hung up. It had sounded like Alder had said "Today or never."

"You think they will get the supplies to us before we run out of time?" Mathers asked, painfully aware that the chance of a delivery getting past the protestors was slim.

"You never know, maybe the army will airlift us in a takeaway and a laser focal plane detector?"

Ortile burst through the door, clumsily stumbling into the room and tripping over a chair. He just about regained his balance and avoided crashing into Mathers. "He's gone again, so is the guard's gun."

Gronan drove towards the White House, unsure how well the assessment he was about to present to the Vice President would be taken. The end of the French Revolution had just started, roughly on schedule against the timescale his staff had predicted. Gronan struggled to word the latest development into his report, the whole situation was so surreal. The *end* of the French Revolution had just *started*. Revolutionaries had just begun to behead French aristocrats in Paris, and at the rate things were going it would be a few hours until this current crisis ended with the *start* of the Revolution.

Gronan was an incredible intellectual, he loved to theorise about how to control the various political incidents he had helped to manage by assessing intelligence and offering options. He was a brilliant analyst who could suggest the action any government needed to take given almost any political crisis, from terrorist attacks to organised criminal groups. He had virtually written the book on how to identify a lone criminal or terrorist with no links to any group or organisation, through advanced profiling and intelligence analysis. He could have a subject profile written within hours, given minimal information, which would help either the intelligence community, or local law enforcement to formulate a strategy to apprehend any criminal or terrorist. The problem was that this was such a unique situation, even he was out of his depth. He had stopped enjoying the theorising now history was the future. His current problem with his level of knowledge and ability to analyse intelligence was that he was presenting his findings to an idiot. The Vice President would fail to grasp the key points of what was put in front of him, and would fixate on irrelevant trivialities. He simply couldn't prioritise the most urgent issues.

Gronan chuckled to himself at the thought that he could confuse the Vice President with the possibility the United States could support the Revolution in line with the beliefs of Thomas Jefferson, or if they should remain neutral as was Washington's policy. He decided against bringing the subject up, the Vice President wouldn't recognise the sarcasm. He decided to avoid too much French revolution discussion at all, and focus on the estimated assessment that the British would be landing in the American colonies within the hour to restart the American War of Independence.

Alder and Mathers walked slowly from the elevators into the reception area, hoping maybe to find Pete Dornel stood watching the demonstrators on the monitors as they had been a short while earlier. Dornel was not anywhere in the foyer. They walked to the bank of monitors and stared at the crowd at the main gate area of the facility. There were maybe fifteen monitors set into a security station just behind the reception desk. Each monitor showed a different perspective of the front area of the facility, and the entrance area to the main building which they now stood in.

"More of them showing up," Alder said as he tapped a screen showing an overview of the protestors from a high mast camera focussed over the main entrance gates. "Looks like they are giving it another shot at getting through those gates."

"They won't take too much more of the pounding those guys are giving them. Think we'll get the army here with those supplies before they have broken through and are running around the compound? I don't think we can do anything more before we get some real food and that equipment."

On the screen the protestors were lining up another car towards the gates. Alder stood quietly watching as the crowd cleared in front of the car. "They will have to deal with whatever is out there when they get here. No point worrying, one way or another they've been tasked to deliver what we need and secure the facility."

Alder stopped speaking suddenly, a lower screen taking his focus from the protestors. Walking along a wide path towards the main gate where the protestors were gathered was a figure Alder instantly recognised. Even in the dim early evening light Alder could clearly see Dornel strolling casually towards the crowd.

Ahren crouched over the police officer. He was barely conscious and bleeding heavily from the gunshot wounds. His face was a bloody mess, he had been coughing blood up as he tried to speak. His right eye had swollen horrifically where Bulmann had thrust his thumb deep into the socket. It looked like the eye of a bug of some kind to Ahren, red and bloodshot, bulging out from the socket. Ahren had seen too many of the soldiers he had commanded injured like this. Men, often barely past being boys, lay dying on a field where some battle for a little more ground or just to gain a tactical advantage had taken place. To him they had been heroes, every one giving their lives for a purpose, to protect Germany. But things had changed. He was watching a man close to death losing a battle that should never have been his to fight. Ahren should have killed Bulmann when he had the chance. The more he had thought about it, the more it was obvious what he was. A killer. Not a soldier. Not a hero. Ahren felt like a petty thief as he ran his hand over the police officer's belt, locating the cuff keys he would need to free himself.

"I am sorry." He lifted the police officer's hand to push onto one of the gunshot wounds, trying to slow the bleeding. It was futile, he could see blood coming from beneath the police officer. At least one of the bullets had gone straight through him, exiting low in his back creating a further wound to lose blood from. The police officer seemed to come back a little when Ahren spoke, his left eye focussing on Ahren's face for a few seconds. "You are the police? Do you know who I am? Did you recognise the man who shot you?"

"Du bist soldaten." *You are soldiers.* The words were forced out of his mouth with all the effort he could manage.

"Ja. We are. We were. Not anymore though, not for a long time." He thought it would be a difficult explanation, not necessary given the situation. "What is happening?"

"The past. It's coming back. Much more than just you." The policeman shuddered with the effort of speaking.

"More? From the war?"

"From everywhere."

Lights of cars moving past him on the road caught Ahren's attention. "Danke. Lay still." He saw movement from the bank where the car that had barely missed him when it had been forced off the road as Bulmann had pulled out into the carriageway had crashed. The driver was climbing from the car. He looked unhurt, but clearly in shock. Ahren stood and stepped towards the driver. "This policeman has been shot. He needs help, will you stay with him?" The man looked scared, and took a step back from Ahren. Presented with a man covered in blood, wearing dirty clothes and stinking of diesel, it was understandable that the driver may be concerned for his own safety. Ahren held his hands out in front of him, a passive gesture to relax the man as best he could. "I did not shoot him, the man who stole his car and caused you to crash shot this policeman, and now he is trying to escape. I must follow him, please stay with him. Get him help."

The driver stepped forward again, and looked from Ahren to the police officer. "He is still alive?" He asked.

"He is, just. Sit with him. Please." Ahren stepped back and started walking towards his car.

"You are going to try to catch the man who did this?" The man stepped forward as he asked, moving towards the police officer and crouching down, a wave of shock hitting him again as he saw how badly he was injured.

"I'm not catching him, not any more. He is going to die, or I am. The police know who I am, when they come tell them the man I was with did this. He is trying to get to Berlin. Tell them I'm going there to find him." Ahren ran back to the car he and Bulmann had been travelling in. It would never keep up with the police car Bulmann was in, but it would get him to Berlin, and he would find Bulmann there.

The heavy double doors of the Oval Office opened in front of Gronan, as a Secret Service agent stepped from the room, followed by the Secretary of State. Gronan looked at the Secretary of State quickly, then threw his gaze to the Secret Service Agent, and nodded an acknowledgement. He was very close to the Secretary of State, but this was not the time to engage in his usual back and forth with her. She was as brilliant as anyone he had ever engaged with, and they shared both a serious professional relationship based on mutual respect, and also a personal friendship based on good natured banter and a small amount of sexual tension. He was almost ten years older than her, and often wondered if she used his admiration for her to manipulate him slightly when she needed some support from the intelligence community. He didn't mind if she did in all reality, he used her influence at times to his own gain at times too. It was a mutual benefit.

"Jim," she said as she stepped past him.

"Holly. How are they in there?"

"Having a great time," she replied from over her shoulder as she walked away.

"They are ready for you sir," a Secret service agent interjected from the doorway. Gronan turned and walked into the Oval Office.

The President stood from behind his desk as Gronan walked into the office, and moved to meet him in the middle of the room. "Holly is going to engage with the Europeans to arrange some support for the scientists that have caused this. It's getting worse over there and they are still isolated. We need some forward movement on this. What have you got?" The Vice President was sitting in his usual space, on a leather sofa just in front of the President's desk. Gronan walked to the second sofa near the desk and stood beside it. He never sat while the President was standing.

"I have the blueprints for the facility, my people will forward them to Holly. We completed a risk assessment today, entry points to the facility, key threats, supply of services such as water and power. They will need a few generators from the nearest army base along with the equipment they have requested already. They have a good enough power supply to run the experiment, but if there are any problems, they may need every bit of power available to keep things moving." He stopped momentarily, and turned the page on a report he was holding. He passed a print out of the facility blueprint to the President, along with a map of the surrounding area. That was the simple part explained. Logistics of securing a building or small external area was an everyday event.

The President looked back to him, gesturing with his hand to continue, making a small circle in the air. *Let's get to the real issues.* He put the blueprint down on a table, and ran his hand across his mouth.

"We think there is a steady rate of movement backwards through time. I have a report with some estimates of the dates and events we are expecting the next jumps to potentially originate from. We are putting ourselves somewhere in the Eighteenth Century at the moment. We have to assume that domestically there is a strong chance we are going to have British soldiers at our shores now, or worse, on land within hours. The French Revolution is in full swing, which is really causing some issues in Paris. We placed ourselves at Seventeen-

Eighty-Nine approximately an hour ago, when a fairly large group of badly dressed starving Parisians stormed the Bastille. We have already seen some disease outbreaks in Japan and Africa. The next concern on that front is the bubonic plague and small pox. We are estimating a timescale of six hours before we start to see infections spread in Europe and Africa."

The President sat on the sofa just across from the Vice President, and ran his hand across his face, from his brow to his jaw. "Ok Jim, I want you in the Situation Room in thirty minutes with a short-term plan for the next six hours, based on the worst-case scenario estimates your team has made for the events we are expecting." He turned to the Vice President. "Go with him, I want you putting the actions in place once you have a full assessment ready. Jim will need to go back to his team while you implement the actions set out. From here on out, we meet every six hours in the Situation Room, with an updated assessment for the expected events of the following six hours, and the actions you aim to put in place. Thank you both."

"Should we go after him?" Mathers was walking towards the doors to the reception area, set into the high glass walled facade of the building.

"It's too late now. There's no way we can safely go out there at the moment the way things are. We're just going to have to hope he doesn't do something stupid while he's out there." Alder touched Mathers on the shoulder, moving him back from the front doors. They walked back to the bank of monitors just as the protestors had moved the car into position lined up in front of the main gates. Mathers shook his head as he watched it start the run up.

The same image was running across the screen in the main gatehouse where the lone inexperienced guard was sitting. He watched transfixed as the car hurled itself forwards towards the gates. He stood and moved away from where he had been sitting to look through the windows at the front of the building across the short distance towards the gates.

The protestor sat in the car had pulled the handbrake on hard, and was revving the engine to the point where the front wheels were beginning to spin, buffeting the front of the car. It was a mid-sized Ford family saloon, at least ten years old. It had a few bumps and dents in the bodywork, but was a solidly built car with plenty of muscle left under the bonnet. The driver looked out through the windscreen, catching the eyes of several protestors stood just adjacent to the car. He was going to be the hero of this protest. The new poster-boy for a new generation of people who would not accept the *old guard* of society damaging the world in the way they had done for the hundreds of years before this crisis. A new world was emerging from the ashes of a failed society which had almost burned up the planet with greed and a vicious struggle for power and the control of others. Now one young man would lead The People into the very grounds of the organisation which had done so much damage to the planet.

The leader of The People nodded from his driver's seat to the protestors just a few feet away from him, and pushed the accelerator pedal down to the floor, the engine roaring against the strain of the handbrake. He dropped the handle on the brake as the accelerator pedal hit the floor, and the Ford raced forward towards the gates. The acceleration was more than the young driver had expected. He was young and had never driven a car this powerful before. It was exhilarating. He was speeding towards his destiny, leading The People into the grounds of The Enemy. A roar burst out from the crowd of protestors, a cheer of support. They were going to break through the gates this time. Inside the car, the speedometer shot upward, the rev counter reaching the red. He changed gears once, and then a second time, red lining the engine as he fought with the steering wheel to control the car, wrestling to hold it in line with the gates. The protestors filled into the gap behind the car as if flew through the gap in the crowd towards the gates, a surge of humanity urging it forward, almost pulled forward along with the momentum of the car.

The hero of The People smiled as he saw the gates loom up in his windscreen, racing towards him as he made his historic journey. He tensed in the driver's seat, preparing for the impact. The car slammed into the gates almost perfectly central to the join between the two gates. The barriers holding the gates together twisted under the strain, momentarily holding before they reached breaking point from the force of the impact.

Inside the car, the driver had a moment of ultimate satisfaction, as the front of the car drove into the gates driving a wedge further into the opening the first attempt to break into the facility had made. The gap was opening up. He was leading The People into the facility. His jubilation was instantly replaced with terror in a split second as both the driver's airbag and the passenger's airbags exploded out in front of him. A split second later his face punched into the airbag. In that split second he relaxed again, as he realised the airbag had saved him. The Airbag saved him from smashing his face into the dashboard of the car and the steering wing wheel. It didn't save him from the five-foot-long bolt of steel which was skewed out from the already damaged gates. The bolt was what remained of a manual secondary locking mechanism on the gates, now twisted and hanging in the small gap between the gates. It speared through the spider web cracked windscreen, pierced the airbag his face had just hit, drove through his skull and embedded itself in the driver's seat headrest.

Dornel walked out onto the road leading towards the gates, watching the sea of protestors parting as the car started its journey towards the gates. He saw the car accelerate towards the gates, the wave of protestors filling in behind it, a swell in the crowd moving towards the gates. He carried on walking calmly towards the gates, maybe twenty to thirty steps ahead of him. The car was building up speed quickly on the other side of the gates, it would reach them while he was still several steps away from it. Dornel thought the situation was becoming a game of will between himself, the gates, and the car. They were on a journey together, all heading for the same destination. It was inevitable they would meet, and either the gates or destiny would decide how this dark game of chicken would play out. Dornel had no intention of moving from the path he was currently strolling down. Either he met the car on his side of the gates and he would be the loser, or he would meet the car when he reached the gates.

Mathers made a small moaning noise deep in his chest, rumbling up through his throat and out of his mouth becoming almost a cry. "Screen seven," he managed to say. The screen showed Dornel walking with purpose along the road towards the gates. He looked like he was daring the car to come through the gates, willing it to try to get to him.

"I think the army are going to be a little bit too late for him now then."

Dornel barely flinched as the car smashed its way into the gates, not missing a step. The car had driven the gates open by almost two feet, but the car itself now blocked the way through the gates. It had become enmeshed in the mangled metal remains of the gates.

The protestors had rushed to get to the gates and push through the newly created gap. They stopped in their tracks as they saw firstly the car wedge itself in place in the gates, and then a solitary figure walking towards the gates from inside the facility. There was something incredibly disquieting to the crowd which had only moments before been baying for blood, to see the lone scientist continue to walk towards them without breaking his stride while the Ford crashed into the gates. A few protestors were still pushing the car from behind, trying to clear a gap wide enough to swarm through.

Dornel walked up to the crumpled bonnet of the Ford prying its way through the small gap in the gates and stopped, surveying the damage. The car was now at an angle, with the front left corner protruding through the gap. He looked from the bonnet to the windscreen. It had been pierced by a long shaft of steel which had bedded itself deeply into the car. His gaze followed the path of the steel bolt from the gate through the windscreen, and stopped on the deflating airbag, which was becoming a loose white sheet limply flapping as the last of its air escaped. It was coming to rest over what remained of the face of the driver, blood beginning to stain it red. He looked up from the airbag, his gaze meeting the gaze of a protestor just behind the car. The crowd was beginning to shout a call out again, but Dornel heard barely anything. He was oblivious to the shouts and abuse being hurled in his direction. Auditory exclusion shutting out everything but his focus on the protestor he now stared at. The man was staring back, unmasked hatred in his eyes.

Mathers and Alder watched Dornel on the screen reach the car, stop just next to it, and then put his foot onto the front bumper where it pushed through the gates.

"Don't tell me he's going to try to just walk out of here through them?" Mathers said as he turned to Alder, confused by what Dornel was attempting to do.

"I just don't know what he's playing at. There has to be maybe a couple of hundred people out there now. They clearly aren't here to show some support to the people inside this facility."

"We have to get out there and stop him, he's in shock. Those people will tear him apart." Mathers started to walk towards the doors, then stopped. He turned back and met Alder's gaze. They both knew the crowd would never listen to them trying to explain what had happened. There would be no negotiating with them, if he was going through the gates, Dornel was on his own.

The crowd began to shout louder as Dornel stood with one foot planted shakily on the crumpled front bumper of the Ford. His eyes remained locked on the protestor he had been staring at. The man was maybe in his early twenties, a ratty beard sprouting from his jaw. He looked like he had been wearing the same clothes for the last week, a stretched faded grey t-shirt, and an old pair of blue jeans. Dornel felt like he looked similar. He hadn't shaved for days, he was in an old shirt he had changed into, and a pair of trousers he felt like he had been living in for far too long. The man he was staring at may have looked similar to how Dornel felt right now, but Dornel was positive he had not made any contribution to society, science, the arts, or any other field of human achievement in the same way that the scientists in the Collider facility had attempted to realise. Who was this man to protest anything? What had he done?

Dornel pushed his weight onto the bumper of the car his foot was rested on, testing its stability. It seemed solid enough. He stepped forward onto the bumper, and from there onto the bonnet of the car. He gripped the edge of the gate to support himself as he stood on the car. He began to hear the crowd, the sound resonating through his feet from the car. His perspective suddenly expanded massively. He saw the crowd as a whole, heard them screaming at him. The ground was rumbling as the protestors pushed forward against the gates, the rear end of the car, and against each other. Dornel looked across the heads of the crowd, scanning for something, anything to suggest these people were worthy of the protest they were making. He saw nothing.

Screams of "Murderer," and "Monster" rose from the crowd. Dornel stood silently as the crowd shouted. He watched some protestors reach up to the gates, trying to pull themselves onto the back of the car and push through the gates. Arms reached through the gap, hands clawing for him. He was safely stood on the bonnet, out of reach by a few clear feet. The noise was now deafening, a constant roar, individual voices indistinguishable from the overall wall of sound. Dornel looked down into the car. The image of the very dead driver inspired no emotional response from him. It was just a bag of meat stapled to the headrest of the driver's seat to Dornel. He looked back at the crowd and realised they meant nothing more to him than the dead driver.

"What did any of you ever do to make you think you can judge me or anyone else in here?" Dornel's voice was quiet. He couldn't hear himself speak. There was no response from the crowd. He spoke again, a little louder. "Do you want to know what we were trying to do in here, or do you just want to stand there and shout incoherently?"

Nothing. The crowd just continued to shout at him, still pushing forward against the gates. A throb of force pushed through the car as more protestors decided they wanted to try to get a little closer as they realised Dornel was stood in front of them. He stood his ground, facing down the protestors. They would listen one way or another. He raised the gun he had picked up before walking out of the bunker. He was holding it above his head, his arm straight up in the air. A signal for silence. He got the opposite. More shouts, screams, and abuse. He pulled the trigger. Nothing. He pulled the trigger again. It wouldn't move. Safety switches. Guns had safety switches. He knew that from films. He brought the gun back down to look at it. It was smooth, thin, and straight. Not a revolver, one of the guns they have in films where they load the bullets in a magazine into the handle. It had a couple of switches on the left side, one sat just above the grip, roughly where a right-handed person would rest their thumb when holding the gun. He turned the gun over in his hand, looking for anything more obvious. There was nothing that looked more likely, so he pushed the switch upwards with his thumb. He raised the gun again to show the crowd, another warning. Nothing. He pulled the trigger. An explosion rang out above him very satisfyingly.

A wave of motion passed back through the crowd in front of Dornel as people tried to dive backwards, some ducking for cover, others trying to turn and run. It was very satisfying to see. He had taken a small amount of power back from the protestors who had attacked the facility. They were not as strong as maybe they had first seemed. As he looked at them his eyes again met those of the young man with the ratty beard stood just across the top of the car from him. He was still stood there, defiant. Unconcerned by the gunshot Dornel had fired.

155

Other protestors were pushing forward again, also unafraid. They stood with the young man Dornel was staring at, and began to shout abuse at him again. Rage filled him, who were they to stand there and protest? He raised the gun, and looked from the crowd to the back of the weapon he was holding in an outstretched hand. In the periphery of his vision he saw the motion of the crowd, beyond his focus which was now on the back of the gun. They were moving back again, but only slightly. There was one of him. He could not force them all away with just one gun, but he needed them to leave. He wanted to leave, one way or another. He would not be staying here.

"I'll shoot," Dornel said quietly to the back of the gun. His focus drew past the gun to the crowd. "I will shoot you." This time his voice was louder, clearer. The crowd reacted in a way he did not expect. Instead of running away from him, seemingly not afraid of what he may do, they suddenly pushed forwards again, the protestors most forward in the crowd slamming against the car, beginning to try to climb through the gates again.

He was trapped. There was no way he could go back, he would not be in the facility when they restarted the experiment. One way or another, he would never go into that building again. The car he was standing on bucked violently with the force of the protestors pushing on it from its rear bumper. Fear rose suddenly again in Dornel, these people would not let him escape. But then, if he did escape, where would he go? The experiment was going to happen again wherever he was. What if it did the same thing to him as it had before, if he was forced to relive the pain of the tumour tearing the inside of his head apart. Months of agony all compressed into an instant of such sheer agony it had all but destroyed his consciousness. It rendered him mute for days, scarred his every thought with the memory of a pain so real and intense he had lost every ounce of his personality, of his very being.

The shell of the man Dornel used to be stood on the bonnet of an old European model Ford he did not recognise, and tried to pull together a coherent thought. He looked along the sight of the gun, seeing the young man he had been staring in his aim. Who was this protesting worthless creature to stop him from escaping from the compound? To keep him imprisoned now, a nobody who had come amongst a crowd to deliver his judgement to men who were not his equal. Dornel looked from the young man, to the corpse in the front seat of the car, and back again.

It was a human. A life which may or may not have great merit. But a life that was not his to take. Dornel could not shoot. The crowd slammed forwards again, driving the car inches further through the gates. They creaked as the pressure mounted. Dornel staggered with the sudden motion. He regained his footing as the crowd pushed again, this time managing to wrench an even bigger gap in the gates, which were folded over the roof of the car, but separating in front of Dornel. They were breaking through to extract their vengeance on the perpetrators of this crime against the planet. Innocent or guilty, good or bad, Dornel could not shoot any of these people. They were unarmed. But there was one thing which may stop them. His hand had fallen to his side as he realised he could not shoot the man he had been staring at. It rose again, swiftly. The gun touched the side of his own head and he fired.

In the crowd, the young man who had been staring back at the scientist from the facility watched in shock, as the man who had been threatening him with a gun stood for a long time with it held out in front of him. One way or another, the young man figured, this man and his friends were going to kill him. Their experiment was killing millions, and was not going to stop. He stood there defiantly as the man had come out of the facility, and then stood at the gates pointing a gun at him. *Go ahead* he thought, *look me in the eyes if you are going to murder me, look me in the eyes and have the courage to kill me while I stand here. I won't back down.* The standoff had lasted for an eternity, as other protestors had scrambled around him and tried to get to the man, tried to push through the gates into the facility. Then suddenly the man on the other side of the gates had done something he never expected. He simply lowered the gun, then lifted it back to his own head. The shot silenced the crowd. All shouting, all pushing, everything stopped. A vaporous red cloud burst from the side of the man's head as it jerked with the force of the bullet, his eyes instantly blank. He pitched sideways, his upper body giving way like a toppling building. He slammed onto the car bonnet, now almost face to face with the dead driver.

The screen in front of Alder and Mathers flashed with the gun shot, the blood cloud momentarily bursting from Dornel's head dissipating quickly as they watched on. Alder gasped suddenly, the shock setting in as he realised what he had just seen. Both men simply stood, staring at Dornel's body sprawled on the bonnet if the car. This was the end of any chance of another attempt at the experiment, they had lost too much now. Three dead from the team of six scientists.

Mathers slowly stepped forward and tapped a screen just above the image of Dornel. He had no idea how much time had passed, the combination of crippling shock from all of the violence they had gone through, the isolation of the facility in lockdown, and mental stress of the experience of the first experiment had rendered the passage of time abstract to both scientists, something they were simply unaware of any more. The screen Mathers had tapped showed that the mass of protestors was thinning, slowly moving back from the gate area. Even the most volatile looking protestors seemed to be mollified by the scene of a man shooting himself a few feet in front of them. They continued to watch as more and more protestors fell back from the gates, some walking away, some simply stepping back from the gates and gathering into smaller groups, stunned by what had just happened in front of them.

Nothing was said, Alder and Mathers just knew nothing more could be done stood in the foyer staring at the screens. They walked back to the elevators in silence, waited for the doors to open, and stepped inside.

Interception

Jason Gillen sat in the safe house in Potsdam, waiting for the images to roll out of his printer. He had been sent old military photographs of Ahren and Bulmann, along with scans from security cameras at the Cracow Glowny train station showing both men. Gronan had called Gillen a few minutes earlier and tasked him with intercepting Ahren, apprehending him, and returning him to the safe house for further instruction. He was being tracked by satellites driving towards Berlin, chasing Bulmann in the stolen police car. Gillen pulled the last print off the printer and walked down to the garage. He entered a code into an alarm panel on the wall by the entrance to the garage from the safe house, and stepped into the dark garage. Sitting in his car, he logged onto the car computer attached to the dashboard. The screen lit up and panned into a satellite image of the area south of Berlin, giving a real time feed with a target type cross slowly moving along a road. He clicked a button, and the computer calculated an intercept route from his current position. A few seconds later, he pushed a button which opened the garage doors, and the unmarked car pulled out onto the quiet Potsdam street.

Gillen was a CIA operative who had been assigned to Central Europe for the past ten years. He primarily worked in Germany, identifying and neutralising foreign investors looking to fund potential terror cells which may target American assets within Europe. This assignment was a huge relief to Gillen, who had spent the last few months stood down. Mostly between assignments he would just spend hours sat in the safe house reading and exercising. Gillen was in his late thirties, in excellent shape, and struggled to spend prolonged periods of time doing nothing. He was the image of a cliché intelligence agent, six feet tall, with strong features and a lean muscular physique. This was unusual in the modern CIA, who had always avoided such an overt appearance. Gillen had been incredibly successful within a limited and very specific role, where his appearance as a presentable all-American had actually been beneficial. It disarmed the type of target Gillen specialised in, who would be alarmed by a rough looking or average person moving about the circles of Embassies where the norm was refined style and subtle intelligence. Gillen had better than average record for identifying and neutralising the conduit bankers who used embassies to move between countries and mingle amongst the benefactors of state sponsored terrorists.

The screen on the computer attached to Gillen's car dashboard flashed a message across the screen. He was being instructed to make contact with his handler prior to intercepting his target. Gillen had been briefed that the situation was fluid, with objectives subject to change at very short notice. This usually meant a decision would be made to arrest unharmed or eliminate, depending on the intelligence assessment at that exact moment.

Gronan hung up his phone and replaced it in his trouser pocket, and penned a quick line on a scrap of paper. He waited patiently while the Vice President finished his own telephone call. The Vice President was showing off, probably talking to one of his campaign investors. He was downplaying the crisis and making vacuous jokes. Gronan had tired of his lack of focus quickly, and was now openly showing his frustration.

The Vice President put his hand over the mouthpiece of his phone. "Have you got something?" he asked vacantly, aware that Gronan was stood at the door, keen to get back to the Situation Room for the update meeting.

"Two somethings," he replied. "The British *are* coming. Several ships sighted a few miles from Virginia. We are assuming they are headed for the Battle of The Chesapeake.

Secondly, traces of volcanic ash are being found in the atmosphere of Japan near Mount Fuji. An ash cloud was observed less than an hour ago. This gives us one of two conclusions. Either Mount Fuji is erupting again, or this thing has gone as far as the start of the Eighteenth century, probably into the Seventeenth now."

"Have your people got any projections for what we may be expecting from the Seventeenth Century?"

"They are working that up now. We are aiming to prioritise threats which may have an impact on the scientists at that facility. Last thing we need is one of those jumpers to wander in there and give them all the plague or some other horrific disease." Gronan didn't wait for a reply, he stepped out of the room and started walking towards the Situation Room. "I'll see you in the meeting, once you finish your call," he said over his shoulder through the closing door.

"Do you think he knew anything about it? Like was it painful, or do you think was dead before his brain could process the fact that he had just shot himself?" Mathers' eyes were bloodshot. He had been sitting for hours in the small kitchen area, numb from what he had seen. He had started to cry eventually, letting himself process what had happened. Accepting it.

Alder sat quietly, patiently letting him deal with the situation as best he could. "I don't think so. I hope he simply switched off, all the pain gone in an instant. It's too much to accept really, isn't it?"

"He was in a lot of pain. I think he was really struggling to continue even before this had happened. Did he ever talk to you about his illness?"

"I knew some of it. I had known him briefly a few years before he was ill. He was always, maybe a bit sensitive. I think being ill made him more fragile. You know how sometimes people who are ill recover and the whole experience makes them stronger? I think with Pete it damaged him, made him less robust than he had been. I just don't think he had the strength left to carry on in here, the experiment showed him something that pushed him over the edge."

"What did you see? Did it bring back anything for you?" Mathers wiped his eyes and stood up, walked to the fridge, and grabbed a couple of cans of coke. He didn't ask if Alder wanted a drink, they had reached a point where they would both pick up drinks and food for each other when they got something for themselves.

"It was strange, I had an incredibly vivid flashback to my wedding day. I could literally taste the meal I ate that day, I could smell the perfume my wife wore, I felt her lips against mine as she kissed me. I could feel her body against me while we danced." Alder stopped for a moment, disappeared into himself. Mathers could see that Alder was reliving the memory deeply within himself, it was clearly a very sensitive topic for him. "You know she died nearly ten years ago now. Then we did that experiment, and she was alive again. I was holding her, kissing her. I could have lived in that moment for the rest of my life, you know it was real. I had her in my arms again. All the people that came through this tear, all those jumpers, you know for a moment I wished she had come through too. Then I realised that if she had, I would have lost her back then. I had her for the best part of both of our lives, and then she became ill. I stayed with her all the way to the end, and then I lost her. Nothing can change that, it's how life goes. But I had a moment with her again, and it was a moment more than I could ever have asked for." He stopped again, holding back tears. Alder looked younger suddenly, more human than Mathers had ever seen him. The look in his eyes was that of a man who had been truly happy, not those of an ageing scientist whose life was entirely invested in this experimental research. "I never thought about another woman, never needed anyone but her. She was lovely. Tell me, what was it you saw?"

Mathers struggled for a moment. How could he tell Alder the vision he had, it would just be poor taste given the gentle story he had told. "It was maybe a little different." He smiled.

"You enjoyed a memory from the young man you used to be, don't worry, you're a lot younger than me, maybe I focussed on an old mans most treasured memory." Alder smiled, realising Mathers' embarrassment at what he had seen. "It's ok, if it was personal to you, we don't have to talk about it."

"I was losing my virginity." Mathers laughed, shaking his head at how stupid it was to be worried about saying it out loud. "I saw her in front of me, she was right there. I could feel her." He flushed momentarily, realising what he was saying. "I saw us together. I met her when I was a teenager. We dated for a year or so, then split up. Teenagers. We dated again a few years later, maybe five or six years after I graduated. I worked in England for a long time after I graduated. She came to visit me there. I saw that too. We were in Stratford-Upon-Avon. Funny, we were in a café. I could taste the wine we were drinking. That was possibly the best day of my life, we walked by the river, drank, ate, made love. It was just a perfect day. I think it must have been July. We saw Hamlet at the theatre that evening. She didn't understand any of it. The language of love, tragedy, life and death, all played out to a young couple in love themselves. Afterwards I had to explain it to her. The beauty of language lost on a world moved on, struggling to recreate art to a viewer unprepared to comprehend its concept. I think maybe that made me love her a little more though. She was very innocent."

Alder laughed. "Did you practice that little speech?"

"No, just spent too much time in the last few days thinking about it."

Street lights began to illuminate the road ahead of Gillen, he was driving steadily through the early evening, gradually relaxing in the leather car seat. He was driving a Five

Series BMW, pacey enough to deliver exactly what he had needed from it this evening. He had been tense as he drove across the south region of Berlin, focussed on avoiding being stopped by either the police or any looters who had taken to the streets every evening since the experiment had triggered a shockwave of unrest through society. He had aimed to be out of Berlin and ready to intercept his target on a main road a few miles south of the city. This would minimise the opportunity for escaping into any back streets or alleyways. No bystanders to either interrupt or interfere if he was to eliminate his target. No witnesses.

The computer screen on Gillen's dashboard flashed onto an incoming call. He reached over and tapped the screen, accepting the call. The face of his handler appeared in the frame of the split screen next to the map.

"New instructions." The voice came through the car radio speakers, replacing the Aerosmith song he had been listening to. "Intercept and arrest Target One, carry to Schönefeld Airport south runway via freight terminal."

Gillen looked at his handler briefly on the screen. He had absolutely no discernible personality that Gillen had been able to identify. An empty vessel, barely capable of any form of interaction with other human beings. He had no interests, no friends anyone knew about, none of Gillen's colleagues had ever been able to hold a conversation with him on any topic other than tasking instructions.

"Confirmed," Gillen replied. "Target Two?"

"Eliminate if encountered. Do not pursue."

"Confirmed. Anything else?"

"Further instructions pending. Make contact once you have the primary complete." The screen went blank for a second, then the map expanded to fill the screen.

"Nice talking to you," Gillen said to the screen, amused at the lack of pleasantries. He glanced at the map, his target blinking only a few inches from his car on the screen. He pulled over onto the hard shoulder of the carriageway and touched the screen. It zoomed into the road he was parked on. The satellite image showed his target driving along the road towards him, no other cars between them. The satellite image showed the car closing in to less than half a mile from him. He wondered where Bulmann had managed to lose Ahren along the country roads. Quickly, he opened his car door and stepped out. He pulled a small bag from the back seat and walked along the road towards the oncoming car. Headlights crested a small rise ahead of him and lit the road dimly. He opened the bad and pulled out the stinger. He tossed the bag to the ditch and threw the stinger out across the road, holding the grip in his left hand as it extended out onto the tarmac. He pulled a flash bang from his pocket, twisted the top to set a timer on it, and threw it to the other side of the road. He took a few steps further towards the oncoming car and set a second flash bang timer, and threw it hard towards the car along the road. Gillen turned and ran along the bank past the stinger, then stopped, dropped a smoke grenade onto the road, and walked into the tree line just deep enough off the verge to set his position. The car headlights flashed through the trees just in front of him. The road was on a slight bend to his right, giving him slightly more opportunity for surprise. The first flash bang burst with an explosion of light and a sudden crack. He saw the car appear behind its lights, speeding along the road around the bend in front of him. The flash bang had exploded just behind the car, clearly distracting the driver, who had swerved slightly, clearly seeing the flash in his rear-view mirror and trying to work out what had caused it. Moments after the flash bang exploded, the car hit the stinger, driving over it at enough speed to cause the driver to have to fight for control as the tyres all burst in an instant. Gillen had deliberately chosen to set his ambush just past the bend in the road to ensure the car was not going too fast to maintain some control. It veered slightly, the tyres flapping loosely on the rims of its wheels. Gillen was impressed by the steady control the driver showed, not suddenly braking too hard or panicking and trying to turn the car. It rumbled a short distance down the road before he saw the brakes gently pull it to a halt. The second flash bang

exploded, lighting the road ahead of the car, followed almost instantly by the smoke grenade

erupting and throwing out a cloud of smoke into the road just ahead of him.

Ahren stepped from the car, scanning from the road to the verge assessing the

situation. He pulled the car door wide open, and then opened the back door, ducking between

the two. He was planning the best route of escape, clearly already very aware of the trap he

was within. Gillen held his nerve, patiently waiting for Ahren to step into the trap. He had

hidden at the tree line exactly where anyone stunned by a trap of this nature would make for.

The obvious cover available against an unseen enemy. Gillen pressed the key in his pocket,

unlocking his car, which triggered the parking lights to illuminate the road ahead of Ahren.

Gillen watched as Ahren broke cover, moving out past his car doors and into the road, but

instead of making for the tree line, he ducked and threw something back into his car and ran

from it, back along the road in the direction he had come from. Gillen held his position,

curious as to what tactic his prey was employing. It only took a few moments to realise what

had been thrown into the car. Ahren had used the car cigarette lighter to set fire to the

something sitting on one of the car seats, causing smoke and flames to rise up out of the open

doors. Gillen decided he had to break cover now, or lose Ahren in the smoke and darkness.

He ran along the verge just inside the tree line, Ahren's silhouette still just visible ahead of

him. He ducked deeper into the trees as he ran, anticipating Ahren to do the same. Ahren held

his nerve, working his way along the road, hearing footsteps behind him. Gillen guessed that

Ahren must weigh something just over two hundred pounds, too heavy for a low dose

tranquilliser to guarantee being effective, he needed him to be incapacitated for at least a few

minutes, long enough to cuff and move into a position where he could speak to him when he

regained consciousness.

Ahren glanced behind him as he ran along the road. He wanted to move into a position of cover where he could reverse the trap. He had identified only one person tracking him so far, and had rightly assumed that a stronger ambushing force would be ahead of his car along the road. Anyone behind him along the road would simply be backup to the primary force, surely less in number and strength if there at all. The fact that he had found no backup suggested his enemy was working alone or in limited number. This would be the place he would move into cover, having drawn whoever was stalking him further from the ambush site, reducing their advantage significantly.

Gillen saw the figure ahead of him flash between trees, ducking into cover as he went. He gambled correctly, impressed by the strategy his target had employed. He fired a flare high directly between the trees he had just watched the figure pass. It burst with a bright flame a few feet above the tree line, lighting the area ahead enough to cast shadows, showing exactly where Ahren was running. Gillen stepped to his right and fired a taser between the trees into the gap Ahren ran into. A web of wires flew out from the taser, at least a dozen spreading out in a wide arc carrying almost fifty thousand volts with them. Ahren's momentum took him between the trees into the web of wires from the taser, unable to stop in time as the flare lit up his position. Two barbs dug into his skin, one burying itself in his arm, the second sitting high in his torso. The voltage struck immediately, standing him bolt upright as every muscle in his body tensed instantly, then dropping him to his knees with the shock, pitching onto his side with the last of his strength as he fell forward into the dirt.

Gronan had walked into Situation Room with the intention of laying out a plan for every scenario his staff had identified as being a priority risk. He was immediately derailed as The President had opened the meeting with news that contact had been made with the Collider facility, and that there had been an incident. They were expecting a conference call with the lead scientists, but that had apparently been delayed whilst the military assessed various scenarios. Gronan could not understand why the facility had not already received military support to ensure security levels were appropriate to manage any external threat. His staff had quietly informed him that one of their sources told them The Vice President had assigned military resources to other areas prioritised above the security of the facility, including buffering local military and police forces in areas where civil unrest had been reported. This was clearly a political move to strengthen his support and influence internationally, he had his sights set on the Oval Office, and any mileage he could wring out of this crisis he would gladly take. Gronan quietly watched as one of the Generals who had been a constant at the briefings spoke to The President. Neither looked happy. The President nodded, rubbed his face, and turned to the table.

"Every priority has now been focussed on the security of the facility in Switzerland as of now. Our military resources in the area have been mobilised, and three units from Patch Barracks in Stuttgart have been deployed to the facility, and are expected there within four hours. General Anderston will be taking charge of the overall security of the facility and surrounding area." An aide passed a note to The President as he finished speaking. He looked at it briefly, placed it on the table leaving his finger resting on it, and took a sip of water from a glass he had been nursing in his other hand. The water was warm and stale, he realised it had been in his hand since he walked into the room some time before. "They are ready at the facility." He turned to the aide who had handed him the note. "Put them through straight away please."

The screen on the wall at the foot of the table lit up, and Gronan recognised two of the scientists who had spoken with The President during a previous conference call. They looked much older suddenly. Neither had shaved, and both seemed drawn, their eyes somehow showing pain and exhaustion, and simultaneously almost blank. They just stood in front of the camera, not acknowledging anyone in the Situation Room.

"Gentlemen, I'm sorry to hear you have suffered another loss. Please excuse my lack of sensitivity, we will all need to set aside a time to mourn once this crisis is resolved, but what is required now is for us all to steady our focus to the task at hand. I hope you can find the strength to continue until we have the opportunity to put our minds to those we have lost." Alder held his hand up, stopping The President without even looking at him.

"Your speech is very eloquent, and I'm sure inspiring to the men and women who wrap themselves in your flag to shield them from the pains of war and loss, comfort them in times of despair, and dress their wounds. I'm afraid we are not wrapped in any flag. Our wound is very open, and no words of consolation, no matter how well delivered, will resolve our current problem." Alder stopped to regain his composure. He knew there was nothing he could say which would fully explain just how far past the point of being able to try to attempt another experiment they had reached. "Earlier today the protestors outside our gates attempted to break into this facility. They almost gained access to the external areas of the facility, and from there, would likely have very little difficulty causing significant disruption to our work. They have been temporarily dispersed, but I believe they will be back soon enough. We simply cannot maintain a secure perimeter now. Your supposed support which was on the way is too late to help now." He stopped again, breathing heavily.

"I understand…" The President started.

Alder interrupted him. "Clearly you don't. One of my men, Peter Dornel is gone. With another of my staff lost, we are simply not in any position to attempt any further work now. I only have two staff and myself remaining here, and three men vital to this work are dead. It's over I'm afraid."

"We have arranged for two of our best scientists in your field to be flown to Switzerland in the next couple of hours. A military transport should have them there by eight tomorrow morning. Military support will be with you before midnight, I have asked that General Anderston who is in overall command of United States Armed Forces in Europe take personal charge of the security of yourselves and your facility."

Alder turned to Mathers, looking at him desperately for the words that would make the Americans understand. He had lost his patience.

"Your men will be very welcome," Mathers said appreciatively, a light, almost imperceptible tone of sarcasm in his voice. "If they could start by picking up the dead bodies at the main gates for us that would be lovely. After that, some fresh food would be appreciated. I can't remember the last time I ate something we didn't have to scavenge from the facility canteen and cook in a microwave. Then the list of supplies we sent to you will need to be delivered before we can start to attempt any repairs on the equipment here. A conservative estimate would be that if your men are fully competent and conversant with the work we have been doing, we could possibly attempt another experiment in a week's time."

The President shook his head, looking down at the floor. "I will offer you both the same courtesy of blunt honesty you have shown me during our pleasant conversations. You will have the support you need as soon as it can be with you. Military support would have been with you sooner, but they were spread thinly trying to stop the civil unrest your experiment has caused. They were fighting soldiers from wars that ended years ago, wars your experiment unleased on the world again. You have lost friends. So have thousands of other people all across the world, bombs dropped on Britain and Germany, disease spread throughout the world without warning, people were torn apart by the phenomenon your experiment caused, literally torn in half. You have brought this planet to the brink of total social meltdown and all-out war. I would suggest your only hope for any future is to focus every effort into whatever work you can do to fix this, and not in a week's time. Now. You will have every single thing you've asked for, and you had better pray that you can fix this while we still have anything left on this planet worth fixing." The President threw the glass of water from his hand and stormed up to the screen, past the table full of advisors, scientists, Generals, and politicians, all shocked by the sudden outburst. The glass had shattered against the floor near to the head of the table where The President had been stood, startling some advisors out of their chairs. He stood in front of the screen, staring directly into the eyes of Alder. "You will do everything you can to fix this now, and after this is over you better hope the worst that happens is that you are not held responsible for any more deaths than can be avoided. I swear to you now that if you don't fix this, I will bring every level of justice at my disposal to bear against you. Switch it off. Now."

The screen went blank.

The early evening pedestrian footfall on Cannon Street was much lighter than usual, due to a curfew being placed on all British cities following looting and sporadic riots breaking out in across the country. A few police officers walked along the road, warning any passers-by that there was only just over half an hour left before the curfew would be coming into effect. The police officers were relieved, the night before the street had been far busier, not bustling with post-work drinkers and tourists the way it had been prior to the events of the past few days, but still busy enough to cause them some concern that the curfew may be broken by groups set on some untoward activity. A sudden heat rushed past the officers on the air, a hot dry wind suddenly swirling between the tall buildings. Just as the officers passed

Friday Street walking towards Saint Paul's Cathedral, the air around them changed in an instant.

Around the police officers and the few pedestrians, the air turned to fire less than a second, abstractly one of the police officers thought of a nuclear bomb exploding in a movie he had watched once, a tsunami of flame washing through the street in front of them. The flames carried on the wind tore through the street, stretching almost all the way back to Pudding Lane, and passing Saint Paul's Cathedral to the west. Both police officers screamed in agony momentarily as the flames overtook them, the sound muted as the air coming out of their lungs turned to fire, filling their mouths and passing down their throats deep into their lungs. In less than a second the police officers and pedestrians on Cannon Street transitioned from living, breathing, sentient beings, to melting mounds of flesh and charred bone on the scorched pavement, which was cracking and breaking under them.

The trees lining the grassy area of Saint Paul's Cathedral ignited, with an entire avenue of Pyrus Bradford trees exploding seconds after they were engulfed in the flames. The grass on the open areas of the courtyard dried and turned brown before melting into the ground.

The doors of Saint Paul's Cathedral burst outwards, flame following them, scorching the stone black around the lower sections of the building. The fire rose up from the road and crowned a halo around the dome of the Cathedral, sending a strange smoke ring into the sky.

Every car and building window between Saint Paul's Cathedral and Monument Station warped and shattered in the heat, the shattered glass melting into the road. Pulses of flame and fragments of shrapnel flew hundreds of yards into the air and out from the fire as the few cars which had been parked on the road exploded. Stretched out along the road, almost four-hundred-year-old piles of burning timber had appeared within the fire, turning almost instantly to ash. The remains of the closely built wooden structures which had been the basis of London's working and middle-class houses in the seventeenth century littered the street burning against an avenue of concrete and what had been glass and steel buildings. A river of molten lead ran from the Cathedral out into the churchyard and park, flowing out onto the road. The vacuum caused by all the soot and dust within the fire instantly being ignited using the surrounding oxygen as an accelerant, sucked all of the air from fleet street in an almost tornado like wind, suffocating the pedestrians who were stood staring at the fire, thinking they were safely outside the blast zone.

The protestors outside the Collider facility had dwindled to just a few small groups collected together and the occasional unstable individual stragglers, though they were more interested in fighting between themselves than making any concerted effort to get through the gates. Between the few protestors a man in brown robes walked from person to person, reading from his bible until eventually being told to move on as each consecutive protestor's patience was lost with him.

The man in robes moved close to the gates of the facility and stood still, quietly waiting. He held up his bible in his left hand, looking up towards it with all the reverence he felt he could muster. He had been stood with some other religious onlookers earlier in the evening, before walking through the protestors spreading his message. Now these onlookers had gathered in front of him, ready to listen to his words. Slowly a few of the protestors walked towards him and joined the group, curious what the unusual man would have to say now.

"This is the tribulation before. We are in the days of Thessalonians, making ready for His return. The days are upon us where Man shall split into two groups, those who follow the lamb, and those who are wicked, assembled before Him for judgement upon His return. We stand now in the Valley of Josaphat. Allow yourselves into his arms and be baptised before it is too late, take Him into you as He shall take you with Him to meet The Lord. Only He can wash away your sins and cleanse your spirit before judgement. Was it not written that the dead shall stand up again? Restored to life for they shall meet with him and together we shall all rise up to meet with The Lord. Prove you are righteous and you shall come with us." He looked half crazy to most of the protestors, stood there in his robes holding out a bible and shouting about the dead rising again. He did seem to attract a few followers though, the protestors who watched on were surprised at the growing size of the group surrounding him.

"How many more signs can we ask for before we believe? Do you need to wait until *Hellfire and brimstone* rain down upon you before you realise *The Rapture* surrounds you, has passed you by? Or will you stand with me now and welcome Him? His touch is upon this place, guiding these events. He moulded the acts of the men in this place to bring about the time of His return, raising His followers from the dead, and raining down fire upon the hive of sinners and the dens of evil." He pointed towards the facility as he spoke, emphasising each point he made.

Gillen cable tied Ahren's hands behind his back and rolled him onto his side, placing him into the recovery position. He wrapped a small tracking bracelet around Ahren's ankle just above the joint, securing it in place and locking it with a key. He stepped back and took out his phone, took a photograph, and forwarded it to a number marked "Confirm". He swapped the phone for a small torch in his pocket, and leant against a tree next to where Ahren was beginning to stir.

"Welcome back. In more ways than one from the sound of it." Ahren struggled to roll onto his back and tried to sit up. "Stay still for just a few moments, let your body get all of your senses back before you move too much. You just took quite a shock. I'm not here to hurt you, we need to talk."

Ahren lay back against the ground and rolled his body slightly, testing the feeling in his arms. He could feel the restraints against his wrists, tightly bound together. His head hurt like hell, he felt like he had been set on fire. "I don't have time for this, if you are here to kill me, do it. If not, let me go before it's too late." He rolled onto his back and used his feet to push himself to a tree, sitting up against it.

"I haven't been sent here to kill you, I've simply been sent to collect you and bring you back to Berlin."

"You are American. Why would you want anything from me? I was going to Berlin, you have been sent to bring me to where I was going anyway. We are wasting time, if you are taking me to Berlin we need to go now. A man is on his way there, a very dangerous man."

"Before we move, just a few things you need to know."

"We can talk in your automobile once we are moving."

"Agreed, but before we move you need to know the rules. You have a restraint on your wrists. That stays in place. You also have a tracking device attached to your ankle. That also stays in place. I have no idea what you are wanted for, but from the sound of it you are important, and they want you alive. I have no intention of hurting you, but I will do what I need to ensure you don't escape from me. Work with me and this will be a nice easy drive."

"Agreed." Ahren pulled his knees to his chest, putting his feet flat on the ground in front of him. He rolled his weight forward by pushing off the tree in a smooth motion, lifting himself to a standing position in one graceful movement. "We go now?"

Gillen nodded and pointed towards the road. He walked a few paces behind Ahren, watching his movement. "Did you feel it when it happened?" Gillen asked, his tone lighter than before.

"When what happened?"

"Well either you look incredibly good for a man who is well over a hundred years old, or you travelled through time this week. You aren't the only one, the world's gone crazy."

"The world has *gone* crazy? If it is any more crazy here that it was where I came from, I would be quite surprised. To answer your question, I was in a tank in Russia, there was war everywhere in the world. Then somehow it was a few days ago and apparently the war was over a long time ago. I can't tell you how it happened, I was there, then I was here."

Gillen nodded, unsure what to say to what he had heard. This soldier had been in the Second World War a meter of days ago, and now he was the best part of a century out of time. A man displaced from his own time, Ahren was for some reason still vitally important to someone, or Gillen would not have been sent to capture him and deliver him to the airfield near Berlin.

"So, you were just a soldier, nothing special?"

"Nothing special, no. You would have called me a normal soldier, I was a General, but one of many in the war. Now all I am is a man. Once I have found the man I came here with and settled that debt with the world, I will work out what else I am."

"You call being a General *nothing special*?"

"I commanded men. I had been a soldier my whole life, just like a lot of other soldiers. I was good at my job, and got promoted. But no, I was not special. I followed orders, and I followed the rules of war. I was a German soldier, but I never considered myself a Nazi, which was why I was rolling into a battle in Russia on a tank instead of commanding a sector in France."

They were walking along the edge of the road, breaking clear of the tress and out onto the smooth tarmac, dimly lit by the moon. Ahren picked up the pace, not wanting to waste any time, he could not let Bulmann gain any greater a lead than he already had. Within a few minutes they were stood at Gillen's car, Ahren impatient to be moving. Gillen opened the front near side passenger door, and allowed Ahren to slip into the seat.

"Turn your body into the car and lean forwards. Give me your hands, slowly and gently."

Gillen took out a small pocket knife, opened the blade out from the handle, and cut the plastic cable tie from Ahren's wrists, then took a step back from the car.

"Pull the seat belt across yourself and click it into place."

Ahren pulled the seatbelt across himself and clicked it into place, then rested his arms across the top of the belt strap on his lap.

"Put your arms out in front of you, put your hands together, and lace your fingers into each other, like you're praying." Ahren followed the instructions slowly, making each steady motion precisely as he was instructed. "Bring your elbows and your wrists together as close as you can." Ahren was sat with his elbows pushed together against his stomach, his hands in front of his face as if he were sitting in church. Gillen stepped forwards, reached into the car, and snapped another cable tie tightly around Ahren's wrists. Then he took a piece of heavy fabric about the size of a handkerchief and placed it over Ahrens hands, wrapping it tightly at the wrists, and then put a further cable tie over the cloth. Ahrens's hands were bound tightly together, and he found he could not separate his fingers inside the cloth due to it being so tightly fixed at his wrists. He could barely even separate his elbows, so simply moved his forearms down and rested them on his lap. Gillen closed the door, walked around the front of the car, and eased into the driver's seat.

"These restraints are different from anything I have seen before. I'm impressed."

"They're practical for a solo arrest and transport. Standard police cuffs and rigid cuffs leave your hands free to grab anything you want, so unless you are cuffed behind your back, they are useless. Even behind your back, you could grab something if you really felt like resisting. They also give you a potential weapon. Like that you are restrained completely, no damage done to you, and I can transport you sitting next to me. You said you wanted to talk, this is your chance."

Gillen started the car and pulled out onto the road.

The entire Situation Room sat silently, not wanting to make any eye contact after the screen on the wall went blank. It felt very uncomfortable to Gronan, sitting in the shocked silence waiting for someone to be the first person to speak. They were seated in thickly padded black leather office chairs around the large oak table, The Great Seal of the United States carved ornately into the centre of the table top. The President cutting off conferences with the scientists in that way was becoming a little more familiar, a blunt ending followed by a blank screen. More monitors were set into the plain walls at even spaces around of the room, each showing different feeds from either news broadcasts or satellite images of various key global locations such as Washington and Berlin. Some of the satellite feeds were live, where others showed images of recent incidents, including a group of German World War Two tanks firing on a lone British tank in the Ardennes. Gronan noticed that most of the people in the room were either busily shuffling paperwork, staring at the screens on the walls, or simply looking down at the dark blue carpet. The President had walked away from the screen and sat down at the head of the table, annoyed that he had let his frustration and anger get the better of him, it was a rare occurrence that he had passed the point where diplomacy would work within a discussion with anyone. Suddenly a phone started to buzz loudly on the table. It was set on silent, but the heavy vibrate function was almost as loud as if the ring tone was on full volume. Then one after another, almost every other phone in the room started to either vibrate or chirp in one way or another.

An aide walked briskly into the room as people started to pick up their phones, and strode directly to the President. The Vice President was talking on his phone, and appeared to be going pale at what he was hearing. Everyone in the room was getting the same briefing simultaneously. The President stood up and asked the aide to switch the main monitor to show a satellite view of Central London. One by one everyone in the room ended their calls, and began to look at the President hesitantly. Before the President said anything, the Vice President ended his call loudly, and stood up from his place to the Presidents left hand at the table. *Buffoon*, Gronan thought to himself as he ended his call, looking down at the list he had in front of him prepared by his staff a few hours before.

"Has everyone been appraised of the situation in London?" The Vice President asked. "Initial assessments are that terrorists may have attempted to set off an improvised dirty bomb amongst the chaos over there. This is one of the scenarios we have been concerned about, cells which we were monitoring before this crisis using this as an opportunity to further their cause. Our resources internationally have been spread so thin we have not been able to continue monitoring these groups to the same level, many have already dropped off the radar."

Gronan shook his head and looked at the President.

"Jim? Something to add?" The President asked, cutting in on the Vice President.

"My people have completed a few assessments and mapped out predicted incidents as you asked. They have been passed on a short while ago, and were on the schedule for this briefing. Based on the location this is not a dirty bomb, as we are reading it from the intel we have so far. It's the Great Fire of London."

The Vice President snatched up a sheaf of paperwork from the table in front of him and shuffled through it, clearly angry at being embarrassed.

"What provenance do you have?" The Vice President was almost stuttering the words out as he searched through the paperwork for the briefing sheet Gronan had given him before the meeting. "How reliable is your assessment, how good is your source? Because we know there have been plans by a cell in London for some time now. You know that as well as I do. If this isn't a bomb that's great, but if it is, we will need to look internally again to strengthen our resources towards identifying any potential group with motivation to use this situation to forward their agenda."

"It is ahead of the estimated schedule we have at the moment, but our calculations are not based on an exact science here. It's not like we have any previous experience of this to base our work on. We have a rough timeline with events plotted against it, which identifies major global incidents and events as requested. I am fully aware of the threats you are talking about, and my people are monitoring those them as best they can with the resources we have at this time."

The main screen lit up showing a live satellite feed of south-east England, with London slowly zooming into clarity. There were co-ordinates displayed across the bottom of the screen, with the date and time showing just below them. The image panned up slightly and centred on London, outlined by various grid references. Gronan picked up his phone and called the central satellite control centre number at the CIA. He called out grid references from the sheet in his hand, and watched as the screen panned in towards the centre of London, the outer ring of the M25 expanding out of the frame of the image, The Thames loomed into the screen splitting London from east to west. The image moved east of Westminster, working its way across the city, with The Thames bordering the bottom of the screen. It settled on four grid squares, with St Paul's Cathedral centred in the top left square, and Cannon street carving its way through the image to the bottom right corner. The image showed the scale of the destruction, fires being fought as best the Fire Service could manage, buildings destroyed and still burning, the normally grey road scorched black. The image didn't show a blast pattern dispersing in the usual pattern expected from any normal urban explosion, but instead there seemed to be a path cut diagonally from the top left of the screen starting at the Cathedral grounds, moving along the roads towards the bottom right of the screen.

Gronan quietly gave some instructions over the phone, and the clock on the bottom right side of the screen started to run backwards. In less than a minute, they watched the image on the screen move backwards through the last hour. Fires which had been put out on the periphery of the screen burst back into life, and the screen grew brighter, then suddenly the light seemed to be sucked downwards across the image, followed by a flash in the bottom right corner of the screen just under the digital clock display as it kept creeping backwards. A moment later the fires were out, and image was simply that of a normal London aerial view. Gronan spoke into his phone again, and the image froze, the clock stopped a few moments before the fire started.

"Doesn't look like an explosion to me," Gronan said, trying not to sound too pleased that his department had been right in their assessment.

The Rapture

The man in the brown robe walked to the main gates of the facility, and stood at the back of the wreckage of the car. He looked over the roof of the car and pointed from the body sprawled a few feet from him on the car bonnet, to the shape skewered in the front seat.

"Look at what these men have led us to. Was it *His* will to hold these gates together and stop the intruders, the transgressors into this holy place? I think it must have been, for these people put his plan into action. These events are *His* making, and guided by *His* hand." He over-emphasised the word *His* every time he used it, looking to the heavens with each reference, making the most of his performance, playing up the pious convert. He looked at the gathered protestors and followers in front of him, revelling in the opportunity to gather more new converts for the journey they were about to undertake. "*He* has set us on the path to Jesus' return, for Jesus to take us to meet *Him* as was promised so long ago. These men were the tools in The Lord's hand to bring us to that great meeting in heaven."

He walked as close to the gates as he could, reaching over the bolt which had driven through the car windscreen into the head of its driver. The lower half of the gates had been forced apart to the height of the car, which had wedged solidly into the gap it created. The gates had remained held fairly close together above the top of the car, still hanging no more than a few inches apart at the top, widening to about ten to twelve inches apart nearer the car. There was a small gap between the bolt, the windscreen of the car, and the gate which the car was wedged against, less than a few feet wide, but enough for the man in robes to lean into, and at full stretch he could reach the car bonnet. His fingertips edged past the top of Dornel's lifeless shoulder, reaching at full stretch. He managed to get a small amount or purchase on the barrel of the gun between his thumb and index finger, and started to slide it across the bonnet. As gently as he could, he lifted the gun and eased it through the gap between the car and the gate.

"Look at the ways of the past." He held up the gun above his head for the small crowd to see. "See how unbelievers were held at bay not by man alone, but by this invention of man, but now we must cast these old ways aside. These symbols of man's mortality are obsolete, the corrupt systems of the old world will crumble to dust as *His* followers are resurrected from dust. We, the *Believers* must become the gates to this holy land." He tucked the gun into his robes.

"So, saying your department's calculations are correct, can we assess how quickly this is moving through time, and how accurately can we predict what we are expecting to be dealing with next?" The President asked.

Gronan slid a sheet of paper across the table to The President, with various events plotted against it. There were dates of the original event, and when they had predicted that event may come through a jump in time.

"We thought we were close to the end of the seventeenth century a short while ago, but we now have an almost exact date from the Great Fire of London, certainly within a week," Gronan replied. "We have that date plotted against two other events, a woman who was literally torn apart by one of these jumps in Italy and the Second World War Royal Air Force bomber which dropped the bomb on Berlin. From the gaps between these events, and then the time between them and the fire in London, there is definite acceleration in the rate we are seeing intervals between events. My guys are describing it as a wave, and the wave is accelerating backwards through time. I can't guarantee that a specific predicted historical event will come through, but you have a full list of Seventeenth Century significant factors we should be at least have some protective responses planned for."

"I think that sounds like a fairly accurate assessment of the situation. What else do we need to be looking at in the next four hours?"

"I had a call from Colonel Grey in Britain a couple of minutes ago," Steve Halt said, slipping into the conversation as subtly as he had slipped into the Situation room. "They dispatched an army unit from Mansergh Barracks in Germany several hours ago. It's only a single unit, but they are solid and will be at the facility within the next half an hour, which is going to be well ahead of our unit. They will simply secure the perimeter at first, and then bolster security once we have a stronger presence. We also discussed a strategy for our navy to intercept the British ships before they reach The Chesapeake. I don't think they are going to be easy to negotiate with, they will be expecting to be taking on a few colonists, the sight of an aircraft carrier in their path and a fly-over is going to spook them pretty badly at the very least. The America is on an intercept now, so we will have feedback from them in the hour. The cholera outbreak in Tokyo is getting bad. We have the facilities to treat and cure diseases like that quickly, but the sad reality of the modern world is that the one woman who brought it with her appeared in the main Tokyo train station and infected hundreds of people. Those people were so geographically mobile that it spread throughout the entire city in a few hours. My concern is that it may have not been contained to Tokyo, all there needed to be was one person getting on an airplane after being infected and that could be an international plague an hour later. We have to look at what other infections could appear in the same way, and get some plans together for infection control."

The British Army unit deployed to the collider facility had used a pair of Foxhound light protected patrol vehicles converted for urban deployment to transport a single squad of eleven soldiers to the facility. Ten of the soldiers were deployed from a regular unit, the eleventh had taken command of the assignment on request directly from the Prime Minister. He was a Major named Freeman who had suffered the misfortune to have been posted to almost every unwinnable conflict the army had engaged in since day one of his career, and this day was no exception. This led him to gain promotion to Major through a wealth operational experience, but limited his further promotion to higher levels of command because of his jaded attitude towards the political direction of those ranks. He had served in both Afghanistan and Iraq, seeing the fiercest action in both theatres. He was looking to serve out the last year of his commission in Germany overseeing the decommissioning of army vehicles returning from The Middle East. British army units from various camps had been returning to bases across Europe, and their equipment was being assessed for maintenance and repair requirements, or marked for decommission. His last job was supposed to be signing off the chit for every vehicle coming through the base, either being reassigned for further use or decommissioned following inspection. Twelve months as a signatory. Then muster out with a decent lump sum and go home. The only real thought in his head for months. Home.

"Time to facility seven minutes," buzzed through their headsets, the soldier in the navigator position of the lead Foxhound turned in his seat and looked into the cabin. "Light resistance has been reported at the site. Currently nothing along the road to suggest we will be facing any resistance prior to arrival."

"Hold position at the main entrance Corporal." He turned to the CO of the unit the squad had been drawn from, sitting behind him in the back seat of the Foxhound. "Perimeter sweep and secure line of sight to all entrance points primarily. Any protestors to be dispersed, no detentions. Minimal engagement is expected, but force is authorised where necessary. Martial law is now in place for a mile around the target location." He looked down at a clipboard with their brief attached to it. "Principals within the facility identified as Alder and

Mathers, contact to be established and ensure their safety is maintained until support arrives.

We have a General Anderston from the United States Army en-route with no current ETA.

Once his unit arrives further assessments will be made. Until then we put a complete hold on

the perimeter."

"Received," Captain Stafe replied.

A mile from the facility the Foxhounds pulled onto the road leading to the main

entrance and slowed to an approach pace. They had driven the last few miles through hills

and countryside, and were now approaching the outskirts of one of the towns east of

Montreux, where the facility had been built. It was at the very border of the town, on a quiet

road which ran from Montreux directly past the front gate of the facility into the centre of the

town.

The high metal fence surrounding the facility loomed ahead of them to their right,

dark and forbidding. It was set back a few hundred yards from the road, behind sporadically

planted bushes and trees on a well-maintained grass expanse. On their left side there was a

large park area, which the road had clearly been cut through when the facility had been built a

few years before. The upper floor windows of larger buildings in the facility were visible

over the fence, but there were no lights on in them, no signs of life at all. As they passed a

sign which told them the facility was on their right just ahead, the first few protestors came

into view on the grass area in front of the fence. They slowed as a second sign indicated that

the turn opposite led to the facility. More protestors stood at the mouth of the drive, watching

the military vehicles slowly roll into view, and then turn off the main road onto the driveway.

Ahead of them was a large pair of gates at the head of the drive, with a single storey

gatehouse built into the fence area running into the facility grounds. More protestors, small

groups and individuals were stood on the grass to either side of the drive. Most of the protestors looked to be startled by the sudden arrival of the military, and many started to walk away from the driveway, some sinking back towards the trees and bushes along the front of the fence, others making directly for the main road, and starting towards the town. They passed the damaged van off to the side of the drive area, sat deserted on the grass verge, and pulled up halfway down the drive, a short distance from the gates. There was a car wedged into the main gates, with a small group of protestors stood just in front of it.

"Potential resistance at the gates, no weapons observed," the Corporal in the navigator position called over the radio.

"Received," Captain Stafe replied. "Three up front, clear any civilians and secure the main gates. Three to the rear, get the drive clear to the road and set a perimeter there." Stafe was blunt, to the point. The soldiers under his command had come to see him as a guaranteed quantity in any situation. No grey area, his thinking was always black and white, in combat any order that is indecisive or unclear can get soldiers killed.

The Corporal stepped out of the front seat of the front Foxhound, and was met by two soldiers from the rear vehicle. They marched towards the gates of the facility whilst three soldiers from the rear vehicle started along the driveway towards the main road. Major Freeman watched the soldiers making their way to the main gates, and saw a small group of protestors part in front of them. Through the path created by the protestors, just beyond the soldiers Freeman saw a man stood at the mouth of the gates. He was tall and thin, wearing some sort of robes, making him look strangely out of place in the oasis of modernity. The soldiers were speaking to the protestors with no activity for longer than Freeman liked, they should be dispersing by now. Some of the protestors at the back of the group appeared to be moving away slowly, backing off from the main gathering, but still watching the scene unfold. He looked out of the rear of the Foxhound and saw protestors being moved away from the driveway and out onto the main road. There seemed to be a core group which were not co-operating with the instructions given to them to disperse immediately.

"Let's get this situation moving," Freeman said to Stafe. "Check the progress moving everyone off the grounds and out onto the main road, and post sentries in line of sight at the main road junction. I'm going to the gates to see what the fuss is." He didn't wait for a reply before cracking his door and jumping down from the Foxhound, and marched off towards the protestors gathered at the main gate at double time. The Corporal glanced back from the group he had been speaking to, and saw Freeman march up and stand a few feet behind the gathered protestors taking in the scene.

"Corporal?" Freeman called.

The Corporal marched back through the group of protestors and stood to attention in front of Freeman.

"Problem?"

"Sir. Passive resistance offered by the leader of the group. Seems they are a religious group that have some strange beliefs about the return of their messiah."

"Did you tell him that this site is now under military authority?"

"Yes sir, even told them we had a Major here with us. Said they don't recognise any authority other than *His*," The Corporal said, and pointed upwards.

"Did you tell him I am in overall charge of this site?"

"Yes sir."

"Well?"

The Corporal fought back a laugh, but a smile momentarily crossed his lips, just long enough to anger Freeman.

"He said Jesus outranks you sir."

"Nonsense. Jesus holds no rank in the British Army, or any other military organisation. Even if he did, he'd be working his way up through the ranks like everybody else. With me." Freeman marched past the Corporal, who fell in behind him and marched through the gap in the crowd to the man in robes again.

"Time's up, martial law is in effect at this site, you and your followers are ordered to disperse immediately."

The man in the robes just stood and looked at Freeman. A few of the followers started to back off, with more of the stragglers at the back of the crowd looking from the gates to the main road, and deciding that maybe they would be safer taking a walk back to town. The crowd started to thin to only the hardcore followers of the man in robes, who remained stood defiantly in front of the soldiers.

"Take my advice, you and your friends here need to move on, now," Freeman said, noticing that gaps were opening up in the crowd around him.

"You have no authority over me, or any other person gathered here today." The man in robes finally spoke. "Your actions will be judged when Jesus returns, stand with us. There is nothing you can do now but surrender to him."

"The British Army does not surrender to fictional characters or figments of your imagination. Move along now or force will be used." Freeman placed his right hand on the holster attached to his belt, unfastening the strap making the pistol ready.

"Your threats don't scare me or anyone else here. Bullets cannot harm his followers now. We are returning, strike us down and he will raise us up again. These weapons are obsolete." He reached into his robe and pulled out the pistol he had picked up from the car bonnet and held it up.

Freeman didn't wait for the man in robes to say anything more. He had taken the safety off the pistol with his thumb as he released the strap, and the second he saw the handle of the pistol coming out of the robes, he was drawing his own pistol. He fired once, directly into the chest of the man in robes. Screams sounded around him from the crowd, and the Corporal and both soldiers stood behind freeman shouldered their weapons, opening out into a small firing team formation. The man in robes' arms flew up to the heavens, the gun falling from his hands as he lurched backwards. A large red patch appeared on the front his dirty robes. His head tipped back, and he fell backwards, dead instantly.

"Don't let me keep you from Jesus," Freeman said, immediately ashamed of the stupid line he had delivered. He shook his head and turned to assess the situation. The crowd was mostly in shock. Some had run as soon as the guns were drawn, others turned and made for the main road at the sound of the shot. Only one or two remained, rooted to the spot where they were stood, mouths open, staring at either Freeman or the body of the man in robes, now flat on his back, his arms straight out to his sides.

Ahren sat quietly in the car as they accelerated through the country roads northwards towards Berlin. He stared straight forwards through the windscreen taking in the change in landscape. They had passed a few small houses and petrol stations as they drove, a truck stop lit up with neon signs advertising chain restaurants and a bar shone through the dusk light. Every new sight re-enforced the reality of the situation to Ahren, the world has changed in an instant around him. He might as well be from another planet for all he knew about the world he now inhabited. As a soldier he had one focus, his mission. But as a man his brain struggled to process every image his eyes fed to it. He had thought maybe the war had driven him mad at one point while he was sitting on the train working its way through Poland. That this was all an imagination. If not that, maybe he had died. He settled on the thought that this world was reality, that maybe he didn't deserve for this to just be a hallucination driven by madness, and that he wasn't lucky enough to have died without knowing it was happening.

Gillen glanced to his right, and saw Ahren sat there in awe of the few simple things they had passed in the short time they had been moving. His face was dull, slack and emotionless. The last thing he needed was for Ahren to shut down now, to let shock overcome him.

"It's real out there," Gillen said gently, trying to bring Ahren back to the alert state he had been when he had been talking to him on the way to the car. "You aren't the only one that's appeared out of nowhere. For some reason you are important though, politically I think."

"I can't think why I would be." Ahren slowly turned his attention from the view outside to Gillen, sitting there next to him. "I told you, I am just a man here. I don't want to think why anyone would want anything from me. I should be dead, long gone and the world better for it. The more I think about this, the more it seems right. Once I have done what is needed, maybe that is all that will be left for me, to join the men I served my country with."

"I don't know for sure, but the way it seems to me, you are going to have the chance to serve your country again one way or another."

"That is all I have ever done with my life, serve my country and my family. If there is something I can do in this world, maybe that will go some way to giving restitution for the damage I have done by following men who had no right to even exist, certainly not to lead a country. I told you I was chasing a very dangerous man. He was one of those men who betrayed my country. I will do what you ask, but I must stop him before we go anywhere else, before we do anything else. He is my only priority right now. I need to know, is it all true. About my country, did we do the things I have been told happened?"

"What have you been told?" Gillen tried to think of the best way to get around this question. How much could he say to someone who had been part of the German Army in the Second World War?

"The killing. Genocide. How many really died? Did we try to wipe out an entire civilisation? I was just a soldier, but was I fighting in the name of something so vile and abhorrent?"

"History is gone, even if it was just a few days ago. You can only be held accountable for your own actions, not what others did. But yes, I think it's true. And probably a whole lot more than you will want to know. But a whole lot more history has happened since then."

"Thank you." Ahren nodded, appreciating the honesty Gillen showed him. "If you are saying I am judged for what I do in this world, then it is even more important to me that we find Herr Bulmann and allow some small amount of justice to clear my conscience. Then I will be yours to do with as you see fit."

Gillen nodded. "Seems fair to me. Hold that thought, I need to confirm we are on our way back to Berlin." He tapped a button on the centre panel of the car's dashboard, the screen lit up with a menu. He touched the screen twice, and a buzzing sound started through the car speakers.

"That sound is strange, have you broken your radio?" Ahren asked. He looked at the panel Gillen was intermittently tapping.

"Wait and see," Gillen replied. "I think you may like the new radio technology we use."

The screen want blank for a moment, and then an image of Gillen's handler lit across the centre of the monitor.

"Confirm contact success," the handler said flatly.

"Confirmed," Gillen replied.

Ahren stared at the screen, then reached forward and touched the edge of the dashboard, running his finger across the smooth surface to the edge of the screen. "Automobiles with moving pictures on a screen. Is this some sort of cinema moving picture?" he asked.

"That's what we use now, it's like a radio or telephone you would have used, but now we have a screen with pictures, so we can see the person we are talking to as well as hear them. He can see us too, say hello."

"Gutten tag. Hello."

The handler glanced momentarily at Ahren, then looked back to Gillen. "Did you encounter the other target?"

"No, still shows as heading towards Berlin on the satellite tracking."

"Confirmed. Any resistance?"

"No concerns so far, we're making good time."

"Good. Continue to agreed destination. Further instructions will follow." The screen went blank.

"Auf wiedersehen," Ahren said. "He seemed rude."

Gillen laughed. "He was pretty conversational there, almost jovial compared to his usual personality."

Major Freeman walked past the corpse spread-eagle on the driveway, and traced the path from the main vehicle gates to the edge of the gatehouse building. When he had shot the protestor, it had started a near panic amongst the rest of the gathered crowd. The soldiers had used the reaction to herd most of the remaining protestors from the area, a tactic they were very used to using. A gunshot will shock most people, and that shock can be used to control their behaviour. The soldiers look for the reaction of crowds to use to their advantage, and also to identify potential threats. Amongst a crowd of civilians, when a gun is fired it is very obvious to identify anyone who is a potential threat, as most military personnel, serious criminals, and terrorists are desensitised to the sound of gunfire. Their lack of reaction makes them stand out amongst the general population, who will have some definite form of reaction. Freeman had watched his soldiers assess the crowd instantly, and go straight into passive policing tactics. No overt threats were identified, so all civilians were cleared from the area.

Freeman looked from the high gates to the building which formed part of the perimeter. A barred window a few feet wide was set into the wall at head height, giving a view out onto the driveway. He had observed two much larger windows at the side of the building within the driveway just past the gates. As he looked through the smaller window, he picked out exactly what he had expected to see. A young security guard, probably his first real job after college, was stood clamped to the wall as tightly as possible, attempting to peak out of one of the windows on the side of the building towards the main gates where soldiers were finishing off moving away the final protestors and starting to set up a perimeter and assess the damage which had been done to the gates. He was slight, and looked like he was in a uniform handed down to him by an elder relative, and which he was a few years from growing into. His hair was cut very short, a buzz cut done with clippers, Freeman assumed with the intention of making himself look somewhat older and more authoritative. Freeman tapped lightly on the window with his knuckles. The security guard visibly jumped and spun towards the direction of the tapping on the window. He stared wide eyed out through the window at Freeman. Freeman held up his army ID card, with one hand, and pointed out towards the gates with the other. The guard seemed rooted to the ground, seemingly not understanding what Freeman was instructing him to do. Freeman shook his head in frustration, pointed at the guard, and then made a walking motion with his first two fingers, then pointed towards the gates again. The guard held his ground for a couple of seconds, clearly scared and out of his depth, then puffed himself up and walked to the door of the building, and out towards the gates.

Freeman met the guard at gate, stood beside the wrecked car. "You in charge here?" Freeman asked slightly sarcastically.

"There was another guard. He had some problems apparently, so it's just me out here now. There are some of the scientists here too. So, I guess I am in charge. Maybe."

"Good, did they tell you we are coming?"

"I got a call from the bunker in the main building the scientists are in about an hour ago, they said soldiers were going to come and help us. You're English though, I was told American soldiers are coming."

"That's true, I am English. The Americans are on their way, and we are here to help until they get here. I think we'll probably be sticking around to be helping you around out here." The guard clearly looked more relaxed as he realised he wouldn't be left on his own outside the facility any more. "Is there another way in round here? These gates look a little jammed."

"There's a civilian gate just the other side of the gatehouse. It's a double door entrance, but I need some sort of passkey or override to get you in through it."

"Make a call to the guys in the bunker and tell them we are here. See if they have the access to let us in through that way. We can start to try to get these gates cleared from inside once we are in. There are supplies on the way with the Americans. Way I hear it, you guys aren't doing too well when it comes to decent food in there."

The guard nodded. "I've been helping myself to food in the canteen for a couple of days, I think it's starting to run out of everything worth eating now."

"Go make the call, come back out here once you've spoken to the scientists in the bunker, I'll be here." He turned from the gates as the guard headed back into the gatehouse at double time, and looked along the driveway. The approach to the facility was clear of all protestors out to the main road, and his section was forming near the Foxhounds. Captain Stafe issuing instructions to the soldiers, who were starting to move out individually to take up positions and sweep the area.

Stafe finished directing the soldiers, looked towards Freeman and nodded. He marched from the Foxhounds to meet Freeman at the gates, smiled, and looked down at the dead man in robes. "We going need to start a morgue up?" Stafe asked.

"Let the Americans worry about that, apparently there are a few more inside that will need storing from what I've heard. Not got many details of what's gone on in there, but from the sound of it the other guard on duty went off camp very badly. Whatever's inside is really not down to us, officially we have taken charge externally. Seems to me that if they are going to set up a morgue anyway then this chap and our former stunt driver in the car there can be put in with the others when it's ready."

"What did we get from the guard you spoke to?"

"Civilian gate, he's going to work on getting it opened up from inside, from there maybe we can start trying get things moving. I'm calling in for update, maybe we can get an ETA for the Americans to come and save us all."

"Where are they coming from?"

"If we're lucky, World War Two. Optimistically, Germany." Freeman smiled and walked off to the Foxhounds to call in their situation over the radio.

At just past seven in the morning Anthony Clarence stepped off the first train on the Central Line arriving at Liverpool Street. He was already running late due to the restricted train service running because of the curfew and public services becoming increasingly restricted. He was totally uninterested in world affairs, and thought that the whole idea of curfews because of some haywire experiment in mainland Europe was beyond any rational reaction. Life goes on. Anthony Clarence was an important man who worked hard, and expected to be able to continue with his life exactly the same way he always had, after all, while the world sorted itself out, why should he lose money? His company was based in an office building just south of Bank Station, but this morning he would have to walk all the way from Liverpool Street as the train he was on had terminated there for some reason. He walked up the steps through the station, rushed through the double width opening past the grey concrete pillars at the mouth of the entrance to the station out onto the path, and froze suddenly. The roads were blocked in every direction, with police and emergency vehicles parked lined up along every road. He looked around, taking in the scene. south-west of where he was stood, he could see smoke rising faintly into the sky. A few of the other passengers on the train walked past him, stopped in their tracks, and turned, looking around themselves and at each other. He walked purposefully towards a temporary barrier at the edge of the road manned by a police officer in high-vis' clothing.

"Why are these roads all closed?" he demanded, wafting an arm around himself pointing roughly towards each road in turn. The police officer was almost a full foot taller than Clarence, but he seemed not to notice this fact as he stood angrily in front of the officer, beginning to invade his personal space. He was angry at being delayed, and now combined with the roads being closed his day was going altogether downhill. He was aware that an itch in his leg was adding to his frustration. The filthy conditions on the Underground had not helped his mood, there had obviously not been any cleaning done in a few days, and now he was suffering with what he thought must be flea bites.

"There was a fire last night sir," the police officer replied calmly, looking down at Clarence wearily. He had long bitter experience handling members of the public who were frustrated with one situation or another, and lacked basic courtesy whilst venting their frustration. "All roads from here to the river are closed, the only people moving in the area are emergency services for the next few hours at least."

"My office is a few roads over, surely there is no reason I can't make my way there," Clarence snapped back. "You can't shut the whole city down for a small fire." He suddenly flinched and slapped at his lower leg twice, another damned flea bite. "Well?" he blurted towards the officer.

"Well, we can shut the area down for the safety of the public sir, and unfortunately it looks like that will be the way it's going to stay for a good part of the day. Have a safe trip back home and take the day off would be my advice."

"I'm not being sent back home by a bloody civil servant guarding a plastic barrier, let me through. My taxes pay for you, this barrier, and this road, and I fully intend to walk past you and your barrier down this road to my office." He stepped to his left, looking around the officer down the road.

The police officer sighed and lifted his right arm out to block Clarence's way past him. "Well I have to thank you for your investment in police equipment services and equipment. That said, unless you feel particularly keen to see how your taxes are spent at the local police station, I would ask that you leave me to look after your barrier here and go back to the train station behind you and catch the next available train home sir."

Clarence looked back at the police officer, craning his neck to stare into his eyes. He started to open his mouth, then realised this officer did not look particularly interested in continuing the conversation or letting him past. "Great, thanks for your help." He turned without waiting for reply, and headed for the station entrance he had come from a few minutes before.

"Safe trip home," the officer replied.

Just passed dawn, Freeman walked through the civilian entrance from the gate house and across the driveway towards the Foxhounds. He had spent a couple of hours working his way around the facility grounds assessing the internal condition of the perimeter walls and fences, and mapped the area roughly to include buildings and potential fortifications should they be necessary. Stafe met him and nodded casually.

"Sentries changed over a few minutes ago, I've put two at a time on stand-down rotation to keep them fresh. I'm guessing we may be here for a while," Stafe reported.

"Send the stand-down lads in to the facility via the civilian entrance and let them go to the canteen. There should be some basic food and refreshments there, and with a bit of luck if they are on usual form the Americans will bring a truck full of supplies and a chef. When they go to the gate tell them to let our friend *Carl the guard* to log them in. He has an override key for the doors now, so he can control movement. Post a sentry by the gate from this morning, we can do with that being controlled by us now."

"Agreed," Stafe said, and returned to the soldiers stood beside the Foxhounds. Freeman walked back to the gatehouse and waved to the guard, stood at the small window watching him. A moment later the civilian entry gate clicked open and Freeman walked inside.

Anthony Clarence stepped out of his local Underground station an hour after he had finished arguing with the police officer outside Liverpool Street station. He was still angry and frustrated, but now he was starting to feel a little ill. He felt slightly weak, and hoped fresh air would clear his head. The last thing he wanted was to be off work with a bout of flu on top of missing a day due to some stupid bureaucrat overreacting to a simple fire. He walked slowly back towards the building he lived in. He had moved into a new apartment a year previously, and had spent less time in it in that year than he had spent in his office. He was starting to wish he had taken the opportunity to set up a home office in the spare bedroom when his son had left for university. Instead, his wife had insisted that they leave the bedroom exactly as it had been so it was comfortable and free for his son's return each holiday.

When he reached the steps up to the front door of the building, Clarence had to stop and catch his breath. He was exhausted from the walk. It felt that the all the strength had drained out of his body in the few minutes he had been walking. He leant against the small wall bordering the entrance to the building along the path, and decided he would go straight to bed. His wife should be home, and she could go to the shops and get him some flu medicine. He would be right as rain tomorrow with a bit of luck. He started for the stairs, and stumbled, losing his footing at the bottom step. He pitched forward and just barely caught himself inches from hitting his face on the smooth concrete of the steps. He sprawled onto his hands and knees, and painfully turned himself into a sitting position. He coughed and almost vomited as his body heaved with the effort of holding himself upright on the step. He sat in the same position with his head rested on his hands for a few minutes, until the nausea passed. He forced himself to his feet and climbed the steps into the building.

Clarence used the lift inside the building to reach the third floor, stumbled out through the doors, and staggered to his front door. As he leant against the door, he pulled his keys from his pocket and tried to push them into the lock. His hand was visibly trembling, and he scraped the keys hard against the bronze lock surround, leaving several deep scratches in the metal. He stopped momentarily, assessed his keys, and used his other hand to stabilise himself against the door. He finally managed to drive the key home into the lock, and almost broke it turning the bunch to open the door. The door pushed wide open with his weight pushed against it, and slammed against the wall of the hallway. Clarence left the keys hung in the lock, took a single step forwards into the hallway, and sat heavily onto the carpet, resting against the hallway wall. His legs splayed out in front of him, and he fought off another wave of nausea, closing his eyes to try to stop the spinning gyroscope his brain had become.

The first soldiers leaving the facility to go back out on patrol following stand-down walked out of the gatehouse and stretched in the warm morning Sun. They marched to Stafe, stood to attention, and received their detailed duty for the next period. They would relieve the soldiers patrolling the entry area to the facility driveway. Before taking up their post however, they had a less pleasant task to complete. Stafe had asked them to move the corpse of the protestor in robes from the driveway to the shade of the trees. He was lay directly in the sun, and would be becoming ripe quite quickly in the summer heat. The corpse in the car was turning particularly unpleasant, but little could be done about that until the car was extracted from the gates. They marched to the body, still spread out on the driveway where he had fell, and stood over him. It looked like a full-size crucifix spread out on the ground.

"Irony," one of the soldiers said looking down at the body.

"He's in a better place, he'll be with Jesus now," the other soldier replied.

"That's what Freeman said."

They took latex gloves from their utility pouches on their webbing, stretched them over their hands, and took hold of both arms and legs. The corpse was dropped off under the nearest tree, and the soldiers marched straight back to the driveway to take their posts.

Private Harper walked back along the drive moments after being relieved to take her turn stood down in the facility. She passed Stafe, smiled, and paused momentarily. She had liked him since being assigned to his company, attracted to his quiet assured style and robust presence amongst the soldiers. He had an ability to support new soldiers without seeming to patronise them, which had given her confidence both completing her duties and fitting into the social structure of an army unit predominantly staffed by men.

He smiled back and nodded. "Get inside and eat. Not sure how good it is yet, but we may as well use up their food before we start working our way through our own scran. Not sure how long our supplies are going to have to last."

"Can I bring anything out for you?" she replied.

"I'm good, I'll be in within an hour to get myself some down time."

She smiled again, more warmly than before, and walked to the gatehouse. The civilian door opened, and the guard she had seen a few times in passing stood in the doorway. He smiled at her shyly. She was pretty, even in an unflattering uniform with no make-up on. She had short closely cut hair, which framed her face and suited the pleasantly rounded shape of her head. She nodded to the guard as she reached him, and saluted in mock seriousness. He seemed nervous.

"Morning," she said. "Can I come in?"

"Yes. Please," he replied, still stood in the doorway absently blocking the entrance. They stood looking at each other silently for a few seconds. He broke the silence clumsily. "You're a woman soldier."

"I am, glad you noticed. Are you one of those time travellers, from the 'Fifties?"

He missed the sarcasm. "No, I work here. I'm in charge of the security. The other guards left. Well, one had some problems. He's dead now apparently. He hurt some of the scientists."

"I heard there were problems. We're here to help now. Do you mind if I come inside and get some food? Carl, isn't it?"

"It is, you can, I'm Carl," he replied, going red in the face with awkward embarrassment. He stood silently staring at her, and then realised he had to move if she was going to be able to get through the door. He smiled and stepped to his right, straight into the door frame. He flushed a darker shade of red, stepped backwards, and held the door for her.

Private Harper walked through the gatehouse and stepped out from a door beside the car wedged in the gates. She stopped and looked at the blood stain on the bonnet where Dornel's body had lay, before it had been moved inside the main building. Her gaze moved up from the stain on the bonnet to the mangled shape still skewered in the driver seat. It wasn't the worst mess she had seen, for most soldiers in her unit dead bodies had become something they were desensitised to, like seeing meat, it was dissociated from a living breathing person.

She heard a distant sound of heavy vehicles along the road, which pulled her attention away from the mangled car. That must be the Americans arriving she assumed. They would do their usual grand entrance and expect to take control of the scene without any form of briefing or hand-over. She decided to go straight to the canteen and avoid them, no point in losing out on her stand-down time by getting caught up in the grand entrance.

Chasing the past

Schönefeld Airport was almost deserted when Gillen had driven to the main terminal early in the morning. He had stopped to speak to a lone police officer at the entrance to the airfield, then driven directly to the main terminal and parked up. The freight entrance had been secured, but there was some minimal activity in the main terminal entrance area.

They had sat for a few hours after parking, waiting for Gillen's handler to make contact again with further instructions. Gillen had taken the time to answer some of Ahren's questions about the world. Over seventy years of world events was quite a difficult subject to fill anyone in on, especially if they had as many questions as Ahren had. Each answer had led inevitably to another question. *Germany had lost the war. What happened to Germany after the war? The atomic bomb was dropped on Japan. Russia and America had become Superpowers. Why had Russia and America become enemies? Europe split between East and West. Who had been on each side? What was the nuclear arms race? Mutually assured destruction. Why had there been a crisis over a small island called Cuba? JFK was killed. Who was JFK? The space race. Men went to the moon. The fall of The Berlin Wall. 9/11. Ninth of November? No, September Eleventh. Why had the world changed focus to wars in the Middle East and terrorism? Science had developed to a point where so many diseases had been cured, many eradicated. Why couldn't they cure cancer then? The collider facility had completed their first experiment. History started to merge with the present. Ahren had arrived.* It had gone on until Ahren banged the dashboard with his bound hands in frustration.

"My family," he said quietly. "I know enough about things that happened to everyone else. I need to know about my family, and we have both avoided that information."

The screen on the dashboard flashed into life, a buzzing sound interrupted Ahren. Gillen looked at the screen and touched a red *accept* panel on the screen. "Sorry," he said.

The screen changed from the call receipt screen to the face of Gillen's handler again. "Hold for Director Gronan," he said. The screen went blank before Gillen could reply. The image of his handler was replaced by a secure office in The White House, with Jim Gronan sitting close to the screen.

"How are we looking?" Gronan asked. He had known Gillen from his first assignment, and had a healthy respect for his skills.

"Instructions completed so far sir. Currently in position at the airport as instructed," Gillen replied. "Say hello to General Ahren." He looked to his right.

"Hello," Ahren said, leaning towards the screen. "You are the reason this man has collected me I assume?"

"I asked for you to be intercepted, yes. How do you feel about helping us, and your own country at the same time?"

"I have something I have to do. A man I need to find. Then, if you think I can help you I will do what I can. What is it you need from me?"

"You are a German General, we are hoping you can help to gain control of a couple of situations. There are a couple of German units in France and Belgium at the moment, from both wars. They haven't worked out that the war is over yet, so they are still fighting, killing people. We need you to talk to them, persuade them to stop. The wars are over, we want to get them home. The German Chancellor thinks you could be of service to your country and your compatriots once again."

"They are still fighting? Who are they fighting?"

"Soldiers. Civilians. The German units in Belgium are shelling Ypres as we speak. People are dying. Innocent people. We can't just walk up to a tank and shout *the war ended* though. That's where you could help. You can talk to them, order them to stand down, and convince them that they don't need to fight any more."

"Agreed," Ahren said, nodding. "Then they can come home?"

"That's what we are hoping for. We are waiting for an available plane to pick you up. There have been a few delays, we think it will be this evening before we can get you moving."

"I want to do something before we go to France. If we are not going to be able to leave immediately, I need your help too."

"Bulmann?" Gronan asked.

"Ja, Bulmann."

"He's in Berlin. The German's are tracking him for us. I spoke to The Chancellor an hour ago. You want him, go ahead. You have eight hours, then you return to Schönefeld Airport and get on the flight."

"Agreed. Eight hours."

"Jason, go with him. Call in once you have Bulmann." The screen went blank again.

"Let's go catch up with your friend," Gillen said. He reached into his pocket, pulled out a small knife, and cut the cable tie from around Ahrens hands, took the cloth off them, and cut the second cable tie.

"We aren't going to be talking to him," Ahren said. "When we find him, I will kill him."

The Prime Minister sat at his desk in the study at Number Ten Downing Street listening to the sound of protestors. There had been a slowly growing gathering of people stood near the gates of Downing Street for the past few hours, the same people he assumed had been stood there the previous day. His frustration was building steadily. What gave them the right to stand out there protesting at a time like this? He heard shouts from the protestors as he stood and walked to the hallway through his open study door. They were shouting abuse at the police who were guarding Downing Street, and intermittently chanting slogans he couldn't quite make out. He walked back into his study, stopped momentarily in the doorway, shook his head and turned, and stormed straight back along the hallway and out through the front door.

The police officer stood on Guard at the front door of Number Ten Downing street turned as he heard the familiar sound of the heavy black door opening. The Prime Minister stood momentarily on the front step of Number Ten, looking between the police officer and the crowd gathered at the gates of Downing Street a short way off to his left. Then he stormed out down the path slamming the door behind him, and walked the hundred yards or so down to the gates, acknowledging the few police officers who were stepping out from the sentry posts near the gates. They fell in behind him and escorted him to where Downing Street's gates opened out onto Whitehall.

As the Prime Minister reached the gates, he began to hear the chanting more clearly. There were protestors with banners scrawled with slogans from *"Not our fault,"* to *"Save our planet from your destructive policies"*. He just made out the constantly cycling chant of *"Save our future,"* and *"Send them back"*, before the crowd spotted him approaching, and the chants turned to abuse and jeering directed towards him.

The Prime Minister walked close to the gates and stood for a moment with his hand raised to the crowd, he guessed a few hundred people. They slowly quietened to a level where he could be heard if he raised his voice to just shy of a shout.

"What purpose does it serve for you to be here?" he asked the crowd. Further jeering and abuse flew from the gathered crowd. He waited for the abuse to die down before trying again. "What do you think can be achieved by protesting out here today?" Amongst the replying chorus of more jeers and abuse, The Prime Minister heard a voice cut through, a woman shouting something about inheriting a broken planet. He shook his head and almost gave up trying to engage with the crowd. "If you want to do some good, to make a difference today, this is not the place to make that difference." He heard his voice wavering between frustration and anger, and tried to pull himself back to the calm public speaking persona he had used for most of his political career. "We need to pull together today, tomorrow, maybe for a long time to come."

The crowd drowned him out again. "What have *you* done?" floated over the abuse this time.

"My wife and children are helping aid workers near St. Pauls Cathedral as we speak. A few days ago, we were all trying to help with the clear up operation in Docklands. What have you done?" The Prime Minister gave up on politics, there was nothing this crowd would hear that would convince them, the only thing left would be to shame them. "There are people without homes today, without water or power. Injured people in hospitals which cannot cope right now. Police, ambulance, and fire crews are on the streets with volunteers as we speak trying to hold this city together. You could be helping them now, making a real difference."

He saw a banner which said "We should not have to inherit your broken world." A "Not our fault" chant started up again as he stood staring at the banner. They were young people, mainly people in their early twenties to mid-thirties from the look of it. Motivated idealists with no concept of the real world.

"It isn't your fault," he shouted back at them, suddenly quietening the crowd again. "It isn't my fault. It wasn't my wife's fault. It wasn't the fault of the men and women who lost their lives in a fire last night either. Or last week when bombs dropped on London and Berlin. You stand here and shout about it not being your fault, but you haven't done anything to help either. You haven't picked up an injured person from the street, haven't cleaned or dressed someone's wounds for them. Have you helped to run a shelter for people who lost their homes? You aren't helping to feed people today. You are standing here waving banners claiming you don't want to inherit our broken world. Well I've got news for all of you. No generation asked to inherit anything, ever. Along with their faults, you are also inheriting the gifts of previous generations. The mobile phones and social media you used to arrange this protest today. A gift from previous generations. The vehicles you came here in, gifts. The houses you live in, the clothes you wear. You don't want the negatives of a damaged world and blame everyone else because it isn't perfect, but you take the gifts technology gave you without thanks. The price we pay for those gifts should be to try to improve the world, but all people like you can do is complain. Well if you aren't prepared to contribute, to pay back for the gifts society has given you, maybe you shouldn't be taking the gifts you have inherited. Why don't you try to going back to the dark ages and inventing mobile phones and social media for yourselves? Though there would be no point until one of you can work out how to make electricity. Or you could contribute to the society that paid such a huge price for you through history, that enabled you to stand here and protest, and why don't you use the technology you do have, and go and help your neighbours, maybe some of the people in crisis in shelters or hospitals today?"

He didn't wait for a response, just turned and walked back towards Number Ten.

Anthony Clarence was slumped in the hall way when his wife had come home late in the afternoon. She had found him leant against the hallway wall, sweat running down his face, but shivering violently too. He was deathly pale and clammy as she helped him to his feet and moved him into the bedroom. He had been sick on the hallway carpet, and the smell was foul, acrid and hanging on the air in the whole apartment. She put him to bed, where he had slept solidly for almost eight hours.

Assuming her husband was suffering with a bout of flu, Samantha Clarence had decided to sleep on the sofa as best she could, rather than spending the night in the bed with her husband. She was woken by the sound of him vomiting shortly after midnight. She forced herself up from the sofa, already able to smell the vomit. It made her feel nauseous herself, she had spent a long time cleaning the hall carpet and the aired out the apartment as best she could afterwards to try to get rid of the smell. She had placed a bucket by the bed, anticipating further vomiting, and was keen to get its contents flushed away as soon as possible.

Walking into the bedroom, Samantha Clarence let out a small groan from her throat as she turned the light on. Her husband had indeed been heavily sick again, but he had not managed to get anywhere near the bucket. She was confronted with the sight of him leant over on his side on the bed, half laying in his own vomit, which had covered a large area of his side of the bed. He was pushing the sheets back and trying to sit up, shaking and sweating. She could hear him moaning as he tried to lift himself up. She started to walk towards him, and stopped suddenly as she saw his body jerk violently on the bed. He fell back against his pillow, jerked violently again, and straightened out, his legs cycling against the sheets, pushing them down his body. His eyes seemed to roll in his head as he thrashed on the bed. After a few moments, as quickly as the seizure had started, he calmed and lay still on the bed, his head turning, seemingly looking around the room in a confused state. His eyes were blank, and as his head turned towards her, she could see he wasn't aware of what was happening. She walked to the bed, placed a hand on his chest to hold him still, and reached for the phone on the bedside table with her other hand.

The ambulance arrived less than an hour after she had called for it. She had initially been told it could take a few hours due to a high level of calls being received, combined with a reduced service, so she was very relieved when the doorbell had buzzed. She used the intercom to allow the paramedics into the building. They were at the front door almost immediately, clearly keen to assess the situation, and either get their patient to the nearest hospital, or on to their next call as soon as was possible. Within a few minutes of the paramedics seeing Anthony Clarence, they knew they would be in for an urgent run to the nearest hospital with the blue lights on. He had developed swollen glands in his neck and groin, there was clearly blood in the vomit staining the bed sheets, and he had black dots appearing in various patches on his skin.

Knew it, Private Harper thought as the first American vehicle rounded the entrance to the driveway of the facility.

"What's this?" Carl the guard asked her, looking towards the camouflaged truck rolling its way up the driveway.

"'Merica reportin' for duty," she said, feigning a southern American accent. "I'm going to go get some food, figure we're safe enough now." She walked away, leaving the guard to greet the American Army at the gates. He looked from her to the convoy of vehicles now pulling into the driveway, and decided the greeting would be better done by the British soldiers posted on the other side of the gates. He walked back into the gatehouse, closed the door, and got himself comfortable at the desk. He guessed he would meet the American soldiers soon enough. He picked up the phone and called the scientists in the main building, guessing they would need to know the Americans had arrived.

"I think we are about to be relegated to guard duty," Stafe said to Freeman casually. He was lent against a Foxhound, watching the American Army transports stopping just short of the two British vehicles. "Looks like they came equipped for D-Day." An American soldier in full combat gear stepped out of an M1126 Stryker Infantry Carrier Vehicle and approached Stafe and Freeman.

"Let's stand to attention for this chap," Freeman replied. "He looks important. Well, he's got eight wheels on his ride anyway." They stepped away from the Foxhound and stood to attention facing the soldier.

The American soldier marched directly up to Freeman and saluted causally.

"Sergeant Tarping, Special Operations EUCOM out of Patch Barracks in Stuttgart, here with General Anderston to provide security and resources for the European Science Directorate facility," the soldier barked at Freeman.

"Super," Freeman replied, smiling warmly. "Freeman and Stafe, British Army. Site is secure already, if your General wants to pop on over, we can have a bit of a tour and sort out a hand-over."

"I have orders to take a unit to recce the area immediately, the General will move into position once we have a confirmed secure perimeter sir."

Freeman nodded and gestured with his arm towards the main gates.

"Be my guest. There's a car stuck in the gates, as you can see. I would suggest you knock on the gatehouse door to get into the grounds of the facility once you have yourself a confirmed secure perimeter."

"Acknowledged," Sergeant Tarping replied, saluted, wheeled round and marched back to the American convoy.

"He seemed keen," Freeman said quietly to Stafe. "Post a second sentry inside the gatehouse with the facility guard, I think he will be needing a bit of extra support. Once their General graces us with his presence I'll run up a patrol schedule with him, we'll base ourselves in the gatehouse and patrol the perimeter, they're welcome to the rest. That was our initial remit, and my ego isn't going to be bruised by sticking to that."

"The American Army and the British Army are both out there now," Mathers said as he hung up the phone. They were sitting in a small office just off the Alternative Control Room. The stark fluorescent lights were making Mathers' head hurt, he had barely spent more than an hour in natural light in almost a week now. "That was the guard, he asked if we are going out there to meet them. The gates are still jammed, so they will need to clear that before the supplies can get through to us."

"Armies, they're like busses," Alder replied. He could see in Mathers' face he needed to get some fresh air. "Hopefully if they've brought everything we asked for we might be able to actually square this circle." He stood and made for the door.

"I'm not sure it's as simple as that classic, at least with that problem you know what the square and the circle are. This feels more like cubing an undefinable shape."

"Either way, we are almost finished. If we get everything we need I think we can have the Collider running in a couple of days' time. If they haven't got what we'll need we won't be doing anything."

"I just want to go home now. Come back and start again next week maybe." Mathers switched the lights off in the office and walked after Alder.

The scientists walked out through the main reception doors and into the warm morning sunlight. It felt a long way from the cool sterile climate deep inside the bunker. The change in temperature felt good, they were back in the real world and out of the isolation they had been locked in for so long. A female soldier walked past them along the path as if they weren't there.

"Still want to go home?" Alder asked as he watched Private Harper walk away.

"I may give it another day or two if she's staying," Mathers replied. "You know what I have been thinking? We run the experiment again as soon as the repairs are done, what does that give us? I mean do you think that running the experiment for a second time will reverse what is happening do you? I don't."

"If we run the experiment again, I have some reservations about what we can achieve. My biggest fear is that we will add to what is already happening making things even worse. Imagine there is a tear in time already, and we rip it apart completely by running a second experiment. I haven't wanted to think about it but that is a very real possibility. Whatever happens, they believe that we need to repeat the experiment, and in some way, I have to agree. We damaged too much equipment the first time round to be able to assess what actually happened. I think the best that we can aim for is that we manage to repeat the experiment without making things worse, and at least if we can get some data, we may be able to start to try to find a cure for what's happening with that information."

"So, we do another experiment just to get some data, then we start again with that data. Great. We're never going home are we?"

"Maybe one day. If we can get anything from the second experiment, I think we may be able to adapt the Collider to reverse what has caused this problem. Unfortunately, my best guess is that we can only stop the tear, we won't be sending anyone back to when they came from. Just no more travellers coming through."

They walked to the main gates without speaking again.

The BMW pulled out of the main terminal of Schönefeld Airport and turned north towards central Berlin. Gillen shifted through the Five Series' gears smoothly accelerating up onto the autobahn and started to pass the few other cars moving towards Berlin. He noticed that the flow of traffic out of Berlin was much heavier than that going towards Berlin, and assumed that the crisis in cities was deepening. It seemed likely that the population of Berlin was going to be significantly more panicked due to the Second World War bombs dropped on the city. The traffic would be a steady exodus of panicked civilians not prepared to wait for any more unpleasant surprises from the past to rain down on them. Gillen leaned over and tapped the screen on the dashboard, lighting up the video screen menu. He tapped the screen twice, and a gentle buzzing sound started to ring through the car speakers. A few seconds later, his handler's face appeared on the small monitor.

"On your way to Berlin to catch up to Bulmann I assume?" the handler asked from the screen.

"Sure are," Gillen replied. "Has Director Gronan spoken to you about providing some support?"

"Select option two on your menu screen, I set a satellite feed to your car navigation with a live feed of the car Bulmann stole. He went to his family home in Hoppegarten a few hours ago, the car was stationary for some time. None of his family live in the area, haven't been for years. He obviously discovered that fact, and started for central Berlin from there. He parked on Niederkirchnerstrasse a few minutes ago. It was called Prinz-Albrecht-Strasse during the war."

"The rat returns to the sewer," Ahren said angrily. "He has done what any good SS soldier would do, he has gone where he hopes to find more of his own, in that *gathsename*."

He looked at Gillen and saw confusion in his face. "A place of suffering. The Gestapo and SS headquarters. He wants to breathe life back into The Third Reich."

"It's not there anymore," the handler said. "The buildings were all destroyed, he won't find anything but a museum. The car just started moving again, I guess he just worked that out for himself. He just took a left onto Wilhelmstrasse, heading north. The police have roadblocks set up before he can get to The Brandenburg Gate and The Reichstag Building if that is where he's going now."

"Keep the satellite on him, we are less than twenty minutes from his location," Gillen said, pushing his foot harder onto the gas. He clicked the screen off and focused on the road, weaving in and out of the lanes to pass cars moving less than half the speed of the BMW.

"He will be even more dangerous than before, the war was everything to him, it gave him power and purpose. Everything he believed in is gone, his family, his Fuhrer, the SS." Ahren looked at the world flying past him through the windscreen. "Everything I had too."

Freeman and Stafe were stood next to the civilian entrance at the gatehouse when Sergeant Tarping marched back up to them. He had deployed American soldiers along the driveway at regular intervals, and posted a soldier with the British soldier at the entrance to the driveway from the main road. He was talking into a radio as he stopped next to Freeman and Stafe.

"Site confirmed secure," Tarping said into the radio mouthpiece on his headset. "Deliver the package when ready, over." He turned to Freeman and saluted.

"Satisfied that we have everything locked down to your standards?" Freeman asked, deliberately not saluting back.

"Yes sir. I have some requests, we need to start to move into the facility as soon as possible. Can your vehicles move away from the gates, we will be using heavy machinery to push the car that's wedged in the gates out of the way?"

"There's no need," Stafe started, but was cut off by Freeman, who raised his hand to silence Stafe.

"We can pull back to give you a clear run at it," Freeman confirmed.

"Acknowledged," Tarping replied. He saluted again, about turned, and marched back towards the main road and the sound of approaching vehicles.

"Why did you say they could bring in heavy equipment to move the car? It's barely wedged in those gates. If the guard in there hits the gate release a couple of guys could push it clear," Stafe asked.

"If they push it free and the guard opened the gates, they would expect us to get the gates repaired and guard them, if they bring in machinery to clear the gates, it's down to them to secure them again," Freeman replied. "Let's go and meet the package."

Stafe looked at the gates and saw the level of damage they had sustained from the impacts delivered by protestors. He nodded and fell in behind Freeman. They marched to the Foxhounds and ordered them to fall back to clear enough space for the Americans' heavy machinery to be brought in. At the mouth of the driveway, another eight wheeled armoured personnel carrier similar to the Stryker that Tarping had arrived in pulled up and stopped. Another heavy-duty vehicle pulled past that, followed by a gunmetal grey heavily armoured articulated lorry. A few smaller armoured vehicles pulled around onto the drive, and then a truck pulling a low loading trailer with some heavy machinery loaded on-board stopped, completely blocking the driveway entrance.

"With a bit of luck there'll be a couple of restaurants in that lorry," Freeman said. Maybe a bar too."

"They certainly brought the whole set up with them," Stafe said. "I saw whole concerts in a small stadium at an American base in Afghanistan when I was out there. We turned up in the desert with a few tents and a mess hall, a few weeks later the Americans arrived and within a week there was a full town with a cinema and a stadium and they were holding rock concerts."

"That's probably why they were late getting here, it takes time to load up all that stuff for a few days deployment."

They walked towards the heavy-duty troop transport as its side door opened and the American soldiers started to step out.

"Is *the package* actually the President, or is this General really important?" Stafe asked.

"I think the General over there is in charge of the whole American army in Europe. He's here to take charge on orders from The President."

The General stepped out of one of the smaller vehicles in the convoy that had just arrived. He straightened himself to his full height, stretched his back, and placed his uniform cap on top of his balding head. He was wearing a camouflage style combat uniform, strangely contrasting to what Freeman had anticipated.

"He's shorter than I expected," Freeman said.

"Never meet your heroes," Stafe replied. "We could always stoop a little if you think it will make him feel better?"

Freeman stifled a laugh as the General clocked them and began to march towards where they were stood. The General marched directly past Freeman, saluting as he went by.

"Anderston, General Anderston," the General said brusquely. "Here on orders of the United States Government to oversee this facility for the foreseeable future." He continued for a few more paces, still marching with purpose. Freeman stood still, watching as

Anderston went by. The General stopped suddenly, seemingly conscious that neither Freeman nor Stafe had fallen in behind him. He turned and walked back to where they were stood.

"Freeman, Major," Freeman replied, standing to attention simultaneously with Stafe in perfectly co-ordinated unison. "Shall we inspect the facility?" he asked.

"What does *keep the satellite on him* mean?" Ahren asked, as the car screamed northwards along Charlottenstrasse, weaving between parked cars on either side of the road.

"We have camera's everywhere now," Gillen replied. "Satellites are like having a camera in the sky, an unmanned reconnaissance plane. We picked the two of you up on cameras at the train station in Poland using security cameras. They automatically recognised your faces, and we used cameras and satellites to track you, with a little help from a drone. Unfortunately, you can't go anywhere these days without someone catching you on camera. Once we have you, we can follow wherever you go. I watched footage of you being pulled over by the police officer, saw what Bulmann did to him."

"He has no conscience. The perfect soldier, yet at the same time the worst type of soldier. He is relentless, nothing will stop him except death." Ahren looked out of the windscreen again, started to take in the scenery as it passed. High fronted modern buildings of glass facades and heavy concrete structures lined the road, filled with shops, restaurants and cafes opening onto the street under colourful awnings. "I recognise this place, but things here are just not right. It's the same, but nothing's the same. Is this what happened to Berlin after the war ended?"

"Berlin is a much better place now than it was after the war ended. I told you Germany was carved in half for a very long time, it took a long time to recover from that. The Russians got here first at the end of the war, and they were ruthless. There was a lot of rebuilding to be done. Berlin is a modern city now though, united and functioning in the way that any capital city should do."

The screen on the car dashboard pinged and zoomed in to focus on a few city blocks on the map. Two dots were flashing on the map, one moving, the other stationary. They turned left onto Unter den Linden barely slowing as they took the corner, the road opening out to a multi-lane carriageway usually clogged with cars and busses, cyclists and pedestrians. It was almost deserted as they slowed and pulled up the kerb, stopping just short of the next intersection. Ahren gasped as he saw the Brandenburg Gate in the distance. Gillen touched the screen on the dashboard and the menu opened momentarily. He tapped the screen a second time, and the screen instantly changed to a CCTV camera view.

"That's Bulmann's car. There's a road block just ahead of us on the next road to the left. He's on foot less than a mile from here. We'll do better on foot." Gillen took a Bluetooth earpiece from his inside jacket pocket, slid it onto his ear, and clicked the connection button. "Going on foot from here."

"I know, you just said that," Ahren said, looking at Gillen, confused. Gillen raised his hand, *wait a second*.

"Received, I've got you on camera," Gillen's handler's voice came through the earpiece loudly. "Drone's up and I'm into all the local CCTV. Should have satellite cover for the next hour too. He's past the road block ahead of you, using a side street to work his way west. Looks like he's about to go towards the gate. The whole Berlin police force is out there around the Reichstag Building from the look of it. A patrol is walking towards you from the west."

"Check." Gillen turned to Ahren. "It's a small speaker and microphone for a telephone." He pulled his mobile phone out of the same inside pocket from his jacket and showed it to Ahren. "Modern technology at its finest. Let's go and help history catch up with him."

They climbed out of the car and started along Unter den Linden towards the Brandenburg Gate. Gillen pulled Ahren along with him and moved into the recessed doorway of a deserted shop. The police officers walked past on the other side of the road, obscured by trees planted in the central reservation of the road. As soon as the police patrol was out of sight, Gillen stepped out and scanned the road, satisfied it was clear, he nodded to Ahren and moved out, staying tight to the frontages of the buildings. They were closer to Bulmann than they had been since Gillen had intercepted Ahren on the road to Berlin. Gillen pulled a pistol from a holster attached to the back of his belt, and handed it to Ahren.

"I guess you are still up to date with your small arms training. Safety is on. No changes between that and a luger, except for the calibre. Keep it out of sight unless you absolutely need to use it. Please don't shoot me."

There was a queue of emergency vehicles and quick response vehicles at the entrance to the emergency bay at the hospital. The ambulance carrying Anthony Clarence slowed as it turned into the main hospital car park, and took up a place at the back of the queue. Samantha Clarence reached across the space in the back of the ambulance and stroked the back of her husband's arm, ran her fingers across the back of his hand gently, and then gripped it. She squeezed it and felt the heat coming from him. He was burning up, sweating and barely conscious.

"We're here now, hold on," she whispered to him. "It won't be long and you will be good as new."

The back of the ambulance was starkly white with bright overhead lighting. She was sitting on a fold down seat opposite the stretcher position. She sat back into her chair as the paramedic moved through the small gap between her and her husband, and picked up a clipboard. He walked back to the head of the stretcher and checked Clarence's temperature again. There was a drip fed into his left arm which had been slowly administering antibiotics intravenously since they had loaded him onto the ambulance.

"It's a waiting game now," the paramedic said to Samantha Clarence calmly. "We are stuck in this queue until they can free up beds in the emergency room. Every hospital is the same at the moment, they've been doing triage from ambulances to prioritise beds when they open up, so we will probably have a nurse on board before we actually go in. Don't panic when they get on, it's happening on every case coming in at the moment."

A gun shot sounded from a short distance along the road ahead of Gillen and Ahren. It echoed along the road of the sides of the high buildings, making it difficult to pinpoint exactly where it had come from. Gillen thought it sounded as though the sound had come from beyond the Brandenburg Gate. His earpiece clicked and his handler's voice came through at an unusually high pitch.

"He just stabbed a police officer in the back at a road block, and then shot another one." A second shot rang out from the same direction. "Another police officer down," a third shot followed quickly. "He just executed the first policeman he shot. The two police officers who just passed you are running in your direction now."

Gillen looked at Ahren, deciding how they should handle this new problem. He pulled Ahren back to the doorway they had just stepped out from. It would take too much time to explain to the police why they were there, armed, and chasing someone from the past. Moments later they saw the police officers run past them along the road towards the direction of the gun shots.

"He's taken a gun and a few clips from one of the police officers he just shot. I think you are going to need to get up there and back up the two cops that went past you. He's moving to the tree line now, by the time they get to the gate he will be in cover and they'll be sitting ducks."

"Received," Gillen replied. "It's Bulmann, he just killed some police officers. We need to move now." Ahren nodded. Gillen saw something in Ahren's eyes when he told him that Bulmann had killed police officers. He thought it looked like a mixture of bitterness and anger, and guessed there was some regret in there that Ahren hadn't killed Bulmann when he had the chance. Ahren had told him that when they were in Poland, he had not shot Bulmann when he had the chance because he couldn't kill him in cold blood, Bulmann needed to face trial for his crimes. They stepped out from the doorway and began to run towards the gate. The officers who had just passed them were far enough ahead not to notice Gillen and Ahren following behind.

They watched the officers reach the Brandenburg Gate and take cover as they passed through the arches. Ahren and Gillen slowed as they approached the gate, they had reached the open area ahead of the gate. Gillen saw the police ahead of them checking their cover and starting to move forward out of their cover.

"I don't have him on satellite or local cameras, I'm switching the drone to thermal," the handler said into Gillen's ear.

"Are we clear to move through the gate yet?"

"Negative, no confirmation of his location yet."

"Holding at the gate. I need confirmation quickly, those cops are walking into a trap." He signalled by hand to Ahren to hold position. "Why would he wait in cover and not move on after he killed those police officers?"

"He is watching. He knows there may be back-up on its way. Basic urban reconnaissance strategy, disable initial defence forces before attacking your primary target. Gain any intelligence you can from local sources. Are any of the police officers he attacked still alive?"

Gillen touched his earpiece. "Has he left any of the police alive up there?"

"Hold for confirmation." Gillen waited patiently. His handler was back to his impassionate normal self. "Confirmed. One police officer is down but movement is visible. It's the one he stabbed in the back."

"He left one alive. Stabbed him in the back and then left him there," Gillen said to Ahren.

"Vile. Paralysed but avoided vital organs. He will have been left to interrogate once any other threats are neutralised."

"Thermal imaging is online, he's in cover beyond the tree line."

"We need to move forward now," Gillen said. "Those two are running into a trap."

Another shot sounded as the first police officer stepped clear of the gate. He spun and dropped to the ground hard as the bullet buried itself into his shoulder. The second officer almost fell out into the street as he stopped and tried to return fire at an unseen target.

The gunshot had seemed to explode out of nowhere just as the police officer ran clear of the farthest left arch of the Brandenburg Gate. His partner was physically spun around in front of him, his legs crunching together as his upper body was forced back by the impact. His feet were planted heavily, making his legs twist from the knees. The officer had paused momentarily just before he heard the shot, stunned by the scene he was confronted with. There were three cops on the ground in front of him, two dead, and one seriously injured. The delay had saved his life. He was far enough back from the open area and the road that when he returned fire blindly, it gave him time to pull back into the archway of the gate before Bulmann fired again. Dust and chips of cement flew from the gate just in front of his face as he fell into cover and dragged himself backwards. He had half collapsed, half tripped onto his arse as he had backed into cover, and was ungracefully shuffling further into cover in a seated position waving his gun out in front of him wildly. Gillen and Ahren reached the archway as the police officer fell backwards into it, and watched as he made his way awkwardly towards them. Gillen traced the wall into the archway and grabbed the cop, pulling him back further into cover. He held him under the arms, keeping a tight grip on his right arm so he didn't panic and turn the gun on whoever had just grabbed him from behind.

"United States law enforcement," Gillen said loudly into the police officer's ear. He leant in very closely to the officer trying to get through to the shocked man who was still waving his gun ahead of him, aiming at nothing. Gillen had said the words *law enforcement* as clearly as he could, as he was worried the cop could easily turn his gun on them in the state he was in as Gillen and Ahren reached the gate.

"Polizei," Ahren said over Gillen's shoulder, realising that the officer may not understand Gillen speaking in English.

"Polizei," the cop replied, lowering his gun to his lap. "Was ist ihm passiert? Was ist los?" *Whats happened?*

Another gunshot sounded, followed by a scream. The scream seemed to echo forever in the arch.

"Hilf ihm," the officer said dazedly as he pulled out of Gillen's grip and stood up. *Help him.* He ran forwards out of the archway, firing twice randomly as he reached his partner. He dropped to his knees on the pavement next to his partner, who was weakly trying to roll onto his front and drag himself away from the direction of the shots. He was bleeding heavily from a large wound in his shoulder, and a second wound in his hip.

A figure moved quickly from the cover of the trees across the road ahead of the gate. The officer saw the movement and fired again, missing badly. He hit a tree as the figure dropped to the ground and disappeared from view. The officer fired again at the area where he lost sight of the figure.

"Get down now," Gillen shouted, edging forward in the archway to try to cover the officer.

Before Gillen could say anything more a shot seemed to come from nowhere. The officer's head flew backwards, the top left side of his skull seemingly exploding as blood burst out heavily. He fell backwards, his legs bent underneath him making his body arch in an ugly final pose. His head was pushed so far back with the force of the shot that his sightless eyes were staring upside down towards Gillen and Ahren. A second shot exploded into the wall of the gate a few inches ahead of Gillen, who threw himself backwards taking Ahren back with him, both collapsing to the ground.

Bulmann ran through the trees which lined the road, moving further into cover. There were at least another two police officers in the archway, and the longer he delayed, the more time there was for backup to arrive. He had caused enough damage to the officers he had shot that they would hold up any backup while their injuries were treated. It would give him time to put distance between him and anyone looking for him. He jumped over a short concrete wall and moved into the park area set back from the road. The dense trees and bushes gave him safe cover as he moved slowly, reloading his gun and taking time to check the other gun he had taken from the police officer he had stabbed. It was an automatic pistol, but he didn't recognise the make or model. The words *SIG Sauer* were engraved into the top slide just behind the short barrel of the gun. It was fully loaded, with twelve rounds loaded in the magazine.

Bulmann tucked the gun into his waistband and walked casually through the trees. The tree line opened out onto the road west of the Brandenburg Gate. The road was densely lined with trees on either side, parkland opening out from his current side of the road, further parkland followed by the sculpted lawns of the Reichstag Building behind the trees across the road from him. He looked along the road in both directions. He was a few hundred yards west of the gate now, safely clear of any wildly aimed shots that may come from the area where he had killed or injured the police officers at the roadblock.

Bulmann broke cover and sprinted across the road, vaulting the short hedge which separated the pavement from the grass bank and the tree line. He moved into the cover of trees and bushes again, working his way slowly towards the criminals who had betrayed the Reich. For whatever had happened in the past, he was going to take revenge now. A new Reich would stand or fall with him.

Time runs out

Samantha Clarence began to worry that they had been sitting in the queue of emergency vehicles for too long. *Surely* her husband was too ill to wait for treatment. She watched him getting weaker as he lay on the stretcher in the ambulance, his breathing seemed to be very shallow and laboured now. It was getting uncomfortably hot inside the ambulance. The rear doors suddenly opened, and a young doctor stepped inside.

"Just here for some blood," the doctor said. "How's our patient doing?" He looked from the body of Anthony Clarence on the stretcher to the paramedic questioningly. "Have we had triage yet?"

"About an hour and a half ago, nothing back since."

"How long has he been unconscious?"

"In and out since we picked him up, but we haven't had any response for the last hour or so."

"I don't like the look of the rash he's developing and the black spots on the skin. Any blood in his vomit?"

"He was sick before we left home, there was blood in it," Samantha Clarence replied.

The doctor started to scribble some notes on a pad he had taken from his coat pocket. He was wearing a long white standard hospital Accident and Emergency coat open at the front. It was hanging loosely off him, very creased, and looked like he had been wearing it for a week. He tapped the pen at the top of the pad as he read back his notes absently to the paramedic.

"Rash on the skin, looks like more dark patches developing. Vomit in blood. Loss of consciousness. Fever. I think we are going to need to test for responsiveness to antibiotics now." He turned to Samantha Clarence as he started for the ambulance doors. "I think we'll bump you up the queue."

It took a few agonising minutes after the doctor left the ambulance before Samantha Clarence felt the engine rumble to life, and then suddenly they started to move around other ambulances in the long queue, and reached the main ambulance bay of the Accident and Emergency department. The doors jerked open stiffly, and an orderly stood looking into the ambulance.

"Straight in," the orderly said to the paramedics. "Bay twelve, they're setting up in there now." He reached an arm into the ambulance and pulled the foot of the stretcher trolley as the paramedic started to push it through the doors.

Samantha Clarence looked around in shock as they walked with the trolley through the Accident and Emergency department doors. What looked like hundreds of people were sitting in chairs, sat on the ground, or stood in any free space in the waiting area. They almost had to force people out of the way to get to the treatment area doors and into bay twelve. The people they passed seemed to mostly be in shock, tired, some were ill, and many were injured. They were all clearly resigned to the fact that the overstretched hospital could not cope with the volume of patients who had been steadily arriving over the past few days.

They wheeled Anthony Clarence on the stretcher into bay twelve where a young and very tired looking nurse was stood. She guided the head end of the trolley to the wall smoothly, kicked the brake onto the wheel, and looked down at her new patient. In one smooth movement she turned his arm over and wrapped a rubber tourniquet around it just above the elbow. She tapped a vein gently, lifted a cannula she had prepared on the table next to her, and slid it into the thinly expanded vein. *Weak pulse* she thought. A moment later she clicked the line from the drip into the cannula, turned, smiled at Samantha Clarence, and slid out of the bay, pulling a curtain around the bay as she left.

Alder and Mathers stood in the sunlight on the main facility road watching as the American soldiers attached chains to the car wedged in the entry gates. There was a lot of shouting and orders being barked by a very officious looking young American sergeant. Freeman and Stafe strolled through the gatehouse doors and walked casually to where Alder and Mathers were stood watching the action. The chains being fitted to the car fed out from a winch loaded onto the back of heavy-duty transport that the Americans had brought with them.

"We should get one of those," Stafe said.

At a command from the young American sergeant, the winch started to whine loudly and there was a sudden grinding sound from the gates as the chain went taught. The car shuddered between the gates, then the piercing sound of metal shearing drowned out the whine of the winch. The rear section of the car and its cabin flew free from the gates, lifting off the ground by a few feet momentarily, landed back on the road and rolled quickly towards the vehicle with the winch. A second metallic snap of chains stopped the car just short of the winch vehicle. The car had been had been tethered to the frame of the gates by more chains, and the force of stopping the car pulled the gates further out of line. The small group of observers turned away and stepped back as the car burst violently free from the gates, surprised by the force of its expulsion from the mangled structure.

"Good job," Freeman said. "I like what they've done with the gates, very smooth leaving the front of the car in there."

Stafe, Alder, and Mathers looked from the torn-up rear of the car to the gates, which still had large pieces of the front wings and bumper of the car torn and skewered to them.

American soldiers quickly began to cut the remaining pieces of the car free from the gates and started clearing the entrance way. Within an hour the gates had been pulled back onto their hinges as best as they could be and then opened fully using the winch. Equipment trucks started to roll through the gates into the vehicle compound a few hundred yards into the facility past the gate area, all overseen by Alder and Mathers with keen interest.

"No going back now," Alder said quietly. "If they brought all of it, we are back in business."

Mathers' previously relaxed face momentarily darkened. "I'm not sure I like that thought. Just about starting to feel human again standing out here, easy to forget there's a world out there while we're working in the bunker."

"Let's get some food," Alder said. "How's the canteen these days?" he asked Freeman.

"I've had worse. The Americans have probably brought plenty of goodies if you don't like the menu in there though."

The spasm shook through Anthony Clarence's body so violently he seemed to lift off the hospital trolley. He had been shuddering hard enough to cause an audible rattle from the frame of the trolley for too long, and the sudden spasm was a step too far for Samantha Clarence to process. She had been trying to hold his hand and stay calm while they waited for a doctor, but he seemed to be getting worse with every minute that passed. A second spasm wracked his body on the trolley, throwing Samantha back as she tried to hold him still. The cannula tore from his arm as he twisted in the bed. A third spasm exploded through his body more violently than either before had. His body seemed to settle, and the shuddering subsided. Then nothing. Samantha lifted his hand in her palm and patted it with her other hand. It didn't shake the way it had been. She placed it limply back on the trolley. He didn't move for what seemed like an eternity as she stood over him staring down at his body. A twitch in his arm shocked her back to reality.

She ran out of the bay into the Accident and Emergency department looking wildly around for a doctor. She tripped over the leg of a patient sitting on the floor and almost fell, blindly stumbling forward through the crowds of ill and dying. She shouted for help, pushing her way through to the triage desk area, and saw the nurse who had put the cannula in her husband's arm a short while earlier.

"He's dying," she said desperately as the nurse looked towards her. "I think he needs to see a doctor now." The nurse looked blankly at her for a few moments, then seemed to remember where she knew this crying, frantic looking woman from. She turned and walked into an office without speaking, then walked back out after what seemed like forever, carrying a large green bag. Still without speaking, the nurse walked past Samantha Clarence towards the bay her husband was lay in, pushing her way through the crowd, most of whom tried to ask her questions or show her injuries as she went.

Samantha Clarence followed the nurse as she walked into the bay, watching her calmly take Anthony Clarence's wrist in her hand checking his pulse. She stepped to the wall and pressed a large red button, which lit up a flashing red light over the bay. A buzzer sounded distantly somewhere across the Accident and Emergency department. The nurse opened the green bag she had brought with her, took out what looked like a transparent plastic bottle with a mouth and nose cover attached to the top, and placed the mouth and nose cover onto Anthony Clarence's face. She secured it in place with an elastic fastener.

"Squeeze this and then release it smoothly once every five to ten seconds like this," the nurse said to Samantha Clarence, demonstrating once by closing her hand around the bottle, which seemed to crush in her hand and then re-inflate as she released her grip.

Samantha followed the instruction, looking down at the face of her husband. His face was ashen.

The nurse took out a blood pressure strap, wrapped it around his arm, and pumped it up, slowly releasing the pressure on the pump and reading the gauge. She took to strap back off his arm, lifted his wrist in her hand and checked his pulse again. A doctor walked brusquely into the room just as the nurse replaced the arm.

"What have we got?" The doctor asked.

"Plague victim from the symptoms he's presenting with, non-responsive to anti-biotic treatment so far, though he hasn't taken much on before throwing the drip. Blood pressure non-existent, pulse through the floor right now. Shallow to no breathing"

"Have we tried adrenaline?"

"None so far," the nurse replied. "We only got him off an ambulance a few minutes ago."

"Let's start with some adrenaline shall we," the doctor said calmly.

The nurse pulled a syringe from the green bag, unwrapped the needle, drew some fluid from a small bottle into the syringe, and looked at the doctor. He nodded calmly as he walked to the opposite side of the trolley, lifting the arm nearest to him and turning it upwards in his hand. He tapped at the inner forearm, and took the syringe from the nurse. The injection was slow and smooth, pushing the plunger steadily as the adrenaline flowed into Anthony Clarence's vein. Nothing. The doctor placed a wad of cotton wool on the arm where the needle had punctured, withdrew the needle slowly, and passed it back to the nurse. He checked for a pulse again, and shook his head.

"Chest compressions please," he said.

The nurse began chest compressions, a steady rhythm firmly pumping through his body. Samantha Clarence watched, still squeezing the bottle in her hand. Releasing.

Squeezing again. There was silence in the bay while they worked, staring down at the limp body on the trolley. The doctor walked back into the bay. Samantha had not realised he had even left. He rolled a trolley ahead of him, placed it next to the bed, and lifted a pair of paddles from it.

"Step back," the doctor said. The nurse obeyed, reaching over and taking Samantha's hands from the bottle, leaving the mask strapped to the lifeless face. They stepped back slightly from the trolley.

The doctor pressed the paddles to Anthony Clarence's naked chest, and a dull thump sounded from the body as it twitched lightly. The doctor took the paddles away, and the nurse stepped forward, lifted a wrist, and checked for a pulse. She shook her head. The same process repeated. The paddles pressed against the lifeless chest. A dull thump, a twitch, nothing. The nurse stepped forward again as the doctor placed the paddles back on the machine. The nurse shook her head. Samantha Clarence stepped forward again, and started to pump the bottle slowly, squeezing, releasing, and squeezing again.

"I'm sorry," the doctor said, lifting the other arm and checking for a pulse himself. He slipped his hand onto the neck of Anthony Clarence and checked again for a pulse. "I'm calling it here, time?" he asked the nurse.

Ahren grabbed Gillen's arm and pulled him forward through the Brandenburg Gate and turned right, keeping tight to the wall as it curved around where the Gate was set into the wall of the next building. The sound of a crowd echoed from the front of the Reichstag Building, just up the road from the Gate. The road blocks had cut off most access points to the centre of Berlin, but some protestors and onlookers had walked through the city and congregated at the front of the Reichstag Building. Ahren and Gillen jogged the short distance along the path between the buildings and the park that Bulmann was swiftly making his way through. Ahren had guessed where Bulmann would be making for as soon as they caught up to him at the Brandenburg Gate. The road opened up at an intersection on the edge of the Reichstag Building. Ahren and Gillen looked to their left along the road between the park and the Reichstag Building, and saw a roadblock set up over the main entrance to the grounds. They ran across the road and started towards the roadblock, suddenly realising that there were no police anywhere along the road. People in front of the Reichstag Building started to come into view as they made their way towards the grounds, some cautiously looking along the road and starting to move away from the grounds trying to see where the gunshots minutes earlier had come from.

"These people are going to give him cover," Gillen said quietly. "Where is he?" he said touching the transmit button on his earpiece.

"Working his way quickly towards a small group of people on the border of the park to your left," the voice of his controller said in his ear. "If he moves much further forward, I should have satellite cover as well as heat source from the drone."

Two gunshots and the sounds of screams broke out over the low murmur of the crowd on the grounds of the Reichstag Building.

"Running from the park now, approximately fifty yards ahead of your position," the voice said in Gillen's ear.

Gillen saw a shape explode out from the park and sprint from across the road, towards the open gardens. He raised his pistol and fired at the shape. He saw the figure dive over a short gate and run towards the crowd. People on the gardens had turned towards the sound of the gunshots, panic breaking out instantly. Some were stood still, looking around desperately trying to find safety, others running wildly in all directions aimlessly overcome by the urge of flight. Ahren saw Bulmann sprint through the dispersing crowd, raised his gun, and tried to find a clear aim through the stampede of people. Before he could take a shot, Bulmann grabbed a woman by the arm, turning her mid step and pulled her in front of him. Ahren grabbed Gillen and pulled him against the wall of the Reichstag Building, pushing him into cover at the corner of the building as Bulmann fired over the shoulder of his hostage. People suddenly ran around the corner almost slamming into Ahren as he tried to see where Bulmann had gone. Ahren stepped back and stood for a minute, allowing the crowd who were running past them to get clear. He didn't want to provoke Bulmann to fire into the crowd.

"Are those people clear yet?" Gillen said.

"Still a few people out there, looks like some have lay down where they are, some running northwards. He has a hostage, satellite shows no clear shot from your position, he's moving with the last of the crowd."

Gillen glanced around the corner of the building, pulled back, and watched the last few people running away long the road.

"Short wall running against a road in front of the building. May be enough cover for us to get a lucky shot off at him," Gillen said. Ahren nodded. Gillen ran from the corner of the building and slid to a crouched stop against the small wall, followed closely by Ahren. The German flag was flying at half-mast a short way in front of the Reichstag Building, fluttering slowly in the wind.

"You won't be able to shoot me from there before I kill this woman, probably some of these other people too," Bulmann's voice roared across the now silent grounds. The woman screamed as if prompted by the threat.

"What do you think this will change?" Ahren replied, knowing he wouldn't make any difference to Bulmann's resolve.

"We were the bricks that the Fuhrer built an entire empire from. He created greatness from nothing, and now those bricks have been turned back to dust under the years of politicians' rule. They left us with nothing. Those politicians tore all that he built down when they betrayed him and surrendered to our enemies. Now I am going to tear what they have built down so Germany can rebuild itself again in his image."

"His Image?" Ahren asked, frustration clear as he shouted at Bulmann. "His image was the image of hatred and death and bringing this country to its knees. He's dust now too, just like the Germany you think you remember. A memory any decent soldier would want to forget. You and he are an abomination to this country and the real soldiers who served Germany. Look at all of the Germans you have killed to get here."

"And how many Germans did you kill with your orders and your weakness?" Bulmann shouted back. "These weak Germans need to be cleaned from the pure image of what we built so that the true inheritors of his Germany can take their place ruling this new world."

The woman Bulmann was holding screamed again and struggled, trying to free herself. She had almost buckled at the knees as Bulmann shouted at Ahren, the shock of the situation more than anything she could have imagined in a civilised society. He was holding a pistol he had taken from a police officer in his right hand, his arm stretched out over the woman's right shoulder, and a second pistol in his left hand pushed into the side of her torso holding her in place.

"You think these few pathetic creatures who call themselves Germans mean something to me?" Bulmann shouted. A police officer who had been shot by Bulmann as he ran into the grounds of the Reichstag Building lay near the flag pole between Bulmann and Ahren, still alive and moaning as he clasped his hands tightly over the wound in his upper chest. Bulmann lowered the pistol in his right hand and aimed at the police officer. "They mean nothing," he shouted, and shot twice into the body of the police officer. The woman Bulmann was holding screamed again, and went limp in his arm momentarily, the world swimming out of focus in front of her. As she found her feet, he pulled her backwards tightly against his chest. "Last chance," Bulmann shouted. "I know you won't join me, but you can leave now and live as a traitor for a little while longer."

General Anderston marched through the gates into the compound and stared at the small group of onlookers watching the proceedings. He made eye contact with Freeman and waited, seemingly expecting to be acknowledged immediately.

"Who is that?" Alders asked quietly.

"The American General," Stafe answered casually.

"He's very important," Freeman added, smiling. "America sent him to take charge over here."

"He seems to be looking at you," Mathers said, trying not to make it too obvious they were all stood staring back at the American General.

Freeman nodded. He snapped off a smart salute at Anderston and turned to Stafe quickly, again nodding, this time a frustrated acknowledgement that they would have to go and speak to the American. They marched in step to Anderston and stood to attention.

"We're moving some equipment in now, have you identified a suitable location for the transport vehicles to unload?" The question trailed off as he seemed to realise that Alder and Mathers were still stood a short distance away watching the conversation. "Who are those civilians?"

"The scientists," Freeman answered. "The older one is Alder, he's in charge here. Lead scientist, it was his experiment. The younger one is Mathers."

"Ah," Anderston replied smiling. The smile worried Freeman and Stafe. "Well let's see if they can get this equipment in place and fix this here problem before it goes too far." He marched between Freeman and Stafe towards Alder and Mathers, stopping short of them by a few paces. Alder looked at Mathers briefly, and put his hand on Mathers' arm. The slowly evolved silent communication between them that Alder would deal with the situation, and for Mathers not to become too worked up. They stood their ground silently, waiting for an obviously increasingly annoyed Anderston to come the rest of the way to them. After a few awkward moments of staring at the scientists, becoming increasingly flustered and reddening visibly, Anderston marched the last few steps to face Alder and Mathers.

"Hello," Alder said, cutting off the American General stood in front of him as he opened his mouth to speak. "Anything we can do to help you?"

"This experiment," Anderston said, his attempt at taking control of the conversation derailed by Alder's casual reaction to him. Anderston was used to subordinates coming to him and speaking when spoken to, not speaking over him. He had developed a tactic of stopping a short distance from people who he approached in order to take the power from them in the situation immediately, by forcing them to come the short distance to him before they could speak. "This experiment," he repeated angrily. "When do you foresee yourself being in a position to have it completed?"

"Did you bring the equipment we requested?" Alder asked calmly in reply. His calmness clearly frustrated Anderston even more.

"Of course. It is ready to be loaded in now."

"Good good," Alder said cheerily. "Follow this main road, second building on your right as you go past the bend up there. Let us know when you are ready to bring it in." Alder touched Mathers' arm lightly as he turned, and started to walk away. Mathers smiled and followed swiftly, neither looking back. Anderston opened his mouth to speak, a small sound coming from his throat, muted instantly by rage. Who were they to speak to him like a delivery boy?

Freeman and Stafe looked at each other and smiled as they saw the scientists dismiss themselves from Anderston's presence and walk off into the compound. Anderston looked visibly shaken and angered by the perceived disrespect he had just been shown as he turned back to the British soldiers.

"External patrol check," Freeman said. They saluted in unison towards Anderston, turned on their heels, and marched away through the gates and out of the facility compound.

Gillen slid along the wall towards the steps leading up to the entrance of the Reichstag Building, trying to gain an advantage of angle to get a clear shot off on Bulmann. He was listening to Bulmann shout at Ahren, placing his distance at less than a hundred feet away. He realised that the voice sounded like it was getting further away, and not closer as he had expected.

"He's pulling back, I don't understand," his controller said in his earpiece. It didn't make sense, why would he come as far as the steps to the Reichstag Building, only to then pull back.

"He's trying to draw us into the open," Gillen said to Ahren, realising that although he had a human shield, Bulmann was gambling on using the risk of moving through open ground, as they had the high ground. If he tried to go directly into the building, they had the advantage of outflanking Bulmann from cover.

"He knew we were making our way here and drew us out once he reached the grounds by shooting that policeman and grabbing the woman."

"Suggestions?" Gillen asked. He knew Ahren would have had the same training as Bulmann and would be able to think like him. Ahren looked at him and read his train of thought.

"He's a psychopath, soldiers do not use civilians as shields. He is as well trained as anyone I ever met, but he's an animal underneath the training. You can't second guess what he will do, for every military technique he uses, he also does something that is pure psychopath."

"Let's hope we can anticipate the elements of his military training that override the animal instincts then," Gillen said, and lifted himself upwards to look over the rim of the wall. He dropped back down a second later. Bulmann was moving away from them fast, working his way towards the limited cover of a group of low hedges lining the left side of the lawn in front of the Reichstag Building. The woman he was pulling along with him was struggling weakly in his grip. "How good is his aim?"

"Good enough in the open, better than mine," Ahren answered.

Gillen nodded. He stood and jumped over the wall, hauling himself onto the top of the steps of the Reichstag Building, and slamming into cover behind a pillar just as he heard the impact of a bullet dislodge some mortar from the steps, followed by the echo of the shot exploding around the lawn.

Ahren rounded the wall at the far end, opposite to where Gillen had jumped up onto the steps and ran towards a short edging wall at the base of the steps. He saw Bulmann raise the gun in his right hand and shoot towards Gillen as he was diving into cover behind the pillar, raised his own gun as he ran, and decided against shooting. Bulmann was too far away for Ahren to shoot cleanly without hitting the woman. She struggled more in his arms as he pulled her along. Bulmann seemed to see Ahren moving as he was firing at Gillen, adjusted his aim at the last minute, and fired wildly towards him. The woman struggling in his arms threw Bulmann's aim off, making him miss badly. Frustration took over, and Bulmann gave up his temporary advantage of cover as a trade off against better aim and mobility. He wrapped his right arm around the neck of the woman as Gillen peaked around the pillar, pushed the gun in his left hand against the side of her lower torso and fired. The bullet tore through the front of her stomach and exited on the right-hand side of her body, gouging a trench through her midriff and tearing a slab of meaty flesh free. She half folded sideways, her hip forced outward with the force of the blast, fell to her side, and writhed on the ground moaning at Bulmann's feet. He momentarily looked down at his victim, turned and ran for the row of low hedges. Gunshots sounded from behind him as he dived into cover, disappearing between the first and second hedge.

Ahren and Gillen both saw the woman fall, broke cover, and ran towards Bulmann, drawn out into the open by the sudden act of extreme violence. As Ahren reached the flag a burst of pain tore through his shoulder, and a force like nothing he had ever felt before spun him and threw him backwards. He lost his footing and fell and the base of the flagpole. He had been aiming at where Bulmann had dived into cover, but the shot seemingly came from further left of where he had disappeared. Questions flew through Ahren's head. *How badly was he hurt? Had he really been shot? Did Bulmann have an accomplice? How else had Bulmann disappeared in one place and Ahren had been shot a moment later from somewhere else?* Then it came to him in a flash of memory so ingrained in him he had not even realised such a natural and obvious thing was being used against him. He heard a second shot. Then a third.

Gillen had seen Bulmann fire at Ahren, from behind a small hedge, then turn his aim towards Gillen as he had reacted to Ahren dropping from the impact of the bullet. Gillen fired as he ran, missing Bulmann who had started to run, jumping over the first hedge and turning as he moved, firing again. Gillen sprinted towards Bulmann, his pulse throbbing hard in his neck. He could feel his heart pumping so hard in his chest it hurt. He passed the woman on the lawn, still writhing in agony, blood flooding from the wide-open wound in the front of her body. Gillen saw Bulmann run between the hedges a hundred feet ahead of him, and then disappear out of view as he dropped to the ground. He fired again, hoping he had found a target through the hedge.

Ahren watched Bulmann dive into cover again behind the hedge, saw Gillen sprinting towards the row of hedges as fast as any man he had ever seen move, and prayed he was right. He pushed himself up to a seating position. Through the tear in his vest he could see that his left shoulder was obliterated by the bullet which had torn through it, the bone shattered. He raised his pistol in his right hand as steadily as he could manage, shaking with the effort and almost blinded by the tears in his eyes from the pain he felt.

As Gillen ran towards the first hedge he swung the pistol in front of him, trying to target where Bulmann had dropped to the ground a few hedges ahead. Suddenly out of nowhere in his peripheral vision he saw a shape burst upwards. He started to turn his gun towards the shape as it lifted guns in each hand towards him. Less than a second from breaking cover the shape was at full height, Bulmann was on his feet and steadying his aim. Gillen had no chance to adjust as he swung his gun.

As Bulmann stood between the rows of hedges aiming at the oncoming target of the CIA agent, he smiled momentarily. Simple strategy had given him victory over these amateurs.

The figure rose into view almost perfectly between the hedges where Ahren was aiming his gun. He adjusted so slightly it felt that the gun had moved from his wrist and not any movement in his body. It still sent a wave of pain piercing through his left shoulder. He ignored the pain, focussed through the sights of his gun, and fired, fired again, and then with the last of his strength, pulled the trigger one last time before falling backwards, nothing left to steady his balance or hold him up.

Gillen saw a burst of red explode high in Bulmann's chest, pushing him backwards. Bulmann pulled the trigger on the gun in his right hand, firing just wide of Gillen. Less than a second later he fired the gun in his left hand, again missing his target. A second gunshot sounded behind Gillen as he stumbled forward whilst trying to adjust his own aim. As Gillen managed to turn towards Bulmann enough to try to level the staggering soldier in his sights, a third shot sounded behind him. A large wound opened at the base of Bulmann's throat where his neck met his body. Blood burst from his mouth, and his arms were thrown outwards and towards the sky as he began to fall backwards. His guns both fired once more as a final spasm forced the muscles of his body tight before they loosened for the last time. He landed on his back, blood running from the open wound in his chest and the wound which had almost separated his head from his body. His dead eyes still showed the cold malice Gillen had seen when he looked at his secondary target in the photograph his handler had given him the previous day. A photograph taken over seventy years ago.

The meeting in the situation room of The Whitehouse jarred with the feeling Jim Gronan had gotten every time he had ever attended in the past. There was a subdued mood which seemed to clash strangely with the anxious and frenetic energy of those who were buzzing between himself and the President. The Vice President was sitting just to the left of the President, quietly reading a report.

"Any word from these European Science Directorate guys yet?" Steve Halt said close to Gronan's ear, pulling him back out of his thoughts about the occupants of the room. He realised he had been watching minions scuttle to and from the Vice President with updates and reports, the expression on the Vice President's face becoming more baffled with each new report or update.

"Our guys got there with equipment a few hours ago," Gronan replied. "We don't have much feedback as to a timescale for repairs and installing the new equipment though. Sounds like they need to test each individual piece of equipment they replace before doing a full system reboot. I'm curious." Gronan turned away from the table to face Halt, lowering his voice. The conversation they were having was attracting more than a few glances around the room. "Why have you come to me to ask about if a military convoy with equipment has arrived at its destination, when the Secretary of Defence and two Generals are stood a few feet away from you?"

"Would you ask Doug Mortin for anything without having more than the equal pound of spare flesh to offer in return? And besides, these days Doug is climbing so far up our all-powerful VP's ass we might as well go straight to the top of that sad little chain for the skewed response than to wait for Doug to get permission to tell us the angle they think we can cope with. Remember, one of those Generals over there has only just been given the National Security Advisors job, and the other wants yours. Neither will say a word without Mortin spelling it out for them first. What you and I brief The President on this situation will hopefully balance out what the VP's little team come up with. That way maybe we can hold off on those Generals flattening half of Switzerland for a few days more."

"Ok everybody," the silenced immediately as The President turned from the National Security Advisor and walked to the table. "I think we are at a point where we need to make a decision on the direction we are taking and what support we can provide. I want an assessment of the chances of the ESD guys' success in completing another experiment with the repairs they are making. We also need to consider if we think they will get enough information from that to tell us what has gone wrong so we can get this damn mess fixed. Doug?"

The Secretary of Defence nodded to the President and stood to address the table shuffling some paperwork in his hands as he rose. It was something that Gronan had seen him do before, completely unnecessary in Gronan's opinion, but Mortin seemed to revel in being the centre of attention.

"General Anderston arrived at the ESD facility eleven hours ago. Our troops have cleared an obstruction at the entrance of the facility, and have been securing the area, with assistance from British military personnel. There was minor resistance from a small group of protestors in an external area of the facility which has been quelled with no injury or loss of life to our people. We expect them to begin to unload the equipment and supplies requested by the facility staff during the next six hours, but the facility have been less helpful in giving some sort of timescale for installation and testing of the equipment."

"Thank you," The President said quietly. The Secretary of Defence started to open his mouth to speak, but something in the look the Vice President gave him stopped in his tracks. The room fell silent for a few moments, Mortin looked from face to face, then awkwardly sat back down into his chair, begrudgingly conceding his momentary position of power to the silent room.

"The timescale issue of installation and testing equipment may not be too significant," The President said, breaking the silence. "Steve, how are we getting on with putting a man into there?"

"Approximately an hour ago I spoke with a scientist named Blancs who works at the Large Hadron Collider facility in Cern," said Halt. He almost seemed to sit back from the table rather than moving forwards to it as he spoke, commanding the attention of everyone in the room without moving from his chair. "Doctor Blancs is an expert in particle acceleration, and has a working knowledge of the original paper submitted by Doctor Alder and Doctor Rosst which formed the basis for the work at the facility which has caused this situation. He will be making his way from Cern to assist with installation and testing, and will then feed back to us an expected timescale for any new work, with an expert prognosis on the realistic outcome of any further tests. He will also assess whatever data they have from their first experiment and feed that back to us to see if it can be identified as to what actually went wrong."

The President nodded slowly, and tapped his finger on a report sitting on the table in front of him. The room sat silently looking at him as he thought. He lifted both hands and ran them down across his face slowly before looking back up to the others gathered around the table. He had left the tips of his index fingers touching his lips, his hands pressed together as if in prayer just in front of his chin. Suddenly he took his hands away from his face.

"What do we have in terms of notable incidents and predictions on where we are historically since our last update?"

"Various small incidents which are tracking the timeline seem to indicate we were comfortably within the sixteenth century approximately two hours ago," Gronan replied. "Soldiers from a Dutch revolt against Spanish Catholicism have been identified as wearing mid-sixteenth century dress and carrying weapons dated to that era. The problem is that we are now seeing soldiers being reported throughout Europe from both the English Civil War and the Thirty Years War between France and Spain from the seventeenth century, on top of others from conflicts right up to the Second World War, which is also causing some concern. It was only going to be a matter of time before a group of soldiers from one time period ran into a group of soldiers from another time period, and we have no further capacity to manage any conflicts. On a relevant theme, we picked up two German soldiers who had come through from World War Two, and travelled across Europe right into the heart of Germany from Russia. One of them was a war criminal, who we can confirm has now been killed. The other is working with one of our field agents, with the aim of making contact with German forces from World War One, currently engaged in military activity in Belgium. Unfortunately, the soldier in question has been injured during the incident where the other soldier was killed."

"Martial law has been declared across almost every continent on the planet right now, but that just reduces the number of civilians on the streets by a small proportion," Gronan took a moment to shuffle some paperwork in front of him, collecting his thoughts patiently while the room waited for him to continue. "We have had our first report of a fatality from bubonic plague, more commonly known as Black Death. A man in London was admitted to a hospital Emergency Room with symptoms matching those of the plague, and died shortly after initially being treated. We have no real control of the spread of infection right now. My Biggest concern is not soldiers from the past killing each other or general population in smaller isolated pockets of violence, it is the outbreak of a pandemic disease which we do not have the capacity to treat on top of the other ongoing incidents. We have already seen cholera in Tokyo, and that is continuing to spread. The Japanese Government have restricted all internal and external movement around Tokyo by their citizens, shut down all public transport and blocked all main highways, but they are still suspected to be trying to manage a cholera outbreak which is affecting somewhere between twenty and forty percent of their entire population at best estimate." Gronan stopped talking and sat back from the table, allowing the impact of what he had said to sink in. He had made his point and there was no need to add any further detail.

The President nodded and stood from the table as everyone sat staring down at the paperwork in front of them, or at their hands or laps, all attempting to avoid eye contact with anyone else in the room. To look up now seemed as if it would be to acknowledge the horrific possibility that they were no longer in control of the destiny not only of their own lives, but fully to concede that the grip on the destiny of the entire human race may be beyond their reach.

"One Hour," The President said quietly. "We meet back in this room for hourly updates as of now. Steve, I want the Chief Medical Examiner and Andy Gearne from the Department of Health either in this room or on conference call in the next five minutes."

Gillen knelt over Ahren assessing the wound to his left shoulder, the bullet had almost certainly smashed bone within the shoulder joint beyond repair. Fortunately, it appeared that though there was some serious bone damage, there was no sign that there was any arterial bleeding. Ahren would live long enough to get to a hospital, if there was any still able to treat him with everything else happening.

"How did you know?" Gillen asked quietly.

"Know what?"

"Where he would be. From that distance you couldn't have been able to see him before he appeared in front of me. I had no idea where he was going to appear, and somehow you managed to shoot him the moment he was standing."

"Something we were talking about before," Ahren replied, looking over towards the bushes where Bulmann's body lay. "We were hoping he would make a mistake or be in some way predictable. He did something his military training instilled in him to do. He dived into cover, and when he landed, he rolled to his left before exiting cover to fire. Basic Wehrmacht training at its best."

"Thank you," Gillen said. He was tearing at the vest Ahren was wearing, clearing the area around the wound. He tore some cloth from his own shirt and leaned forward. "This will hurt."

"I know," Ahren said calmly, before letting out a scream of pain as Gillen wrapped the cloth tightly around the wound in Ahren's shoulder. Ahren almost fainted at the sudden shock and increased pain bursting through his body.

"Sit forwards now," Gillen said, supporting Ahren under his right arm as he felt him going weak. "Let's see if we can keep you from going into full shock if we can. There is something I need to tell you anyway, so I guess you will need to stay with me."

"Ja?" Ahren asked, lifting his head to look at Gillen, an effort which made a wave of nausea pass through his body momentarily.

"I asked my handler to do some research while I was tracking you and Herr Bulmann, to give me some point of reference to where you may be going. Homes, family, that sort of thing."

"I had assumed my family had," Ahren paused, looking down again towards his feet, his chest rested against his knees as he sat. "I assumed that as we had not won the war, my family was gone."

"I am sorry," Gillen said. "Your wife died some years ago. She survived the war, and brought up your daughter here in Berlin. Your daughter is still alive, she lives a few miles from here."

Ahren gasped sharply, the gasp sending another surge of pain through his body making him spasm. He barely seemed to feel it as he tried to stand, his legs still too weak to support him. Gillen held his grip firmly under Ahren's right arm and guided him gently back to a seated position.

"Hospital first," Gillen said. "I have her address. It is martial law here with a curfew apparently now, so she should be at home. I will see if I can get us cleared to find her once you are patched up."

Alder and Mathers stood quietly watching American soldiers unloading flight case after flight case of equipment from several army vehicles parked just in front of the doors to the main facility building. Two back-up generators had been parked on flat-bed trailers next to the building and were being hooked up to the main facility power supply in sequence. The main generator was also being repaired by army technicians as the offload was being completed. No matter what happened during the experiment, there would be power in relay to all of their original equipment as well as to back up monitoring equipment, the vital data from the first experiment which was not captured would not be lost for a second time. One way or another, they would know what had happened within the Collider to cause the tear in time.

"Are you Doctor Alder?" Private Harper asked suddenly from a short distance away. Mathers jumped as she broke the silence, having not noticed her walk up next to them.

"That would be me," Alder replied.

"Information from Major Freeman sir," Harper said formally. "An American scientist is on his way here now. Doctor Blancs from Cern. The Americans have said that he will be here within the hour."

"Ask the Gatehouse to call down to me when he arrives please," Alder said, turned, and without speaking again, walked away into the Collider building.

"Sorry," Mathers said, confusion clear in his face as to what had just happened. It wasn't like Alder to be so brusque. "I'm Mathers, I work with Doctor Alder. Jules Mathers. I don't know why he was rude then, it must be the strain of the last week. I am sure everyone is here to help us." He smiled awkwardly at Harper.

"I'm sure they are," she replied.

"I'm Jules by the way," he said holding out his hand.

"I know, you said that already," Harper said as she shook his hand quickly. She saluted and started to turn from him.

"Can I show you around?" Mathers asked, stepping towards her. "We don't have much in the canteen, but maybe I can offer you some coffee at least?"

Harper turned back slowly and looked at Mathers. He smiled again, fumbling at his shirt as he tried to work out what to do with his hands as she stared at him.

"Thank you, but I am on duty."

"Maybe if you have a break?" he tried hopefully.

"I don't think socialising with staff here is something which would be right at the moment," Harper replied. "I doubt I will have many breaks while I am here." She looked at him, uncomfortable and dishevelled stood in front of her. "I am sorry, it just wouldn't be right," she repeated. "After all, I'm sure you are very busy at the moment."

"I could make some time," he tried.

"Haven't you done that already?" She said. His face looked slightly flushed at that comment, almost more hurt by the minor rebuke than the initial rejection. "I'm sorry, it is nice of you to offer, but at the moment the people employed in this facility are not exactly the most popular people in the world, you know. And if I am seen as distracting you," she trailed off. Mathers nodded slowly. He realised that this wasn't just going to be something that would just *blow over* if they ever did manage to repair some of the damage they had caused. He nodded to Harper, turned, and walked after Alder.

The Vice President knocked on the door of the Oval Office quietly and hearing a murmur of acknowledgement, walked slowly into the room. The president was sitting behind his desk shuffling paperwork in front of him. There seemed to be growing piles of reports spilling across not only the desk, but on the coffee table too. The President has always been incredibly neat and organised when it came to filing and official reports, but over the past number of days there had not been any opportunity to even attempt to catch up on administrative tasks such as filing reports which had already been read. Most reports were being picked up again and re-assessed a day or so after they had been handed to The

President, with assessments changing so fast at times that most departments were struggling to collate updates and information consistently. Anarchy was reigning within every government in the world, as society began to crumble into mass disorder.

"I need one thing from you," The President said, barely looking from the report he had picked up to acknowledge The Vice President. "We need to put personal agendas aside right now, and work together. If I see competition between staff in a meeting again, I will have them removed from the room, even if that means yourself. Before each hourly briefing I want you to meet with all section heads and ensure that there is no confusion in what our best course of action will be, based on a combined threat assessment. Steve Halt will be in that meeting with you." The President put down the report he had been holding and stood from behind the desk. "I will not be the person who has to collate conflicting analysis from multiple agencies and departments just because of your ego and their petty aspirations of a little more power." The President pointed around the room at the reports strewn across every flat surface. "This ends now."

"It is their job to present every possible assessment," The Vice President argued weakly. "There is no right answer to this situation, these are just best-case scenarios."

"I am not saying you have to make any final decision, I wouldn't want to jeopardise you politically. I just want the options laid out in each meeting without bias. Do you think that is achievable within your limitations?"

The Vice President started to speak, then stopped momentarily. He had never seen The President reach this point. He had seen anger, frustration, even rage in White House from The President, but it had never been singularly directed at him in such a way.

"I am not to blame for this," The Vice President said lamely. "I will ensure ego is put aside though."

The President didn't reply, silently walking out of the Oval Office leaving the door open behind him.

Mathers caught up to Alder at the doors to the elevators in the foyer of the main facility building. Alder was simply stood waiting quietly, and it took a few moments for Mathers to realise that Alder had not yet called the elevator.

"Are you ok?" Mathers asked.

"Good," Alder replied, almost startled by the question. "Why wouldn't I be?"

"I don't know, you walked away when the soldier told us Doctor Blancs was coming. Is that a problem?"

"Not in the slightest," Alder replied. "We are going to need his help if we are going to succeed this time."

"Succeed?" Mathers asked, confused by Alder's choice of words.

"The pressure inside the Collider chamber is going to be greater than before if we can manage to run the experiment again successfully. The greater the mass of the particle, the greater the gravity within the chamber. The fish which we found inside the control room, it didn't just move through time, I believe that it moved geographically too, the result of the greatly increased gravity. It moved from the lake. Doctor Blancs is the only other scientist I have spoken to who understands the levels of gravitational force and impact that this type of experiment will be put under. He also understands the theory of time being pulled through itself when a point in time becomes fixed. When we stopped the train so to speak. He understands the theory of that momentum from the past catching up to us."

"Then why did you walk away, having him here will help us, won't it?" Mathers was becoming more confused with every question.

"He will have his instructions and an agenda given to him by our friends the various governments we have spoken to recently. He will be of great use to us, but he may also have a very different view of this experiment and how it should be completed. We discussed my theories a long time ago, when Doctor Rosst and I initially published the paper which secured funding for this very facility. He did not believe that we would be able to accelerate any particle to anything close to the speed of light, and that there was too much danger involved in our way of searching for a different perspective on the ever-popular *God Particle*." Alder shrugged as he pondered the best way to explain his disagreement with Blancs. "Our experiment contradicted his own experiment, contradicted many laws of science that he is not prepared to question. We were looking for a way to create an environment where a particle with actual mass would behave in the same way as a photon. If that was even *possible*. The theory behind that possibility was awesome, and would open up whole new worlds of scientific research and advancement. If however, we could reach the same speed and it did *not* behave in the same way as a photon, to be able to study that reaction would be equally interesting. I had my ideas on what this may entail, and sadly so did Doctor Blancs. Unfortunately, we disagreed on these ideas, and also on their validity."

Alder reached forwards and placed his finger on the biometric reader next to the elevator. The doors opened quietly in front of them, and Alder stepped inside. Mathers realised the conversation was over, and followed Alder into the elevator in silence. The doors closed behind him, and they started moving down into the heart of the facility.

The sharp end of the past

The city of Târgoviște sits on the bank of the Ialomița River in an area of Romania once known as Wallachia, more commonly known to the world as Transylvania. Martial law had not been enforced in Târgoviște to the same degree as the more densely populated cities of Romania such as Bucharest, as there was simply not the police or military presence to enforce any restrictions on the population. The population of Târgoviște had simply continued with life as normal while the rest of the world seemed to be falling into chaos. The news of events in the outside world were reported on television, but with no signs of anything having happened in or near the city, why should there be any need for interruption or restrictions on people whose lives did not need to change.

Ioana Rancaciov walked casually along the verge of the road leading north away from the monastery of Dealu towards the open countryside and the mountains far away in the distance surrounding Brașov. She was studying medicine at the University of Valahia in Târgoviște, and enjoyed walking out into the countryside each day both before and after she had studied at the university library. It was a peaceful area and she would take the time to clear her head so that when she returned to her room on the university campus in the evening she was always refreshed. It seemed to help her retain the vast amount of information any student of medicine was expected to absorb.

A young boy ran past Ioana along the road, skirting between small trees as he jumped across a ditch at the side of the road and into a small field which bordered the road. She stopped to look at her phone which had buzzed in her pocket, another update from one of her

258

friends which she had been tagged in. Signal had been intermittent at best over the past day, and she had been surprised enough to look at her phone in the expectation that something interesting may have finally delivered. She lost interest instantly, it was a photograph of her at a concert the week before, a band she had no real interest in seeing, but had been convinced to go for the sake of a night out with her roommate and some of their friends. She started to walk again, replacing her phone in her pocket and looking at the mountains in the distance again. Her phone buzzed again, distractingly. She watched the boy who must have been no more than ten years old running away through the field, then looked down to turn her phone off. As she was looking at the phone the world in front of her seemed to darken instantly, and she heard the boy scream.

A forest of large wooden spikes seemed to have silently been planted around Ioana Rancaciov in the blink of an eye as she looked up from her phone. The smell was instant, repulsing her to the point that she nearly vomited, feeling herself heave and lurching back a step. It was the smell of hundreds of corpses, a smell she recognised but magnified infinitely beyond anything she had experienced in her four years at medical school, even during trips to the local mortuary. Impaled on every spike around her was a human body, or at least some part of a body. There had been no sound, other than that of the boy screaming. No vibration or tremor under her feet as the hundreds of spikes had been planted in the ground. They simply *were* where they had not been a moment before. She turned and saw that the spikes were somehow also mounted into the road, forced through the tarmac causing cracks to open out from the wooden stakes like lightning bolts cut into the road. The boy screamed again from somewhere within the field she had been standing next to. She turned back to the field and started the make her way through the forest of the dead, covering her mouth and nose with her sleeve, her lower face pressed into the crook of her elbow to mask the stench which had suddenly invaded the air. Flies buzzed between each trunk and across every decaying limb. There was nowhere to look in order to avoid the horror of what surrounded her. The ground was suddenly awash with blood and lumps of severed flesh which hung from the trunks of the morbid trees, bodies were impaled at eye level in front of her and everywhere around her, and flies seemed to be swarming downwards from the sky to feast on the carrion. As she moved through the spikes the bodies seemed to be getting fresher, with wet blood dripping from limbs which seemed less decayed than the first bodies which had been surrounding her. She stepped between two particularly closely mounted corpses on spikes trying to make her way clear of the bodies, and felt an arm brush against her shoulder. She turned to see a man mounted prostrate on a spike, his limp body leaning grotesquely backwards, arms spread out to his sides, his head hanging backwards at his left shoulder, facing the sky as if searching for something in the clouds. The spike was staked through his back, protruding through his upper chest at his right shoulder. Fresh blood was running from wounds on his body, and was dripping from the fingers of his right hand. He somehow managed to move his left arm again, momentarily reaching towards her, and then it fell to his side again.

Somewhere behind her the boy screamed again. Ioana Rancaciov stepped clear of the newly planted forest of corpses, trying not to look back at the bodies she had made her way through. Where had the boy gone? He had run past her no more than a few minutes before, so must still be within the field she was stood in. She looked to the tree line at the far edge of the field and saw fleeting movement, it was him. She began to run towards where he was, shouting for him to wait for her. As she crossed the field, she realised why he had screamed again. Another body was partially mounted on a newer spike, a body still writhing in death throws. At the foot of the trunk the body was staked to, was the corpse of a child. The impaled man seemed to be trying to lift himself from the spike which was planted through his torso at the waist, with his stomach uppermost, his legs and feet parallel with his shoulders and flailing head. His efforts to move seemed to be driving him further onto the spike as he tried to lift his arms to gain purchase on the wood enough to grip it and pull himself upward. She turned away again, remembering that there was a small child out here who she could help. Her medical training would do nothing for any of the dying without equipment.

Again, she saw the slightest glimpse of movement, and Ioana set off chasing the boy. She caught up to him as he fell to his knees at the edge of the field where the tree line merged with thick undergrowth of the edge of a small wood. She crouched and touched the boy's shoulder. He started as she touched him, trying to get to his feet again. She held him back and quietly said to him that she was not going to hurt him. His eyes darted from her to the body impaled close to them, back to her, then across the forest of corpses at the other side of the field and into the road. He was in shock, and unable to speak. She asked him his name, and again he failed to reply. She pointed to herself and said "Ioana." His eyes did not register any understanding. She stood, keeping a hand rested on his shoulder, then reached down and took him in her arms, lifting him back to his feet. They were going to have to find a way back to Târgoviște through the fields and avoid the road for as far as they could, until she was sure they were clear of any more impaled bodies.

The phone next to Mathers buzzed twice before he picked it up. It was the security guard at the main gate house, asking if Mathers or Alder would go to meet Doctor Blancs, as he had just arrived at the main gate area. Mathers said he was on his way, and hung up the phone. He looked at the phone for a moment, thinking if he should call the guard back to ask for Doctor Blancs to be escorted to the main building by one of the soldiers. He decided it would be better for him to go and meet him at the gate, it would give him an opportunity to meet Doctor Blancs on his own, and an opportunity for Alder to make any preparations he needed prior to his arrival.

"Doctor Blancs is here, he's at the gate," Mathers said to Alder. "I said I would go there now to collect him."

Alder nodded without replying, patted Mathers on the shoulder, and turned back to a monitor mounted in the control console. Mathers took his silence as begrudging acceptance that they would be working with Blancs whether Alder liked it or not. He walked out of the control room and headed for the elevators.

It took a few minutes for Mathers to reach the main gate area, where Doctor Blancs was stood beside an American military transport vehicle with some of the British soldiers who Mathers and Alder had spoken to earlier that day. As he reached the small gathering, he realised that they had stopped talking as he approached. He stood back from the group momentarily, as if to wait for an invitation to join. Nothing was said. He walked to the group after a moment's pause, just enough time to avoid interrupting whatever conversation they may have needed to finish.

"Mathers," he said quietly. "Collecting Doctor Blancs."

"Blancs," a smallish man said from the centre of the group, reaching out his hand in return, proffering it to Mathers welcomingly. "Jules Mathers, isn't it?"

"It is, yes. Welcome Doctor, thank you for coming." Mathers had never met Blancs before, and was surprised how normal he appeared to be. He was not a tall man at all, but seemed to have good bearing within his smaller frame, and something Mathers could not put his finger on. His suit didn't seem to sit quite right, as if it was a suit he had bought when he was a little heavier, and then lost enough weight that the suit jacket hung loose at the shoulders in an odd way, making him look not dishevelled but almost casually dressed. There was something unusual seemingly hidden in his rather ordinary facial features, causing Mathers to stare slightly more than he would have intended to. He was totally at ease chatting to the soldiers from what Mathers could tell, socially comfortable in an extremely abnormal situation. Something Mathers had tried to do when talking to the new visitors to the facility, and failed miserably at.

"I was just discussing the drive over here," Blancs said conversationally, as if he had been talking about a trip to the shops. "You know they have told everybody to stay at home? It is like the world is deserted out there. Apart from the road blocks that is, soldiers everywhere. I hear there were some protestors here," Blancs said lightly, changing the subject. "They have made a mess of your gates."

"We did have some unrest outside the facility," Mathers replied a little embarrassed.

"A Little unrest," Freeman interrupted, laughing as Mathers flushed red in the face. "You had everything from anarchists to religious maniacs celebrating the return of *The Lord* camped outside."

"That was quite the interesting idea," Blancs said. "Apparently there are some sections of society who believe you and my friend Doctor Alder have been the catalyst for the *second coming of Our Lord and Saviour*. Talking of Doctor Alder."

"He's in the main building, testing some equipment in the control room," Mathers replied. "If you are ready, I will take you to him now?"

"No time like the present," Blancs replied politely, trying to stifle a smile at his own poor humour, the pun clearly lost on Mathers. "Thank you for your hospitality," he said to the soldiers. "After you."

Mathers nodded at the soldiers, turning and leading Blancs away from the gate and into the facility.

"So, has he come out his shell at all recently?" Blancs asked as they walked through the grounds of the facility. "Losing his wife was a terrible shock, even though she had been ill for a while. I think he just expected her to pull through. A shame, all that knowledge in science, and yet I know he felt so impotent in his attempts to understand her illness."

"He spoke a little about her recently, but that is the first conversation I have ever had with him on the subject," Mathers said, slowing his pace a little to allow Blancs to catch up to him. He had realised that Blancs was walking almost deliberately slowly. He was uncomfortable talking about Alder's personal life, and did not want to still be having the conversation when they reached the main building, and certainly not when they were near the control room.

"She was his first passion, science was simply something to focus his mind when she was not there. This was his greatest achievement you know, and I have to admit I think it is a shame that she was not here to see him succeed."

"Succeed?" Mathers asked, somewhat baffled by the way Blancs phrased the comment. "We have torn time apart, I'm lost on how that is success?"

"The experiment itself succeeded, your equipment undoubtedly accelerated a sub-atomic particle with a measurable mass to light speed. The tear in time was not success or failure, it was simply one of many results of the experiment." Blancs stopped walking altogether. "You seem confused my friend. For Doctor Alder, for myself, and a great many others, science is not about the unfortunate side effects or extraneous secondary results, but of testing the original theory, proving the hypothesis. This unfortunate minor glitch may result in untold advances for humanity, we just need to tweak the finer points of the experiment itself to ensure that the equipment can handle the extra gravitational load and we will have this time problem sorted in, well, no time at all."

Minor glitch? Mathers head was filled with questions, how could Blancs call thousands of deaths a minor glitch? The experiment *was* a success? It made no sense, they had almost destroyed all of their equipment, had barely managed to register any readings before they lost all power and were trapped in the bunker. They still hadn't retrieved any usable data, and now Blancs was saying that they could fix the tear in time, as it was changing a tyre on the spare wheel of his car. Mathers mumbled something about needing to do more that pop on a new wheel in reply even he wasn't sure made sense as an analogy, and started walking towards the main facility building again.

Steve Halt watched the Vice President walk into the Situation Room, followed closely by the National Security Advisor and the Secretary of Defence. Advisors jockeyed for position behind them, all trying to get close to the table vying to be noticed by the most powerful men in the United States as having been useful during a crisis. They would make careers off the back of this opportunity, and every one of them seemed almost too obviously to have an aspiration to take a place of power at the table in the near future. Halt looked across the table to where Gronan had been sitting. The chair was empty, and Halt wished he had waited a little longer to return to the room too. The minions and climbers buzzed around him continuing their conversations whilst trying to make eye contact with him or the Vice President, barely acknowledging their counterparts as they circled the table like young Beta male lions, looking for either an ally amongst the Alphas or trying to spot a weaker old lion to displace. He thought they would be welcome to his seat if they were so desperate, he could stand at the back of the room hidden by everyone else, and knew he would still be sought out when there was a need for his input. The worst part was that he was starting to lose interest in the job. Gronan was right, these people were dangerous and would destroy anyone and anything in order to advance themselves. A murmur spread through the room, and Halt looked up to see Gronan walk back into the room casually, his usual understated presence unnerving the quietened audience. They watched as he dropped some papers on the table in front of his seat, took his jacket off, and hung it loosely across the back of his chair. He didn't look at anyone in the room, simply placing his hands on the back of the chair and resting his weight forwards slightly. A moment later the room fell silent as the President walked through the door, the Secret Service closing the door behind him.

"I need Alder on teleconference immediately," The President said. A technician moved to a small desk at the side of the room, picked up the phone, and whispered instructions into it. "I want to take as balanced a view as I can on this, but we have reached a point where the United States navy has just been forced to destroy a British warship in Chesapeake Bay, the growing plague and cholera pandemics are currently wiping out entire towns and causing whole cities to be quarantined, armies are running rampant across Europe, and I have just been told that hundreds of corpses have been found impaled on spikes in a town in Romania. The balanced view is that right at this moment I fear that if we take no immediate action to rectify this situation, very soon there will be almost no one left alive on this planet except the people who jump forwards in time from the past, bringing nothing but anarchy with them."

The technician stepped across the room to where the President stood, and quietly waited to be acknowledged. The President looked at him and just nodded, before walking to the table and facing the screens, all currently showing the Great Seal of the United States against a blue background. The screens suddenly lit up with Alder's face, behind him stood Mathers, and then further back another man who no one in the Situation Room recognised.

"Mr President," Alder said politely. "I have been on hold as I was instructed, awaiting your call. How can I help you?"

The President twitched slightly at the impertinent politeness and courtesy in Alders' voice, as if he were a call centre advisor speaking to an annoyed customer. He paused for a moment before reacting, running his left hand slowly across his face, and tapping his right-hand index finger on the table in front of him.

"You have an hour. Not a day, not a week. An hour. In one hours' time, we will be speaking again, and you will be either telling me that you will be beginning your experiment within the following hour, or we will be seeking an alternative option to end this crisis. I need a single word from you, yes or no. Can you have your equipment repaired in that time in order to complete this experiment?"

Alder looked back at Mathers and Blancs, and shrugged. He turned back to the screen and nodded. The President reddened noticeably in the face.

"I will assume that is a yes?"

"It is," replied Alder. "Yes, I will speak to you in one hour."

"Let me make it clear to you now, this experiment had better give us an explanation of exactly what has caused this tear in time, and you had better have an answer to the question of how we fix this. I am still of a mind that you be held accountable for every single death since the first experiment you attempted, and that is something which will be on your conscience for the rest of your life."

"If you will excuse me then," Alder replied. "I would appear to have a lot of work to do, and an hour to do it." He leaned forward, pressed a switch, and the screen momentarily went blank in front of the President, before the Great Seal returned.

"An hour," Mathers said quietly. "Can we get everything in place within an hour?"

"Let's not waste any more of that hour talking about it," Blancs replied. He had already been in the control room for a little over an hour when the call had come through telling them that the President needed to speak to them urgently, and had been putting together a secondary power generator backup to ensure they would be able to continue the experiment if there was a power surge similar to the surge created by the first experiment. He had spoken briefly to Alder, and Mathers had felt uncomfortable immediately upon bringing

Blancs into the control room. He had opted to leave as soon as he saw the frosty reception Alder had given Blancs. A short while later Mathers decided to venture back into the control room, hoping there may have been a thawing of the atmosphere. He had been greeted by a surprisingly agreeable discussion between the pair, with Blancs suggesting that the drain in power had led to a breach in the gravitational shield within the collider, allowing the resulting reaction to tear the hole in time. This was not something which was in Blancs' opinion, the fault of anyone at the facility, as it would have been impossible to predict that the power company could not maintain a consistent supply of electricity required, and just how quickly the original back-up generator would fail. He was unsure if a second experiment would give them anything solid to work with in terms of a solution to the problem, but as he had explained to Mathers on his return, an understanding of where the collider had torn into time may give them a starting point to repairing at least some of the damage. It may even give them some indication of the explanation as to how time worked, beyond being the concept used to explain why everything didn't happen all at once.

"So, what do they expect us to do once we manage to run the experiment?" Mathers asked awkwardly whilst initiating the start-up procedure for the monitoring stations in the control room. "There are four of us with Doctor Blancs added, even if we take a couple of stations each, we will be risking another breach if someone does not permanently monitor the pressure within the Collider itself, and Doctor Rosst was the only person I knew who." He stopped himself saying any more, and looked at Alder, who had reddened slightly.

"I can monitor the pressure within the chambers of the Collider remotely from here," Alder said firmly.

"If I may?" Blancs interjected. "I had felt it would be beneficial for you to monitor the particle acceleration rate and resulting data from the command suite once you have completed the initiation process. Jules and Steve can control the test cycle and ensure everything is running smoothly from the control room. I think I may be of more helpful to you if I go into the outer chamber tunnels and monitor pressure and gravitational stability from there. That way I can make any adjustments and try to maintain the power supply manually if necessary."

"If something goes wrong though," Mathers said.

"If something goes wrong, I will be in just as much danger up here young man, and if we do not succeed, I have a suspicion there will not be much to live for much longer anyway."

At exactly an hour since the President spoke to Alder via teleconference, the screen in the Situation Room momentarily went blank again, changing from the Great Seal of The United States to the faces of four scientists in Switzerland. The President sat at the large table, with only the Vice President, Gronan, and Halt also sitting at the table. The rest of the room was eerily still and empty. The President had tired of arguments between the NSA, CIA, National Security Advisor, homeland, and every other agency that felt that could make a little mileage for themselves out of this incident, and had dismissed everyone who would not serve an immediate purpose. Even the Technician had stepped out of the room, leaving Halt to accept teleconference feed once the line was established.

Gronan wondered to himself who the fourth face on the screen was. Another scientist at the facility he did not recognise. He had been told that the new face he had seen in the last conversation was Blancs, the scientist brought in by the Americans to help restore some semblance of stability to these rogue European scientists. The new face looked weary, tired in the same way Alder and Mathers looked, as if thoroughly defeated by the world which they had created. Steve Ortile had entered the room silently and slipped behind Blancs and Mathers as Alder had made the connection to the President. He looked like he hadn't slept for days, his clothes dishevelled and his hair a wild mess. His appearance momentarily derailed Alder's train of thought on how he would address this conversation with the Americans. It was shocking how much he appeared to have aged in the space of just over a week.

"One question," The President said. "Again, I want a one answer, yes or no. Can you complete the experiment?"

Silence.

"Yes," Alder said finally, firmly. "We start the countdown within the hour. You will not hear from us and we will not be able to respond to you until this is complete, one way or another."

The President started to speak, but the screen went blank in front of him before he had managed to say anything. The Great Seal of The Unites States stamped itself back onto the screen marking the end of the conversation.

"Little bit rude," The Vice President said slowly, turning from the screen to see the other three men's backs as they walked through the door of the Situation room and out into the corridor.

The Last Experiment

Eleven days had passed. From what felt like an eternity where time was both meaningless and the only focus in the world, Mathers realised that in those eleven days an entire planet had changed. Civilisations had been irreparably damaged, altered beyond recognition, maybe even ended in some cases. In some way five centuries of existence seemed to occupy the exact same moment, the here and now. Mathers wondered how you fixed that. It wasn't as simple as pulling the ends of a piece of string which had become knotted to straighten it out again, but that seemed to be what was expected of them. He wondered why Blancs seemed so positive that what they had done was in some way a success, that things could be salvaged. They had restarted wars where peace had been the status quo for many generations, dropped bombs on unsuspecting innocent people, and set long forgotten soldiers amongst populations wholly unprepared for invasion. Mathers focussed on a single incident he had heard about days before on the news, which seemed somehow more horrific than all of the war and violence they had brought upon the world. Reality had hit him hard as he processed the situation in his mind. What *they* had caused. A young girl, innocent, simply walking home after an evening at work had been torn apart, literally half of her body torn through time and dumped on the same side of the road the rest of her body had been found so long before, tragic bookends of a hole in time. He could barely bring himself to watch the news after that, guilt eating him up every time he saw another story of death or destruction they had caused, and every time thinking back to the lone girl who died because of what they had done.

The door opened behind him and then sucked closed again, the air moving slightly. It didn't feel as crisp somehow now in the control room. The power was fully restored, everywhere seemingly so much brighter bathed in newly restored white artificial light. The dull emergency lighting had seemed so much more appropriate to Mathers. Alder stood at his shoulder, resting his hand gently on the back of the chair Mathers was sitting on. They had reached a point where conversation almost seemed unnecessary now, they had both gone through so much in the past number of days, friends dying in front of them, the world collapsing around them, being at the brink of success and then being blamed for the collapse of civilisation. Once you had shared that sort of experience, small talk seemed to be unnatural.

"Blancs is running a test charge through the magnets to check our power supply from the main grid and each of the backup generators," Mathers said, not looking up from the screen. "No failures yet."

"If this doesn't work," Alder said. "I mean, if things don't go to plan here today, I wanted to say thank you. You have stood by me and what I have done, and that has been something I will never forget."

Mathers turned slightly in his chair, surprised by the humble words, he had never even thought about blaming only Alder for all that had happened, this was something they had all done together, and it had been an honour working with such great scientists. Unfortunately, there had been something which had gone wrong, and now they were going to do everything they could to fix it. The guilt was shared, not laid at a single door. Alder looked at him as he started out of his seat, nodded, and turned to walk out.

"It was all of us," Mathers said. Alder stopped momentarily. "We wanted to improve the world, we all did this."

"No, I am afraid it wasn't all of us. I wanted to make the world better. You have no part in the guilt of what has been done, just me." Alder walked out of the room before Mathers could say anything in reply.

Mathers sat silently waiting again, listening to Steve Ortile moving slowly around behind him stitching monitors from test setting to live feed as he went. There was a gentle hum in the air as all of the equipment which had been lifeless for so many days picked up speed, drawing more and more power from the local grid, devouring enough electricity to light a whole street even at this idle stage just to run the electro-magnetic field which shielded the collider tunnels from the immense gravitational forces which they were to endure during the experiment. Mathers looked down at his hands, clasped together on the console in front of him. They were shaking slightly, not in the same nervous way that he had noticed himself shake when they first ran the equipment up to full speed to complete this experiment previously, not an excited shake of adrenaline, but a fatigued tremor caused by the duress of so many days underground witnessing ordeal after ordeal. The stress has crept into his body in a way he could never imagine himself recovering from.

"We are at full power now," Ortile said quietly. "All systems are showing stable power supply, and all temperatures are remaining stable in the tunnels."

"All systems at full cycle speed confirmed," Mathers said confirming to Alder that they were ready. It was going to happen now.

"Received," Alder's voice boomed through the speaker at the front of Mathers' desk, Alder's face clear on a small monitor in front of him. He was completing his final equipment checks in the Command Suite. He thought momentarily about his wife, he missed her. He thought about everybody else who had been lost recently in his life, Rosst dying right here in front of him so violently. Enlan too. Was it really worth it? He put the thought out of his mind, it was a moot point now anyway. "Shall we begin then? Do we have confirmation from Doctor Blancs that all is in place where he is?"

"Everything confirmed as correct from here," Blancs' voice buzzed through a radio transmitter from the Collider tunnels. "Ready when you are."

"Jules," Alder said quietly. "Go ahead when the test cycle is complete. Good luck, thank you again my friend."

Mathers looked at the control desk in front of him, no LED lights had illuminated this time, the Collider was at full speed for the test cycle, just one button to press. He reached forward, trembling even more now.

"Test cycle initiated," Mathers said as loudly and clearly as he could manage. He pressed the small silver button to the live position, and heard the same pulse of energy rumble far beneath him he had become familiar with when they had first started to test this equipment at close to full capacity. It was normal.

The LED light on the control desk had changed from red to green as soon as Mathers confirmed the test cycle was a showing all levels within the agreed safety parameters. Alder would have been able to see the same readings from the command suite. Everything was as it should be. Exactly how everything had been as it should be at this stage during the first experiment. Alder had confidently entered the pass key into the control panel as soon as Mathers had confirmed the same readings he himself was looking at. Mathers paused, staring at the green LED. Next to it was the button which ignited the nuclear reaction in the feed chamber, hurling sub-atomic particles into the focus tunnel. If Blancs was correct, those particles would pass him where he was positioned in a small chamber outside the focus tunnel at light speed. There was nothing more Mathers could do, he stopped thinking, reached out his hand, and without making a sound, lifted the small cover above the switch, and pressed it forwards. A small click was all that Mathers heard. The same small click that the switch had made days before. A second LED lit up. Green. Everything was fine, the reaction had fired in the correct sequence, and there had been no breach of the electro-magnetic field shielding the tunnels. Mathers remembered to breathe, realising it had been several seconds since he had pressed the button and had not taken a breath since the first LED had turned from red to green. Everything was as it should be.

The warning light did not illuminate. Nothing happened the same way the first experiment had done as far as Mathers could tell. Just one green light, then another. Everything normal. And then nothing. All of the lights went out again for just a moment, yet there *was* still light. It made no sense to him. The crack seemed to be something that was all around him, through him, almost imperceptible, but there like looking at the finest cut into a soft cheese, both sides around the cut absorbing the divide and then returning together as if they had never been parted. The sound in the control room was almost nothing, a slight whine in the distance as far as Mathers could tell. He tried to turn his head, and saw dust rising up in his peripheral vision from the floor, from the surface of the desk in front of him, from every surface in the room in fact. It was like seeing dust in a weightless atmosphere. Then a pen from the desk in front of him began to lift too. It seemed to break through a wave of dust as it gathered momentum. His perception altered again, from dream-like slow motion to a car crash in high definition. He was lifted out of his chair and his right leg caught on the leg of the fixed workstation desk he was sitting at. He grabbed at the desk and caught a loose grip on the metal frame next to where his leg had caught, just as the left side of his body swung free of the desk, stretching him out from the desk like a starfish. His head seemed to snap round with the motion so hard it seemed his neck would break, and he saw Ortile finally, brutally accelerating across the room, vertically lifted at least four or five feet from the floor, and seemingly propelled towards the front wall of the control room. He passed Mathers at a pace beyond the strength Mathers had to move his head, spinning in the weightlessness and being pulled by such a great force his arms and legs pulsed jerkily forwards and backwards as he tumbled. The sound of the impact rang in Mathers' ears. It was the crashing breaking sound of a window smashing, but there were no windows in the control room. Mathers' head finally caught up to where Ortile had ended his short flight. The wall of monitors which had displayed every reading from the collider inner chambers had shattered with the impact of Ortile's body, leaving what looked like glass dust floating next to each screen, the screens themselves propelled outwards, and then returned to the monitors by the same force which had taken Ortile. His body had impacted against a number of monitors, smashing each of their thin LED screens with the energy, and he had been separated from himself with each monitor division. The larger part of the top of his head was being forced into the highest monitor, parts of his torso dividing into lower monitors as it tore apart. Mathers could see no blood on the floor, it had simply smeared on the metal frames of the monitors and been sucked into the wall, the very molecules of his blood beginning to separate with the force, as his body had upon impact with the monitors.

In the outer chamber around the focus tunnels Blancs had been stood silently listening to the changing sound within the massive section of tubing he was stood next to. All of his equipment showed an increasing pressure within the tunnel, and it almost seemed to Blancs that there was an increase in the air pressure around him in the outer chamber. His hair felt like it was standing up on his head, a strange electric feeling as if he were in some way in contact with a very low voltage live cable. There was definitely a raising whine within the focus tunnel, it was audible now more so, as if the reinforced metal was being stretched at its molecular level, but that was impossible. The tubing was metres thick and designed to contain a nuclear reaction. It could not be possible for the tube to move even a millionth of a millimetre. He stepped close to the tube and placed the palm of his hand gently against it. There was a strange shuddering sensation coming from the tube. It reminded him of the feeling of driving a car over freshly laid tarmac. That was the last thought he managed to process. A few short moments after he had placed his hand on the tubing an ear shattering scream burst from the focus tunnel, and the pressure in the outer chamber increased way beyond his perception. Blancs' body was subjected to a force hundreds of times that of the normal Earth's gravity in that moment, propelling him along parallel to the focus tunnel, accelerating instantly to the fastest speed any human being had ever experienced. Blancs did not survive long enough to revel in the experience. A bloody hand print was left smeared along the outer casing of the focus tunnel for a short distance. Blanc's body tumbled out of control countless times as it was projected along, being pulled apart as it went. Parts of his body began to separate from itself, arms and legs first tearing free, closely followed by his head. The limbs and head flew along with the dismembered torso, followed closely by a horizontal raining mass of blood. The body managed less than a half circuit of the Collider tunnel loops before the molecular disintegration completely took over, his body being torn apart to such a degree his bones had been turned to dust. Blancs had become a flying red cloud of microscopic particles in less than a complete second. Alder looked from camera to camera in the Command Suite watching the cloud flying through the outer chamber and trying to work out why Blancs had disappeared. As the idea that the cloud *was* Blancs occurred to Alder, the screaming whine pierced his ears and the room seemed to swim around him. It seemed that the walls were warping, becoming convex all around him, as if being sucked into the centre of the room somehow. They were definitely flexing. Similar to Blancs final thought, it occurred to Alder that what he was seeing was impossible, solid concrete walls cannot flex, especially not those installed in a nuclear bunker. But concrete dust was coming loose from the walls as they moved around him. He felt the pressure rise in the room, then the lights went out. A snapping sound seemed to fill the world around his body, and he was flung helplessly against a disintegrating wall.

Outside the bunker the soldiers walking around the Collider facility felt what seemed to be an earthquake under their feet, the ground trembling deep beneath them at first, growing steadily into a full shock wave shuddering and pulsing, heaving the very ground from under them. Private Harper was hurled off her feet suddenly, taking Stafe out as she fell. She looked along the ground and saw a trench tearing itself into the earth, pulling tarmac roads and deep layers of earth apart. The trench tore through the entire facility in an instant, ripping buildings apart with it, eating up the huge American transport vehicles as if they were nothing. An explosion sounded in one of the furthest buildings, as the tear in the ground reached it and immediately pulled the building's very foundations apart as if they were made from paper. Another building quickly followed, blown apart in an instant, throwing lumps of steel and mortar out across the facility and leaving nothing but a crater where moments before a five-story building had stood. The main facility building seemed to implode as the soldiers looked on, frozen by the insane image in front of them. Glass shattered in every window in the entire facility. Amidst the explosions and collapsing outbuildings, a loud siren seemed to be cutting through the air from within the still growing trench in the ground, along with another sound. A higher pitch than the siren, seemingly just a constant whining noise, as if a great force was twisting and tearing through tonnes upon tonnes of metal. Then a final explosion sounded, hurling what seemed like hundreds of tons of smashed concrete and glass miles up into the air, along with a number of the soldiers. The trench tore even further apart, swallowing almost all of the last of the soldiers along with the remaining vehicles and what was left of the crumbling buildings. From their undignified heap on the ground, Stafe and Harper saw Anderston plummet into the trench, his face caught in a shocked expression of helplessness.

Anderston seemed to freeze mid fall in the trench as Stafe and Harper watched him fall, and then a light surrounded him, seemingly pierced him as it passed upwards through his body out from the depths of the crater. Stafe and Harper felt nothing, it was instant. One moment they existed, the next, they were simply disconnected atoms floating on the wave of the explosion. The light which had flooded out of the crater seemed to flash brilliantly across the entire facility for an instant, and then as suddenly as it had started, disappeared. It left what remained of the buildings, the trees, grass, and tarmac of the interlinking roads all scorched black. Ash began to lift from the crater in the ground, simultaneously beginning to also fall from the sky, where rubble and plants, as well as a number of the soldier's bodies had been thrown hundreds of feet upwards before being burned to nothing but the pure white ash which gently now hung in the air. The facility transformed from an erupting exploding scene of collapsing buildings and earth tearing itself apart to a peaceful winter park, white with snow like ash coating the ground, and flakes of ash hanging in the air as if snowflakes so light and pure they almost defied gravity as they descended to the ground. The facility was still, silent.

In California the San Andreas Fault shuddered momentarily. Then without warning the entire fault tore itself open to almost a mile wide, as if either side had never been in contact with each other. The Fault slit apart for almost its entire seven-hundred and fifty-mile length, tearing a new sea into the west coast of America, separating almost a hundred miles of California from the mainland from San Francisco to San Bernadino to begin a short-lived new existence as an island, surviving only a matter of a few hours before being swallowed whole into the Pacific, and leaving Death Valley as the new west coast of America. At almost exactly the same time, the few metres wide gap between the Eurasian and American tectonic plates which project up above the ground in Iceland split apart, tearing the entire country into two pieces for a few moments, before the Atlantic Ocean swallowed the entire country as if it had never existed. As a result, minutes later tidal waves wiped miles off the coasts of North America, Greenland, Hawaii, and Britain. Inactive volcanoes across the planet erupted simultaneously as the Earth shook to its very core and destabilised fragile geological systems, throwing molten lava and chunks of red-hot magma into the sky, killing thousands of unsuspecting people in mere seconds, freezing their bodies into statues encased in the hot ash spewed from out of the volcanoes, agonisingly reminiscent of the remains of Pompei, baked solid as if they were clay in an oven.

The entire planet seemed to be vibrating from its deepest layers, the inner core of the planet seeming to be pushing itself out towards the crust, shuddering as gravity seemed to at once tear the world apart and simultaneously crush it in on itself with an enormous unseen pressure. Those who had survived the earthquakes, floods, tidal waves, explosions, and eruptions, and who were still physically capable of moving outside saw hundreds of shooting stars in the heavens above them, the sky in a constant state of change. Clouds seemed to pass overhead as if in slow motion on a motion-capture camera. The sun and the moon both seemed there, yet not there, with an unnatural light seeming to mix with the yellowing dusk light of an early spring evening at one moment, melting into a brilliant blue mid-winter morning the next.

Mathers came to in darkness, his body alight with intense pain, tearing him from dull unconsciousness to agonisingly fully conscious in an instant. He felt the leg of the chair he had been sitting on resting under his leg, which he thought may be broken. His ribs felt like they had all been smashed to a million pieces, and the taste of blood was unmistakeable in his mouth, deep in his throat making him gag violently. He lifted his right arm to try to right himself using the desk, but his shoulder turning in his socket seemed to rip what was left of his ribs and away from his sternum. Alive. He must be alive if he felt this bad, no matter how dark and painful the situation was, maybe there was some hope that he could survive. Then the reality hit him, there had been a catastrophic breakdown of the collider safety shields. It was the last warning light he had seen on his monitors before the room turned black along with his consciousness. A nuclear meltdown? Unlikely, the focus tunnels were sealed within re-enforced chambers hundreds of metres underground, at worst, any breach would be contained within these chambers, which were currently a few floors below him in the bunker. If he was still alive, surely any nuclear breach in the collider itself would be contained for long enough to seal off the area and put contingency plans into place. He lay still in the darkness, his mind ablaze with every possible idea of what he could do to escape from the bunker, and then to try to activate the lock down procedure for the bunker. A full contingency plan had been set out by Alder and Rosst in the months before the collider facility had been completed. A backup generator was located in a completely isolated chamber at the far edge of the bunker, which powered a number of additional blast doors, and which could be activated either from the command suite, or remotely from within a number of escape shafts built into the four corners of the bunker. In the event of a potential meltdown, every member of staff had practiced an exercise where they collected a torch, a containment suit with breathing apparatus, and a small Geiger counter, and walked in darkness to each of the separate escape shafts, accessed the shaft, and moved up towards ground level, where they would activate the blast doors. This procedure would essentially seal the bunker, cocooned in isolation underground until responding government agencies could enable nuclear meltdown protocols to contain the incident. Every member of staff was aware that they were strictly prohibited from attempting to rescue anyone else underground in the bunker, but were to simply access one of these shafts as soon as possible, with the first person to activate the blast doors essentially sealing the bunker, and anyone else remaining inside. But Alder was between Mathers and the nearest shaft. Alder, in the command suite, would be vital to assessing if there was any possibility of accessing the bunker again once it was sealed. It seemed unlikely to Mathers that Alder could have survived, but on the tiny chance that he may have done, Mathers could not bring himself to consign Alder to this concrete grave. It was clear that the collider experiment, the facility, and any chance of reviving the equipment or any further experiment or attempts to understand what had happened was dead. He started to try to lift himself again, the pain now dulled by a wave of shock and adrenaline that passed through Mathers at the realisation that everything in the bunker was likely to already be dead, and he would be too if he didn't get to one of the shafts immediately.

It took Mathers almost an hour to lift himself to a standing position and find his way to the cabinet in the control room which held the containment suits and emergency torches. The room was in perfect darkness, with absolutely no light source for his eyes to adjust even vaguely to while he struggled to negotiate the obstacles in the control room. He had fallen twice over objects he could not identify in the darkness. The room was strewn with debris, making his treacherous journey all the more difficult. The whole time he moved invisible noises seemed to tear at his very heart, which was thudding hard and fast inside his chest. The walls seemed to be creaking and flexing around him, a pulse in the air seeming to press on his chest with each groan of the steel which covered the walls. He leant against the cabinet, its cold steel door soothing the burning sensation in his face from the sheer effort of lifting himself to a standing position, and then the agony of moving across the room on what he had increasingly become sure was a broken leg. Sweat ran over his eyes and down his nose and cheeks, dripped from his chin onto his raggedly torn shirt, and soaked uncomfortably into the fabric. He rubbed his upper arm over his face, taking the worst of the sweat onto his sleeve and clearing his eyes.

The torch was not where it should be. He had managed to pry open the cabinet doors, which seemed somewhat buckled on their hinges, and had stubbornly resisted his initial attempts to open them. His hand frantically searched the shelves of the cabinet blindly, running over each surface until they reached an unidentified object, examining the object with his hands as a blind man would learn a new object's qualities. Every manor of tools, paper, stationary, and what he guessed to be some random personal items of the now forever departed staff of the facility like a watch and set of car keys. With each new item, his heart raced even more, the panic that he would not be able to find a torch becoming an increasingly likely scenario. He had barely managed to negotiate a small room in the blackness, without a torch and in his current physical condition, there was no way Mathers could make his way to an emergency escape shaft. He doubted he would even be able to safely locate the door of the room he was currently in. he plunged his hand deeper into the cabinet, his wrist hitting what felt like a cold metal tube. He heard something hard bang against the side of the cabinet, and in his panic, he drew his hand back sharply in an effort to locate what he had hit. Again, he hit the object, which again banged against the inside of the cabinet, rattled along the shelf, and clattered out onto the floor somewhere by his feet. A heavy cylindrical metal object. A surge of adrenaline rushed through his body, a torch, it must be. He didn't register pain in his leg as he dropped himself awkwardly to the floor, and started to pat his hands vertically straight down onto the floor. He had enough control of his actions to realise that if he flailed his hands around wildly in his search, he was likely to further roll the torch away from him. He brought his hand down hard on the broken wheel of an office chair, then the outer case of hard-drive from one of the servers, and then with his third pat of the floor, his hand set around the cylinder. It was solid, dense metal. Heavy as he lifted it. Impatience overtook Mathers, he hauled himself back to his feet without resting, and searched the sides of the cylinder. His fingers clicked against a switch pushing its way out of the cylinder. He closed his eyes, and pushed the switch upwards. When he opened his eyes, a beam of light cut across the room ahead of him.

Once out into the corridor, Mathers moved slowly, with exact purpose. He leant against the wall where he knew a short distance ahead of him along the corridor the door to the command suite was located. The light from the torch revealed the scale of the damage to the facility. He had been lucky in a sense, he thought to himself. The route to Alder was at least clear, where the opposite route to a nearer escape shaft was entirely blocked by a collapsed roof. Small fires burned amongst rubble and debris, and the smoke hood he had located with the use of the torch helped him breathe, but did little for his vision. He finally found the entry to the command suite, a single door hanging at an angle out into the corridor, held in place by a single hinge low in the door frame. He shone the torch into the room, and held his breath. The room seemed to have been torn apart by much the same force which had thrown his body around the control room. Lying in the middle of the detritus was a motionless body. Alder.

It took Mathers almost half an hour to pull the unconscious and badly injured Alder from the command suite out onto the corridor. He sat down gently next to his mentor, and lifted him to a slightly more comfortable seated position. Alder's breathing was rapid but becoming more regular, and Mathers had placed a smoke hood over his face to keep him from breathing in any more of the smoke which seemed to be floating towards them more thickly now. He heard Alder cough through the smoke hood, and jerk convulsively against the wall. Then he spoke.

"Is it over?" he asked. His eyes still seemed to be closed under the hood.

"Yes, it's over now," Mathers replied. "There is nothing left we can do down here." Alder's eyes opened, bloodshot and distant under the clear plastic covering of the smoke hood, looking out towards Mathers.

"Go," he said simply.

"Go where?" Asked Mathers in reply. Where do the people who destroyed civilisation go once they are finished?

"I don't know, anywhere. Just don't sit here and die with me."

"Neither of us are sitting here and dying," said Mathers slowly. "You made me complicit in this," Mathers shouted suddenly, grabbing Alder's attention. "You didn't ask if I wanted to change the world." His snap of temper abated quickly, his mind simply unable to take the stress. He had been in shock for what felt like days now, and he was simply unable to process the enormity of the reality which had unfolded around him. "Whatever the world looks like out there, we are going to at least breath the air and see natural light before we give up."

Alder shook his head, but Mathers simply shrugged, and started to pull Alder from the floor. Alder seemed to resist weakly, his body more passively resistant, almost limp as to be a dead weight. "If you want me to leave you, that's not happening. I won't let you stay here and not face whatever is outside. So, we either sit and die together down here like you said, or you get up off the floor and walk with me, because I can't carry you."

Alder nodded again, and Mathers felt him bear down against the floor with the last of his strength, and stood fully, leaning weakly against the wall, his hand on Mather's shoulder. He momentarily seemed to lose his balance, and again Mathers had to support more weight than he thought his leg could bear to hold Alder upright.

"I can't go with you like this, neither of us will make it out of this corridor, let alone out of the facility."

"Then neither of us leaves, like I said, we both live or we both die," Mathers said quietly, honestly. Tears ran down his face, frustration mingled with pain and anger, his emotions toward his mentor both dull and blunted, whilst at the same time agonisingly sharp and still alive within him.

Alder sat quietly, considering something which looked just beyond his grasp to Mathers. "Do you remember those god-awful fruit and nut bags Piers Enlan used to eat all the time?" Mathers nodded, slowly. I was sitting in the office we shared when we were building this facility, just Piers and me, working away in my own little world. Listening to him crunch distracted me, threw me off for a minute or so. I started thinking about my wife. How much I missed her, how much pain she endured in those last days. Then it happened. He broke wind. You know, like he always did, trying to hide it under a scrape of his chair on the floor, or clearing his throat. Right there I broke, she was gone, the world stopped making sense, and here was this idiot, god rest his soul, stinking and crunching. The world is so random in its cruelty. And I thought, *maybe it could be better*. I lost too much, carried on where maybe I should have just allowed myself to be lost, but I carried on. And when the first experiment failed, I just carried on, reached right through the hole and pulled everything that was left through. It's finished, all of it. I'm so sorry." He paused, coughing violently, tasting blood again in his mouth. "You're right, we will both live or we will both die. I like to think both, and I think I owe it to you to face it out there with you." He sat back against the wall for a moment, his eyes closed. Mathers thought he had never seen a man so utterly broken.

"Which way?" Alder opened his eyes and looked into the darkness the way Mathers had come, turned and looked along the corridor where Mathers had focussed the light from the torch. He had looked for just a moment into Mathers' eyes, and shame had overtaken him. Not far ahead of them was the sealed door to an escape shaft. It was barely visible through the thickening smoke, even with the faint illumination of the emergency light which seemed to be fading out with each passing moment.

The short distance to the escape shaft left Mathers again sweating and faint, the world seeming to grow opaque around him. They stopped at the doors, Mathers' face pressed against the door frame. He summed up all his strength and pushed the override key from his personal set of keys into the lock. It was a magnetised key, and sunk into the lock with little effort from Mathers. Nothing happened for a long few seconds, then a slow suction sound sighed from the seal as the doors parted. They had reached the end of the road. Both men fell through the door and collapsed into the escape shaft elevator. The doors sealed behind them, finally and eternally isolating the collider bunker from the outside world. Mathers vomited on the floor as the force of the independently generator powered elevator sped them to the surface.

Mathers helped Alder out through the burnt rubble of what remained the Collider building, into the smoke and ash filled compound. The other buildings in the facility were either entirely destroyed or set alight, fires burning almost everywhere, eating up the remains of a once great scientific prospect. Alder held weakly to Mathers as he limped further into the night, making their way clear of the wreckage of collapsed buildings and what had once been their dreams.

"Do you think the religious thing might be right after all? The lord came back, brought his followers back to life? Because this looks more like hell than heaven to me." Alder was slowing, unable to keep the pace even with Mathers supporting him. Mathers assumed he had gone as far as he could, and stopped to answer the question, letting Alder rest momentarily.

"I like the scientific possibility we may have proved that there is no God after all. Maybe this whole existence is just a big loop?"

"You think we just reset the Big Bang?" Alder coughed and laughed at the same time as he asked the question. "I like that idea, I always did. Maybe we are just about to go all the way around again, but maybe do it a little better the next time. That was my hope, anyway."

"If we do, I hope next time we meet again. Maybe we could be doctors instead though, or maybe teachers? Something less stressful than this end of the world stuff."

"I'd like that." Alder smiled as he started to walk again, stumbling with every step. Mathers held on to him, wondering how far they would get. The mangled gates at the entrance to the compound were clear, sitting limply on the floor just outside the main entrance. No soldiers or protestors could have survived the explosions if they had remained near to the facility. A fine grey dust covered the floor, settled for miles around having been spewed out of the strange pulse like ash from a great grey volcano.

They stopped just outside what was left of the gates, standing at the edge of the road which was bordered by a once beautiful park. Alder pointed upwards, his head now rested on Mathers' shoulder. It was late evening; the sky was beautiful. A blue grey expanse stretching forever, going nowhere. Clouds made their way over the heads of the scientists, as if there was nothing unusual about this night. A summer's night like any other. Suddenly the Earth shook violently, a tremor so deep that Mathers thought it felt like the Earth had crashed into another planet. The shock separated the scientists, throwing them hundreds of feet apart.

Mathers regained consciousness with a jump, he had no idea how long he had been out. He saw Alder lay on his back some way from him. Mathers tried to stand, a shot of pain searing through his lower body, his leg now undoubtedly badly broken. He collapsed back to the ground, deciding not to try again. He slowly dragged himself to where Alder lay. Alder was facing the sky, still blue grey and beautiful, but now with other colours seeping in, the colours mixing into a collage like no artist had ever created. Mathers reached Alder, and lay next to him, staring up to the sky watching the show. He took Alder's limp hand in his own.

"If this really is the Big Bang, I'm glad I saw it at least for this moment. See you next time around, only a few billion years to wait." The colours in the sky darkened suddenly. The blue grey turned a blood red, then into a strained purple. A tear opened up into the sky, dark, then every colour Mathers had ever seen, light and dark at the same time. Everything and nothing flashed in front of Mathers' eyes within the tear, then there was no colour at all. Everything stopped.

Author's note.

This book is dedicated to A, A, and T.

Firstly, thank you if you are reading this, for reaching this far. I genuinely hope you have enjoyed this book, and look forward to us meeting again at the end of my next book, due out in 2021.

The research within this book was all completed by myself. Any errors are mine, and mine alone (as a certain famous author often states in his own note at this point). This book was then scrutinised by HG, ably offering critique on a number of errors either factual or in storytelling. Hopefully anything which remains in terms of error, is there purely to aid the story, and not too distracting if you are either a science or military purist.

A quote from a DVD cover stuck with me throughout the writing of this book. It went something along the lines that 'all of the characters are conscious that they are not going to arrive at the end of the film alive'. I wanted this overarching feeling of helplessness to play out in many of the characters in these pages.

Printed in Great Britain
by Amazon